THE BEST OF WOMEN

By Anne Evans

1

Published in 2008 by YouWriteOn.com

1

Published by YouWriteOn.com

Chapter 1

Queenie had never planned to go shoplifting that Thursday afternoon . On her way to the bus stop she`d remembered that she needed cornflour for her shortbread recipe so she`d popped in to O`Riorden`s for just that single item . Then , walking round the aisles she`d begun to feel the familiar sensations which presaged the action to which she had become addicted. Her heart began to race and she could feel her cheeks flush and her breath quicken . As she dropped the small tin of crab into the folds of her umbrella , a rush of adrenalin completed the buzz .

Then she`d turned and seen both Mr. O`Riorden and his ginger haired assistant glaring at her from the end of the aisle .Had they seen what she had done ? Through a haze of fright she had watched the shopkeeper hissing whispers to the girl on the checkout but she was unable to hear the words. The two of them had then seemed to assume a militant vengeful stance as if awaiting their chance to pounce on her. Terrified , she had taken a second turn around the shelves and ,in the concealment offered by a display of floor cleaners and detergents , she`d removed the tin from her umbrella and then shook from her sleeve a narrow packet of chocolate biscuits placing both of these items in the bottom of a plastic bucket which was conveniently to hand.

She approached the checkout quite brazenly then and gazed serenely into the hostile stare of the Sweda operater as she paid for her cornflour and jar of sweet pickle. Mr.O`Riorden stood by whilst these purchases were made breathing heavily , the buttons of his white coat straining across his stomach.He made no attempt to detain her then . Instead he had followed her to the shop entrance and, in a low voice but quite pleasantly , had requested that she do her shopping elsewhere in future. "I think you know what I mean Miss Mack " he had added . The words spoken in his soft Irish brogue did not sound at all censorious .Nevertheless it was the look of disappointment on his face which would haunt Queenie for weeks to come . Deeply ashamed , she left the premises hurriedly her cheeks burning . Once outside she had to force herself not to break into a run . She scurried to the bus stop, a small slight figure incongruously dressed in a long waxed raincoat and matching wide brimmed hat , attracting curious glances from passers by.

Since then Queenie had been too embarrassed to go within a hundred yards of Eamonn O`Riorden`s shop which was a nuisance since it placed the Co-op opposite out of bounds too . There was only one other grocery in the area and it was notoriously pricey , so there was nothing for it but to take the bus into town and do her shopping there. She did this for several weeks managing to curb her inclinations to take anything by reminding herself of Mr. O`Riorden . One Thursday though , almost without her realising it , a tube of glue found its way into her bag . It was partly the price of it that made her do it she reasoned afterwards . Ridiculous to pay a pound for such an item .

During the next half hour in Boots , Woolworths and even the butchers , she`d seemed to have gone berserk she thought later . A large slab of chocolate and a packet of mints were followed by a tin of carpet dye in Woolworths and a packet of curtain hooks. Some special offer deodorant , fragrance free , and a pair of tweezers came from Boots . Then , for the life of her she couldn`t think why , whilst the butcher was trimming her stewing steak she had flipped down a packet of stock cubes from a display and then casually picked them up as if she were tying her shoelace .

Unpacking her shopping on the kitchen table , Queenie felt deeply ashamed and also rather frightened . Things seemed to be getting out of control. After all , it was not as if she could not afford to pay for these items . The scaring thing about it all was that she did not need most of them. She required neither carpet dye nor curtain hooks and there was a container of stock cubes in the larder. So why had she taken them?

Queenie made herself a cup of tea and took down the biscuit tin from the high shelf where her mother had always kept it to deter casual dipping . It had not occurred to her to alter this arrangement though her mother had died seven years ago . Thoughtfully she munched on a digestive . Something would have to be done . It was one thing to take things she actually needed ; This she could understand . But the other unnecessary items proved that something was definitely wrong . Was this the beginning of madness ? Could hardening of the arteries be the cause? Although Queenie was fascinated by medical matters her knowledge of them was limited to articles in the Sunday press and women`s magazines . Another reason struck her . Could it b e because she spent too much time alone ? This fact had never ben a cause of concern to her but other people remarked about it.

Since her mother had died of an embolism some years ago , Queenie`s life had changed completely. Mrs. Mack had chivvied her daughter constantly as she had her late husband. Without the dynamo of her presence, the persistant exhortations to do this or that , go here or there, Queenie had slumped into delightful inertia . After she`d taken early retirement from her job in the Treasurer`s dept. of the Town Hall , something her mother would never have countenanced , life became even more loosely textured . Then she was involved in a car accident which injured nobody but badly frightened her and put her off driving forever.

At first Queenie had missed her usual social activities but after a while this failed to bother her . There was no point in buying smart clothes when you don`t go anywhere or bothering with expensive hair cuts . She began to wear track suits around the house . If there was somewhere she particularly wanted to go she would beg a lift from friends or Bert next door . As time went on she seldom went out in the evenings particularly during winter months . She attended daytime classes at the local further education college when there was something that interested her . Other than that her main hobby was collecting things or " hoarding junk " as her friend Iris termed it .

She supposed it was a bit of a cliché really – middle aged woman living alone , never been married , three cats .... And then there were the books . People definitely thought that was odd. Having two whole rooms given over to books and piles of magazines . In the beginning they had been confined to shelves but as the collection grew cardboard boxes had accumulated and then tea chests . Queenie had lost track of the extent of her book collection long ago but could not bring herself to part with any of it.

Years ago her mother had encouraged her collection of childrens books believing it to be a worthy hobby as long as it was confined to Queenie`s bedroom . Since her death however Queenie had branched into other forms of literature too . At first it had been general contemporary fiction . If she admired a writer it became necessary to own the complete works , second hand of course . Then she had the idea of obtaining maps and guidebooks to every county in the country. This accomplished , she`d branched out into collections of classical literature, specialising in those with tooled leather bindings . These had long been consigned to tea chests as had the collection of encyclopaedia .

Then she had begun her collection of paintings; mainly watercolours to start with collected partly for the attractiveness of their frames . There must have been at least 50 of them stacked against the garage walls .But her especial interest most recently was old china , a selection of which was displayed on shelves throughout the house , By now there was a serious shortage of storage space . The garage had been the ideal repository now Queenie no longer had a car but that soon became too full and now the utility area which led into it had become a storage depot too as had the cupboard beneath the stairs and one of the bedrooms.

Queenie had become concerned about the clutter and promised herself she would do something about it soon . Meanwhile she rarely missed the fortnightly auction held locally and made sure she was au fait with every jumble sale within walking distance.Then there were the car boot sales held regularly in the grounds of the local school which always yielded some booty.

The phone rang at this point ending her reverie . It was her friend Iris wanting to remind her about the Ladies Club meeting tomorrow and offering transport there . Queenie agreed with pleasure . " Why don`t you come early and have supper with me first ?" she asked Iris who was agreeable to this arrangement . During this conversation Solly ,the oldest of Queenie`s cats began to make a fuss for his food . Due to his insistency and the pressure of his claws through her jersey she was obliged to cut the conversation short and attend to the cats . This job done it was time to see to her own sustenance.

There was a pot of pea soup made yesterday which she planned to enliven by the addition of a spicy sausage . She decided she would follow this with some toasted cheese . She tried to co-incide her evening meal with "The Archers " if possible . She kept a radio in the kitchen so that she could listen in whilst cooking or doing household chores. Her worries temporarily forgotten , she hummed happily to herself as she prepared her meal.

Chapter 2

Iris replaced the telephone receiver furious with herself . The last thing she wanted to do was have supper with Queenie tomorrow Why had she agreed to do it ? She was fond of her old friend . They had known each other since school days . But , she had to admit it , Queenie was becoming more and more odd these days . It was not just her behaviour which had always been on the eccentric side . Lately she had begun to look very strange as well . In the past few weeks she had dyed her hair a peculiar shade of orange . There was no other word to describe the colour . It had not even been dyed properly Iris thought, leaving Queenie with an odd , piebald look Iris , who never passed remarks as a rule, had no choice but to tell Queenie how strange it looked because it was positively embarrassing to be seen out with her . She had thought at first that Queenie was unaware that the dye had not taken   properly . Amongst her other eccentricities was a refusal to wear glasses although she had clearly needed them for some time. When the subject of the hair colour had been raised however , Queenie had merely laughed and said

" Yes, I know it`s a bit funny but it will soon grow out." Then, aware of Iris` scandalised expression she added " For heaven`s sake Iris . It`s nothing to fuss about ."

Then there were Queenie`s clothes : Iris was particular about her own appearance . She insisted on quality . She would prefer one well cut skirt from Jaeger or Aquascutum than any number of inferior make . She was not a fashion plate but she took care of her clothes and liked to think she was always well turned out . At one time , certainly in the days when they had worked together , Queenie too , had taken great pride in her appearance .Her hair had always been well cut and she had dressesd well . This had all changed since her retirement   . Now the word that would best describe her appearance was well.....bizarre . She frequented charity shops , buying the most outlandish and unsuitable garments purely because they were bargains . She even boasted about picking up clothing bargains at jumble sales ! It was all completely unnecessary as far as Iris was concerned   She happened to know for a fact that Queenie`s parents had left her very comfortably off so it could not be financial reasons which forced her into these actions . But it wasn`t merely her appearance which had deteriorated . Her general attitude and behaviour had altered too .And it wasn`t as if she was that old .Only 57 .

Iris remembered the last time Queenie had asked her for supper about two months ago. Queenie could not be described as a good cook . She was too slap dash and unmethodical and tended to veer towards the exotic which did not always come off . Now and then she managed to produce something really tasty On occasions Iris had tasted wonderful curries and once a superb chilli .

On this occasion , unusually , Queenie had served fish – halibut it had been with some kind of herby crust in a creamy sauce. Iris had taken one mouthful and then put down her fork. Queenie merely said "Damn I thought that cream wasn`t quite right but you know I can`t smell properly with this cold. Serves me right for buying it after its sell by date.To Iris` horror she had then told her that whever she went to the market she always bought things from a trader who specialised in selling such items .

"They`re so cheap you wouldn`t believe it " she enthused " And most of the time they`re perfectly all right if you use them at once . I suppose I was taking a chance with cream though."

They continued the meal by eating the vegetables which were plentiful and well cooked. Afterwards Queenie had apologised for the fact that there was no proper pudding but had produced individual pots of yoghurt instead. .Iris could not help herself . She inverted the pot and looked at the date not caring whether Queenie was offended or not .

" No thank you Queenie . I`d really rather not " she had said . "Quite frankly I really can`t understand why you have to go to these lengths to economise . It`s not as if you`re hard up ."

"It`s not a question of money " Queenie had replied " It goes much deeper than that . When I get a bargain I feel rather like a hunter who`s caught a wonderful piece of game . It sort of justifies the time shopping around . After all , I`ve nothing better to do ".

"Then you should have " Iris had answered her . "There are lots of really worthwhile things you could be doing ." She began to enumerate them.

"You know I don`t like good works Iris " Queenie had said looking rather annoyed " I leave that sort of thing to people like you who love them ." And there the matter had rested .

Iris did not want to upset her friend . She remembered only too well the occasion when she had called on Queenie a few weeks after the death of her mother . She had gone equipped with a number of large black plastic sacks with the idea of helping her friend dispose of her mother`s wardrobe . She herself had been very grateful when a friend had helped her with a similar task following her own mother`s death .To her surprise Queenie had been totally affronted by the suggestion that her mother's belongings should be removed and a general coldness had been evinced which lasted for weeks. As far as Iris knew the clothing remained hanging in Mrs. Mack's wardrobe, even though almost seven years had now elapsed since her death .

Iris remembered that she had to go to the library before it closed . Tuesday was late opening night and she had quite a collection of books to return. Apart from her own , she changed the books for her two elderly neighbours who were housebound . However she did find it a chore choosing new books for them. Mrs Simey needed large print books which were in short supply in the library and she was particular about her reading matter. She enjoyed romantic fiction but only the very old fashioned type where no impropriety took place . This sort of book was increasingly difficult to obtain Iris found , and it meant that she herself had quickly to skim through likely books to vet them for sex scenes or bad language . Mrs. Simey was inclined to hold her personally responsible for a book which did not meet her standards .

Miss Geram on the other hand , was interested only in biographies or travel but here too Iris had to be careful. She still had not been forgiven for supplying her with the biography of Rock Hudson a book which she had assumed would be quite innocuous . Unfortunately , the book was in the modern genre of " warts and all " and made no secret of the subject's sexual proclivities .Miss Geram had been scandalised saying that the author deserved to get 10 years in prison for writing such filth . In vain Iris had tried to explain that people had always led scandalous lives , it was just that people were more frank about it these days . Ada Geram would not accept this . As far as she was concerned depravity had begun in 1960. Iris did not resent helping her neighbours in this way because books were important to her and she could imagine how bored she would be if she had nothing to read She just wished they were easier to please.

She combed her hair in front of the hall mirror .The face that looked back at her did not look much different than it had when she was 18 although that was 40 years ago .Her skin showed the usual sagging and fine lines that had accrued with age but the eyes still looked much as they always had , innocent and gentle . As a young woman dissatisfied with her appearance she had longed to look sophisticated believing that this was something one acquired She combed her hair in front of the hall mirror . The face that looked back at her did not look that as one grew older . She had comforted herself with the thought that one day she would achieve this , seeing it as a sort of self knowledge that made one aware of how to make up and style your hair – how to look grown up in fact . But at 58 she still retained the nondescript hairstyle and unmade up face and was still buying the "safe" clothes she had always bought . Oh well , she thought , I may not be sophisticated but at least I don`t look peculiar like Queenie . This was some comfort .

She decided to walk to the library although she had a heavy bag of books. She welcomed the outing having been kept indoors because of rain . More importantly , her elderly labrador needed the exercise . Nellie was only too eager to accompany her mistress making impatient noises whilst Iris was putting on her jacket One advantage of having an old dog , thought Iris is that there are no behaviour problems. Nellie trotted happily at Iris side not requiring her lead which she carried in her mouth . She stopped obediently at each crossing . Passers by nodded approvingly at the dog . Reaching the small parade of shops Iris decided to pick up an evening paper. " Wait here Nellie " she commanded and the animal immediately sat down outside the shop .

A youth was behind the counter in the newsagent`s engaged in conversation with another teenager , a small blonde girl . Neither of them took the slightest notice of Iris . She glanced at the papers on the counter. "Bishop to probe sex scandal in local church " was the headline in the local paper. "Randy chef gave waitress extra portion" was the headline in the" Sun" . Iris looked away. The two continued their conversation so Iris gave a slight cough ."Er, could I have an evening Echo please ? " she asked diffidently . Seconds passed. Neither person took the slightest notice . Eventually, Iris removed a paper from a pile and placed her money on the counter . As she was leaving the shop the youth acknowleged her by shouting familiarl "cheers love ."

She seethed inwardly even though telling herself it was pointless to get annoyed . It was probably quite natural that she should seem invisible to teenagers . Nevertheless , thinking back to her own teenage years , she would never have dreamed of behaving so rudely and even if she had the older person would have swiftly reminded her of her manners – so why hadn`t she done this in the shop? It wasn`t just her innate dislike of causing a scene or drawing attention to herself , she thought . It was that she knew the young people would have been unspeakably rude or worse and she just could not face it .

Nellie sprang to her feet and they continued their wallk to the library . Outside the building Iris tied the dog`s lead to a post much to the animal`s disgust . "Be a good girl because I don`t know how long this will take " she admonished and the dog obediently sat down .A notice on the door said "Notice of altered opening times " regretting that due to cuts in staffing etc the library would no longer be opening on Thursday evenings . This really was a retrograde step thought Iris . Times were hard in the fifties too but libraries had managed to stay open for 12 hours a day except at weekends.

Faye, the librarian looked harassed.

" I expect you`ll want to sign the petition " she said producing a clip board "Everyone 's signing but I`m afraid it wont make any difference."

"I'll sign certainly "said Iris " But , as you say , what good will it do?" she was used to having these conversations with Faye about the deteriorating standards in the library . Although she felt just as strongly about it too , she felt that it was just one of a host of things that were not once as they had been. Just when you thought things could not get worse they did , but gripped by a terrible apathy caused by previous blows people felt powerless to do anything about them .

" Libraries are such soft targets " Faye continued "So few people care what happens to them ."

Iris had to agree. She went straight to the returned books section and saw to her great delight two books she had been coveting for ages – the Philip Larkin biography and the latest Barbara Vine . What a treat ! With a spring in her step she began to search for books for the ladies . .

Chapter 3

Shortly after 6 o clock Iris arrived at Queenie`s cottage. She`d had a brainwave after leaving home . She would take Queenie a pudding . That way she could avoid being confronted with one of Queenie`s bargains . The Spar shop was en route so she called there and picked up a Vienetta. Queenie was partial to icecream she knew. .Before she closed the car door Iris heard Queenie`s front door open and turning , gasped in surprise. Queenie stood there dressed in a most becoming wool dress in a lovely shade of sea green . The most surprising thing of all was her hair . Instead of the grey and orange mass Iris had last seen , Queenie`s hair was a uniform shade of sandy gold , cut much shorter than she normally wore it and perfectly straight . She looked ....fantastic

Iris stared in bewilderment and Queenie burst into delighted laughter.

"I know . It`s unbelievable isn`t it? And the incredible thing is it didn`t cost me a penny ."

"Whatever do you mean ?"

"Well , this morning I was looking in the window of that hairdresser in the High St. You know the one I mean . It used to be called "Elaine`s"  but now it`s called " The Headmaster" and it`s really swish . I was just looking at the price list and thinking how outrageous the prices were when a man came out and asked if I`d liked to be a demonstration model .Of course I said yes "

" Trust you " said Iris following her indoors . " Something like that would never happen to me ."

"Actually" said Queenie " It was a bit embarrassing . The man treated me like dirt. He made sit in front of all his staff and told them my head was a perfect example of badly dyed hair. Some of them laughed when he pointed out the worst bits."

"Well he was certainly right there " Iris put in ." I did tell that myself but you wouldn`t have  it . Perhaps now you`ll believe me when I tell you things for your own good ."

"Anyway , " said Queenie , ignoring Iris` remark. " I was so delighted when he`d finished that I went straight to Oxfam and got this dress I`d seen it earlier but it seemed too dressy."

"No " Iris disagreed . "It looks lovely . "You look lovely " she added honestly." Really Queenie, it does pay you to make an effort you know .You look so...She searched for the right word and found it "sophisticated ."

During the meal which this time was a successful risotto , Queenie debated inwardly whether she should discuss her "problem " with Iris . She had lain awake for hours last night worrying about it . Eventually she decided against it. Iris was so shockable . She`d be horrified to discover somebody she knew was a hardened shoplifter.

"You`re very quiet Queenie. Is something wrong ?" Iris sounded so concerned Queenie was immediately tempted to tell her everything but restrained herself. "Er , I`ve been thinking actually, wondering whether I spend too much time alone. " She said finally "I read an article somewhere that said it was bad for you at our time of life."

"You mean you`re feeling lonely? "Iris questioned "Well I`ve asked you often enough to come with me to an evening class .Or you could help with meals on wheels , or volunteer in a charity shop . Then there`s the ladies sewing club . I really enjoy that ."

" I don`t fancy any of those things  somehow . Anyway I`m not lonely . It`s just that some people  think it`s odd that I live alone . I know VI next door does . She says I should get a lodger but I`m not keen ."

"Oh no !" Iris wrinkled her nose at the thought of a lodger " But there are lots of useful things you could be doing " She began to enumerate them again . It became necessary to change the subject quickly .Queenie thought fast

" Oh , I know what I wanted to tell you You`ll never guess who I met in the health food shop yesterday . Thelma Riley.You must remember her from school . She was that odd, fat girl who left school early. She`s just come back here to live apparently , in one of those new bungalows on the rise. She`s been in Portsmouth for years ." Queenie`s ploy was successful. Iris was most interested in hearing about Thelma and they discussed her until they realised that they`d have to rush if they were to be at the village hall for seven thirty .

The speaker at the ladies club that night was a local health worker who spoke about advances in health care during the 20th century . She showed many slides and the talk was both interesting and informative . Afterwards there was coffee and a variety of home made cakes. Iris and Queenie sat at the back of the hall with Rose Deacon another woman who , like them ,lived alone . It was strange how the single women stuck together thought Iris.Rose and Queenie exchanged animated whispers and giggled frequently much to Iris` irritation because she could not hear their words. In the past year or so she had become rather hard of hearing – not bad enough yet to seek advice – but enough to make her feel rather isolated on occasions like this .

When the meeting came to an end , the three were approached by Selena Duncan the chair .

"I wonder if you three ladies would mind staying behind to clear away ?" She inquired in a voice which brooked no refusal .

"Not at all . We`d love to wouldn`t we girls?" Rose answered . Selena gave her a sharp look. "Now Rose , I rely on you to ensure that everything is secure when you have finished . Just push the keys through Mr. Mitten`s letterbox after you`ve locked up." She moved away.

As the room emptied Rose began to chuckle

" Typical of Selena to assume that because we`re all single we don`t mind staying behind " she laughed . "The others all have husbands to hurry home to and must not be delayed ."

"But I don`t mind staying behind " protested Iris .

"No more do I . I just resent the assumption behind the request" She laughed again . They looked at her in surprise .

"For all Selena`s knows I could be returning home to a big, black lover. Anyway , if I had to return home to Selena`s husband I`d be glad of any excuse to stay behind I can tell you ."

They all laughed unkindly . Selena`s husband was a pompous little red faced man who was dwarfed by his heavily built wife . Picturing them in her mind`s eye , Queenie was greatly amused . The three women had cleared the crockery from the tables and were now in the kitchen where Rose elected to wash , Iris dried and Queenie put away . They worked efficiently together. Queenie glanced at Rose approvingly . She was just the sort of woman she most admired .Positive , full of character with a good sense of humour .

"It`s funny really" Rose said "I don`t know about you two but I think we`ve such a lot to thank the feminists for . I was always against those very strident feminists when the movement first took off but what a difference they`ve made to women like us ."

"How do you mean exactly ?" asked Queenie . Both she and Iris looked at Rose inquiringly . "What I mean is this" said Rose wringing out her dishcloth . " At one time single women like us were treated rather contemptuously.We were definitely second class citizens then. Other women despised us or pitied us – we couldn`t get a man and they could – that sort of thing . It`s only in the last 15 years or so that people have come to realise that single women have their own place in society and that place doesn`t need to be in the home or as an adjunct to a man. " Here she paused for breath .

"And now ? "queried Iris . Rose smiled

" Now people daren`t make any such   assumptions. Just because we`re single doesn`t mean we don`t live with men . Or we could be lesbian of course . But our single status is totally irrelevant now .We`re simply people in our own right ." Privately , Iris disagreed with her . Rose might feel like a person in her own right but she was speaking for herself of course . Not everyone had her confidence . Better change the subject she decided but suddenly Queenie blurted out

" I went to a marriage bureau once."
Rose gave a great whoop of delight

" How wonderful . Tell us all about it"

But Iris glared at Queenie in astonishment .

" You never said . When was this pray ?" Then she realised just how accusing her own voice sounded

"Oh   ages ago now . When I was about 45 I suppose" Queenie looked embarrassed . She was already regretting her outburst but she continued , rather red in the face .

"Rose is   right .That`s exactly why I did it. It didn`t seem right to be single. My mother kept on at me to do something about it . She`d even suggest likely people . People I couldn`t bear the thought of . Other people made remarks too . In the end I thought I`d give it a try …" her voice trailed off . She couldn`t look either of them in the eye Iris noticed.

"I know " broke in Rose "Why don`t we all go to the "Rose and Crown"? We can chat in comfort there."Iris looked doubtful .She did not really enjoy pubs particularly in the evening ."I don`t think so Rose . We really ought to be going home ." But Queenie looked at her pleadingly ." Oh please lets go Iris. I`d really enjoy it ." Reluctantly Iris agreed .

The ladies collected their coats . Iris looked admiringly at the cashmere wrap Rose draped around her smart suit . She knew how to dress . By comparison her own Burberry just looked dowdy , whilst Queenie`s waxed raincoat simply spoiled the effect of her new dress and smart hair do . Rose locked the door of the hall , did as requested with the keys , and the trio

walked across to the nearby pub .

Iris was pleasantly surprised by the public house . It was neither crowded or smokey .two of the things which had always put her off pubs . A large open fire burned at one end of the room surrounded by comfortable armchairs and it was here that the ladies decided to settle themselves. .Rose wen tfor the drinks

"Isn' t this nice Iris? Queenie remarked " I can't remember the last time I was in a pub in the evening."

Iris almost retorted that she had probably been in plenty during her marriage bureau episode but thought better of it . No point in upsetting Queenie at this stage . She wanted to get to the bottom of the whole business .There was a small group of men at the bar laughing amongst themselves and Rose , Iris noticed , had just fallen into conversation with them , effortlessly , unselfconsciously . Iris watched as Rose , making some laughing comment , drew herself away . It all looked so easy . Natural, normal social intercourse but she herself could never have done it she knew . Nor could Queenie. They neither of them had the knack . She wondered why but at this point Rose returned with their drinks , suspiciously large looking gin and tonics for herself and Queenie and orange juice for Iris .

"Those men thought we were from the ladies bowling club " she said laughingly " I had to disillusion them . Said I'd never bowled in my life They said they'd teach us but I told them we were too young for bowls . That's why they were laughing " She raised her glass . Of course , realised Iris , Rose lived within walking distance and would not be driving home .

Rose sat back and sipped at her drink . She looked at Queenie expectantly .

"Well Schererezada , tell us all ." she commanded . Queenie reddened and laughed nervously

" Well there's not much to tell . I just met a few men and nothing really came of it ."

" Oh no " Cried Rose "We're not letting you off so lightly .We want to har the whole story don't we Iris?" Iris agreed . She definitely wanted to hear more .She had been amazed by Queenie's revelation and it made her regard her friend in a new light . If she could keep that to herself for years , what other secrets was she hiding ?

Queenie began to recount her first experience which had taken place in the station car park in Winchester . She had been told that the man she was to meet was a "high flying" civil servant who was a bachelor interested in music and growing rare orchids . He was described as "handsome in an understated way " which she could not quite get to grips with . He had telephoned to arrange the meeting , suggesting that they should have lunch and she had set off for the encounter in a state of great anticipation , having bought a new outfit especially.

It had come as a shock therefore, to be greeted by a short , balding man in a dirty raincoat who had suggested that they should eat at a Wimpey bar he knew in the high street . To add insult to injury she ended up paying for the refreshment herself ." He was so awful" she related " He quizzed me all about my financial situation and got really annoyed when I wouldn't discuss it . Then he had the cheek to tell me that he thought we didn't have enough common interests. I was just glad that I'd never have to meet him again ." The ladies laughed uproariously.

It seemed that all of the men – there had been five of them altogether over a period of about 9 months – had been wildly unsuitable whilst the final one had seemed to be frighteningly unstable and had even threatened her . It was this last encounter which had persuaded Queenie to give up the idea completely. All the time she'd listened to Queenie , although she'd laughed just as much as Rose , Iris had been thinking how demeaning the whole thing was.Trust Queenie to allow herself to be taken advantage of she thought . She felt angry on her behalf too .

"Just how much did all this cost you Queenie ? " she asked finally.Queenie went red again. " About £2000 altogether " she admitted "But I didn't have to pay it all at once. "

"Well I think you were exploited " Rose said " I always imagined that you only paid if you married as a result of joining . I should have refused to pay a penny in view of the rubbish they supplied you."

"Oh but it doesn't work like that " Queenie protested "You had to pay half in advance. Anyway , I know it sounds crazy , but in a way I don't begrudge any of that money . It made me realise that I was happy being single In fact I just felt grateful that I wasn't married to any of those dreadful men ......what's so awful about being single anyway ? "

" Nothing at all "cried Rose" Lets all drink to it girls . Here's to the single life !" They raised their glasses . Iris was the only one of them with misgivings.

Chapter 4

Driving home later after leaving Queenie at her gate , Iris brooded over her friend's revelations concerning the marriage bureau. Her emotions were mixed On the one hand she could not help feeling hurt that Queenie had never broached the subject with her before, on the other she was shocked by the audacity of her behaviour. There was also , she had to admit to herself , a strong element of envy . If only she could summon up the courage to do a thing like that . Not that she wanted to find herself a partner necessarily but she would love to have the confidence to branch out in some way or other , even if it was something as simple as going on holiday alone .

She switched on the radio . Somebody was being interviewed about their early life "Of course , as somebody who was a teenager in the swinging sixties you must have wonderful memories of your youth... " She switched off the radio . The sixties did not swing for her she recalled or anybody else she knew for that matter. She remembered the Beatles of course. Never quite understood what all the fuss was about though .Perhaps she was already too old when all the pop scene began .That famous Larkin poem could almost have been written with her in mind. " Sexual intercourse began in 1963 . Which was rather late for me..." She had never liked that poem although Phillip Larkin was special to her . She had read that he was a reclusive bachelor , extremely shy and afraid of women . She felt they had such a lot in common .His death had been a real blow.

A picture came into her mind – herself in 1963 . She must have been 22 when some of the younger girls in the office had persuaded her to go to the theatre with them to see a famous pop star.......Cliff Richard perhaps . Strange how she could not remember. She had never liked him or any other pop star for that matter but at that time it had been important to her to fit in with the crowd The other girls had regarded her as odd because she was interested in her career and studied for the local government examinations which needed to be passed to proceed to the highest grades in the service , and because she didn't have a boyfriend . When it was suggested that she be included in the outing she had feigned enthusiasm .

The plan had been to finish work and use the office cloakrooms to get ready for the evening and it was there that two of the girls had decided to "do" Iris' hair . In those days it had been fashionable to wear mohair sweaters over short tight skirts and very high stiletto heels . Iris had all these items . The shoes in particular had been a source of friction between herself and her mother who regarded them as both unsuitable and unnecessary. "Doing " Iris` hair consisted of backcombing it into a ball of frizz and then smoothing some top hair over the mass of frizziness. The result was horrifying to her but the girls insisted that it was " Fabulous ".

They then proceeded to make up her face, using liberal applications of very pale foundation followed by copious use of black mascara , eye liner and eyebrow pencil .These were cosmetics Iris never used having a dread of any kind of ostentation When the grotesque caricature of her own face stared back at her from the mirror above the hand basin she could have died with shame but when she tried to protest the others said she looked " great " and "Fab ".The group of girls had then gone to a pub in the town centre and drunk "Babychams" and "Ponies " until it was time for the show . There had been some mild flirting with a similar group of young men in the pub . The girls had giggled and shoved each other and thoroughly enjoyed the badinage . Although she was much the oldest girl in the group Iris had felt gauche and unsure of herself . To compound her misery , she kept catching sight of herself in the mirrors which lined the wall of the pub and her appearance only confirmed her fears of how she looked .

People were always saying that she should "get out more" and " have a good time ".This presumably was what they meant .In the theatre things became worse . She sat amongst her screaming colleagues , some of whom were practically hysterical in their excitement , feeling as though she was acting a part and acting it badly into the bargain . She was terrified too, in case her disaffection became obvious to the others so was obliged to clap her hands and show signs of enthusiasm. She could not bring herself to scream though – that was simply asking too much – but she feigned enthusiastic delight .Yes , it was a wonderful night .Yes , the music was fabulous , all the time praying for the evening to end and wondering bleakly what was wrong with her .Why couldn`t she enjoy herself like the others ?

Afterwards there was another pub and more Babychams and flirting but by now she was so pleased that the worst was over she was almost light hearted When closing time was announced it came as a shock when , with lots of meaning looks , some of the girls indicated that one of the young men wanted to see her home. Within minutes she was standing at the bus stop with the young man in question who told her his name was Jeffrey James . Iris felt awkward and tongue tied but it soon became obvious that not much was required of her in the way of conversation . When the bus came Jeffrey steered her upstairs and sat next to her placing his arm around her shoulders. She shrank immediately but he seemed to like this .

"You`re a shy girl aren`t you ? " he observed . " I like that ."

He had then proceeded to tell her all about himself . He was a confident young man , proud of his job as a draughtsman in a local engineering firm and full of his plans for the future .During the short bus journey Jeffrey attempted no undue intimacy and Iris began to feel quite relaxed in his company. When they approached her stop he helped her to her feet and down the stairs .They walked the short distance to Iris front gate and he continued his monologue .By now he was boasting about his prowess on the rugby field and telling her how fit he kept himself . This involved much training apparently .

Iris became anxious. She wanted to say goodnight but didn`t quite know how to do it without sounding rude. Eventually she indicated that she was home and ,opening the gate , attempted to thank him for escorting her home . It was then that his manner changed completely. " Oh no you don`t " he`d said as she tried to dismiss him. .With both hands on her shoulders he`d clamped his mouth over hers . She submitted briefly only for him to grab her right hand and place it firmly over the bulge in the front of his trousers whilst his other hand scrabbled up her sweater to locate her breast . With a squeal of outrage she broke free and ran up the garden path , his shout of " bitch " echoing down the street . Iris let herself in praying that her parents were in bed . Thankfully her prayers were answered . Hours later in bed , she realised that there was one consolation to the whole fiasco of an evening . At least Jeffrey James would never recognise her again .

In the darkness of the car Iris shivered slightly .The clarity of that memory surprised her , as did its power to make her feel uncomfortable after all this time .There had been other equally unsuccessful encounters with the opposite sex over the years . Every now and then some female acquaintance would take it on herself to " bring Iris out " whatever that strange expression meant . It involved supervising her choice of clothing on shopping trips , suggesting new hair styles or make up and organising visits to ballrooms and nightclubs even , Iris remembered , on one dreadful occasion a "Singles " weekend in Paris.The sole purpose of all this was "meeting someone" . Iris was unable to explain that she did not want any part of it partly because she knew it was not her style but mainly because she found it deeply demeaning Somehow however, she always ended up taking part in the stupid charade whilst at the same time despising herself for not making her real feelings plain

Then there were the invitations to dinner where , supposedly unknown to her , some lone male had been roped in from somewhere with the idea of   pairing them off . Iris lost count of the number of times she had returned home from these sort of occasions and cried herself to sleep . It wasn't just the no hopers with whom they inevitably paired her which upset her but something within herself , some paralysing condition which made her close up like a shell fish when confronted with a man . Sometimes to her great relief she recognised this same condition in the other person too which made the experience less of an ordeal .

By the time she'd reached 45 these occasions had fizzled out altogether. She supposed then that her status as a " spinster ", that horrible word , was confirmed . Her parents , she realised later , had colluded in this idea , albeit unconsciously ." Oh Iris is a home bird. " they would tell others "She's not one for going out . She likes to be with us . "

Queenie though , had been quite a different kettle of fish Iris recalled . In spite of a domineering mother she had gone out and about and other people had never felt the need to "bring her out ". Iris supposed this was because she appeared to have an active social life and   many interests although these never seemed to include the opposite sex .It was not until she , too, had reached middle age that the two of them had been paired off together as the office spinsters , condemned to be invited to all social occasions as a couple . An intimacy had developed between them almost by default Iris mused . Still , over the years she had come to regard Queenie as a close friend and knew she was seen by her in the same light.

Chapter 5

The village of Godney had originally consisted of a long winding street halfway down a low hill in Hampshire .Two nearby hamlets , High Godney on the rise and Low Godney in the valley flanked the village .Four miles away was the market town of Mitthampton .Once separated from the village by acres of lush pasture , development over the years had joined the whole area together and the Godneys were now little more than suburbs of the town though efforts were maintained to declare their separate identity.

On this spring morning ,Rose Deacon was brushing her teeth prior to leaving the house . She had been born and raised in the area but , after leaving home to join the WRAF at the age of 18 ,had returned infrequently After the death of her parents there was no reason for her to ever come here again but , as her retirement loomed closer , she'd made the decision to return .Tall and almost mannish in build with large square shoulders and narrow hips , her style and demeanour were feminine . She had large regular features which combined well to present an attractive face and crisp curling hair which was almost grey now but immaculately shaped . As a young woman in the WRAF , Rose had been almost fanatical about details like hair , shoes and general appearance and now it was second nature to her to be well turned out .

She noticed a trace of blood on her toothbrush and forced herself to acknowledge at last that one of her back teeth was definitely loose She had followed the instructions of the dental hygienist to the letter but it seemed inevitable now that the tooth would go . It was one of the aspects of ageing that simply could not be ignored . It wasn't that she was vain about her teeth but losing the first one was a definite milestone in the ageing process . Still , she had done well to reach the age she had and keep all her teeth she supposed .

Today was one of her days for working in the bookshop so she had no time to hang about thinking about ageing . It was particularly important that she should be early this morning because Gerald Carey the proprietor and her good friend was leaving her in sole charge for the day whilst he went to London . The original arrangement had been that Rose would work in the shop each Tuesday and Thursday but lately Gerald had taken to ringing her on the off chance to come in and work some half days as well. His partner Eric was in poor health now and Gerald wanted to spend as much time as possible with him.

Rose smiled to herself as she remembered how she had met Gerald Carey. It had been when she'd first come back to live in Godney almost three years ago now . Her next door neighbour had called on her the very first evening and given her the lowdown on everybody in the street . Rose was bemused by all the names and descriptions but some of them had stuck in her mind .The good looking man called Gaye , a family called Pickles and a glamorous red haired divorcee called Myra Maysmore .

Later that week , when a tall , distinguished man of striking good looks had raised his hat to her in the street she had known immediately who he was .

"Good morning . You must be our new neighbour " he'd said extending his hand. "

"And you're one of the Gayes " she'd replied " I'm Rose Deacon . How do you do ?"

His expression had startled her for a moment but then he'd burst into a great roar of laughter .

"Oh dear me " he said finally " Wait until I tell Eric. No. You must come and tell him yourself ." Rose had realised her gaffe immediately but could think of no way of retrieving the situation without making it worse .Before she knew what was happening Gerald had propelled her into the bungalow and introduced her to Eric where he repeated the story to the great amusement of them both.They were both so pleasant and friendly Rose soon lost her discomfiture .

After the joke had been thoroughly enjoyed she was made to stay for coffee and both men provided her with their own view of the neighbourhood and its inhabitants which she found highly entertaining .A mutual interest in Bridge was discovered and the men promised to introduce her to the local club . As the weeks went on Eric began to help her to transform her garden and eventually Rose had found herself helping out in the bookshop at first for just a few hours to help out in an emergency and unpaid , and later as a definite arrangement .

After spending many years overseas with the WRAF , Rose had anticipated her retirement with.pleasure . She had not planned to take on any employment . Within weeks of arriving however she had found that all her spare time was accounted for . She'd joined the WI first of all and , as soon as people got to know that she was retired with time to spare , she was inundated with requests to make use of it .On Monday morning she helped out in a local charity shop and in the afternoon did a session with the C.A.B. Every other Wednesday she was a guide in St. Stephen's church which had many visitors because of its antiquity . Inevitably , Saturday morning saw her in service at a jumble sale , coffee morning or bazaar. Since she`d begun working at the book shop Rose had to make a  conscious effort to keep Fridays free to ensure she had time to attend to her  shopping and the garden Before she`d begun her retirement she had envisaged it as a time to take up new hobbies , visit old friends and take extended holidays , but so far it had not worked out like that . In fact , life now seemed busier than it had been before but she had no complaints about this.

Rose thought back to last night . How funny Queenie had been recounting her adventures with the marriage bureau .Even Iris had had to laugh . She wondered idly about Iris. She remembered her from school of course , Queenie not so well since she was a year or so younger . Iris had always been the retiring type . Did she have a secret romance in her past ? She seemed the sort of person who might have remained unmarried out of devotion to elderly parents . Or could there have been some tragedy ? A broken engagement perhaps or even the death of a fiance . There was something innocent and virginal about Iris .

Still , you never could tell , mused Rose thinking back to her own experiences . For more than 20 years Rose had been the mistress of a senior Army Officer . The affair had continued in spite of difficulties such as both of them being in different continents .They had always managed to meet up for snatched weekends in unlikely locations even when George was in Hong Kong and she was in Cyprus . Perhaps it had been these very obstacles that had kept the passion so intense .Naively , she had believed George when he`d promised that one day they would be together always . First it had been  " when the children  are  at school I`ll ask Moira for a divorce ." Then " As soon as the girls are off our hands I`ll definitely leave " . Until there came a time when he`d stopped promising anything . Even then , she`d been fool enough to cling on to the relationship until a close friend had told her that George` wife had divorced him and that he was about to remarry a much younger woman – oddly enough also named Rose .

Rose thought of herself as a fairly hard boiled person . She`d been 46 when she finally accepted there was no future for her with George Of course there was her own career to think  about .Before she was 44  she`d become a Wing Commander and later that same year been awarded the O.B.E.. Her success at her job had tempered failure in other areas. Because her disillusionment with George had occurred so gradually she had shed no tears then or since . She`d grow accustomed to living alone , even liked it .

When she was younger friends had often said   "What a shame you never married Rose .What a waste ." At the time she'd been inclined to agree . Now nobody would dream of making such a remark to a single woman she thought . People simply assumed that you remained single because you chose to . She had no regrets for what might have been now . In fact , some years ago , when she had bumped into George and his mark two wife whilst shopping in London she had felt only amusement at his obvious discomfiture and was surprised to discover that she did not envy his wife in the least .

She took her jacket from the hall stand and heard a click and then a bang as Evie Piper , the cleaning lady let herself in . Evie was windswept and rosy cheeked , the bulky down jacket she was wearing over two jerseys giving her a deceptively buxom appearance .

"Morning Rose . I'm glad I caught you before you left the house " The glow on her face was not surprising given all those garments thought Rose , watching her divest herself of the top layers . Then she realised that Evie was blushing

" Is something wrong Evie ? " she asked .

"I'm so sorry Rose but I'll have to stop working for you after next week". Evie said apologetically . " We've just found out I'm pregnant you see and Stan's put his foot down ." Rose was surprised but delighted . Evie , she knew , had long since given up hope of having a second child . In fact , Darren her son was 18 .

"How exciting for you . Stan must be thrilled . " Rose smiled warmly.

" He nearly died of shock ! Well , to be honest with you so did I . I thought I was in the change . I went to the well woman clinic to ask about HRT I was feeling so bad , and then the doctor gave me an internal .When we worked it out it seems I'm almost 5 months gone". Evie still looked surprised . " I cried when they confirmed it . The nurse said don't worry , at your age you can get a termination no problem. She didn't understand , bless her . Mind , we haven't told our Darren yet . I don't know quite how to broach it . And I'm so sorry about letting you down ."Evie looked embarrassed again . " I'll miss the money too . It came in handy ."

"Don't give me a thought " Rose answered "You're the important one now I'll never find anyone as reliable as you I know , but I'll put a card in the newsagent's this morning and see what turns up ."

"Well , matter of fact , I think I know someone who might suit . That's as long as you don't mind someone young ? It's Hayley , our Darren's girlfriend .

"But I thought you'd said you didn't approve of her " Rose vaguely remembered a conversation about the girl some months ago .

" That was when we first met her . I must admit we were n't keen . She's from that rough estate near the brick works and Stan had the idea she'd put ideas in Darren's head , but now we've got to know her I quite like her . Only she lost her job when the chicken factory closed down last month and I don't hold with these youngsters hanging about doing nothing .If you like I'll spend the first morning with her showing her how you like things done – just so she'll know how to go on. " Evie was buttoning her overall now .

"That sounds grand , but you only spend two mornings here . Is that going to be enough work for her ?" Rose liked the idea of giving work to an unemployed teenager .

"Well I'm hoping she 'll take over all my ladies if they'll have her . The thing is I'll be really glad to have this job back as soon as the baby is a few months old . If you've no objection I'd bring it with me , so in a way Hayley would just be holding the fort. I reckon to be back at work inside six months ."

" That sounds an ideal arrangement all round . But have you asked her yet ? Rose enquired

" Well no . As I told you , we haven't mentioned anything to our Darren yet I worked all this out in bed last night . I was too excited to sleep much .Poor Stan didn't get much either ." the two ladies laughed .

"How about if I brought her here on Friday ? She's desperate for a job so I know she'll jump at the chance."

Rose was pleased to agree   .

Chapter 6

Iris was hanging out her washing when she heard the telephone ring. It was still quite chilly even for April but there was a good drying wind .With luck everything should be dry by teatime she thought . She sighed with annoyance at the interruption and made her way indoors . As she had suspected it was her neighbour Ada who had an unerring knack of ringing at the most inconvenient times . She wanted to know if Iris would come and have tea with her that afternoon and , should she just happen to be going near the shops , could she pick up her prescription and a large box of unsweetened muesli .?

Actually , I hadn`t planned to go shopping at all today . This is what Iris would have liked to say. Instead she told Ada she would do it , telling herself that she might well be housebound one day and be glad of a kind neighbour . She had to take Nellie out anyway , she justified to herself and it wasn`t that much more trouble to take the route near the shops. Anyway , she could take the opportunity to pay the paper bill which had arrived that morning Another item in the morning`s post was an invitation to a school reunion which would take place in September . Iris had tossed this aside . She didn`t fancy it in the least . In her experience the only people who turned up at these events were those with something to boast about and she had no wish to be patronised yet again .

Something else had come this morning too – another thing to worry about . There had been a card from the health centre inviting her to attend for a smear test . There had been a previous invitation about three years ago which Iris had ignored . She could not bear the thought of being examined

" down there ". Also she was unsure whether the test was applicable   for somebody of her status She had the idea that you did not need it if you were unmarried . She would not allow herself to name the word " virgin ". Who could she possibly ask about this without causing herself untold embarrassment ? No doubt the test would be painful or uncomfortable too , even if it was necessary ? On the other hand she knew it was foolish to neglect this aspect of her health since there was a family history of cancer.

Why was life so complicated and difficult ? The obvious answer was to discuss the matter with somebody but it would have to be somebody she didn`t know and how could you talk of such things with a stranger ? She really didn`t like thinking about it much less talking about it . Therefore she would simply ignore the problem and

27

end up despising herself for doing so. This apt self analysis made her so cross she banged shut the kitchen door causing Nellie to leap up from her basket in surprise.

These weren't the only reasons why Iris was out of sorts . Ever since she'd finished reading the Phillip Larkin biography she'd been in a of daze of disappointment . At the same time she realised the stupidity of this reaction . Ridiculous to be so upset about somebody you never even knew she told herself . But her disillusionment was acute . She had admired – no , more , - revered the poet for many years . She had identified with him , feeling that they were kindred spirits with everything in common . Now , having learned of the many unpleasant traits of his personality and the way in which he'd treated women she would never be able to enjoy his poetry again It had been like being robbed of something precious she felt .

This and the other niggling problems made her feel out of sorts so that when she called on Ada at teatime she was short tempered and preoccupied . As usual , the door was locked and Iris fetched the key from under the flower pot where the Home Help always left it despite being warned not to do this .She called to Ada as she let herself in ."Come on in my dear " the mannish voice answered Ada was often taken for a man when speaking on the telephone . Her voice was almost baritone.In person though , she was of very feminine appearance with a large bosom , small waist and shapely hips . Only her swollen ankles and misshapen feet gave away her disability.

The mobile hairdresser still called weekly to attend to her blue rinse and twice yearly perm and Ada was fond of jewellry , never without a string of beads and a brooch though she could no longer wear her rings . She still liked to bake her own bread and scones occasionally although she was barely able to bend down to the oven these days .Ada could still clean her silver and dust her ornaments if they were placed within her reach and this was something Iris occasionally helped her to do . But the bungalow , once so spotless and immaculate , no longer smelled of beeswax and once gleaming surfaces were now smeared or lightly filmed with dust . The place could not be described as dirty or even neglected , it was just not as it had been .

Fortunately the decline had coincided with a deterioration in Ada's eyesight so that she was unable to tell the extent of the problem but she was still aware that her home was suffering through lack of care . Ada knew that the Home Help had neither the time or the inclination to take the care she thought was necessary but , since she refused to employ extra help , there was nothing to be done about it .Iris saw a cobweb hanging from the hall light fitting and knocked it down noticing as she did so the grubby marks on the paintwork and the skirting . Entering the kitchen to fetch the teatray , she saw that the work surfaces had become stained and that there was ingrained grease at the base of the gas cooker and in the corners of the units . The place needed a complete spring clean . She could not blame the Home Help who only spent an hour each morning with Ada , and was kept busy helping her to wash and dress before washing a few dishes and then dashing about with the vacuum cleaner .It occurred to Iris then that she should offer to do some cleaning but she dismissed the thought immediately. Where would it end ? After all , Ada was well able to afford to pay a cleaner.

The old lady was avid to hear everything that had been happening in the close and was disappointed that Iris had no particular gossip to impart . She questioned her closely about the local shops and their inhabitants , the progress of the protest about the by pass and the state of the flower rota in the church . Iris tried to be as entertaining as she could but her heart was not in it today . Sensing this , the old lady became annoyed and was soon poised to find fault . Ada was a retired head teacher of an infants school . She had trained just after the war and had never adapted to the laissez faire days of the sixties . She was a firm believer in learning by rote and sitting still at desks and had very firm ideas of how things should be outside the classroom too . After retirement she had occupied herself with the parish council and her duties as a JP , but then arthritis had struck and she`d been confined to her house with nobody to dominate but her neighbours and the cleaner .

Although she was fond of Iris and thoroughly approved of her , Ada could not resist the temptation of an argument . Today she had the perfect excuse – an unsuitable library book .The book in question had seemed quite innocuous to Iris – an autobiography of a well known poet – and she had taken the precaution of looking through it beforehand to ensure that there was no cause for offence . Because the writer was in the same age group as Ada she had felt confident that all would be well . Unfortunately there was a chapter describing a wartime encounter with a prostitute and Ada took great exception to this. As far as she was concerned it was just another example of falling standards all round ." Why was it published at all ? " she demanded , " At one time the library would never have stocked such a book . Decent people don`t want to read about these things ." She sighed and went on   "There used to be such nice writers years ago . People like

Beverly Nicholls for example . Now he was a thoroughly nice person .I met him once at a garden party . 1958 it must have been . He signed a copy of one of his books for me . He was absolutely charming ." Iris said nothing . She had heard this story before and even been shown the book – a copy of "Down the garden path " still in pristine condition .

Ada continued   " And what about Joyce Grenfell ? She was a really nice woman as well as being very clever .And she was funny , too , without ever being vulgar . There was no need for vulgarity then so why is it needed now?

" Why ask me ? "Iris thought irritably .Anyone would think it was my fault . She struck back , tired of letting Ada always have the upper hand .

" Everyone knows that Beverly Nicholls was a notorious homosexual , " she said angrily."So was Godfrey Winn , that other man you admired so much . As for Joyce Grenfell , no doubt she was a lovely person but you may be sure she had a dark side too . Everyone does."

" I don't believe a word of it . For one thing , even the Queen Mother admired Beverly Nicholls. I happen to know that for a fact ." Ada said this as if it settled the matter.

" Well , I can prove it, " said Iris thoroughly nettled. "They have Beverly Nicholls' biography in the library. According to that he's a self confessed homosexual . That's one of the reasons I've never brought you the book ."

Ada was really angry now . " Nasty , jealous people always accuse decent people of unspeakable things . It's a pack of lies you can be sure . They deserve to be prosecuted in my opinion . And I'm surprised at you , Iris You're not usually so argumentative and... and .." she struggled for the right word " ...aggressive . I'll put it down to your time of life ." This was the spark that really fired Iris' temper .

"For heavens sake Ada! How can you be so blinkered ? You read the papers and see the television .You must know these things go on . Only an idiot could be so unaware . If you must know , I'm hard put to find you a book that will suit you , you're so out of touch with reality. "

" Well , really !" Ada was lost for words but soon recovered herself   " I've never known you be rude before , Iris.I'm very surprised and disappointed ." Ada's eyes were full of tears . " I can see I've become a nuisance to you .Please don't bother to fetch me any books in future. I'll do without ."

" Oh Ada " Iris reached out and touched her hand . " I'm sorry I lost my temper . You know it's no trouble at all to fetch your books . Please don't be cross with me . I'm out of sorts today .Forgive me please ." Eventually , mollified , Ada began to talk of other things .

Back at home Iris mulled it over . In a way she could sympathise with Ada's point of view . For that generation things had been so different . Everything was black or white . Homosexuality was never a topic for discussion . Many women must have gone through life without knowing anything about it .As for bisexuality , for a good part of her life Iris herself had never even considered the possibility of such a thing – though from everything you read nowadays a third of the population were that way inclined – or so some people would have you believe .

Some years ago she had read about the marriage of Harold Nicolson and Vita Sackville West with incredulity , partly because of what she read and partly at what it revealed about her own ignorance and naivety . At the time she had comforted herself with the idea that such people were rare and that their behaviour had to do with them being artistic , creative individuals leading bohemian lives unlike the common herd . As time went on though it seemed that more and more people in the public eye were moved to reveal sexual secrets in their lives which must mean that such behaviour was common and even normal .

Even so , Iris could still not believe that this applied to the circles she moved in. She thought about her own family . Her own father for instance . Could he have been a latent homosexual ? The idea was so ludicrous that she almost laughed out loud . She remembered him playing cricket with her brother in the back garden " Don't throw the ball like that " he instructed ." That's the way girls and sissies throw it ." " Sissies " and "Nancy Boys " was the way homosexuals were described then .To Iris those names had just meant a man who was effeminate in manner .

There had been a curate everyone had joked about because of his long wavy hair and falsetto voice . He was particularly popular with old ladies she recalled . Would they have been so fond of him if they had really understood about his proclivities ? More recently too , revelations about various people in the public eye had caused her to question her ideas . Modern day icons like Leonard Bernstein , John Cheever , Stephen Spender and many others seemed to have led double lives . No one seemed to be shocked or censorious about it although she herself had felt appalled on learning these facts . What did this say about her ?

She seemed to be very similar to Ada in her point of view . Did this mean that she was old fashioned and out of touch ? She was a

31

middle aged spinster after all . If she were honest , she had to admit she was inclined towards Ada`s way of thinking in many ways .People went on about being open and honest about these matters but surely things were better in more innocent days ? Well , it was five o clock . She was relieved to turn on the radio where the PM programme took her mind off this conumdrum .

Chapter 7

Hayley Beale was watching " Style Challenge " on the television . The girl they were making over had been given a completely different hair style which transformed her pudgy features. Hayley went up to the mirror over the fireplace and stared discontentedly at her own reflection . Apart from a few pimples on her forehead she had an attractive , elfin face . She pulled her dark ,frizzy hair this way and that trying to achieve a similar look to the girl on TV but gave up scowled and returned to the sofa. Rita , her mother , entered the room searching for her handbag on her way out , her bottom huge in the polyester trousers she wore under a too short denim jacket .

"Are you going lie there all day watching that telly ?" she challenged "You should be down the job centre looking for work ." Hayley shrugged .

Rita wasn't really interested in getting answers to her questions .She was worn down with the struggle of coping with three recalcitrant teenagers without a husband to support her , as well as chronic bronchitis and her part time job in the brewery ." I've got to take our Wayne to the law centre . You could at least wash a few pots and run the hoover around . Sandy wants her video changing too ." Rita glanced in the mirror and ran a hand through the back of her hair . Better wear a scarf she decided .

" And don't make faces at me behind my back because I can see you in the mirror . Cheeky Cow! " she shouted , her temper flaring . " I'm just about fed up with you and your moods ."

" All right . All right . Don't keep on to me " the girl's voice was truculent but Rita took no notice . She found her handbag lying behind the door and left the house . Hayley looked around the room in disgust . She was fed up . She hated this house , clapped out furniture , old , ugly curtains and smelly stained carpet . She hated Rastus , the old German Shepherd her mother kept as a burglar deterrent . As if anyone would be daft enough to burgle this dump .You could spend all day here cleaning up here and it wouldn't look any better afterwards . Why couldn't they live somewhere decent ?

It was only in recent months that Hayley had begun to question her own life style . Since she had started " going " with Darren Piper in fact . His house had been a revelation to her. True , it was just a council house like theirs , but everything there was looked after properly. Their garden was full of spring flowers now instead of rusting bikes and old fridges like round here . The grass was cut regularly and the front door was newly painted . Indoors it was even nicer , everything was sparkling clean and smelled fresh The family ate their meals at a table and the food had been cooked by Mrs . Piper and not brought in from a takeaway or in a box from Tesco ready to heat in the microwave .

Hayley found it a pleasure to wash the dishes in the Piper's kitchen where everything had its place and had actually volunteered to help Mrs. Piper when she planned to do her spring clean . She began to spend more and more time there .Her mother would have been shocked to the core to see how domesticated her daughter was in somebody else's home .Both Darren and his parents had hinted more than once that it was time he visited Hayley's home and this prospect was a continuing source of anxiety .The problem was that Hayley did not dare to invite Darren to her house . It was so different to his. What would he think ? The closest he had been was to the end of the road . At first it had been easy to fob him off with tales of a strict mother who didn't agree with boyfriends ,but that story had worn thin The truth was that she was desperately ashamed of her home feeling , perhaps unreasonably , that Darren would somehow blame her for the squalor . She didn't dare take the chance anyway .

After she'd been to the Pipers for the first time Hayley had returned to her own home determined to do something about the conditions there . After four hours in the kitchen , having washed down all the paint work and scrubbed the cracked floor tiles until her shoulders ached   , she had acknowledged defeat .It simply didn't make any difference . The only thing that would work would be to have the whole place gutted and everything renewed . It was completely beyond her.

Later that day , sitting on the sofa together beforer "Coronation Street " had finished and feeling a rare sense of intimacy with her mother , she had confided the problem . Rita was truly baffled .

" Why can't you bring him here ? I don't mind .What's wrong with the place ? I know we haven't got the money to be posh but it's nothing to be ashamed of ." Then angrily "I never took you for a snob Hayley ." Rita was flushed with annoyance . Then she began to cry with the sheer injustice of it all . There was no gratitude , nothing to acknowledge the hardship she'd experienced in trying to " make do ". She'd done the best she could , she thought .

" You ungrateful little cow ! Have you any idea what a struggle it is trying to put food in your mouths let alone have the place decorated and buy fancy furniture ? If you and our Wayne got off your idle arses and brought some proper money in it would help but all you do is take , take ,take ! Then you have the bloody cheek to tell me this place isn`t good enough for your fancy boyfriend . Do you think I like living like this ? It`s not my fault your father buggered off .” Hayley had cried then too.Tears of frustration and fury . Why didn`t her mother understand ?

After a while Rita got up and wiped her eyes . She went to the kitchen and returned with two mugs of tea . She hated to see her daughter`s misery but concluded it would be a good thing if the young couple went their separate ways . Whoever he was, he was no better than them and he was obviously giving Hayley ideas – making her turn against her own family . It wasn`t right. Who did these people think they were anyway ? They only lived in a council house same as she did , even if his Dad did work for the council .There were several boys living in this street who would be just as suitable for Hayley instead of making herself miserable about Darren bloody Piper . Rita fumed .

She handed Hayley a mug .“ Come on .No point in carrying on like that .Let`s watch “Heartbeat “You can come down the club with me later on if you want . They have Bingo for the last hour .”

Hayley brightened . She`d never been to the club before .Under 18s weren`t allowed but she could soon make herself look 18. She took the mug from her mother noticing that there was a nasty chip in one place , but said nothing and drank from the other side .That had been last Sunday ; Hayley had accompanied her mother to the club and even joined in with the sing song which was a feature of that night`s entertainment before bingo. Rita had hoped the upset had been a storm in a teacup but since then , Hayley`s mood had not improved . Rita couldn`t help noticing her disparaging looks , particularly towards herself when she was getting ready to go out of an evening . She had seen the way her daughter`s lip curled when meals were discussed “ Count me out . I`m going round Darren`s “ she`d said more than once and her reply when she`d been asked to hoover round the house

“ What`s the use ? It wont look any better.” It was all the fault of that boyfriend Rita knew and she determined to do somet hing about it .

Her chance came sooner than she expected . After she`d been to the Cash And Carry , Rita called in at O`Riorden`s where corned beef was on special offer as well as thick sliced white on a two for one promotion . Rita bought four . She took her purchases to the checkout and stood in a short queue . A woman approached and stood next to her .There was something about the way she glanced into Rita's basket that Rita didn't like . She stared back at the woman belligerently and suddenly realised who she was – Mrs . bloody Piper – she was almost certain of it .

" You Darren's mum - Mrs Piper ? " she asked truculently .The woman started . She had been day dreaming . She looked back at her questioner in surprise .It was somebody she knew by sight , a plump , dyed blonde woman in too tight trousers , whose perm was badly in need of renewal .

" I'm Hayley's mum ." Rita continued belligerently .

" Nice to meet you " Evie replied , smiling hesitantly " Your Hayley's always round our house. " Rita's face darkened ." She's a lovely girl "Evie added hastily " Ever so helpful .I hope you don't mind her coming round so often ? " She smiled again feeling threatened by Rita's hostile gaze

" S'matter of fact , I do mind . I don't hold with our Hayley mixing with people who turn her against her own family , making her think we're not good enough for your precious Darren ." Rita almost spat out the boy's name . .Evie was aghast .

" I'm sure we've done nothing of the kind . We've always made Hayley welcome and I wouldn't dream of…." But Rita cut her short . She had worked herself into a rage now .

" Oh yes you have. You and your home made lasagne and your door chimes I've heard all about you . Teaching our Hayley to make flaky pastry and look down on us . I can't afford a dish washer nor a food processer . But I haven't got a husband who work for the council " She paused for breath " Who the ##### hell do you think you are anyway ? " she shouted . " You're no ###### better than us ." Evie flinched at the foul expletives .A hush had descended on the shop.Rita's face was so close to her now Evie could see the broken veins on her cheeks and the mark round her chin where her make up ended .

From the corner of her eye Evie saw several customers watching the entertainment with obvious enjoyment . She felt totally mortified . To be accosted and screamed at in a public place like this with other people gawping and listening .And what had she done to deserve it? The sooner Darren got shut of that girl the better . If this was a sample of her family Evie wanted no part of them .She would have liked to make some dignified reply but reasoned that the other woman was quite capable of continuing her tirade of abuse or even attacking her. She placed her wire basket on the ground and attempted to turn away but was obstructed by Mr. O`Riorden who had heard the commotion and come rushing down from cooked meats .

" Ladies , ladies whatever is going on ? I can`t have customers causing a disturbance like this ?"He was pink in the face . Neither woman answered .Evie pushed past him rudely and made for the exit her face flaming . Rita coolly turned towards the checkout , ignoring the customers who continued to stare at her and whisper amongst themselves . She felt very pleased with herself . It was wonderful luck that her chance for confrontation had come so soon . She`d seized her opportunity and made good use of it .

Waiting for the bus , Evie played over the embarrassing scene in her mind She was trembling with shock . She would not have Hayley in the house again . Stan wouldn`t allow it anyway . Not once he knew what had happened . She`d always had her misgivings about the girl ever since she`d said where she lived . Hayley couldn`t help her family of course but Darren would be better off without her .They were only kids anyway , when all was said and done .

Then Evie remembered Rose and the cleaning job . Well , she`d just have to think of something else . There were always people looking for cleaning jobs Good thing she hadn`t had the chance to say anything to the girl ...then again , it wasn`t the poor girl`s fault that her mother was so awful. The bus hove into view at this point . Evie assembled her shopping and located her purse .Her hands were still trembling she noted .

Chapter 8

Just north of the old station , opposite the open space where the brick works had once been ,was a straggling row of 40 council houses. In the days when they had all been owned by the council they had presented a uniform picture of green front doors with window frames picked out in cream . Since the right to buy however , great changes had taken place . More than 30 of the houses had been bought by the occupants and these properties flaunted their independence in a variety of ways . Several of them had since been repossessed but not before irrevocable changes had taken place .

Some had been extended either front or back and most had had their windows replaced with plastic framed double glazing . Some had removed their front privet hedges to make way for a drive in . Others had been encased with imitation stone cladding . The front doors were a variety of colours now too – some of them were even glass .The overall effect though was spoiled by most of the properties which were not owner occupied Several of these were empty and boarded up but even some occupied ones had boarded up windows and old rusting appliances lying in their neglected front gardens .

Yards of grafitti executed in lurid colours of spray paint disfigured the low concrete wall in front of the old brickworks . There was a small playground with broken swings and a rusty slide which now seemed to be used as a dogs toilet . At the end of the road where once there had been a corner shop there was now a burnt out shell , windows covered with corrugated iron which rattled in the wind .The street was called Berringer Row after a former deceased councillor .

Shortly before 8 .30 am , a middle aged man emerged from one of the houses . Nobody looking at Cyril Gotes could guess at the squalor which lay behind his front door . He was a dapper figure , smartly dressed with an impeccably ironed shirt and highly polished shoes . He had a military haircut and sported a well kept , gingery moustache . As an ex-serviceman he was particular about his appearance . He was not an attractive looking man however despite his smartness .He was short and stockily built with a low forehead and broad simian features . These , combined with a grizzled , balding head and red complexion were not appealing to the eye .

He walked smartly for about 100 yards looking straight ahead , the metal tips of his shoes ringing out against the paving , ignoring two elderly women who stood gossiping at a gate . He wanted no truck with neighbours . He turned left into the cul de sac where the lock up garages were . His was the first in the row and , when he unlocked it , presented a model of tidiness . Just inside the door was a hook where his brown warehouse coat hung. Carefully shaking it first , Cyril donned the garment and climbing into his van reversed it out of the garage , turned off the engine and went back to the garage to retrieve some tools and lock up .

In the house Cyril had just left , Sandy Gotes was in bed . She and her husband occupied separate rooms . His was the small bedroom next to the bathroom where there was barely space for more than a single bed and a chest of drawers . Hers was the master bedroom . She lay in the centre of a double bed with a cat and two kittens on one side of her and a small mongrel dog cuddled into the hollow behind her knees , The room was in semi darkness because the curtains , long since parted from their hooks , were held together with large safety pins . Heaps of clothing , most of it soiled , were piled onto every available surface. On each side of the bed were cups , plates , empty mineral bottles and piles of old newspapers and magazines .

Paper backed books , toast crusts and the remains of a fish supper still in its paper wrapping lay about on the floor . Cats had relieved themselves at some time in this room and this sharp , unmistakable odour dominated the other smells of stale air , mouldy food , mildew and the sweetish smell of dirt .In the midst of this malodorous den Sandy dozed oblivious to the smell . She was an enormous woman , all 20 stone of her. Strangely , the fat which encircled her body from the neck down had avoided her face so that her delicate features remained unblurred . She was a pretty woman still and looked younger than her 38 years .

19 years as an army wife had taken Sandy to various locations around the world until her husband's retirement from service four years ago. When the family had acquired this house she had been delighted to escape from the rigours of occupying a service quarter which was open to inspection at any time and expected   to be maintained to a high standard of cleanliness on pain of disciplinary action .Never a house proud person , she had felt obliged to co-operate to a certain extent although her efforts had never met with the satisfaction of her husband .He was the one who stayed up until 3am ensuring that the cooker was free of grease and the windows gleaming before a march out inspection . On moving into her new home Sandy had declared her independence and had done no housework since.

Always a large lady , her weight had increased by about 5 stone since she had moved here .She took no exercise at all spending most of her time in bed . Indeed she had not left the house for over two years. Her sheer bulk made it impossible for her to walk for more than a few yards and Cyril refused to allow her to get into his van . As for shopping she simply did not do any . Cyril looked after himself entirely while Sandy relied on her next door neighbour Rita to bring her what she required . Rita had a card for the Cash and Carry which enabled her to buy the vast quantities of crisps , coca cola and chocolate biscuits which formed the large part of Sandy`s diet This was supplemented by fish suppers and take aways from the local Chinese and Indian shops . Sandy paid dearly for these because Rita`s teenage children were not willing to collect the meals for her without a substantial cash bribe.

Even if she`d wanted to , Sandy`s health did not allow her to do much these days . About a year ago when she`d suffered a severe attack of bronchitis the doctor had warned her that she was digging her grave with her own teeth . He had offered a period in hospital where her weight loss could be medically supervised and , when she had refused , had sent the health visitor to persuade her. When this proved unsuccessful he had involved the Social Services . For several weeks Sandy had been visited by Miss Welch , a pleasant , older lady who tried to tell her that she was really suffering from depression . Eventually she , too , had given up and for the last six months Sandy had been left in peace Even Cyril didn`t bother her these days . In fact, although she could hear him pottering around in the evenings , whole weeks would go by without her having to set eyes on him . This suited them both very well . Every Friday , an envelope containing some folded notes was left on top of the bathroom cupboard . This was Sandy`s "housekeeping money ".

Once in a while Hilda , Sandy`s sister would call round . Deeply mortified by the squalor she would attempt to deal with the worst of it . On these occasions Sandy would have clean sheets and it had even been known for Hilda to persuade her to have a bath although her sheer bulk made this quite a performance. Hilda had no truck with Cyril and he kept well out of her way too. If he saw the white mini parked outside the house he took care to stay away until it had gone .It did occur to Hilda to wonder why her brother-in-law tolerated the situation but she knew better than to discuss it with Sandy . Cyril was " not right ". All the family knew that . Sandy had been warned not to marry him even though she`d been pregnant at the time. Now she was paying for it. It was the children Hilda felt bad about but both of them had had the sense to leave home as soon as they got the chance . Young Cyril was in the army and Karen was working in a hotel in London and took care not to come home for holidays.

Sandie stirred in her bed as the bell rang . She heard Rita shout "Only me Sand " and struggled to sit up in bed . Rita entered the room wrinkling her nose

" Christ . It stinks in here!" The dog , recognising that her voice meant food jumped down from the bed and began to nose around her feet . "I'm early this morning." Rita explained " Only I've got to take our Wayne to the law centre for 9.30 and I thought I'd go from there to the Cash and Carry .You're low on cat food . Now tell me what else you want ."

"My throat's bad " Sandy croaked. "Don't get me those fags again I'd better have something milder . Just get me the usual stuff , but ask your Wayne if he'll take my video back . They charge double if it's not back by 3.30."

"Well , I'll ask him " Rita sounded doubtful "But you know I can't make him if he's in one of his moods . Best ask him yourself . Ring at lunchtime . By the way , Sandy , I shall want some money."

"All right . I'll get it for you . What about your Hayley then ? Would she change my video?" Sandy persisted , struggling with her pillows in an attempt to locate her purse. Her movements exposed a large portion of her chest and upper arms .

"She's watching telly , little cow ! She's been in a right mood all week . I'm fed up with the lot of them I can tell you . You're lucky yours are off your hands ." Rita answered staring at Sandy's exposed flesh .

" Coo , you've got a terrible rash there Sandy . Looks like measles or something .You want to get it looked at."

"It's nothing " Sandy said defensively , pulling up the stained covers .

"How much money do you want Rite ? Do us a favour will you and feed the dog and cats ? They're starving ." On cue , the animals followed Rita downstairs . Sandy took the opportunity to have a really good scratch . Then , finding the remote control of the television she switched on in time to catch the start of " Kilroy ".

Chapter 9

Thelma Honeyspan put down the magazine she had been leafing through and wandered over to the window again , the third time she`d done so in the last 30 minutes , The view had not altered . Her neat front garden stretched in front of her . The other houses in the quiet suburban close remained unchanged . There was nothing new to see . Inside , her immaculate sitting room was like a furniture showroom . Everything was new and meticulously arranged and , apart from the magazine on the sofa , there was nothing out of place . 18 months ago , Thelma thought , if anyone had told her that she would be living in a bungalow like this with all the time in the world to enjoy it she would have laughed in their face .

The same thing applied to her appearance too.She looked at her nails . She`d had a manicure that morning though even that could not disguise the 30 years of prior neglect . The painted nails looked incongruous at the end of her clumsy , reddish fingers and no amount of hand creams would restore the shape of her hands , swollen and battered through years of hard work .Her hair was the biggest difference of all . She , who had never set foot in a salon before the age of   55 , was now a regular patron of the most expensive hairdresser in the area Her hair , once pepper and salt and dragged back into a bun , was now a delicate shade of ash blonde which framed her heavy features attractively .

Her face had not changed . Somehow she could not come to grips with cosmetics . After all she had never been used to using make up and 57 was too old for learning new tricks in spite of the beauticians who urged her to try various products . Mother had called it " painting " and had never allowed it in the days when Thelma might have been tempted to try . Her figure had not altered either . She was still stockily built , broad in the beam and thick waisted with heavy legs . The majority of plump women had good bosoms Thelma had always observed . But here again nature had cheated and hers was disappointingly meagre which caused problems when buying clothes .

As for her feet .... well the least said the better , but what could you expect after all those years pounding hospital wards?The wardrobes   in her bedroom were full of new clothes but Thelma did not really like to wear them . Every morning , if she hadn`t anywhere special to go , she put on the same old skirt and jersey .When you`d worn a uniform for years it was hard to stand in front of a wardrobe deciding what to wear . In the past it had not been a problem .Now she understood the expression " spoiled for choice" Before of course this sort of choice had just been a fantasy .The strangest thing of all though, was that now she had the things she`d  always  craved Thelma found she did not really want them after all . There was something missing still but she didn`t know what it was.

Perhaps she had made a mistake in moving back to this area but , after all she`d been brought up here and  she supposed this was were her roots were. .30 odd years was a long time to be away from anywhere  though  especially if you hadn`t bothered keeping up with people you used to know. Occasionally she saw the odd person she remembered from her schooldays and sometimes they were friendly , Queenie for example , but on the whole Thelma could not help having doubts over whether her decision to return here had been a wise one .

Before she`d moved back  here ,she`d planned it all out in her mind She would join the golf club , not that she`d ever played the game but she knew you got a good class of person there . She would start attending St. Stephen`s church and perhaps join the Ladies Guild . She would make new friends and entertain them at luncheon parties just like Mrs. Oliphant , the lady her mother had once cleaned for had done . People would ask her about her past and she would refer casually to " my late husband ".

Only somehow it hadn`t quite worked out as she`d planned . When she`d enquired about joining the golf club she`d been told there was a two year waiting list . At St. Stephen`s nobody had spoken to her . The vicar had made his introduction and welcomed her to the parish but had seemed too preoccupied to listen to her tell him how she had been confirmed there in 1955 . She asked him about the Ladies guild but apparently it was long defunct . "Sadly , most ladies seem to have jobs these days " he had told her . " even my own wife runs a playgroup although she is , of course , heavily involved with parish work too." There was a young wives club and an old folks weekly luncheon club but nothing , it seemed , for her particular age group . As for her entertaining plans – whom do you entertain when you know nobody ?

Thelma had been to the local library and discovered there were heaps of clubs to join but they were all geared to particular activities . She could not play bridge and had no interest in archaeology , photography or bell ringing . There was something called the Housewives society but she didn`t regard herself as a housewife . Anyway it sounded rather down market and unappealing she thought . On the other hand , The University of the Third Age which apparently was desperately seeking new members , seemed far too high powered and beyond her reach. It was all very disappointing but then she had become used to that .

On the polished drum table was a large , silver photograph frame containing a picture of an elderly man . This was Graham Honeyspan , her late husband . She looked at it fondly . Thelma`s marriage had lasted only seven months and been uncomsummated into the bargain . Graham had left her all his worldly goods however , which she reckoned was a very good exchange for nursing him in his final days before the stomach cancer finally killed him . In the space of a few months she had become a woman of means and a woman with a past – two things she had always craved but never expected to achieve . And she`d got them without having to do any of the nasty things which would normally be involved in achieving this status . It was better than winning the lottery Thelma thought .

There was no point flaunting her wealth in Portsmouth . Too many people knew how she`d  acquired  it to make her situation viable there .Some of her colleagues had been downright jealous , hinting at horrible things she had refused to acknowledge . She hadn`t said a word when Graham proposed but it was amazing how news got around .She`d noticed them sniggering in the canteen  and how conversations suddenly stopped when she entered the room .Some of the younger ones had been particularly offensive , asking her about her trousseau in a suggestive manner .Then there was that book they`d left in her locker “ The Joy of Sex “ or some such filth . It had gone straight into the bin anyway . She`d taken care that none of them knew when the wedding was due to take place .

The biggest delight of all was when she `d handed in her resignation  form . In the space headed “ reason for leaving “ she`d put “marriage ” in great printed letters. Oh , the satisfaction she`d felt walking out of the hospital after her last day of work .There`d been nothing to compare with it before or since .

Of course Graham had been very weak by then . Much too ill for a honeymoon . For Thelma though , it had been almost like a holiday living in Graham`s huge old house , gloomy though it was . While he`d rested in the afternoons she`d spent hours rummaging through drawers and  cupboards . Some of them hadn`t been touched for almost 20 years . All the clothing of the first Mrs. Honeyspan remained in the wardrobes though she`d died in 1979 . Thelma had boxed most of it up to send to charity shops but had kept the furs and jewellry .

After Graham died Thelma had sold the house .The new owners planned to turn it into a nursing home and had been glad to buy most of the furnishings from her . Mr. Addicott her solicitor had advised her to put the furniture in for auction but Thelma could not imagine anyone wanting to such dark , heavy stuff and had been glad to dispose of it for whatever price she was offered in spite of the solicitor`s demurs .

Then she had made a point of buying the most modern bungalow she could find in this neighbourhood .It was one of a small , exclusive development of what were described as "executive homes ". Hers had gadgets and fittings she was not even aware existed until she`d seen them here . She had " central dust extraction " for example which made a conventional vacuum cleaner redundant and other extras such as triple glazing and solar powered heating .All the windows were fitted with security roller blinds and the gardens had been landscaped .

The whole place was so labour saving and efficient to run that Thelma could have kept it immaculate herself with less than 10 minutes work a day . She had always dreamed of having help in the house however so had felt compelled to engage a "daily ". The trouble was that there was very little for her to do . She made Thelma feel uncomfortable anyway .

Mrs. Norish seemed much too grand to be a cleaner .Thelma felt,   ridiculously , that she should be waiting on her. She couldn`t help feeling too , that Mrs.Norish sensed that she was not used to having help and could see through her façade of gentility . Perhaps it was her own fault for being too chummy with her but how were you supposed to behave towards your daily help ? Thelma did not know . She determined that she would dispense with Mrs Norish soon and find somebody more down market . She had the perfect excuse after all . There was simply not enough work to keep a cleaner occupied . But she had to have somebody . Apart from anything else she needed the company

Thelma had always dreamed of foreign travel but that , too , had been a source of disappointment .It was simply no fun on your own . It was only in Mills and Boon novels that lone women had exciting adventures on holiday abroad . The reality was that you had one lonely drink in the hotel bar surrounded by people who were all enjoying themselves , then dinner which you ate alone before retiring to your lonely hotel room . Graham Honeyspan owned a timeshare apartment in Florida which now belonged to Thelma and this was where she`d spent the loneliest holiday of her life . And that was her problem now decided Thelma . She had never had time to be lonely in the past , but she was lonely now and had to do something about it. .

Chapter 10

At the bottom of the recreation ground in the vandalised hut which had once been home to the bowling club , Hayley and two other teenaged girls were sharing a " joint " . Since the major bust up with her boyfriend Darren two weeks ago , Hayley had taken up with her girlfriends again . She`d hung around the house crying for two or three days , getting on Rita`s nerves , until boredom had sent her down to the shopping centre where the girls hung out during the day and she`d got talking to them .They were suspicious of her at first . After all you can`t just drop people because you`ve got a boyfriend and then just expect to take up with them again when you feel like it .

But the girls did have a lot in common . Besides all living in the same street , they had attended the same school and all three of them were unemployed although Sharon had worked until recently on the checkout at O`Riordens. An incident concerning a missing £20 note had put paid to this , her first venture into the field of employment , whilst Hayley and Michelle were out of work .This was the first occasion that Hayley had ever tried a

" joint ". The other girls claimed to be old hands at the experience but the truth was that they had only tried it twice before . Before graduating to cannabis they had all indulged in glue sniffing but now were all agreed that glue was just for kids . Cannabis was far more sophisticated and not much more expensive.

For her part though ,Hayley could not see what the fuss was about. The stuff smelled unpleasant and tasted worse but the other two seemed to like it so she supposed she should persevere After all , cigarettes were foul too until you got used to them .In fact , the stuff which had been sold to them by Duane the local pusher was not cannabis at all but an ersatz mixture which he always palmed off on people he knew could not tell the difference.The three girls were all in this category. .Eventually they would wise up , there was no avoiding that but until then he could afford to laugh to himself when they made their purchase .

It was dark in the hut and smelly too , but there was also something exciting and dangerous about it . There was no definite arrangement but it was quite likely that some boys Sharon knew might turn up later . At least Yozzer had hinted they might come when she`d told them her plans .Outside it was damp but , in here , with the sound of rain pattering on the tin roof it was almost cosy . The three girls were huddled together on a pile of old chair cushions which , though smelly were virtually dry . Hayley produced a bottle of extra strong cider chosen especially because of the screw cap . " D'you nick it ? " queried Michelle . She had lately dyed her hair in three different colours and had plucked her eyebrows to the bone which gave her a strange , alien look . There were three studs in the base of her each of her nostrils .

Hayley , by contrast , had no facial jewelry but her hair was now arranged in hundreds of tiny plaits   , each one of which terminated in a brightly coloured bead . Sharon had spent most of that day doing this arrangement for her . Rita would baulk , Hayley knew , but since they were no longer on speaking terms , her reaction was a matter of complete indifference to her daughter. Hayley had not spoken to her mother for a fortnight . Ever since she'd heard about the scene in O'Riordens in fact. What made it all worse was that her mother had not even mentioned the matter to her. .It was Mrs. Piper who'd told her and Darren had elaborated on the story later , which had led to their argument and subsequent break up . She'd then heard a different version of the story from Sharon who'd been an eye witness to the scene in the shop . None of the stories relected well on her mother .

" Nah . I got the money from Sandy for getting her fish and chips ." Hayley replied " she always gives me a pound ."

" She's married to that funny bloke inshe ? " Michelle asked . She continued " He's dead weird .Give us a go at the cider then . Yeah , our Cher says he used to park his van outside the tennis courts to watch the girls playing . He used to stay there for hours . The girls didn't half have a laugh about it.Some of them used to undo their front buttons to give him a show and pull their skirts as high as they could .Miss Martindale sussed it in the end and called the police to have him moved on." They all laughed .

" He offered me £20 quid once " Sharon volunteered . " whaffor ? " both girls asked eagerly ."Give you three guesses ." she replied derisively " but he's a dirty bugger all right . I told him straight it would cost him a lot more than that and he just walked away . Anyway , I couldn't fancy him even if he offered a hundred quid."

There was a sound outside and all the girls froze .What if it were a policeman ? But then the voices they heard came nearer and they recognised the raucous tones of Yozzer , Paz and Chink..

"Quick . Hide the stuff . They'll only try to nick it." Sharon hurriedly extinguished the joint and pushed the bottle out of sight . Perhaps the boys would have their own "stuff".

"Look who's here lads." Chink , a tall Chinese boy whose father owned the local takeaway was first into the hut . He was carrying a bottle of whisky . The two other lads burst into raucous yells when they spied the girls . One had two bottles of coca cola . The other a supply of cigarettes .

" If we had some music we could have a proper party. " laughed Sharon.

"We don't need music to have fun." said Yozzer ." Move over girls and let us in ." Obligingly they did . At first , none of the girls liked the taste of the whisky , even followed by a swig of cola , but within a surprisingly short time they were all enjoying themselves enormously .Chink had his arm halfway up Hayley's sweater and she didn't mind in the least . When he first began to kiss her she thought of Darren and felt sad . She knew she shouldn't be kissing someone she didn't love . In spite of herself though , she was soon responding enthusiastically . She couldn't help feeling surprised because she'd never taken to Chink when they were at school . He wasn't that bad looking really but his clothes always smelled of cooking oil and he was foreign too .But now none of this bothered her in the least .She saw out of the corner of her eye that Sharon was practically stripped off now and couldn't help giggling to herself . It was all so funny . She didn't know when she'd had such a good time . When Chink began tugging at her underwear she raised no objections .

Chapter 11

It was Monday morning . Rose was in the charity shop showing Thelma the ropes . It was a chilly morning and both women were shivering as they stood in the backroom of the shop sorting out piles of clothing .

" It will warm up when the heating gets going ." Rose promised Thelma .

" But I'm glad you came in so early Thelma . It gives me a chance to show you what's what before we open up .You know there are always three of us on duty here – May will be here any minute – and that means we never have to get in a panic if there's a sudden rush ."

Thelma looked on sceptically .Rush... in a charity shop she thought. Who does she think she's kidding ? She fingered one of the garments in front of her disparagingly saying " Does anyone ever buy this stuff ? " She herself would never have been caught dead anywhere near a charity shop even in the days when she'd been really hard up . There was stigma attached to such places as far as she was concerned Of course it was different on the otherside of the counter where she now found herself .

She'd been in a quandary this morning .What did you wear to work in a charity shop ? She had no idea but in the end had eventually settled on a knitted suit . Now , comparing her apparel with Rose who was wearing a sweater and trousers , she felt overdressed . She kept on getting this wrong . She wondered again whether volunteering to work here was a good idea even if it was only one half day each week . No doubt it would end up as a disappointment as most of her ventures seemed to do . She frowned , which made the flesh at the base of her cheeks crumple like the corners on a badly wrapped parcel .

" Oh yes of course ." Rose was surprised by Thelma's question . " Some of the things we get here are really good quality and often they've never even been worn . Queenie my friend has picked up some wonderful bargains here . Of course , being a size 10 helps . All the really smart things seem to be in small sizes – unfortunately for you and me ."

Thelma sniffed and said nothing but thought to herself .....if she thinks I would ever lower myself to buy anything here .....Instead she said

"Oh do you know Queenie too ? We were in the same form at the grammar school ." Rose was surprised again . " Really ? But I was there too and I don`t remember you at all .Of course I`m four years older than Queenie."

Thelma blushed . " I left school early " she said . It was a very sore point with her . " I missed almost a year of school through having TB . Then I was 15 and my mother thought I might as well get a job ." She hated owning up to this and had never forgiven her mother for it. Rose merely answered

" What a shame for you ."

The shop door pinged loudly and a high pitched voice trilled

"Here I am like a bad penny ." The owner of the voice was a diminutive white haired lady and she was followed immediately by an even older , shrivelled looking woman with long white hairs hanging from her chin . The first woman smiled brightly at them both . Surely she is rather old to be volunteering for shop work Thelma thought . As for the really old lady she looked as if she could be senile judging by her vacant expression. Presumably , it being a charity shop , there were no regulations about the age of the volunteers .

"I`ve brought mother with me this morning" explained May after Rose had made the introductions . " She loves a morning here . It does her good to have an outing . She might even do a bit of ironing for us later on. She gets bored at home by herself ." Mrs. Crowe, May`s mother , turned out to be stone deaf and rather vague in manner but she smiled happily enough as May led her into the back room .

Thelma was still thinking about Queenie however . It seemed unfair that she had retained her slim figure . She remembered their schooldays and those humiliating gym lessons . Navy blue knickers which cruelly exposed her own protruding belly and lumpy dimpled thighs . Mottled and suet like , they were a bitter contrast to the other girls like Queenie whose figures were so neat and legs pale and slim . Thelma railed at the cruelty of fate which had decreed that not only would she be born poor and underprivileged , but plain and fat into the bargain. It was all so unfair .

There were other humiliations which came to mind now too . The hand me down school uniform donated by parents whose child had outgrown it , issued through the school supposedly in confidence but everyone knew where it came from . The free school meals and the shame and embarrassment at the beginning of each term when everyone else paid for theirs . The form mistress would come to her name on the register and say

" Ah yes . Thelma. Yours are free aren`t they ?"

She remembered school outings she could not participate in because of the cost . As for school trips abroad – they were simply out of the question Girls like Queenie had been able to take part in everything and just took it all for granted never appreciating how lucky they were . Queenie`s mother had been something to do with fund raising for the school , Thelma recalled , and had been a prominent figure at bazaars and choral evenings . Iris Claye`s father was another one . He had been chairmen of the governors as well as a JP. Her own mother had kowtowed to them – had been only too glad of the chance of earning extra money by turning up in the evenings to serve Mrs. Mack and Mr. Claye with tea and biscuits at some out of school function .

Still , the tables were turned now and no mistake . Imagine Queenie coming here to buy her clothes ! Thelma smiled maliciously . She couldn`t get over it . Just wait until Queenie had a really good look at her bungalow . That would give her something to think  about . Queenie still lived in the old  thatched cottage that was her childhood home ..Enlarged and modernised by Queenie`s father , the garden led down to the river and it was a picturesque spot . As a girl Thelma had thought it an idyllic place and had envied her friend`s good fortune . Now she wouldn`t look at it twice . It wasn`t a patch on her lovely home . Old fashioned  , no modern conveniences such as she enjoyed and probably damp too no doubt . Well Queenie was getting her come uppance now that was sure .She would invite her round soon . Let her see that she couldn`t be looked down upon and patronised now . .She smiled again .

"That`s what I like to  see , A nice , cheery face !" May patted Thelma on the arm " You`ll fit in well here , wont she Rose ? We`re a happy crowd ."

" Yes indeed " Rose agreed . Privately she had her doubts about Thelma . Still , give her a chance. She might improve on getting to know her better. When she`d called into the C.A.B. for advice on how to fill her time she`d cut rather a pathetic figure . So many middle aged women were left at a complete loss when they were widowed . It seemed that Thelma had panicked too and moved house immediately after her bereavement . These hasty decisions were often a mistake in Rose` experience but perhaps Thelma would work things out .

May was a good old soul but she was so determindly cheerful and matey that it had the effect of depressing her , Rose found . Even more irritating was her habit of saying " wonderful " and " marvellous " to whatever remark was made to her . And she would drag her poor old mother along with her whenever she came to work in the shop. Rose was certain the old lady would be happier at home .Now the poor old thing , who must be well into her nineties , was shoved into that chilly back room without even a comfortable chair to sit on . Goodness , I`m becoming really uncharitable , Rose chided herself , determining to put this mood behind her .

"Shall we have some coffee before we open up ? " she asked the others   " We have time . It`s only nine thirty five "

" Wonderful " enthused May . " Not for mother though . Not good for her waterworks . I`ll get her some Ovaltine later . Now I must show you the lovely  things  Margaret O`Riorden has given me to sell in the shop .She says she`s cleared out all her cupboards  and there`s no end of stuff here ." She indicated a bulging carrier bag and two large , black bin bags .

This was the fun part of working in the shop , Rose had explained earlier to Thelma . You never knew what was going to come in . Once they`d gingerly opened a scruffy old cardboard box brought in by an old man to discover two beautiful pieces of Georgian silver . On the other hand , a parcel brought in by a very grand looking lady had proved to contain some items of well worn underwear and an old dressing gown.

They drank their coffee whilst they unpacked Mrs. O` Riorden`s offerings. The carrier bag was found to contain a chromium fireside set and a few brass ornaments .May tutted over this . So few people had open fires these days . Would they be able to sell it ? They then unpacked several pieces of glass and china including a splendid old soup tureen complete with lid . This cheered her . A large number of books both hard and paper backed came next , then various items of table linen and some curtains , unfortunately faded down one side. " Isn`t it strange ? People don`t seem to use tablecloths any more ."May observed .

" I think they still do for special occasions " Rose disagreed " But most people have modern kitchens with wipe down surfaces , breakfast bars and so on . I suppose it`s all to do with labour saving . That`s why we get so much table linen in the shop ."

They continued digging into the plastic bags whilst Thelma looked on . In a Tupperware box were several ornamental egg cups . souvenirs of holidays on the Costa Brava . " They`ll sell like hot cakes " May opined " Margaret loved her souvenirs ." Cushion covers in an unpleasant shade of puce , one side satin the other velvet , were unearthed by Rose next .

"Those look brand new " May said accusingly . " Why ever did Margaret get rid of them ? Look there`s a price tag. "

" I expect they were an unwanted gift " Rose said . Most of their new stock came into that category . She was not surprised that they had never been used Still , they were bound to sell People bought the most surprising things . To prove her point May said

" Do you know , I think I shall buy those myself . Mother loves that shade "

Two pairs of evening sandals , a black sequinned top and several taffeta skirts seemed to indicate that Margaret O`Riorden`s dancing days were over.

" Margaret must be 68 now. "May said suddenly as if reading their thoughts. " Doesn`t time fly ? We were at school together you know and in the land army . We did have some fun .It`s such a shame she can`t go dancing now.Eamon`s hip plays him up these days and his sight`s poor too. That`s one of the reasons he`s thinking of retiring . I`ve told Margaret many a time that I`d go dancing with her whenever she wants . They have a tea dance in the masonic hall every Wednesday afternoon . It`s mostly ladies of course but I don`t think she`s keen on the idea . I do know it`s not the same dancing without a man but still ..... " May`s voice sounded wistful .

Rose visualised the scene ; plump , elderly ladies dancing together One manning the record player and two in the kitchen attending to tea and scones . She found it very depressing. Then May said hopefully

" Do you like dancing Rose ? "

" Oh May , I`m far too busy for dancing . Anyway Wednesday `s my C.A.B. day ." Rose tried to keep her voice neutral " But what about you Thelma ?"   "

" I`ve never danced in  my  life . My mother didn`t agree with it . " Thelma`s voice was flat .

Rose suddenly had a flash of memory . Of course she remembered Thelma now . Her mother had worked in the school canteen , a dour , over weight lady who`d belonged to some strict religious sect which believed that people should not enjoy themselves . On wet days the girls had been allowed to play records and do ballroom dancing in the school hall and she recalled how Thelma had once been pulled out by her irate parent for daring to participate . It must have been very embarrassing for her . She`d been a plump , plain schoolgirl too , Rose recalled , whose looks weren`t enhanced by the thick spectacles she wore . Oh well , it explained a lot . She felt a stab of pity.

May continued " Of course , years ago we danced the night away . During the war there was dancing every night for anyone who wanted it if you knew where to go . There were always men to spare .We used to have such fun I remember when.....".

" I think it`s opening time ladies " Rose  interrupted thankfully . She had heard May`s war time reminisences many times before and did not want to hear them again his morning.

" Everything ready ? " She went to the door to reverse   the "Closed " sign whilst May took up her position behind the counter and. Thelma looked on uncertaionly .

Chaper 12

Queenie woke with a start , glanced at the alarm clock and realised with dismay that it was only 4.20 am . Another broken night . This was happening all too often lately . In fact , her insomnia had become such a problem that she had consulted Dr.Jarvis about it some weeks ago   but the young, lady doctor had been most reluctant to prescribe the sleeping tablets Queenie had requested

" I'm afraid that drugs only suppress the problem . " she'd said . "Then they can be habit forming too ." She had a lovely Scottish accent , rather like Janet from "Dr. Finlay's casebook ." There's obviously something on your mind . Can you think what it might be ? "

Queenie knew only too well , but how could you tell your doctor that you had a problem with shoplifting ? After ascertaining that her patient had no health problems which could affect her sleep pattern , Dr. Jarvis had suggested that Queenie should attend her insomnia hypnosis group which met weekly , saying she'd found that six sessions generally did the trick . There would be a vacancy occurring soon she'd told her , but Queenie never got round to arranging attendance . She knew in her heart that it wasn't hypnosis she required but the ending of her " habit ".

She was absolutely wide awake now so there was nothing else for it but to get up .With a sigh she groped for her slippers , found her dressing gown and stumbled downstairs . The cats made muted welcoming sounds as if aware that this was not an appropriate time for their usual , noisy morning greeting and Solly jumped up and rubbed himself against her ankles. Queenie filled the kettle and switched it on , then changed her mind and put some milk in a sauce pan . This sleeping problem was really getting her down . Either she lay awake for hours after first going to bed or fell asleep immediately only to become wide awake during the early hours as had happened just now .

After drinking her cocoa she remained so alert it seemed pointless to return to bed . This was the time for doing one of those boring jobs she never found time for during the day , like turning out the shelves in the larder – a job that was long overdue . She was about to stand on a chair when she thought better of it and went to fetch the steps . This wasn't the hour to have an accident . She began with the top shelf and soon became engrossed in her work .Almost two hours later , she sat down exhausted . Three shelves done and lined with fresh paper and what a good thing she had finally got round to doing the job . There were things here that should have been thrown out years ago .

She found some carrier bags and began to fill them with various half empty jars and packets . There was a carton of dried beans with "Use before end 87 " stamped on it .Queenie giggled . Iris would have a fit ! It was useful having this large larder with such wide , deep shelves but it did encourage her to hoard things . She had found items she had forgotten ever buying – those tinned mangoes for instance – she would use them tonight.Then there was all that China tea that her mother had been so fond of and the jars of pickled pears She had no use for them now .She decided to save the two remaining shelves for another sleepless night .

Queenie thought about Iris then . Funny how she had been so miffed because she hadn`t been told about the marriage bureau before . Queenie could just imagine her reaction if she had decided to confide in her at the time . Incredulity followed by shock and horror . Iris was so conventional . She had never meant to say anything about it to anyone but it had just popped out , probably because of Rose . She seemed so easy to talk to . Queenie decided she would ring her soon and invite her to tea .

Her mind wandered back to Iris again . Although she`d known her at school they were not in the same year group and they`d never been really close then nor even in those early years at work . At one time Iris had been her immediate superior in the Treasurer`s department and there was no question of confiding in her about intimate , personal matters . It was only much later , when their status as single women was confirmed , or to put it more bluntly when they were the only spinsters in the office that any intimacy began to develop .Funny how some people hated that word spinster Iris loathed it Queenie knew , but it didn`t bother her in the least .

It was strange about Iris really . Queenie suspected that she would have loved to be married so why hadn`t she done anything about it  ? She`d certainly been attractive in a quiet sort of way but she had done none of the things young women do to find boyfriends , going to dances or belonging to clubs . She`d seemed to be quite contented living quietly at home with her parents . Queenie thought back to her own younger days . There had been boyfriends but as soon as they became serious she had invariably lost interest. As a young woman she had enjoyed a varied social life which involved the tennis club and the local amateur dramatic society .The problem was that although she had enjoyed the company of the opposite sex she disliked physical contact with them .Her mother was always urging her to go

56

out to meet people and openly longing for the day when her daughter would get married . On a holiday to the Middle Eastin 1965 she had returned home with yards of Damascus silk which she had presented to a startled Queenie telling her that it was for her wedding dress .

She had been a very great disappointment to her mother Queenie acknowledged . She was able to admit to herself now that she had never had the slightest desire to get married and that any attempts to do so had been half hearted and purely to placate her mother .No , Iris was the one who should have gone to a marriage bureau Queenie decided . What a pity her parents had not encouraged the idea when she was younger . Still , if that had happened and she`d found a partner they would never have become close friends .They had been thrown together by default in the way women without male partners often were . There was an unspoken sisterhood between women like them Queenie acknowledged . Women who were not on their own would not understand this . But , come to that , she doubted if Rose would understand it . She appeared to have led rather a different life to them although she was a spinster too. Apparently she had been in the RAF which perhaps accounted for it .

Queenie was about to replace a small jar of yeast extract in the larder when immediately her worries came flooding back . She had " taken " this item – even in her mind she refused to say the word stolen – from O`Riordens about seven months ago . She could almost date the occasion . Whatever was she going to do about it ?

She made herself some toast and a pot of tea and took the tray into the sitting room . If she watched the early morning news for a while perhaps she might nod off , she thought . She settled herself on the comfortable , old sofa and one by one the cats joined her . In the early morning light the room looked charming . Queenie had a good eye for colour and several nice old pieces of furniture . The walls were papered in a primrose coloured paper and her chintz curtains were patterned in blue and yellow . The carpet , once dark blue had faded to a far nicer shade than it had been originally , Queenie thought . A few years ago she had acquired a beautiful silk rug in shades of blue and silver grey and this , combined with her various pieces of china , added to the pleasant effect . As the daylight grew however , the mistakes in Queenie`s wall papering were exposed as were the worn patches on the chair covers and various stains on the carpet as well as a patch of damp in the corner of the ceiling She drank her tea and , surrounded by the cats , eventually fell asleep.

Chapter 13

Sandy was sitting semi upright in bed toying with the Kentucky Fried Chicken Rita had brought in earlier . Most unusually for her , she did not feel hungry . In fact she was feeling very unwell .She had not felt really well for a long time but this wasn't just the usual lethargy. She felt hot and out of sorts and , worryingly , she could not even fancy a fag which meant that something must be wrong .

After a few minutes she pushed the box of food towards the dog who crouched expectantly at the side of the bed . He made a noise of gratification , something between a squeal and a growl and gripped the box firmly in his jaw One of the cats attempted to sniff the contents but he growled so ferociously it slunk away . Sandy threw a book at him

" Christ 's sake shut up Skipper " she shouted irritably . Shafts of lemon coloured light filtered through the gaps in the badly closed curtains giving the animal an exotic , gilded look. As she leant back in bed she caught a glimpse of her face in the smeared mirror of the dressing table . That too , had a yellow tinge .

She picked up her copy of " Chat " again . This week' true life story " I was raped by my own GP " did not interest her . Nor could she raise any enthusiasm in learning " 20 ways to turn on your man ". She threw the magazine on the floor then rooted through the foetid bedding searching for the remote control of the TV . Her search located an empty crisp packet , coins of various size and an old tennis ball which was a favourite toy of Skipper.There were also several old chips , as well as fluff , cat fur and other unsavoury items all of which she threw to the floor

The remote control was eventually located under her pillow but it took several attempts before she succeeded in turning on the TV . The batteries must be on the blink she decided . Once on , the programme turned out to be an old American situation comedy about teenagers . After every character spoke there was loud canned laughter . Sandy sighed and scratched her left armpit so vigorously that she gasped in pain . Pulling down the stained flannelette nightie she observed that the rash she'd first noticed two weeks ago had now spread all over her body . It was then that she began to feel scared .

She dragged herself out of bed . Her toenails rasped against the pile of the nylon carpet and she winced as the sole of her foot trod on something small and sharp . It could have been a splinter of chicken bone but she did not have the energy to bend down to investigate .

Slowly, her fat thighs rubbing together with every step , she made her way to the bathroom where she relieved herself and then stood in front of the begrimed hand basin looking in the mirror . Her hair , lank and greasy was plastered to her head , her eyes were dull and bleary and her muddy complexion had a definite yellow tinge . Tears sprang to her eyes .

She made her way back to the bedroom .In bed again she shifted about uncomfortably Her ribs were sore , she realised and her chest felt tight . Oh God . What was the matter now ? She'd have to have the doctor here again but she didn'nt think she could bear it . He'd been so horrible to her last time . He pulled no punches at all and had no compunction about insulting her and hurting her feelings. Last time , he'd told her she'd feel a lot better if she cleaned herself up . He'd wanted to talk to Cyril too , but he'd made himself scarce as he always did when anyone came to visit her .

Perhaps she should ring Hilda and see what she had to say ? She'd once worked in an old folks home and had picked up some medical knowledge . Trouble was , Hilda wasn't on the best of terms with her at the moment . She had made it plain last time she came that her patience was wearing thin . Rita was getting fed up too . She hadn't actually said anything yet but she soon would . Sandy knew she had far too many worries of her own to become involved in hers . Clint was in Youth Custody and Wayne would probably follow him there in due course .Now Hayley , who'd always been a good kid was playing up .She was on bad terms with her mum and had left home at one point though she was back now.

But if she could not even rely on Rita who could she turn to ? Tears ran down Sandy's face which she wiped on the sleeve of her grubby nightie . She picked up the can of coke standing on the bedside table and took a long swig , wincing in discomfort as it went down .On the TV screen Richard and Judy were talking about " women who keep their man appeal ". They were going to interview Tina Turner next. .Sandy flung the empty can into a corner of the room and continued to weep .

After a while she picked up the phone and dialled Rita' s number but it just rang and rang . Then , like a miracle , she heard the familiar voice shout from the front door and was so overcome with relief that her sobs came even louder

" Christ's sake Sandy , what's the matter ? I only called in because I forgot to leave your dog food earlier on . I'm just on my way to the brewery now." Rita looked concerned . She looked dreadful too

, Sandy noticed . She had bags under her eyes and her face looked drawn .

" I don't feel well Rite , I'm all hot and I've got pains all round here see ." She indicated an area around her vast middle .

" Join the bleedin' club . I didn't get a wink of sleep last night and my chest's playing me up something chronic ." Rita sat down heavily on the side of the bed

" It's that little cow Hayley that's got me all upset . She's always on at me about the state of the place but wont do a hand's turn when I ask her to And now she's working as a cleaner . That's rich innit ? " Rita would have gone on but she could see that Sandy wasn't taking much notice of her .

" What's up then love ? " she asked kindly . "D'you think you've got 'flu or what ? " Sandy began to sob again , great fat tears which ran unchecked down her cheeks .

" I thought you were getting fed up with me.Thought you might say you wouldn't come round here no more ."

" I'd never let you down Sand , you know that " Rita replied stoutly She meant it too.

" I don't know what I should take Rite . I've only got aspirins and " Night Nurse " here ."

Rita looked at Sandy more closely then . She noticed the sallow complexion and bleary eyes and thought , she'd feel a lot better if she had a bloody good wash but said

" Perhaps you need a good clear out ? My mother used to swear by Epsom salts .I'll get you some ." she added " All that foreign muck you eat can't be doing you any good either. I wouldn 't touch it ."

"All right " Sandy was doubtful but she was willing to try anything .

" Better me get some pain killers too Rite . I saw some on the telly. You know the one with the woman with the back ache ? "

Rita knew the one she meant .

" OK . I'll bring it round later . I'm not back till after 6 mind . Our Wayne's working by the way ." She added proudly rising from the bed

"You'll never guess whose given him a job ?" She didn't wait for Sandy's response . " Your Cyril ." But Sandy was not interested .That pain was catching her again. She simply looked at Rita. .

" It's only temporary mind , but at least one thing's going right . See you later then . " Rita left the room . After she'd gone

Sandy realised she should have asked her to bring in a bucket . Just in case . She was beginning to feel nauseous .

Chapter 14

Queenie , in " Buy it All " , was about to help herself to a small packet of batteries when she felt a hand on her shoulder . She froze , then almost wet herself with fright . She had already " taken " a box of staples and stuffed them up her sleeve . Somebody must have been watching. .She turned around terror stricken , and found herself looking at Rose .

" Queenie I`m so sorry .I didn`t mean to frighten you ."

" Oh it`s all right Rose . I was miles away . How nice to see you ." Queenie felt so relieved she could almost have embraced her friend .

" I saw you from the street and wondered whether you`d like a lift home ? Or perhaps you`d like to come back with me for a bite of lunch ? I can drop you off later on my way to the church . It`s my guide afternoon . That`s if you`re ready to come now ? "

" I`d love to . Come home with you I mean .Funny you should have come now because I was just going to catch my bus " The two left the store . They made an odd couple strolling along side by by side , Rose tall and elegant in an immaculately cut suit and Queenie diminutive in her long , waxed raincoat and incongruously , green wellingtons .She had put them on earlier that morning to go to the end of the garden in the pouring rain and then , since the rain had continued had decided to keep them on . Then of course it had dried up and now the sun was shining .That was April for you .

They chatted on the way back , Rose telling Queenie about the young girl who had just begun to clean for her . Apparently she had quarrelled with her mother and left home and was now staying with her boyfriend`s family . The mother of the boy had been  Rose`s cleaner previously but was now expecting a baby at the age of 45 . According to Rose the two families involved were at loggerheads . Queenie found it all very interesting " It all sounds rather like Romeo and Juliet ."she remarked . " No " Rose said , laughing " More like " West Side Story ". Anyway , you might meet her this afternoon . She`s due at 2   O clock . Evie always came in the morning but Hayley prefers the afternoon . It doesn`t make any difference to me since I`m out anyway ."

Queenie sat at the kitchen table whilst Rose rustled up a snack . They had a delicious home made soup to begin followed by cheese with crusty french bread .

" I do like your kitchen"   Queenie said sincerely ." In fact I love the whole house . It`s all  so pretty ." Itt was . Rose had spent a lot of money bringing the small property up to date and she had the same high standards for her home as she did for her personal appearance . " I`m sure your house is to. " Rose said. "It certainly looks it from the outside ."

" Well you`ll see for yourself when you come to tea on Sunday " Queenie said . She had already invited Rose by telephone. " I think I`ll ask Thelma to come too.Perhaps I`ll call there on my way home later. She seems so lonely ." Rose agreed that was a good idea .

Looking at Rose` well kept house reminded Queenie that a thorough clean up of her own home was long overdue and , with visitors arriving for tea in the next few days , she ought to do something about it . She would start tomorrow by cleaning all the windows first she decided , and then go through the house room by room ending with the kitchen .

They finished their meal and Rose looked at Queenie .

" Well , I`m glad to see you`re looking better now . You looked ghastly when I met you earlier . Weee you feeling ill ? "

" I`m fine . Really .You just gave me a fright ." Queenie blushed  , wishing with all her heart that she could confide in Rose . She felt sure she`d be able to give her some really useful advice but even as she thought this she knew she would never be able to bring herself to do it .Unable to sleep last night , she`d lain for hours mulling over her problem until she had promised herself that she would never  "take" anything again . It simply wasn`t worth all this worry . Yet within a hour of being out this morning she was up to her old tricks again .She didn`t know why .It all seemed to happen without her even thinking about it . Now she knew what that hackneyed expression   "something came over me " meant because it described exactly what was always happening to her . Perhaps she really was going mad . And look what had almost happened this morning . It could well have been a store detective who had accosted her instead of Rose . What would have happened then ?

This was such a worrying train of thought that the only way Queenie could cope with it was by banishing it to the back of her mind . She deliberately thought of something else , fixing her eyes on an unusual ornament she spied on top of the hall cupboard .

" That`s an interesting thing " she remarked . " I`ve never seen anything like that before ."

"Yes .It`s a Chinese incense burner ." Rose told her " I brought so many knick knacks back from the Far East. he house is full of them .Come and see ." They walked around the house and Queenie found it all so interesting that within minutes she'd completely forgotten about her worries . Then Rose looked at her watch and realised that she'd have to go .

As they were about to leave the house Hayley turned up . Queenie looked at her with interest .Yes , she was quite a pretty girl , she thought , in spite of that peculiar hair style. She wasn't pleased to see them though , that was obvious from her scowl which didn't diminish even when Rose told her that they were just leaving . " I think she's just terribly shy " Rose explained as they were driving off . " And of course she hasn't got used to me yet . But she seems to clean very well ."

Queenie had been right . Hayley wasn't pleased to see them . She'd bven given to understand that she would work here unsupervised and seeing that pair had spoiled her afternoon . She liked to pretend that this house belonged to her and Darren and part of this fantasy involved her putting the key in the door and walking into an empty house. She loved working here. This house was even nicer than Evie's . It didn't seem fair that Rose Deacon should have it all to herself .

For a few moments Hayley pictured her own family living there then common sense immediately banished the fantasy . Just as if ! Within days the garden and even the kitchen would be littered with Wayne's motor bike parts . Her mother would neglect the cleaning . Wayne and Clint would lounge all over the furniture in their dirty clothes even putting their filthy shoes on it too .Things would break and never get repaired . Then there would be people banging on the door wanting bills to be paid . Her mother would sell off anything saleable for whatever she could get .And everywhere there would be the smell of cigarettes and stale fat . It was a different world they inhabited . And it just wasn't fair .

For the past week both Evie and Rose had been trying to persuade Hayley she should return home. The Pipers had no wish to antagonise Rita further and Hayley herself knew that she had hurt her mother very much by walking out . In spite of everything she loved her mother .It was just the life style she wanted to discard . But how could she do that ? When she'd tried moving things that littered up the house and suggested that they ate different foods her mother had accused her of getting above herself . There was no way that her family and Darren's could ever become on good terms she knew.

On her first morning here Evie had told Rose all about the situation Hayley herself had not minded this thinking that Rose might offer some advice .But after listening to it all she had just said

" Why not go home and apologise ?Your mother will be so pleased you're back she wont say a word ." She did not understand the real situation But she couldn't stay with the Pipers much longer even though Darren tried to tell her it was OK . To her employer it was just a quarrel about a boyfriend . She just didn't get it .

Although she'd tried to ingratiate herself in various ways , Mr. Piper was not keen on her presence she could tell , but he tolerated it because he believed that Evie needed her help about the house . Everyone knew that she could not remain there indefinitely .Oh there was no use thinking about it all . She supposed she'd have to return home tonight .In a thoroughly bad temper , Hayley dragged the vacuum cleaner from the cupboard and began to work .

Chapter 15

Iris was feeling put upon . The fact that it was entirely her own fault only made it worse . All because of her inability to say no . She'd planned to go shopping with Rose on Saturday to buy a new outfit . She'd particularly wanted Rose to accompany her , not just because she had such good taste but because Rose was so decisive whereas she herself was just the opposite . Then , earlier this morning Ailsa Croombeck , the vicar's wife , had telephoned . She'd been let down by one of her Christian Action collector's for Saturday morning , she'd said . She knew she could always rely on Iris in an emergency . Would she step into the breach ? Ailsa was so appreciative of Iris' good nature that somehow, without even realising what she was doing , Iris found herself saying yes .

"I knew you wouldn't let me down ." Ailsa said triumphantly " You're an angel Iris. " Iris felt far from angelic now. Why hadn't she said she was too busy to help out? Why couldn't she be more assertive ? she asked herself . This would have been her only free Saturday for weeks and now she'd be spending it on the High Street , rattling a collecting tin It would probably rain too . She would have to ring Rose now to cancel their appointment. Rose would be cross no doubt and who could blame her ? It was Iris who had initiated the outing in the first place . What on earth could she say to her ?

Rose was not at all understanding

" Why on earth didn't you tell her you had a prior engagement ? That's what I did when she asked me ." she asked crossly .

" You mean she asked you too ?" Iris was very taken aback .

"Of course . Probably several other people too . Not everyone is such a pushover as you " Rose did sound exasperated . Iris couldn't blame her After all , she had suggested the shopping trip . A busy person like Rose had probably altered her plans to oblige her . Iris could have cried with annoyance .

"Are you still there ?" Rose asked ." I've just thought of something. I know just the person to stand in for you . Thelma . She's always complaining she has nothing to do at weekends . I'll ring her now ."

" Oh do you think she would ?P erhaps I should ring her myself ? " Iris dithered .

" I've got a better idea . Ask her if we can call round this afternoon . She's never stopped pestering me to come and look at her bungalow   .   She'll be thrilled to have two visitors so we`ll be doing her a favour in a way ." Iris` heart was lightened .

Rose though , replaced the telephone with the greatest irritation . God ! Iris was so wet ! She could hardly control her impatience with her Thank goodness there was time to nip round to see Eric and have a sensible conversation with someone normal . She went to fetch her coat but saw through the glass of the front door Evie walking up the path . She looked harrassed and tired when Rose let her in ."Whatever `s the matter Evie ? I wasn`t expecting you today ."

"I`m that upset Rose .I don`t know whether I`m coming or going."Evie sighed .Rose went to fill the kettle .

" Sit down on a comfortable chair Evie and we`ll have some tea. Then you can tell me all about it . Darren and Hayley were causing problems again . It seemed that Darren , who had told them that he had finished with Hayley had been seeing her on the sly . Not only that , but he`d arrived home last night bringing the girl with him because her mother had thrown her out again. When his father had objected , Darren had threatened to leave home himself . The upshot was that Evie had had hysterics and told her husband that if he made her son leave home she would go too .

"Poor old Stan " Rose said at the end of this saga . " He had to give in then . But do you think you were wise allowing the girl to stay after that terrible row you had with her mother weeks ago ? She sounds the sort of person who might do something nasty "

" That`s what Stan said . But what  could I do ? Darren`s too young to leave home . If his dad makes him leave the two of them might end up in some awful bedsitter together and who knows what that might lead to ? I`m praying the whole thing will blow over after a few days and her mother will let her go home   Honestly Rose , it`s all made me wonder whether I`m doing the right thing having another one . We never had a bit of trouble with Darren until he turned 16 and now look at the worry we`ve got .The one good thing is that you`ve given Hayley the job .She can stay  can`t she ?

" Of course she can . Now as soon as we`ve finished our tea I`ll take you home . Poor Stan must be worrying himself sick about you working yourself into a state in your condition . I hope you`ve made your peace with him now ?" Poor Stan Piper had his hands full thought Rose , feeling thankful that she had no teenage children to worry about .

Rose had been right . Thelma was delighted . Both with the prospect of visitors and of having an occupation for Saturday morning . Weekends were the loneliest time of all she had found But she ought to go shopping at once she decided . She would need to give her guests a really special tea Something that would show them both that she knew how to do things . How fortunate that she had just taken delivery of the nest of onyx tables . She went into the sitting room to admire them again . They were edged in gilt and had elaborately carved legs , also gilded . They really added something to the room she felt . She looked around in satisfaction .The Chinese rugs , also recent purchases , looked so opulent lying against the carpet as they did .

The carpet was Thelma`s pride and joy . She had told the factory the design she wanted and the carpet had been made especially to her requirements . This service was only available to particularly discerning customers she had been told . It was predominately bottle green with huge bouquets of pink cabbage roses at intervals of every square yard . Years before Thelma had coveted a similar carpet she had once seen in somebody`s home and promised herself she would have one just like it one day. Of course hers was far better . It took a really large room like hers to show off such a carpet to its best advantage she acknowledged .

She gazed around her . Everything was perfect but perhaps some fresh flowers might add that something extra ? She made a mental note to call in to the florist and see if they had any of those huge , curly chrysanthemums . Everyone knew they cost the earth . They would provide the finishing touch . Now she would have to get a move on . It was already 12 –20 and her guests would be arriving at four . It was so very satisfying to feel so occupied .

Three hours later her preparations were almost finished and the tea trolley was loaded – or was it overloaded ? Had she gone over the top she wondered ? There was a selection of canapés , smoked salmon , cream cheese and she had even purchased a small jar of caviare. Then there were various cold meats arranged artistically on a long   , oval platter with a selection of continental bread , to say nothing of the various variety of gateaux . She had made a special trip to the Viennese pastry shop for these even though it involved a considerable detour by taxi.

She had done her guests proud she decided .That made it all the more disappointing then , when neither Rose or Iris had eaten much although they had both seemed surprised and awed on seeing the spread she had prepared for them .Rose was going out that evening she explained so she daren't each much for fear of spoiling her supper . Iris had nibbled some canapes and then refused anything more on the grounds of a small appetite . Nor had either of them expressed much enthusiasm or admiration when she had taken them on a tour of the property explaining what everything had cost. She had not expected naked envy exactly but some sort of reaction would have been in order . What did vex her more than anything was the niggling suspicion that ,contrary to her expectations, they didn't envy her in the least .

After her guests had gone , Thelma cleared away the uneaten food and washed the dishes It was only 5..55 . What was she going to do with herself now ? She had hoped that Rose and Iris might have stayed longer but no doubt they had things to do – unlike her . Rose always seemed to be out and about but then she was a bossy boots and a nosey parker , Thelma thought . The type who had to be involved in everything . Still , she had been an officer in the RAF whereas Iris was only a tuppenny halfpenny clerk in the town hall from all accounts , so what gave her the right to be so superior questioning her about her job and whether she was a state registered or state enrolled nurse ? It was none of her business .

She would bet her life on one thing . She was the only one of them who knew what hard work really was . Thelma had lied anyway and told Iris that she had been Sister in Charge at her last job and had run the hospice. .In   fact , she had begun to train as a nurse comparatively late in life , when she was 37 . She had been a State Enrolled Nurse but there was no need for anyone round here to know that . It was all very well for them .If she had had all their advantages and been able to complete her education who knows what she might have achieved ?

If she had her time again , thought Thelma , things would be very different . When she had left school at 15 they had moved to Portsmouth and she had simply taken Mother's advice and gone to work in the old age home which was affiliated to the chapel they attended . For years Thelma had toiled - that was the only way to describe her labour . She realised now that she had been taken advantage of . She had worked long hours for low wages and nobody had suggested she should get proper training . Mother believed she was doing the Lord's work and that she should be satisfied with her lot .

It was the visiting doctor who had told her that she was a born nurse and that she should start training . He was mystified as to why she hadn`t done this before and had even convinced her mother that she should do so . Even after she`d qualified she`d been stupid , Thelma now told herself . There was no reason why she couldn`t have gone on with her training , gained further qualifications and achieved a high position but she had been stymied by a combination of lack of confidence and her mother`s low horizons for her . Mother saw no reason why Thelma should want to improve her status .The Lord did not want it . Consequently she had stayed at the general hospital for years mostly choosing to work nights because it paid better , until her mother had   become too ill to be left alone   She had taken compassionate leave then to nurse her .

Eventually , Mother had gone to the hospice to die and , after this , Thelma had returned to work . She was too old to think about promotion then but it still galled her having to take orders from some slip of a girl young enough to be her daughter . Especially when she knew inside that it was she who should really be in charge .Then , by a pure stroke of luck or it could have been the hand of fate , she was transferred to the private wards where she was to meet her future husband . She smiled thinking of this and her face was transformed for a moment before it sank back into its usual sulky expression .

Those two could be as superior as they liked but she was the one with the beautiful home and the money to do what she wanted with.   Nobody could take that away from her. She went to her bedroom to look again at her clothes . This often cheered her up when she was feeling down in the dumps . Of course , years ago you could tell a really well off person simply by looking at their clothing . What a pity that was not the case now , Thelma thought regretfully .Nice as they were , none of the garments here marked her off as a person of means . What she should have was a mink coat – ranch mink , full length . She pictured herself in such a garment .That would show them all , no doubt about it .Then she came down to earth . Who would dare wear a mink coat these days ?

Chapter 16

Iris was up and about early even though it was Sunday . She`d woken with a niggling background headache behind her eyes which she`d thought that walking Nellie to the paper shop might clear , but it had not gone away .She decided against going to church .Her concentration was too poor and the paracetomol she had taken for her headache had left her feeling slightly nauseated . After sitting quietly with her paper she began to feel better but it was too late for church now . The drizzle had now turned into a downpour so she was better off at home she reasoned . Anyway there was plenty to occupy her here this morning . There was the sponge for Queenie`s party to bake for a start .

Iris went to her bedroom and began to strip the bed . Old habits die hard she thought . Her mother had always changed the beds on Sunday and she had continued in the habit even though she did not regard Monday as washday now .She went to the airing cupboard . High time I sorted this out she told herself . Some of the contents had been airing here for months . She pulled out some sheets from the back of the cupboard and was surprised to encounter wetness . Digging deeper now , everything felt wet . Panic stricken she began to pull everything out , flinging things on the floor higgledy piggledy . When the cupboard was empty there was no mistaking the large wet patch or the slow trickle of water which was leaking through the insulated jacket which covered the tank .

What on earth should she do about it ? How did you get hold of a plumber on a Sunday ? She supposed it was a plumber she required . Their old family plumber Fred Wesley had died years ago and Iris had never had need of one since her parents had died . Exasperation filled her . It was always the same . This was the nuisance of being a woman on your own . At least a man would have some idea about effecting some kind of temporary repair but she did not have the faintest idea what to do . There was nothing else for it . She would have to go across the road and ask Len Haskett if he`d come and have a look . At least he could advise her what to until she could get a plumber .

Iris was not on intimate terms with the Hasketts . She had been welcoming when they`d first moved in two years ago but one look at Beryl Haskett had told her that they had absolutely nothing in common . Beryl was an emaciated peroxide blonde with a haggard face . From a distance of 100 yards or seen from behind she could be taken for a young girl . She wore mini skirts although her skinny shanks would have been far more attractive covered up and in hot weather , skinny rib tank tops . In winter she had a penchant for fake fur , particularly leopard . Close up though , her face could best be described as " lived in " and the improbable shade of her hair only added to this impression . She and her husband ran a number of launderettes Iris had learned . Ethel had once told Iris that she`d heard that they were not really married at all but this was probably just malicious gossip .

Len was always pleasant and friendly when Iris saw him working in the garden but on one occasion when he`d begun a conversation with her Beryl had called him indoors very sharply and since then she had barely nodded at Iris when she`d passed her in the street .For this reason she felt very diffident about approaching them . But there was simply nobody else she could ask so , reluctantly , she found her raincoat ignoring the imploring eyes of the dog and walked across to the bungalow opposite .

Beryl Haskett did not like it . That was obvious to Iris as soon as she had made her request for help . This morning Beryl was wearing leggings made of some very shiny fabric and a low cut , clingy top which did nothing for her lack of cleavage . She glared at Iris rudely and did not ask her indoors in spite of the rain but merely turned on her heel to relay Iris` request to her husband . Len was obliging though and offered to come right away much to Beryl`s chagrin .

"He was just sitting down to his paper " she said accusingly ."It`s only on Sunday he gets the chance ."

" I`m so sorry to trouble you " Iris said apologetically " Of course you don`t have to come at once Len . Any time will do. It isn`t that urgent really " .Beryl looked at her through narrowed eyes. Her eye brows had been almost completely removed , Iris couldn`t help noticing , and then pencilled in again crudely with a brown eye pencil . They looked ridiculous . She quickly looked away before Beryl noticed her staring .

Len insisted on coming immediately though and went to fetch his coat . Beryl seemed to reach a decision then .

" I`m coming with you ." she said to Len . Iris felt disconcerted . Good heavens , she thought . Does she think I`m going to seduce him or what ? " It`s very kind of you both " she just said weakly . Then , repeating herself , " I hate to bother you on a Sunday but I just didn`t know what else to do."

Once he`d taken a look , Len was reassuring about the problem . He told Iris that it did not constitute an emergency but that

72

she should call in a plumber first thing tomorrow. Meanwhile , he made a Heath Robinson type arrangement to control the leak . Beryl took the opportunity to have a really good look around the bungalow while Iris and Len were occupied with the airing cupboard . She was not impressed . No fitted carpets , no wall lights and all that old fashioned furniture . As for those chairs in the sitting room ..well, give her a dralon suite any day . She wouldn't give that stuff house room . And imagine just leaving your walls white like these . She gazed at the back view of Iris disparagingly , Pathetic really the way she always wore those old fashioned clothes . You'd think she'd do something about her hair too . Grey was ageing . Still , what could you expect ? She was only a spinster after all . Having decided that Iris constituted no threat whatsoever , Beryl could afford to be magnanimous .

" Now remember Iris " she said as they were leaving ." any problem at all and Len will be only too glad to help , wont you Len ? "

After they'd gone , Iris made some coffee and sat flipping through the yellow pages. There seemed to be lots of plumbers listed locally but how did you know which was the best ? You heard so many horror stories about tradesmen . She supposed it was best to have a personal recommendation . Perhaps Queenie or Rose might know of somebody? Staring towards the fireplace Iris noticed how dusty the overmantle was . Her carriage clock , the prized trophy of 35 years local government service , was also covered in a film of dust . She must stir herself . If she wasn't careful her house would end up looking like Queenie's . I wonder what they gave her when she retired she thought . Funny that she couldn't remember .

During her working life it had been Iris ` job to make the collection for leaving presents . Sometimes this was a difficult chore if the person concerned was unpopular . She thought of Martha Thexton , cordially detested by everyone in the office . Only the kindest hearted people had been willing to contribute anything and even then Iris had only managed to raise £2 .60. Martha had had the cheek to request a piece of Royal Worcester china . Only someone as brassnecked as her would have the nerve everyone said . Iris had been at her wits end over what to do and had worried for days over the matter . In the end Mr. Parfitt , her immediate line manager , asked her what was wrong and when she'd told him said leave it with him .The next day he'd turned up with a piece of the required china – Iris suspected that it came from his own home – and she'd been able to use the cash to buy a bunch of spring flowers. So after all Martha ended up with a very acceptable gift much to the chagrin of some of her colleagues .

Iris` own leaving party had been quite a different affair she recalled with pride . There`d been a catered lunch for 50 people in the Town Hall with the Chief Executive himself in attendance . There had been speeches , some of them embarrassingly fulsome , and then Iris had been presented with a gift beyond her wildest expectations . She had specified a clock when asked what leaving present she would like , but the antique carriage clock she had been given was so beautiful and valuable she had been quite overcome with emotion . She suspected that Ian Parfitt had a hand in choosing the gift because he was a great auction enthusiast .

" It`s no more than you deserve Iris " he had said when she`d protested to him later . " I`ve never known people give so generously . You must look upon it as a measure of what we think of you here . We`re going to miss you and this is our way of showing it ."

Well , thought Iris . That had been more than four years ago now . She had been enthusiastic when the idea of early retirement had first been mooted .The terms had been so tempting for one thing and her colleagues had kept on telling her to go for it and remarking how lucky she was to get the offer . Somehow , though , things had not turned out as she`d hoped . If she were honest with herself she missed her job . She had reached a senior position in local government and had found her work interesting and rewarding . But more than anything she missed the day to day interaction with her colleagues . The little snippets of gossip , the office feuds and intrigues and the feeling of being a valued member of a team . She could never admit it to anyone – least of all Queenie who had jumped at the chance of retirement like a starving rat – that she now believed she had made a mistake .

" Do keep in touch " everyone had said and , at first she had done so . She`d met her particular friend Maggie for lunch several times and she and her husband had called on her regularly until they`d moved away . Mr. Parfitt still rang for a chat every now and then even now but , one day about a year ago , she`d called at the Town Hall on spec and the receptionist on the desk didn`t know who she was and had told her that members of the public weren`t allowed to use the lift . When Iris had told her she used to work there the girl had just repeated herself . You don`t work here now so keep away her attitude had implied , and Iris had not been back since .

Iris` birthsign was Gemini , one of whose characteristics she had read somewhere , was a fatal inability to make up one`s mind. When she looked back at her life she could see that this flaw had dogged her throughout her life . Why had she taken a job in local

74

government in the first place ? Much better things had been expected of her . She remembered Miss Ingram , the Headmistress of the girls grammar school , expressing disappointment when learning of Iris` decision not to go on to university .

" Anyone can get a job in the Town Hall Iris . You can do much better than that . I hate to see such a waste of ability " In vain her parents had been summoned to the school to be harrangued by Miss Ingram and Iris` own form mistress . Iris had wavered but Ted Claye , her father , detested being told what to do by bossy school teachers . He had been totally in favour of Iris leaving school . If she`d been a boy now , things might have been different . As it was , the Town Hall was a very suitable place for his daughter he thought . What Iris could not explain , either at home or at school was that the Town Hall was not meant to be a career . For her it was just meant to be a stopgap before her future life claimed her .

At 18 she was not at all sure what this future would be but she knew it was something wonderful and exciting . Somehow though it had never happened . Years had gone by , other Town Hall employees had come and gone but Iris remained . Where had the years gone ? She remembered starting work . Her first job had been in the Surveyer`s Dept .Her mother had bought her a navy suit and two drip dry blouses from Marks and Spencer to mark the occasion . She had been known then as "Young Iris" because there was another Iris there .An older , married woman who seemed so mature and sophisticated compared to her .

Other young girls in the office had stayed for a year or so and then left for more glamorous jobs or to get married . In those days girls did leave their jobs to get married . They then turned up a year or so later to show off a baby . She remembered the two girls from Rates who`d gone off on the hippy trail and how daring she`d thought they were . One of them married an Israeli and never returned to England . The other came back with a little , dark skinned baby . The town had been agog . Now both she and her son , fully grown now worked together in the covered market selling incense and ethnic items . When she`d  seen Iris  one day years before her  retirement  she`d said " My Gawd . You`re not still working at the Town Hall ?" In tones of great incredulity . And even that must have been more than 20 years ago .

The first indication that she`d reached maturity was when the junior clerks began to refer to her as Miss Claye rather than her christian name . Iris couldn`t really remember when this had begun . It had certainly not been initiated by her . She had mentioned it to Ian Parfitt laughingly but he`d said that she should look upon it as a mark of respect .After all ,he`d said you are much older than them . She`d had to agree it was true .The strange thing about getting older , she mused is that you can see it happening to everyone else but don`t feel it is affecting you .

Her present life was full . She kept herself busy and she tried to be a helpful member of the community . Why was it at times like this a voice from within kept asking her " Is this all there is ? " Iris found these thoughts so uncomfortable that she quickly turned on the radio and went to find a duster .

Chapter 17

Thelma , wearing an unbecoming beige velour housecoat , walked aimlessly around the house . She wandered from room to room , sat down for seconds in the sitting room , picked up a magazine , replaced it then went to the window . As usual there was nothing to see . She could have screamed with boredom . Sunday was the worst day of the week as far as she was concerned . There was absolutely nothing to do , especially at this time of the year when it was still too cold to do anything outdoors . Not that she was keen on outside activities anyway.

At least during the week the monotony was relieved when Rona ,the latest cleaner , turned up but she didn`t come at weekends . Thelma was tempted to pay her extra to come but there simply wasn`t the need and she did not want Rona to know how much she relied on her company . In fact , she had given her to understand that her weekends were rather busy with entertaining or visiting friends . She couldn`t bear the thought of Rona pitying her .

Truth to tell , she was becoming rather concerned about her relationship with Rona .She was using her more and more as a confidante . It didn`t do at all she knew to become too intimate with " help " but Rona was so easy to talk to . And they had such a lot in common .Like Thelma , Rona had cared for her elderly mother for years until her death and missed her just as much as Thelma did her mother .

She thought back to the old days . She had always tried to have Sundays off . There was always someone only too glad to swap a duty because of the extra money . Mother had liked to have her at home on Sunday . They always went to the morning Service at the mission hall and then came home to their Sunday roast dinner . In the afternoon Thelma had caught up with her knitting and any mending that needed doing in front of the TV . Mother had loved a nice old film . Well they both had . She had mellowed in later life and allowed film watching so to her all the old films were new , as they were to Thelma too .

Then there was the high spot of the week , Sunday tea , with all the little luxuries that were kept for this occasion . More often than not , two or three ladies from Mother`s OAP club turned up and after tea they always used to switch on for " Songs of Praise and sing along . Once , even Pastor Mawson had come for tea . During the summer they used to go to the evening service at the mission too but when the nights drew in mother preferred to stay at home .Whatever they did it was such a happy day.

Of course Queenie had invited her to tea today so at least there was that to look forward to but it was only 9.20 am and there were so many empty hours to fill in before 4 o clock . She had thought of going to church this morning but the rain was so heavy she just could not make the effort . What was the point anyway ? People simply weren't friendly there . It wasn't like the mission where you knew everyone . Had she made a mistake in coming back here ? Thelma worried again . Well , there was no going back now . Rona had suggested that she should buy herself a little dog but she had never been fond of dogs or cats for that matter . And there was her beautiful home to consider . Animals made such a mess.

She wondered who else would be at the tea party and what Queenie would give them to eat .None of that foreign muck she hoped . She had once stood behind Queenie in the health food shop and seen her buying all manner of peculiar items – black olives , mung peas and something in a jar called Tahini paste that looked just like wet cement . She shuddered . That day was the first time she had seen Queenie since she'd moved back here and they'd known each other at once even though 30 years had passed . Annoyingly , although friendly enough ,Queenie had not seemed surprised to see her and asked her none of the questions she had been bursting to answer .

Then the other day , it had been exactly the same when Queenie had called round to invite her to tea . Naturally she had invited her indoors and watched eagerly for her reaction to the splendour of the premises . She had expected surprise and delight , even envy , when she'd showed her around but Queenie's reaction had been infuriatingly non commital . She didn't ask the price of anything and when asked for her opinion just said that it was "very nice ". Annoyingly , she hadn't so much as glanced at the expensive crystal chandeliers which Thelma had chosen so carefully and Rona was always enthusing about . According to her they were the finishing touch .

Thelma sighed and the deep lines that edged her plump cheeks set her mouth into a frown . Nothing seemed to work out as she planned it to .A few weeks ago she had gone to the Citizens Advice Bureau to ask for information about filling in her spare time . She'd seen this suggestion offered to somebody in the agony column of her weekend magazine . The person she'd spoken to had been very helpful but none of the things she'd suggested really appealed . She'd said they needed volunteers to help out in the geriatric hospital . How could she know that Thelma herself had only recently escaped from such an environment ? Then she had mentioned the friendship circle where various ladies befriended lonely old people and called on them regularly. Thelma felt she could have benefited from the friendship circle herself . She couldn`t see herself visiting some senile old lady . She wanted to receive visitors herself . In the end , to avoid looking like a fool , she`d felt more or less forced to agree to helping in a charity shop where , it turned out , Rose Deacon her interviewer herself worked . Well she had been there for three sessions now . It filled in a morning but that was the best she could say for it .

Queenie had told her that Rose Deacon would be coming to the tea party too . Apparently they were pals . Well , it takes all sorts Thelma well knew , but Rose was just a bit too bossy for her taste . She remembered her from school although she hadn`t admitted it . Rose Deacon had been a prefect – very high and mighty . Typical of her to be involved with everything in in the town the way she was . Why should she give herself such airs ? She was another one she`d like to show . Well one thing was sure – she had more money than any of them despite their superiority .

She decide to look through her wardrobe and choose something to wear that afternoon . She would pick something really showy she thought Something that would let them all see she knew how to dress . There were a variety of garments that came into that category . She dithered over a black dress , tastefully draped and trimmed with fur at the neck and sleeves. Too funereal she decided remembering that she had worn it for just such an occasion . After much consideration she eventually settled for a wool dress and matching jacket in a very tasteful shade of silvery blue . Perhaps she should wear her pearls too thought Thelma , or rather the pearls which had once belonged to the late Mrs.Honeyspan . Mother would not have approved of those . " Gilding the lily " was the way she described the wearing of adornments . But then she had never been in Thelma`s position nor mixeda society where jewelry was commonplace .

Should she wear a brooch too ? Or was that too much ? She decided it was and then replaced the navy calf court shoes she had chosen to go with her outfit with a pair in black suede and a matching clutch bag . She hung her outfit on the back of the cupboard door with the shoes underneath and the bag on the bed . Now all she need do later was attend to her hair but how would she fill the rest of the morning ?

As she was leaving the bedroom she heard the door bell ring . She rushed to the door her heart leaping and as she opened it remembered , too late , that she was still wearing her housecoat . Two men stood there dressed in what Thelma recognised as their Sunday best .They both removed their hats on seeing her in spite of the drizzle . The older one spoke first .

" Good morning Sister . We are about the Lord`s business . We are here to talk to you about Jesus ."

" Alleluia " said the other man .

Completely forgetting now about her deshabille , her fear of "strange men" and the uindesirabiltity of inviting strangers indoors , Thelma led them inside.

Chapter 18

Queenie was getting ready for her tea party . She drew the curtains in the sitting room and turned on the lamps . It was really too early to do this because it was still light outside but the room looked so much better when the lighting was not too harsh . She had just removed the scones from the oven and there was some clotted cream which she had " taken "especially yesterday .Whilst clearing out the larder she had come upon a jar of home made strawberry jam , probably bought at some fete or bazaar she couldn`t remember when, unfortunately there was no date on the label . She seemed to remember though that jam improved with age or was that whisky ? Better open it now she thought just to be sure.Otherwise it could be embarrassing . Once opened , it smelled all right but was jam supposed to be quite so viscous ? She tried some with the tip of her finger and decided to risk it .

The piece de resistance was a splendid dundee cake which she had been saving for just such an occasion as this . Iris had telephoned earlier saying she would be bringing a victoria sponge and Queenie did not have the heart to tell her that it was not really required . Iris was so good natured she had probably decided to make it just in case Queenie`s own baking did not turn out properly as had been known to happen in the past . She was using her best china and taken the trouble to wash and iron her old lace trimmed table cloth and napkins Dainty sandwiches were already prepared and now waiting in the kitchen under a damp cloth . What else was there ? Oh yes , better put the cats in the back porch now in case anyone was allergic or simply didn`t like them . She had an idea that Thelma disliked animals .

She thought about Thelma . When she called on her the other day she`d been so pleased to see her it was almost embarrassing . She`d felt forced to stay much longer than she`d planned and even then Thelma wasn`t pleased because. she`d wanted her to stay for supper . The bungalow was opulent indeed .Everything in it was new and had been bought at vast expense although it wasn`t to Queenie`s taste . Thelma had obviously married someone very well off she decided , which was nice for her when you thought about her humble background . Her mother had been one of the school dinner ladies recalled Queenie and they used to live in the council flats on the main road by the brickworks . Even when newly built in the 1950s the flats had looked ....slummy somehow . They were probably perfectly adequate but it was something to do with the concrete facing which had acquired   large , wet looking stains like greasy patches within months of being built .

Queenie had always pitied Thelma for living in such an ugly place . The flats had been pulled down when the new road was built years later . Thelma had not discussed her late husband with her which was odd considering the way she had boasted about everything else. She did not seen to be at ease in her surroundings either somehow . And why on earth had she chosen such a large bungalow living alone as she did .Well , no doubt she would find out all about it in due course .

She went into the kitchen to fill the kettle suddenly lthinking about an embarrassing moment which had occurred yesterday .Iris had telephoned and asked if she would call into O`Riordens and pick up some oat cakes which were ordered especially for her

." I wouldn`t bother you Queenie but Mr. O`Riorden rang especially and said he`d had them in for over a week only my car`s having its MOT and I can`t pick it up until after six this evening" she had said . Queenie`s heart had sunk . She didn`t dare go anywhere near O`Riordens but how could she tell Iris that ? Instead she`d been forced to lie and promise to collect them . There was nothing else for it but to lie again today and tell Iris that she`d forgotten about them . She would be irritated no doubt and who could blame her ?

Goodness how difficult life became when there were all these problems to contend with . It was all her own fault too .Queenie felt really annoyed with herself . She had been making an effort to control her impulses lately but sometimes events overtook her . There was the clotted cream yesterday but that did not really count because she hadn`t  planned to "take it ." The queue at the checkout had been so long that it seemed ridiculous to wait with just that one item so it had gone in her pocket .This morning`s behaviour though there was no excuse for she acknowledged .She had picked up her Sunday Times as usual and then noticed an " Oldie"magazine which she quickly tucked inside the bulky paper . She then made her way to the counter where Sid Leasowe had smiled pleasantly and just accepted the usual money .

Outside the shop it had suddenly struck Queenie what she had done. She liked the Leasowes who were struggling to make their business pay . This made her actions all the more disgraceful as well as inexplicable . Why had she done it ? The only way she could cope with this conundrum was by banishing it to the back of her mind but it returned to haunt her every now and then throughout the day . Was all this worry worth it for the price of a magazine ? It all just confirmed her secret fear that matters were spiralling out of control .But what was she going to do about it ? Her head was beginning to throb with all the anxiety . Fortunately at that moment the bell rang so she went to welcome her first guest . Iris stood on the doorstep holding a large tupperware box and there was Thelma coming round the corner . Most relieved at this diversion , Queenie welcomed them in .

Soon the tea party was in full swing and all the ladies were enjoying themselves . Thankfully , the strawberry jam had proved to be delicious and the scones were light . Queenie could never be sure how they would turn out . Even Iris had two she noted . Thelma had eaten very little at first but seemed to gain her appetite later . Queenie couldn`t help noticing a slight atmosphere between Rose and Thelma . Nothing she could put her finger on exactly but  nuances such as Thelma`s scornful expression when Rose expressed an opinion and a look on Rose` face when Thelma had told them all about her late husbands` former mansion near Chandler`s Ford and gone on to discuss his extensive business interests.

It seemed that the late Mr. Honeyspan had been a man of means . Perhaps not quite the international tycoon Thelma`s boasts would have you believe , but certainly very well heeled .That would explain Thelma`s outfit which was rather out of place at a suburban tea party Queenie thought .It would have been far more appropriate at a smart wedding . Although it seemed that her late husband had passed away comparatively recently , Thelma did notseem like a bereaved person either . More like one of them really .

Strangely , in spite of the marriage bureau episode , Queenie herself had always had an inner knowledge that she would never marry and had known this since she was a young woman . In the same way she had known that she would never have a child , and this knowledge had never upset her . Not that she disliked children . Rather she had just taken this knowledge for granted as a fact of her life like the size of her feet or her eye colour .

During tea , Iris had told them all about her problem with the leaking tank and Rose had recommended a plumber she had used last year . "He`s not a particularly nice man " she said . "In fact I didn`t take to him at all . But he was quick and efficient and charged so reasonably . The main thing was that he was able to come right away . Gotes is his name .You`ll find him in the yellow pages ."

"That`s an easy name to remember ." Iris said  " I`ll try him first thing tomorrow ."

"I don`t suppose you noticed when you saw my bungalow " Thelma butted in ," But all of my plumbing is in special rust resistant pipes that are guaranteed to never need attention And of course , because the property is so new everything is guaranteed for 10 years anyway ."There was no reply to be made to that .

Rose had made them all laugh then telling them funny stories about the builders she`d used when she`d first come back here . Thelma told them some more totally irrelevant details about her home and then Iris told them all about Beryl Haskett and her peculiar attitude when her husband had been asked to help with the leak . This set them all off on the experiences encountered by women on their own - always a good topic of conversation .

Glancing at the clock Queenie saw that it was 6.15 . She felt very gratified .Her party was a success . Then Thelma suddenly introduced a controversial topic. Didn`t they think it was disgraceful she asked , the way these pregnant young girls were given council flats and government hand outs whilst poor old OAPs had to scrape along on a pittance ? She certainly had very strong feelings on the matter thought Queenie , but for somebody who was supposed to be a Christian did she have to be so judgemental and vindictive ?

This led to quite a spirited debate amongst the ladies . Each of them had their own ideas about teenage pregnancy. Iris thought the girl should get married whilst Queenie , much to Thelma`s horror , was in favour of abortion and Rose thought that each case depended on its merits . Thelma said that the old fashioned way was best , mother and baby homes until the child was born and then compulsory adoption. This caused a lull in the conversation .

It was quite a relief when Iris managed to change the subject by asking Queenie whether she`d received an invitation to the school reunion . It turned out they`d all had one except Thelma . She was very intrigued to hear about it though and said she`d definitely like to go . Rose then told them that she was on the committee organising the reunion .Thelma shot her a poisonous glance thinking " trust her ". She`d make sure that Thelma received an invitation , Rose added , saying that a little later on they would be canvassing people to offer accommodation to those who were coming from a distance .

Iris said , quite shortly , that she had no intention of attending . Then she`d said she had to break up the party because she had to get home to take Nellie out . Within minutes it seemed , all the ladies had taken their coats and gone .Later , when the washing up was done , Queenie sat before the fire surrounded by the cats . For most of the day she`d managed to banish her problems to the back of her mind but at quiet moments like this they invariably came to the forefront . What was she going to do about this stealing ? There was no point in calling it anything else she decided .   Talking to somebody might help but she knew she never could bring herself to do this . The thought of broaching the subject with somebody she knew – Iris for instance – appalled her . On the other hand discussing it with a total stranger was even more threatening somehow . But what could she do?

She worried over the problem like a dog with a bone. Hours went by .Then a kind of solution occurred to her . Perhaps if she went to the central library in town there might be a book about it ? Some kind of self help manual ? Relief washed over her . Yes that was the best plan . If there wasn`t such a thing she would have to think again . If only there was somebody to confide in .

Then again , perhaps that wasn`t such a good idea.? The library staff all knew her and might wonder why she should want to borrow such a book. Much better to go to a bookshop where nobody knew her . There was a second hand book shop in the high street which she had never been in . That would make the whole thing more anonymous . Meanwhile she could banish the problem . She would watch TV for an hour whilst finishing the Sunday papers . Then she would relax in a hot bath with the radio on for "A Book at Bedtime ." Feeling quite happy again , she rose from the sofa and switched on the TV .

Chapter 19

Rose was working in the bookshop again . Tuesday was usually a quiet day Lately though , most days had been quiet. Gerald didn`t seem unduly bothered by this but then he had other things to preoccupy him now . Eric`s health was giving cause for concern . According to Eric Gerald suffered from ME although he himself had never discussed his health with Rose . Privately , she wondered whether he might have AIDS . It was likely that Gerald did not wish to disclose this and it was nobody`s business but theirs . Nevertheless , Rose felt sad that her friends felt unable to confide in her. Perhaps they feared her reaction to such news .

She decided to sort through some boxes of books which had been brought in earlier that week. Most of the stock came from auctions and private house sales but more recently Gerald had been given the opportunity of buying up local authority library stock. This present lot seemed to have been stored for a long period in some council warehouse judging by the smell .The books were not damp to the touch but gave off a faint scent of mildew .She lifted them out . Mazo de la Roche , Ethel Mannin, Naomi Jacob , Warwick Deeping , would anyone want to read these books now ?

Gosh , this was interesting – Frank Tilsley and here was Ernest Raymond . How much she had enjoyed these writers years ago .They had been literary giants in the nineteen fifties.Now they were forgotten . Would the same thing happen to Melvyn Bragg or Martin Amis? Anyway , she would enjoy re-reading them . Gerald had earmarked these books for the 20 pence boxes , saying they could be donated to charity shops if they had not sold by the weekend . Then Rose had a good idea . They would be ideal for an old folks home .She knew that few old people enjoyed contemporary fiction.

A young girl walked in at this point .She had ginger hair and was carrying a large box full of paper backed books .

" Would you like to buy these " she inquired "or do you do swaps ? They`re practically new and they`re all Mills And Boon ."

"I`m sorry but the proprietor does all the buying here and he`s away at the moment . But anyway , we don`t sell romantic fiction . There`s a second hand book stall in the market though . You could try there."

The girl looked crestfallen . "I`m trying to sell these for my neighbour . She`s sort of an invalied and can`t get out herself and she reads a lot .Perhaps if I came in on another day I could ask the boss?"

" I`m afraid Mr. Carey definitely wont want them but you might find something for your friend to read in those boxes outside . They`re only 20 pence each. "

" She wont have hard backs . They`re too heavy to hold in bed ." Sharon was cross . Sandy had promised her £I if she returned with some fresh reading matter . Now it looked as though she had lugged that box all the way here for nothing .

Then there was a diversion : Queenie walked in .She looked surprised to see Rose. " I was just passing by and saw you through the window " she lied . "I did n`t realise it was here that you worked . I thought it was Dillons in town."

" Dear me no . This is much more fun than Dillons . But how nice to see you Queenie ." She noticed that her friend looked rather pale and that the ginger haired teenager was staring at her oddly as if trying to place her.Queenie was in a state .She had recognised the girl from O`Riordens immediately but had hoped the girl had not noticed her .She turned around and began scanning the book shelves mindlessly all the time repeating "Please don`t know me " like a mantra .

Although Queenie had told Rose she was "Just passing " she had come to the book shop quite deliberately . Whilst shopping for cat food it had suddenly occurred to her that this might be just the place to find the book she was looking for , so she had walked to the end of the High St , an area she did not normally frequent because there was little to interest her there .After you`d passed the Methodist church there was only a wholesaler of motoring parts , a baby linen shop and an upholsterers before a boring line of hoardings led to the bookshop. She had been taken aback to find Rose there although that was nothing compared to the shock of encountering the ginger haired girl .

The bell pinged as the girl made her exit and Queenie exhaled with relief . Obviously there was nothing to her liking in the 20 pence boxes thought Rose as she waited for the kettle to boil , keeping one eye on the shop door meanwhile . Queenie had suddenly begun to look better she noticed watching her browse the shelves.

Saying a silent prayer of thanks that the girl had gone . Queenie scanned the shelves . There seemed to be quite a selection of books on criminology and look , here was the very book she needed " The Psychology of Criminal Behaviour ". Queenie pulled it out and looked at the index . There were several references to shoplifting . She glanced at the pencilled price on the fly leaf . £ 5. 50 . Not out of her price range but how on earth could she explain to Rose why she wanted such a book ? It looked so odd . Queenie sighed ,Why was everything so difficult ?

She would have to give some thought to this . Then it came to her in a flash . She would simply borrow the book , read it and return it tomorrow.That certainly wasn't stealing was it? Fortunately it was a slim volume although hardbacked , but she was easily able to slide it into her shopper. Just in time too because Rose then appeared carrying a tray. She had rather a strange expression on her face Queenie noticed. Rather surprised looking .

"Queenie , I did try to ring you yesterday to thank you for the tea party but there seemed to be some fault with your phone " She said.

"I know. It was my fault . I hadn't replaced the receiver properly and didn't realise until last night"

"I really loved your cottage" Rose continued "You have some lovely things and you've made it all so cosy."

"You've seen hardly any of it though . You must come again soon and have a really good look around . Most of my stuff is packed away because I've nowhere to put it . I've been collecting china for years and there are boxes and boxes of stuff I keep meaning to sort out . I once though I'd rather like to have a second hand shop , one side for books the other for bric a brac. The only thing is I'd hate to have to sell it . I couldn't bear to part with something I really like so I wouldn't do much business would I ?

Their conversation was interrupted by the arrival of a number of young customers from the local further education college. They had questions to ask Roseabout the stock and Queenie enjoyed the opportunity of observing them . How things had changed since she was their age . The girls were dressed casually in trousers and padded jackets .They wore sensible , comfortable shoes and had soft easy hair styles . She remembered the stiletto heels , beehive hairdos rigid with lacquer and those awful push up bras and horrid roll ons which were de rigeur when she was a teenager . Most of all though she was aware of the easy attitude between the sexes. They seemed to be on genuinely friendly terms with each other . Perhaps that came from co-education ? In her day , even when she was 17 or 18 she would cross the road rather than confront a boy face to face , such was her terror of the opposite sex. Going to an all girls school had probably caused this . If only she'd had a brother things might have been different . Yet Iris had a brother . It had taken years of working with the opposite sex to develop a normal attgitude towards them and she knew that it had been exactly the same for Iris . She envied this generation their freedom .

Since Rose continued to be occupied Queenie made her farewell . She had accomplished her mission and planned to spend the evening studying the book she had "Borrowed " .There was a good 20 minutes before her bus was due so she decided to turn left away from the main road . She had not visited this area for years . The neighbourhood had deteriorated . This was obvious by the litter in the street and the poorly maintained houses . There were two straggling back streets each of which had a shop on the corner .One of these was an off license which she passed by with no particular interest . The other was one of those open all hours shops which cater for the improvident housewife .The sort of shop where you could buy shoelaces at 10 pm or a frozen joint of meat on a Sunday morning

An Asian man adjusting something in the window gave Queenie a broad friendly grin and she smiled back. She stopped to have a closer look at an advertising display in a glass case . A card took her eye immediately . It depicted a gypsy lookibg woman shielding part of her face with a fan as she gazed into a crystal ball.he words beneath said "Leah . Claivoyant. By Appointment only. One visit could change your life." Queenie`s neck hairs prickled . This was something which greatly appealed to her . On many occasions in the past she had been tempted but had never had the nerve to actually consult a fortune teller.

A voice startled her " You are interested in Leah ? I can arrange for you if you wish ." It was the Asian man , surprisingly short now he stood next to her .but looking so pleasant and friendly Queenie forgot to be scared . He spoke English extremely well with no trace of a foreign accent she noted.

"Oh I don`t know really . It`s intriguing but I don`t know if I really believe in it . Do you ? Is she good?

"Of course . I know Leah very well . But it depends what you mean by good Some people think a good clairvoyant is someone who tells them what they want to hear . Leah is a true clairvoyant . She has the genuine gift . I speak with some confidence because she is also my good neighbour." The little man had the most amazing eyes , dark liquid brown with hidden depths that seemed to hold her gaze and prevent her from looking away . He had the dark skin of an Indian with the slanted eyes of a Chinese but his physique was that of an adolescent boy although he appeared to be middleaged . His hair was streaked with grey .

"Do you mind if I ask you where you come from? Queenie asked shyly .

"Not at all . My family are Asian mongrels I suppose . Part Indian , Chinese and Hebraic I believe from a long way back . We regard ourselves as orientals . I came her from Indonesia but was raised in Penang. " He spoke with no shyness "One set of my grandparents came from the middle east so you can see there is a really good mixture there " he laughed and so did Queenie . " You may not know this but all orientals have a well developed sense of the supernatural . We take it for granted that such things exist . Leah has read my palm many times . She is of Gypsy origin of course and , like we orientals she has the sixth sense ."

Queenie was impressed . The man sounde so informed . Somehow she had always regarded fortune telling as something disreputable but he made it sound respectable .

" Does she live in this street ?"

"Nearby . But she never receives casual callers . You have to arrange an appointment in advance . I shall be happy to do this for you."

Queenie thought quickly . She wouldn't dare to do this on her own and she knew that Iris would never countenance it . But perhaps Thelma could be persuaded ? She fumbled in her bag ."I'll just make a note of your number and then let you know . A friend might want to come with me ."

"Please follow me Madam and I will give you Leah`s card . A delicious smell compouned of a myriad of spices emanated from the shop . Queenie sniffed appreciatively . "What a wonderful smell .It really makes me feel hungry ." she thought. The man was a mind reader " I can see you like Indian food " he remarked . "Perhaps you would like to taste something ? My mother would be pleased to let you taste our food ." He shouted something and a plump smiling lady appeared from behind a curtain . The man said a few words to her in a foreign tongue then smiled at Queenie .

"Now you are our guest ." he said .

"No really I couldn`t " she began , covered in confusion . But the man was so pleasant it seemed rude not to respond.

"Now I must introduce myself " he said " My name is.... He said something unpronounceable but added "But my friends call me Jimmy because it is easier .My surname is Ng " he spelled it out .Queenie tried to say it ."Ung " she managed .

" not bad , but Jimmy will do I think . And now .. what is your name?"

" Um ..Queenie Mack " She replied blushing . She always felt embarrassed telling people her name Somehow it sounded even sillier repeating it to a foreigner.

"Ah , A nice eay name but I have not heard it before . So Queenie How do you do ? he held out his hand .

Jimmy ushered Queenie into the back room where she was relieved to see three ladies , two seated at a table and one at the sink . They were introduced as his mother, auntie and sister . The older ladies spoke no English but Jimmie`s sister was able to speak it well . Soon she and Queenie were deep in conversation. After a few minutes Queenie was offered a steamimg plate of what looked like an omelette. "This is a doser " Jimy said " a   favourite lunchtime snack ." It was delicious . Queenie realised that she would have to take a later bus now bu that did not matterbecause of this wonderful adventure .She could hardly wait to ring Iris and tell her all about it . Meanwhile she listened attentively while Gishri explained how to prepare the spices for the dish .

Chapter 20

Rose had been right Iris decided . There was definitely something unpleasant about Cyril Gotes .He`d arrived promptly enough to assess the job after her telephone call this morning -she had to be fair about that – but there was something about his manner which grated on her .He did not seem at all surly as Rose had described though . On the contrary, if anything he was obsequious . After examining the leak he`d told her that a replacement tank would be required – would she want a new one because he might be able to get hold of one that had been reconditioned ? In any event it would be a few days before he could obtain either and the job would take at least half a day , perhaps longer . Did she understand that the water supply would have to be disconnected during that time ? He`d then said that he would telephone her later that day and tell her when he could begin the job , probably Thursday morning he thought .

At this point Iris began to feel rather annoyed . After all she`d merely asked for an estimate and here he was assuming the job was his .

" I had intended to get several estimates before I decided anything ." She told him . He laughed derisively

" Please yourself Madam , but I think you`ll find there`s nobody locally who can do this work as quickly and cheaply as me .You can`t expect anyone to come immediately . I`m only here because I was let down on a job Plumbers round here are booked up for weeks and your is a job that should be done as soon as possible .God knows how long that slow leak has been dripping into your walls ."

He glanced at his watch making it obvious that he had no further time to waste . This decided her . After all , his estimate was surprisingly reasonable and Rose had said he was efficient .

"Miss Deacon recommended you " Iris told the man " And I always prefer to deal with a local person ." Cyril flicked his eyes up and down her and sniffed Was it this that she found so unpleasant thought Iris or was it that horrible thin ginger moustache or those eyes which seemed to look right through you . There was something calculating about his look , as if he was making an inventory of everything she was wearing and putting a price on it she thought crossly .

In fact , Cyril Gotes had made a thorough assessment of Iris but not quite in the way she had imagined . Nice figure still , he observed even though she was a bit of an old maid . Long , slim legs .

Bet she was dying for it really . Would she be a virgin ? He pictured her in bed masturbating and then imagined what he could do to her . Bet she wouldn't say no if itcame to it . His penis stirred and he shifted his posture slightly , flicking his eyes over her again . " I beg your pardon Madam ? " he said obsequiously .

"I was asking if you worked alone ? Only it seems quite a heavy job for a man by himself ."

" Oh no . I have a boy who works with me . Strong young lad . Is that settled then Madam ? I'll ring you this evening then as arranged ." Cyril spoke politely . He remembered Miss Deacon well . Supercilious bitch . Put him in mind of a C.O.'s wife . Very hoity toity and full of herself Practically stood over him while he did the work and did'nt even offer him so much as a cup of tea !

After he'd gone Iris planned her week . She'd have to be at home whilst the work was done which would mean missing the flower club . If the men hadn't finished by 6.30 she'd miss the sewing circle too , which would be annoying . The speaker this month was a well known local author and she'd been looking forward to his talk . She supposed she should look at her household insurance now too . Just in case there was a chance of reclaiming some of the cost .First though , she'd ring Queenie and thank her for the tea party and hear her news .

The phone rang and rang before Queenie answered it . She sounded breathless .

" I've been chasing Solly round the garden " she explained . "He'd caught a grey squirrel but by the time I got to him he'd killed it ." Iris shuddered . She couldn't understand how Queenie tolerated all those cats

. " I've had such a busy morning " Queenie continued " I spilt a bottle of cooking oil and it leaked into all my cupbards so I had to turn them all out . It was a good thing really because there were things I never use now so I've decided to throw them all out. There's a fish kettle and some really huge old saucepans . Would you like them ? "

" No thank you " Iris was emphatic . " But its good to know you're having a clear out at last . Why don't you go right through the whole house while you're at it ? " although she was pretending to be humorous Queenie knew she meant it and felt annoyed .

" I haven't got time for that .Vi brought me in some seville oranges this morning so I'm making marmalade this afternoon."

Iris thought it time to bring the conversation to a halt . Next thing would be Queenie offering to make marmalade for her and , having tried it in the past , she definitely did not want any .

Because of the accident with the cooking oil , Queenie's plan to go back to the bookshop had to be postponed . She decided to leave it until Wednesday after she finished at her wood carving class Meanwhile she had the marmalade to get on with . She had a busy afternoon in the kitchen and decided to have an early meal before relaxing in front of the TV . She made herself a tray of finger food and settled herself on the sofa leafing through a magazine while she nibbled . The other day she'd brought home a stack of glossy magazines she'd found in a charity shop . She enjoyed reading them even though she would never dream of buying them new . After reading through a handful she was left with the same sated feeling she had when she ate too much chocolate . There was simply too much of everything . Too many cosmetics to learn about , too many revolutionary beauty treatments and too many items of clothing to look at

Now though , she had come across something riveting .It was in a recent copy of "Marie Claire "and was all about positive thinking . An American woman (it had to be one of those) thought Queenie , had written a best selling book which supposedly had taken America by storm . The gist of the book was condensed into three or four pages of the magazine and it was so enthralling that she determined to order the book from the library at her first opportunity .

She read through the article quickly then turned back to the beginning to peruse it more thoroughly . " Transform you life with the power of positive affirmation " read Queenie . In a nutshell , the theory of this is that the innermost beliefs of the individual steer him or her towards certain actions or patterns of behaviour . In other words we create our own reality by our thoughts If you are constantly thinking " Life's awful " , then sure enough your life probably will be awful . She read on deeply interested . The writer suggested that these self destructive patterns of behaviour could be reprogrammed by bombarding them with bright , positive messages . These could be in the form of notes which one posted around the house , on the bathroom mirror for example or the door of the fridge .

The writer suggested various forms the notes could take. " I am a powerful sexy lady " was one . Queenie disregarded this immediately . Too American by far . Besides , she did not want to be a powerful , sexy lady. However , " I can and I will " took her fancy as " money flows into my life "and " I will succeed at everything I undertake".

The writer then advised " if you are scared people will laugh at you , put your positive messages where nobody will see them ,

95

inside a drawer or in a book you use frequently . " Queenie had no such qualms . She rose from her chair completely forgetting about the cat who`d been snuggled into her lap and went to fetch pen and paper . Within minutes there were messages stuck to strategic surfaces around the house . She then took a handful upstairs and soon there were messages all over her bedroom and bathroom too .Even if it did not work there was no harm in trying it she reasoned . Then she pinched herself mentally . That was a negative attitude if ever there was one . It would work . She lay in bed later and visualised , as the article had advised , a huge blackboard with the words " I can do anything " written in huge letters and eventually she fell asleep .

Chapter 21

At the end of his last job of the day Cyril Gotes climbed into his into his van and made for home .He smiled grimly to himself as he remembered the parting remark of Mrs. Yates whose lavatory he`d been unblocking for the umpteenth time . Her mentally handicapped son had a habit of throwing his toys down there . Cyril had made some remark about the cold weather to which she had replied

" Never mind . I expect you`re going home to a nice  hot meal ." He`d made no answer but the only hot meal he would get would be one he provided for himself and after a hard day`s work a man did n`t feel like cooking .

He fantasised , as he so often did , about returning home to a different sort of wife - probably a youngish , shapely blonde – and a clean cosy house where an appetising supper awaited him . He pictured her welcoming him home and sitting him down to his hot, home made meal . Afterwards she would be an eager participant in some of the antics he saw in his porn magazines .Then reality broke through .

Cyril knew that the neighbours talked about him , particularly those like Rita next door , who knew exactly what his home circumstances were and this knowledge infuriated him but there was nothing he could do about it On one occasion , Bernard Eccles , the neighbour on his other side had cornered him in the " Flying Goose " and had the nerve to ask him point blank why he put up with it . He had soon shut him up though . They should mind their own bloody business . The truth was that Cyril would have liked nothing better than to get shut of his fat ,slovenly wife but he was scared of losing his army pension for which he`d worked so hard . He`d heard that a divorce would mean he would have to share everything he owned with Sandy and he would see her in hell first .

He would certainly have to sell the house and share the proceeds with her , to say nothing about the business which he was trying so hard to build up .Why the hell should he ? No . He had decided to bide his time . There were other ways of killing a cat as they they say . And if he played his cards right she would dig her grave with her own teeth as the doctor had warned It was only a question of waiting . His army training stood him in good stead in that respect hard though he found it to tolerate the living conditions that life with Sandy entailed

His own room and belongings were immaculately kept and he tried to turn a blind eye to the filth in the rest of the house , hard though it was .He pulled up at the Spar shop and went to find something for his supper .He foraged around the chilled food cabinets for a while but nothing took his fancy . It was all the usual foreign muck anyway . Lasagne , chop suey , chilli or chicken madras . Why couldn't they sell something English ? He abandoned the frozen foods and went to look amongst the tins . The woman at the till was ugly but she had good tits he thought , staring at them offensively whilst he made payment .

Emerging from the shop with a tin of Fray Bentos steak and kidney , he then went into the shop next door where he knew the proprietor kept hard porn magazines behind the counter .He obtained three and also came to an arrangement about exchanging those he already had . Then he climbed into the van and went home.

In Berringer Row a small group of teenaged girls were hanging round the derelict former shop .They all stared as Cyril's van slowed to turn round the corner. One of them was Bernard Eccles'daughter he noticed .She had the same ginger hair as her dad . She was jail bait . Sharon raised her skirt and assumed a provocative pose leaning against the corrugated iron , then burst into a f it of giggles. Little cock teaser he thought , someone wants to teach her a lesson . He stared coldly at the group of girls with no expression on his face and continued driving towards the garages .

As he entered the front door , Wayne Beale , the scrawny adolescent from next door was just coming down the stairs .

" Just brought Sandy her chinky meal " he said to Cyril ." Wouldn't catch me eating muck like that .My mate said they kill cats and eat them ." Cyril made no comment to this but nodded at Wayne politely enough and went into the kitchen .Privately he hated the lad but took care not to make this obvious . On occasions he was useful to him when he had jobs where extra help was needed . Wayne was happy to accept a few pounds for his trouble and Cyril had none of the hassle of employing anybody .

He placed his purchases on the kitchen table . This was his domain and as such was clinically clean . All the work surfaces were bare . Indeed the kitchen could have been a room in an empty house . Cyril left nothing on show and always cleaned up after himself meticulously . This room , his bedroom and the downstairs loo were " his " and were looked after accordingly .The rest of the place was Sandy's and was left to fester . Cyril made sure the door to the bathroom was kept shut when he was around such was the squalor within . Likewise the sitting room although it had been months since anyone entered it . Even Hilda seemed to have given up any attempts to put it to rights . He heard the television blaring away from Sandy's room and even here in the kitchen you could smell the odour emanating from there.

Cyril closed the kitchen door firmly . There were certain tasks he had to undertake before he began to prepare his evening meal . First of all he stripped down to his underwear and donned an old tracksuit . Then there were his shoes to polish .He brought the box with his polishing kit from the bottom of the broom cupboard and spent a good ten minutes attending to his shoes army style He then placed them in the cupboard ready to wear the next day .

He plunged his shirt into a bowl of soapy water and after scrubbing the collar and cuffs with a nail brush he rinsed the garment thoroughly then hung it outside to drip dry . He set up the ironing board then and attended to the crease in his trousers examining them carefully first for any spots or stains . After hanging then up he carefully brushed his sports jacket after first replacing the handkerchief .His underwear and hankies were washed in the machine at weekends .

These tasks completed , he peeled three potatoes and put them on to boil and opened a small tin of peas . He began to feel more cheerful . After his supper he would watch his new video and then he had the magazines to read in bed . He rummaged in one of the kitchen drawers and found a cassette "Country Sounds " which never failed to cheer him up . Soon the sound of Tammy Wynette singing "Crystal Chandeliers " filled the kitchen . An appetising smell emanated from the oven where the steak and kidney pie was cooking and the windows began to steam up as the potatoes bubbled on the stove . Almost contented now , Cyril opened a can of Carlsberg and sat at the kitchen table to have a thorough perusal of the " Sun " .

Chapter 22

Although it was the middle of a Sunday afternoon , Rita Beale was busy in the kitchen. Hideously crammed into too tight jeans and bursting out of a teeshirt belonging to her daughter , she was rubbing at the stainless steel sink with a brillo pad when Wayne wandered in . He was surprised to see his mother in the kitchen . Usually of a Sunday Rita didn`t come downstairs until nearly teatime . After a Saturday night down the club she needed hours in bed to recover .

" What`s up with Sandy mum? " Wayne asked his mother .

"I dunno . Whajermean ? "

"She didn`t want no chinky meal on Friday , or last night and I`ve just been round there now and she don`t want nothing , not even a video ." Wayne was put out since he had been relying on receiving some cash from their neighbour .

" She`s off colour I spect . Listen Wayne , I want you to move some of that stuff from the alley ." There was an outraged  " Whaffor ? "   But before he could continue Rita went on "And get rid of those motor bike bits over there . Our Hayley`s boyfriend `s coming round here for his tea . We`re trying to get the place cleaned up ." Rita sounded harrassed .

" That prick ! " Wayne remembered Darren Piper from school "Why you bothering for him? What`s wrong with the place anyway ? "

Rita saw his point entirely but forebore to comment . No need to tell him that his sister Hayley was turning into a right little snob . She was only humouring her to keep the peace . She`d been that moody lately . "Anyway , she said she wants you out of the way when he comes . Wants me out of the way too. She`s cooking him a meal she said . I`m going down the club ."

" Suits me ." Wayne said . " I can`t stand the prick anyway . Proper mummy`s boy he used to be . Still is probably ." He glanced out of the window then and began to hoot with laughter.

"What`s so funny ?" asked Rita . She went to the window too . Hayley was outside in the street with a broom , sweeping the pavement .

" Christ " said Rita " All we want now is a red carpet . Does she think Prince William `s coming here or what ? "  They both curled up with laughter but at the same time Rita could not help feeling worried . It was all wrong making this stupid fuss .The lad should take them as he found them and if they weren`t good enough - tough !

Hayley was going over the top . She didn`t look well neither , all white and drawn looking .

"Look Wayne ,please move your bike gear .You can see it means a lot to her , this lad coming round here. Don`t spoil it eh ? "

Hayley was exhausted . She`d been up since 7 this morning because she`d felt so sick . It must have been a dodgy curry they`d had last night . Since then she`d be busy trying to get everything ready even though Darren was n`t coming until 5 o clock .. It was obvious she couldn`t have her mother there after what had taken place in O`Riorden`s shop . Time enough for Darren to meet her at some future date . Wayne would only say the wrong thing and embarrass her or even worse , say something to provoke Darren , so she didn`t want him around either . She looked around her . If only there was something she could do to make the street look better . She looked at the broken down fences , boarded up windows and graffiti marked wall and thought the only answer would be a bomb . Wearily she picked up her broom .

Wayne had gone into the sitting room now and was staring round in surprise . Rita followed him and gawped too . The room looked totally different and , Rita had to agree it was vastly improved .For a start . all the clutter that was normally lying around had been completely cleared . Hayley had draped an Indian throw over the settee . Where had that come from ? The table was covered in a pretty lace cloth Rita had never seen before and a vase of fresh flowers had been placed in the middle . Overall there was a smell of lemon pledge .

"Christ Almighty . "Rita was overcome . She had to discuss all this with somebody. She decided to go next door and see Sandy. .She shouted from the front door as usual and heard a faint reply . Unusually , there was no noise from the radio or TV . No sign of Cyril downstairs neither . He must be down the pub . Sandy was lying back in bed .She tried to raise her head but was unable to do so . She looked bad thought Rita. It was obvious that Hilda had not paid her a visit recently because there were no signs of any clean up .It was apparent too that Sandy had not been given clean sheets or a fresh nightie for some while .

"You still feeling bad ? " She enquired " Did you try those Epsom Salts like I said ? "

"They didn`t do no good ." Sandy wheezed . " I don`t know what`s wrong with me Rite . I don`t fancy anything to eat , haven`t for days . I`ve got pains all round my middle . I rang the doctor but he wouldn`t come . Said Cyril had to take me to the surgery ."

" It might be just a bug . Our Hayley was ever so sick this morning . Said she'd had a dodgy curry . I never eat any of that wog food . Our Wayne won't touch it neither . What about them pain killers I got you ? They no good ?

" I'm just taking aspirin now . Them others made me feel sick ."

" What about if you had a bath Sand ? I could run it for you and while your in I could change the bed . You'd feel ever so much better . " Rita coaxed although she didn't fancy the job in the least .

" I dunno . I don't feel like . Perhaps tomorrow ." Sandy shifted her bulk uncomfortably in bed . She didn't know what she wanted . It would be nice to fall asleep for a long , long time she thought .

" You got any sleeping pills Rite ? "

"Yeah . I'll go and get them now ." cheated of her opportunity for a chat about Hayley but relieved to be of service , Rita left the room . In the kitchen Hayley was unwrapping two polythene wrapped parcels as her mother entered .

" What you got there ? " Asked Rita . Hayley blushed .

" This one 's coq au vin and the other is Viennese strudel . Miss Deacon let me take them from her freezer ." She lied . In fact Hayley had taken both of the items without the permission of her employer . She had also taken a lace tablecloth but she intended to return this laundered , later in the week as she would also return the items of cutlery and glass she had " borrowed " for today's occasion .

"Don't fancy any of that foreign muck ." Rita grimaced . " But I suppose our kind of food's not good enough for Darren bloody Piper ."

Hayley made no answer and Rita went upstairs to fetch the pills for her friend . Her daughter had been busy in the bathroom too judging by the smell of air freshener . She noticed new towels were laid out there and a tablet of fancy French soap . Attempts had been made to disguise the marks under the taps in the bath . She shook her head. It was all over the top .

As Rita returned to number fifteen , Cyril appeared around the corner from the direction of the garages . He would have liked to ignore her but she waited deliberately until he reached the gate and then accosted him

" Sandy's not well , Cyril . "

" So what ? " he answered shortly , continuing up the path . Rita followed him as he opened the front door and went inside .

" She`s really ill Cyril . She hasn``t eaten anything for days . I think she needs a doctor ."

"Perhaps she `ll lose some weight then . Not before time either . Anyway , it`s nothing to do with me ." he answered . He went into the kitchen and shut the door firmly in her face .   Defeated , she went upstairs to Sandy

"I`ve got the pills here Sandy , but I`m only giving you two . " Rita said . It had suddenly occurred to her for what use they could be employed . Better not take any chances she thought ." You might feel a lot better after a good night`s sleep " she suggested hopefully . Sandy merely grunted . Then said

" Get us a can of coke Rite will you ?"

Chapter 23

Rose was cross . She had noticed for some time a deterioration in standards of cleanliness compared with the days when Evie had cleaned for her. Dusters were not washed , surfaces looked grubby and things seemed to be missing here and there . An inventory of the bungalow revealed that several things had disappeared from the freezer as well as minor items of toiletries and cosmetics. Hayley had to be responsible . Rose was cross. She had had misgivings about the girl when Evie had first introduced her . Now they seemed justified .

It was her appearance and demeanour that had put Rose off . Hayley was an attractive young woman with her pale skin and long dark hair which looked much nicer now it was released from the ethnic looking braids but her face was always set in a sullen expression and she would never look her in the eye.

From what Evie had told her , Rose knew the girl came from a deprived background . Apparently her mother was a single parent who was still struggling to bring up two others besides Hayley . Evie , initially worried when Darren had first brought the girl home , had become quite fond of her now and spoke highly of her . She would never have recommended her otherwise Rose knew . But from the very beginning the girls attitude had grated on Rose .

She did not expect her to wear the overalls that were Evie`s choice of working apparel but she could not help noticing how dreadful the girl looked in the skin tight leggings and cropped tops she wore , especially lately when she`d seemed to have become rather plump.She had tried to make conversation with Hayley during the few minutes when their paths crossed but the girl made it obvious she did not want to talk to her .Rose had no complaint about this whilst she was doing her work properly . Evie had shown her the routine to follow and initially her work had been faultless . It was only lately that Rose had cause to be dissatisfied but how long had Hayley been helping herself to items from the house ? Thinking back , there had been several puzzling discrepancies for which she had blamed herself .

Only last week a litre of orange juice had disappeared though Rose could have sworn she`d only just opened it whilst she had often wondered why she seemed to use up her bath essence so quickly .Cleaning materials seemed to last no time either . Well , she would have to confront the girl this morning unpleasant though it would be . She took her newspaper into the kitchen and sat down to wait .

Hayley was both surprised and annoyed to find Rose still on the premises . As usual she blushed and lowered her eyes when Rose greeted her . Inwardly though she was furious . She had not bargained for her hanging around whilst she did her work . It wasn`t fair . After muttering something in reply to Rose` greeting she turned her back and went to the sink.   " I`m glad you`re early Hayley " Rose began " I rather wanted to have a word with you."She paused then continued "About some things that have gone missing recently . Mainly from my freezer ."

Hayley did not turn round but Rose could see the blush covering the back of her neck .

" I think you`ve let down Evie dreadfully don`t you" ? There was no answer

" Don`t you think you could look at me when I`m talking to you". Hayley turned slowly and as she did so Rose noticed something about the swell of her tummy . Good heavens !the girl was pregnant . Hayley caught her glance and reddened again . Then she burst into hysterical tears .

Over mugs of coffee at the table , Rose questioned the girl gently all questions of missing items forgotten . Hayley had feared she was pregnant for some time but had discussed her condition with nobody until she had told her boyfriend last night . He had commented on her altered shape which forced her confession . She said she had hoped the problem would " go away" She did not know for sure how many periods she had missed , three or even four she thought ..She cried pitifully

" It`s not fair . I don`t want a baby ." How ironic , thought Rose . Evie trying for a baby for years and now her son has almost beaten her to it . This pregnancy must be only slightly less advanced than Evie`s .

" What does Darren say ? " she enquired

" S`not his "Hayley hiccupped "That`s the trouble"

" Then who ? " Rose was taken aback .

" There was three of them that night .That`s why. I was half drunk or I wouldn`t have done it . Darren thinks it`s his  . He wants to get married" Hayley`s face was a mask of misery .

"Perhaps you`ve made a mistake ? Perhaps it is Darren`s ? " Rose said hopefully .

"You don`t get it do you ? " Hayley spoke as if to a child . " What happens if it turns out the baby is half a chink ? Because it might be for all I know ." There was a long silence . Rose did not know what to say . The dilemma was something so far outside her own experience she was lost for words . Eventually she enquired " What about your mother ? couldn`t you confide in her ?"

"She`ll kill me . I couldn``t do it to her . She`s always told me not to bring any trouble home .If it was Darren`s baby I`d want it . If I went for an abortion he `d never forgive me . What am I going to do ? If I tell him what really happened he wont want to know me ."

"There are various things you can do . It certainly isn`t a hopeless situation Hayley. " Rose tried to sound positive . "The first thing you need is proper advice .There`ll be somebody in the Social Services Dept. who can help you I`ll ring them now." Rose went to fetch the directory. "We`ll make you an urgent appointment . I`ll come with you if you like ." For the next twenty minutes Rose tried unsuccessfully to get through to the local office but the number was constantly engaged . There was only one thing for it . " Right Hayley , grab your jacket . We`re going down to that office now ."

Wordlessly the girl did as she was asked and the two left the house.

Chapter 24

Queenie looked out of the window , saw that it was a lovely sunny morning and , for the thousandth time blessed the good fortune that allowed her not to have to go to work any more . She was finding retirement the best time of her life and had no regrets whatsoever about giving up her former daily routine . Retired people were allowed to attend classes at the local further education college at reduced rates and Queenie had taken advantage of this opportunity to enrol for several different courses . Last year she had tried both wood work and upholstery and samples of her handiwork were on display in her home She was continuing upholstery this year but had given up the wood work classes in favour of wood carving which Mr. Noonan had tactfully suggested as a more suitable alternative .

Queenie had experienced problems in coping with some of the equipment . In fact she had been terrified of tools like the jigsaw and router and frequently had to appeal to her classmates for help . She was not the only lady in the class but the two others were super , confident types who had made her feel totally inferior . One of them had boasted about building her own garden wall and plastering   an outhouse – whilst the other turned out to be a qualified mechanic .Although nobody had said anything , some of her classmates had indicated that she was de trop so she had been relieved at Mr. Noonan`s intervention .

Woodcarving was proving to be an enjoyable occupation . There were other congenial ladies in the class and they could talk amongst themselves as they worked . The objects they were working were usually smallish , manageable things like teapot stands or wall plaques which could easily be carried home when finished . Queenie herself was attempting something more ambitious – a fire screen . Then she remembered , she would have to go back to the bookshop to return the book she had " borrowed " . She had not found it particularly helpful after all because though it explained various types of deviant behaviour it did not give the information she required about how to stop it .The book was more of a text book for students .

Really she should have had more sense she reasoned . Just as if anyone would produce a manual telling you how to stop shoplifting . It would be just as silly as a manual to tell serial killers how to stop murdering . She giggled to herself then , imagining a series of manuals on the library shelves called Mack`s Self Help series – particularly in demand in prison libraries . How to stop committing arson , How to stop car theft , etc . No , it had been a loony idea .

Returning the book meant that she would have to go to the High Street straight from the college if she wanted to catch the 1pm bus home . This could be difficult because she would be carrying the firescreen . Perhaps she should leave the book until tomorrow ? But that would mean that she could not take the bus into town as she liked to do on Thursdays . She pondered over her options as she went downstairs . She particularly wanted to be at home tomorrow afternoon because there was an old film on TV she was dying to see again" The Secret Life of Walter Mitty." She`d been about 12 when she`d seen it first time around . It was always interesting to see old films again she found Often they were disappointing but sometimes they stood the test of time remarkably well . The VCR had been unusable for some time and Queenie had not got around to having it fixed.

The postman had been but she could tell by looking at the mail that it was all junk She gathered it up anyhow . It was something to read whilst she had her breakfast . First of all thoughshe had to deal with the cats . She opened the kitchen door and all three of them surrounded her at once , rubbing against her legs . Oh dear , one of them had brought in a fledgeling . The floor was littered with tiny blue and yellow feathers and there was the small mangled body in front of the cooker . She shouted at Solly crossly as she cleared away the mess but the cat ignored her .

Queenie sat down to her breakfast . She had decided now that she would return the book this morning and she would leave the class about twenty minutes earlier than usual to allow herself time to catch the bus home The matter settled in her mind she paid attention to the eight o clock news just beginning on the radio as she ate her bran flakes .

Arriving at the college shortly before 10 a m , Queenie was surprised to see Thelma in the foyer.It turned out that she did a Keep Fit class on Wednesday mornings . She was dressed for the part too , thought Queenie .The bright pink tracksuit would have looked fine on someone with a smaller bottom , but in Thelma`s place she would have settled for something in navy or black or perhaps not even worn a tracksuit at all ......But then what would you wear instead ?

Queenie was so engrossed in thinking this out that she missed a remark Thelma made and had to ask her to repeat it .

" I was asking if you`d like to come back home with me afterwards or perhaps go and have lunch somewhere in town ?" Unknown to Queenie , Thelma was thinking almost identical thoughts about her friend`s appearance Somebody as short as she is should not wear her skirts so long , she thought. And that velvet cloak is really ridiculous Who does she think she is ? As for that hat ! It looks completely incongruous . She wondered whether Queenie might be turning slightly batty Normal people didn't draw attention to themselves by dressing so bizarrely . Yet she seemed sane enough to talk to .

Queenie thanked her for the offer but explained about having to leave he class early because of some business she had to attend to . Impossible to tell her the real reason. .Immediately , she could tell by the cast down look on Thelma's face that she had said the wrong thing . She thinks I'm trying to put her off , she thought and sought desperately to say something to remedy the situation . Before she could think of anything though , Thelma said

" I don't know . I thought I'd soon get to know people here if I got involved in things but people just aren't very friendly ." She sounded so aggrieved and miserable that Queenie felt an immediate rush of sympathy .

" Oh yes they are Thelma " she said . "Just give them a chance.The trouble is a keep fit class isn't a good place to make friends because you're all too active to talk . In a class like mine we have a chance to talk to each other . Next term you must change . And you should join the Ladies Club too . Iris and I both belong and so does Rose . It's in the village hall on the last Wednesday of the month ."

" Perhaps I will then ." Thelma seemed mollified ." But do call round and see me anytime Queenie . I get so lonely and I'm sure you must do too . " Queenie did not disagree with her although , in fact , she never felt lonely and promised to do so . Then a jangling bell summoned them to their respective classes .

At 11.45 am Queenie left the college and walked towards the High Street . She was encumbered ,the fire screen under one arm and her large straw carrier in her other hand . The bag was surprisingly heavy . Iris always laughed at her saying it was full even before she began shopping. She herself seemed to manage with the smallest handbag you could imagine but if you didn't have a car you had to be prepared for all kinds of contingencies Queenie had found . Accordingly she carried in her bag a folding raincoat and a small umbrella , a paper backed book – you never knew when you might be stuck somewhere with nothing to read – a few items of cosmetics and a small bag containing her wallet , coin purse and various personal documents as well as her house keys Today of course , she also had the book she was planning to return to the shop .

Although it was bright and sunny there was a chilly wind blowing and Queenie wished now that she had worn warmer clothes . As she reached the corner of the High Street a gust of wind caught her hat and , when she attempted to hold it on , blew her cloak completely behind her exposing her cruelly to the cold air . She was forced to take shelter in a shop doorway to sort herself out , much to the amusement of some teenage lads who were loitering in the bus shelter outside . They were dressed completely inadequately she noticed with incredulity in jeans and thin cotton tops , yet seemed unaware of the cold . She trekked on up the street . The fire screen was heavy and difficult to hold comfortably and she now regretted her decision to return the book today .

Entering the book shop at last , Queenie was completely taken aback to see a man standing behind the till . Although no longer young ,he was the most handsome man she had ever set eyes on .There was something so suave and distinguished about him he did not look right in this setting somehow . He looks like an actor she thought . A cross between Cary Grant and Rex Harrison . She stared stupidly and for a few seconds was quite dumbstruck .   The man looked at her inquiringly but she could only stare back .

" I thought I`d find Rose here . " she said at last .

" Ah no. Rose isn`t here on Wednesdays I`m afraid . " he had a rich fruity voice . An actor`s voice that put her in mind of Donald Sinden . " But can I be of service ? " he continued .

"E r no . Not really . That is , thank you but I just wanted to look around ." Queenie was thoroughly discomfitted .

" By all means do so ." He bowed from the waist. Now what was she going to do? She couldn`t possibly replace the book whilst he stood watching her . She would have to wait for a bit and hope that somebody would come and distract him . She wandered round the shelves pretending to look at the books whilst the man looked on . Gerald was amused . What an odd creature . Rather exotically dressed for these parts he thought . Rose knew all kinds of strange people of course . Look at how quickly she`d palled up with him .

" I see you`re interested in natural history . I`m afraid we don`t have a very comprehensive collection .This isn`t a specialist book shop as you probably know ." the fruity voice intoned. Queenie looked at him in bewilderment . Was he talking to her ? He must be as she was the only customer in the shop . For about three minutes she had been staring at the books withoutlooking at the titles . Now she realised that she was in a small section of natural history books. She picked one up at random , replaced it and then had a brilliant idea .

" Excuse me . I`m feeling rather strange . Could you possibly fetch me some water ?

Gerald was instantly solicitous .

" My dear , I`m so sorry . Let me fetch you a chair. I`ll bring some water for you immediately". In an instant a chair had been dragged across the room and Queenie was settled in it . Gerald went to the back room to fetch some water . At once ,Queenie was on her feet . She quickly removed the book from her shopper and within seconds had returned it to its original place on the shelves . She barely had time to resume her seat before Gerald appeared with the water . He seemed rather bemused in manner and had lost his previous air of suavity . She took a few sips from the glass then put it down .

" So.....And are you a good friend of Rose ? " he asked .

Queenie stiffened , sensing the beginning of an inquisition .

" Do you know I`m suddenly feeling so much better . For a while I felt quite giddy but it seems to have passed off . Thank you so much for the water ." She rose to her feet flashing him a dazzling smile " Goodbye ." And left the shop .

Gerald stared after her in astonishment . Then he went straight to the shelf where Queenie had been and pulled out the book he had seen her replacing there. " The Psychology of Criminal Behaviour." It didn`t make sense . He was well used to customers pinching books but had never come across anyone who donated them . Obviously the woman was as rum as she looked .He must remember to ask Rose about her . Turning , he noticed a scrap of paper lying on the floor near where his customer had been sitting . He picked it up and saw that it was actually a large , sticky label with some writing on it .He looked at the words wonderingly. Printed in felt tip pen in large capitals were the words " I can and I will ."

Chapter 25

Iris was in the sitting room writing letters at her desk when the plumbers arrived . They were early so she was pleased that she had taken the precaution of filling the kettle and several saucepans with water before the supply was disconnected . Workmen seemed to need so many cups of tea . She had also filled the bath with water in case the lavatory needed to be flushed although she hated the thought of Mr .Gotes or his assistant using her lavatory .

She kept out of the way whilst the work was going on and was annoyed when the door opened and a youth appeared . " We was just wonderin whether we could have a cuppa tea ?." he said , looking round the room with interest . Wayne Beale was always on the lookout for a likely place to turn over He found Iris` home disappointing in that there was no video or obviously expensive electrical item and nothing that was covetable from his point of view.

" I`ve already explained to Mr.Gotes that you were to help yourselves . Surely you must remember when I showed him where everything was ? " Iris was convinced that the lad was just being nosey but would have been horror struck had she known the real reason for his appraisal . "Cheers then ." He replied oddly and went away . She could hear the blaring noise from their radio even through the closed door . How could they tolerate such a racket ?

In the middle of the afternoon Iris had to leave the house to take Nellie out She`d hoped the men would have finished by now because she did not like leaving them alone in the house –not that she did not trust them exactly – it was just the idea of strangers being on her territory she supposed. When they`d stopped for lunch Iris was annoyed to see that the youth had stripped down to his bare chest and sat himself down in her front doorway reading " The Sun ". It wasn`t even that warm a day .He was unpleasantly hairy but worse than that , there was a tattoo on his diaphragm which disappeared down the front of his trousers . She`d wanted to say something to him but held her tongue because she did not know what his reaction might be . She worried though that one of her elderly neighbours might take exception to it . Old ladies did not like that kind of thing . Sure enough , as she passed Miss Gerram`s window she saw the old lady beckoning to her . As she feared it was to complain about the bare chested youth and Iris could only apologise and tell her it would not happen again .

She walked the dog to the newsagent to pick up an evening paper and then took the path to the common .Nellie was too old to run around but she enjoyed a walk and a good sniff about . Iris always enjoyed the walk too if the weather was reasonable and today it was pleasant . Returning home about half an hour later , she noticed to her annoyance that the old tank had been dumped carelessly in the back garden flattening part of her herb section. Near the back gate a clump of daffodils had been trampled on too . Really it was too bad she thought .

Indoors there was no sign of Mr.Gotes` assistant . When Iris made her complaint to the plumber he was apologetic ,

" I`m very sorry madam , I did tell him to be careful where he put that old tank but you know what these young people are like . I let him go early since we`d finished the heavy stuff . The job`s finished now so I`ll make good whatever damage has been done before I go home . "

Although Iris had not shown the plumbers where she kept the cleaning materials they had found the dustpan and brush and vacuum cleaner and made a very good job of cleaning up . She would have been happy to do this herself disliking the idea of the men ferreting around in her cupboards but could not really complain . After all , she had left them alone in the house and not many work men would have bothered to clean up without being asked .

" Thank you very much for cleaning up Mr Gotes .I didn`t expect you to you know ."

" I wouldn`t dream of doing anything less . I`m noted for my clean work . Word soon spreads around if you do a good job you know . That`s why I was recommended to you ."   Cyril replied self righteously .

" Well , thank you anyway . Now I should ask you about payment . Do you send me an account ? " Iris wished that he would not stare at her in that unpleasant way . It made her feel most uncomfortable .

" Well actually Madam I glad you brought that up because I really prefer cash in hand . It makes it easier all round that way ." Now he was deliberately looking away she noticed .

" But I never keep large sums of money in the house ." She objected " I can give you a cheque immediately ."

" Oh there`s no need to pay me now ," He interrupted " Tomorrow will do fine . I can call round tomorrow on my way home . Say about 5 ? That will give you time to get the cash ."

" Very well " said Iris " I`ll have the money ready for you then ." She was immediately cross with herself . There was obviously some sort of fiddle going on . Income tax probably . Why did she allow herself to become party to it ? But if she refused to pay cash he might refuse to work for her again and you never know when you might need a plumber .

"Oh , by the way , " Mr Gotes said " I found these in your airing cupboard after the shelves were dismantled . They must have fallen down the back ." He pulled from his pocket a pair of white cotton knickers and handed them to her , staring her right in the eyes as he did so . He seemed quite unfazed by her blush and obvious embarrassment .

" So I`ll be round tomorrow afternoon then . " He said , moving towards the door . He turned round before leaving and added , smirking horribly

" My name`s Cyril by the way ."

Iris said nothing . She was shocked and mortified . What a perfectly horrible man she thought . Cheap and efficient he might be but she now heartily regretted ever using his services . She threw the underwear in the broom cupboard for use as a duster . She hated the thought of such intimate apparel being handled by such a person . It was just another of the hazards of being a lone woman she thought . If she`d had a husband he would never have dared to initiate such familiarity.

Later she spoke on the telephone to Rose to discuss arrangements for the following evening They were going to the theatre with a number of others . She went on to tell her about Mr. Gotes and how he had requested payment in cash but didn`t mention his offensive manner regarding her underwear .

"Oh , he tried exactly the same thing with me but I sent him packing" " Rose said ." I told him he could please himself - it was a cheque or nothing . And I insisted on an itemised receipt too . He would soon have climbed down if you had insisted ."

This left Iris feeling very despondent . Why hadn`t she insisted ? She knew too , that the plumber would never have dared to be familiar with Rose because she would never countenance it . It must be something about me , she thought . Why do people think they can get away with it with me ? The trouble was that whenever she tried to be assertive she could never carry it off .People like Mr.Gotes seemed to sense it and took advantage Unreasonably Iris felt annoyed with Rose but when she tried to analyse why could only come up with the fact that Rose made her feel inadequate .

Chapter 26

After Iris` telephone call Rose returned to the kitchen where she was blanching vegetables for the freezer .A large cardboard box had been lying on the back step when she arrived home.It was full of broccoli , parsnips and leeks Eric had probably deposited it there earlier . She would call and see him tomorrow . Luckily there was space in the freezer because she was so busy at the moment there was no way she could use the vegetables up otherwise . I could have offered Iris some just then , she thought and decided to put some aside to take to her tomorrow night .

Why did she always feel so irritated after talking to Iris ? She was a dear really , but such a worrier . Almost a caricature of the proverbial spinster . Completely different from Queenie who didn`t seem to worry about anything . Rose could not help feeling concerned about what had taken place in the shop yesterday . She had seen quite clearly Queenie removing a book from the shelves and concealing it in her shopper . There was a ceiling mirror in the shop for the very purpose of detecting shoplifting . Few people expected to find such a device in a shop such as theirs which made it all the more effective .

Rose was not at all naïve about shoplifting . The most unlikely people were often the worst offenders she knew. Gerald had once had to ban a certain vicar from the shop for that very reason .When Queenie had gone to use the loo Rose had quickly taken the opportunity to retrieve the book from her bag to see just what sort of literature it was that had made Queenie resort to shoplifting . The title had made her almost choke with laughter .Hurriedly she`d thrust it back. She`d been barely able to compose herself when her friend returned and had to keep turning away . She was surprised by Queenie`s behaviour nonetheless . It just did not seem to be in character somehow .

A face appeared at the kitchen window. It was Gerald , pantomiming a pouring and drinking gesture . Rose signalled that the door was unlocked and he entered .

"And why are you in need of a drink ?" she enquired " Was it such a hard day in the shop ? "

" I can see you`re busy Rose but please remove your pinny and come with me . We want you to join us for a drink and then come to "Alfredo`s . We`ve booked a table for eight o clock ."

" I`ve just finished blanching all the vegetables you so kindly left me . At least , I presume it was Eric or you ?"

" Yes . But please finish now and do as I say . I don`t want any nonsense about not being ready to go out . You look perfectly fine to   me   ."

" But what`s it all about . Are you celebrating something ?"

" In a manner of speaking . Helen has come to stay and you know her presence takes some dilution . You are the ideal dilutant if there is such a word and you don`t mind being described as such ."

Gerald looked particularly suave this evening , formally attired in a smart , dark suit .Helen was Eric`s younger sister . Rose had met her before and knew exactly what Gerald meant.

Helen was overbearing , opinionated and self important . Recently retired from a senior nursing post in London , she had begun to pay regular visits to her brother and had even spoken of moving to the area . " We`re hoping she `s only staying for a day or two ." Gerald said " That`s where you come in . Bath is her next port of call . You must persuade her how very pleasant it is   there compared to this area Trouble is , she seems to have convinced herself that Eric needslooking after and that she is the one to do it" ."

Rose ran upstairs and quickly ran a comb through her hair and then powdered her nose. How fortunate that she was already wearing her good woollen dress .What a good thing this wasn`t her Townwoman`s Guild evening She loved impromtu outings like this. It was no novelty to her to be called into service when Eric`s sister visited which seemed to happen every three or four months . The two men were only too glad to have another lady around at these times .

" Just let me make sure everything is secure ." she said to Gerald and minutes later they left the house .

Helen Lawrence , Eric`s sister , was a large lady . She was tall and built on a grand scale with a large bosom and enormous hips . She had "big hair " too , set in a dated 1960s style which required much lacquering and back combing to keep it in shape . Rose thought how odd it was that her brother Eric should be so slightly built - almost feminine – whilst Helen towered over him . It was almost as if God had mismatched their physiques by mistake .

Although their bungalow was kept in immaculate order , Helen liked to preserve the idea that her brother and his companion were totally inept at housekeeping and required her womanly skills to keep things in order . Several years younger than her brother , she also persisted in referring to the two men as " the boys ". They had lived together for more than 30 years and one might have assumed that her years in nursing would have dispelled any naivety as to sexual matters , but despite this Helen also seemed to affect the idea that the men were simply chums , a pair of bachelors waiting for the right woman to come along .

At first Rose had thought that this was some kind of sophisticated joke .Then she had conceded that perhaps it was wishful thinking on Helen's part .That perhaps she was a person who could not bear the thought of homosexual behaviour Later though , she had come to realise that Helen had always hankered after handsome Gerald and could not allow herself to believe that he was forever out of her reach . Gerald himself had told her stories about Helen's behaviour over the years . Her habit , for instance , of asking him to escort her to the annual hospital dinner dance and invariably taking great umbrage when he made his excuses which he did every year .

From the first time Rose had met her Helen had seen her as a rival for Gerald's affections,   This caused great amusement to Rose who would make a game of paying him great attention . He played up for all he was worth too , adding to the fun . He would make remarks about preferring older women , compliment Rose on her hair or dress and generally do what he could to annoy Helen . Sometimes he went too far , Rose thought .

This evening , as it was an occasion , Helen was dressed to the nines and her hair had been coiffed extensively . Wafts of Arpege met them as they entered the sitting room . Gerald grabbed Rose` hand as they walked in but she pulled it away . Helen greeted her coolly but Eric more than made up for that with a big , bear hug . Rose was struck by how frail and thin he seemed although his spirits seemed high enough . He handed Rose a huge gin and tonic

Helen smiled lovingly at Gerald

" You do look smart Gerald .I love that tie . So few men make an effort to smarten themselves up for an evening out these days . And as for the women …..trousers , even tee shirts .. ..you wouldn`t believe some of the outfits you see girls wearing in London . One even turned up at my leaving party wearing climbing  boots , at least that`s what they looked like . When I was a girl we took so much trouble with our appearance Do you remember Eric ? I used to spend the whole of Saturday afternoon getting ready for a dance at the tennis club . You must have been the same Rose ? "

" I suppose I was ." Rose agreed " But in a way it was a bit of a waste of time , looking back . I rather envy young women these days . It`s so much easier for them and …

" Oh I don`t agree at all . " Helen interrupted  rudely . " They just don`t want to make the effort that`s all . It`s like everything else these days . Standards are slipping everywhere ." she appealed to

Gerald " As a man of the world Gerald , don't you agree that a woman is not a real woman unless she presents herself as feminine ."

" Does presenting yourself as feminine mean sporting a beehive hairdo and stiletto heels ? Rose countered " Surely there are other ways of showing your femininity ." She was damned if she was going to allow Helen her own way over this .

"You certainly present yourself as feminine Helen . Nobody could argue about that ." Gerald said desperately , " But talking about oddly dressed women a really strange bird came into the shop today . She was asking for you Rose . Said her name was Queenie ."

" Oh , she's a dear " said Rose " And she doesn't always dress oddly She can look very smart . She's just got rather an eccentric streak Did you talk to her at all ? She has an amazing collection of books at home ."

" No , she was suddenly taken ill .Then she seemed to recover and couldn't leave quickly enough. That was after she'd donated the book though ." They all looked at him in surprise

" Yes , it really was rum . She asked for a drink of water because she felt faint and when I went to get it she took a book out of her bag and placed it on the shelf . I saw her in the ceiling mirror ."

" Did you notice what it was called ? " Rose enquired. " It wasn't "The Psychology of Criminal Behaviour " by any chance ? "

"Yes , it was . What's this all about Rose?

" I wish I knew . .She came in onTuesday and I saw her take the book . I actually thought she'd stolen it . Now it seems it was only borrowed I'm relieved about that at least ."

Helen appeared to be scandalised

" Do you hear this Eric ? Rose actually watches somebody shoplifting – a friend of hers apparently - and does nothing about it ."

Eric said quietly " These things aren't as simple as they seem Helen as you would know if you'd ever worked in a shop . I rely on Rose's judgement "
Rose flashed him a grateful smile .

" I'm rather glad I didn't do anything about it now since it seems she was only borrowing the book , although it would have been better if she'd asked first . I did say she had rather an eccentric streak ."

Gerald was laughing now to Helen's horror .

" That's not all Rose . When she'd gone , I found this on the floor " He produced the sticky label and unfolded it so that they all could read the message . Everyone laughed now except Helen .

118

" I don`t think its funny . " she said " To me it`s disgraceful .
I can`t condone stealing and neither should you Eric and I`m surprised
at you Gerald . At one time you`d never have countenanced it ." The
implication was plain but once again Eric stuck by Rose .

" There`s probably a completely innocent explanation as I
am sure Rose will discover in due course . In any event no harm has
been done . Now we really must be on our way . You know how
temperamental Alfredo can be if we arrive late ." Eric downed his
drink and within a few minutes the quartet left the house .

Alfredo greeted them effusively with much hand kissing and
back slapping . The two men were regular customers and tipped well
and Alfredo treated them accordingly . Rose loved Italian food and
was set to enjoy this unexpected treat . The trouble was that everything
was so delicious it was difficult to choose . Helen , of course , had to
make a nuisance of herself . First by specifying no garlic with her
starter of baby squid and pastina , and then by telling everybody
within earshot of her allergy to red wine . She had an unfortunately
loud , carrying voice which tended to draw the attention of others and
made Rose shrink . Gerald raised his eyebrows to Rose as Helen
spoke and looked pointedly at her but Eric simply said

" No problem dearie . We`re having one of each ."

Towards the end of the meal , after the ladies had finished
their tiramisu and zabaglione and just after Gerald had ordered coffee ,
the atmosphere which had been convivial suddenly took a downward
turn .The conversation had been about Europe and the Common
Market and from there had veered to patriotism . Helen remarked that
nobody celebrated being British any longer and asked why there
wasn`t a national holiday to celebrate Britain .

" There always used to be . You must remember Empire Day
? " said Rose who had very clear memories of marching around the
school playground clutching the union flag . They used to give
schoolchildren a half holiday she remembered . " Everyone used to
celebrate it . Most people hung flags from their houses and there used
to be lots of organised events . Of course , just after the w\ar people
were very patriotic ."   Helen stared coldly at her .

" You may remember it Rose but I can`t say that I do You
are considerably older than me you know"

" All of eighteen months " Gerald whispered to Rose .
Unfortunately Helen heard him clearly .She folded in her lips , cast
down her eyes and took no further part in the conversation . Eric too ,
was very quiet now . He looked very frail and tired Rose thought .

119

" We shall have to go home soon so I might as well tell you our news now " Gerald announced ." Especially as it concerns you Rose . We can't go ahead without your cooperation." Rose stared at him in surprise and Helen cast her a poisonous look .

"The thing is " Gerald said . " Arnold Finney has invited us to spend a few weeks in Mykonos .It would be so good for Eric but it means asking you to take care of the shop whilst we're away . Would you Rose ?" Gerald had the grace to look embarrassed Rose noticed .

" How long will you be away ? " She asked , her heart sinking . She really did not want this responsibility . Much as she hated to let down her friends she did not feel able to take on such commitment At such short notice too . It really was rather naughty of Gerald to take her for granted in this way . Obviously this evening out was a ploy to soften her up.

"Oh no more than six weeks at the most ." Gerald said hastily . " Naturally we wouldn't expect you to open up every day as long as you kept open on Saturdays and market day . And we do realise you'd need help . Feel free to take on somebody to help you ."

" Oh well . I think I could just about cope with that ." Rose spoke resignedly now " As long as it is only six weeks ." How could she refuse ? She knew she had been set up by Gerald but how could she let them down when Eric looked so white and drawn . But there was no doubting his pleasure at her agreement to the proposal He beamed delightedly and said

" I knew we could count on you Rose ."

" Bravo Rose ! " Gerald jumped to his feet , grabbed Rose and hugged her exuberantly much to the enjoyment of the waiters and Alfredo who applauded loudly . Helen rose from the table .

" Do excuse me " she said coldly , making for the ladies room . Alfredo waylaid her after she had proceeded only a few feet .

" Is a wedding soon I think ? " He asked laughingly . She did not deign to reply but behind her the three others laughed hysterically .

Chapter 27

Iris sat at the kitchen table making a list of gardening jobs . She found it best to do this otherwise it was so easy to get sidetracked and end up doing something that was not really necessary . Before you knew where you were the time had gone or it had started to rain .She had new plants to dig in and fertilizer to apply before she began to prune back the winter jasmine and roses and started in on the weeding . Apart from snatched half hours here and there this would be her first proper day of gardening this year and it was so pleasant outdoors

Today she had a happy feeling of anticipation of the day ahead. There was another treat this evening too . The theatre club she belonged to were having a trip to the theatre in Southampton and there would be supper afterwards . It would be the perfect opportunity to wear her new suit.As soon as she finished breakfast she would go straight tothe garden centre to pick up her supplies . She could afford to spend an hour there browsing around . Then she would go to the bank to collect the cash for Mr. Gotes .

The kettle boiled and Iris made a pot of tea .Now for her next treat. Yesterday Ada Simey had given her a loaf of her special , home made bread This was a gift she bestowed infrequently because baking was a real effort for her these days . The late Mr. Simey had been a baker and had obtained this particular recipe from a German POW . The bread was dark , densely textured and delicious with a faint hint of caraway seed . Iris really did appreciate it . She decided to have one slice with unsalted butter and another with honey .

On the radio two MPs were arguing about the crime rate . “ The people know that we are the party of law and order.” said the Tory MP . “ Yet millions of women and old people are frightened to walk the streets at night .“ countered the labour MP .

“ I`m afraid that`s all we have time for .” John Humphries interrupted . Iris was still mourning Brian Redhead ; It had been almost like a personal bereavement when he died . Stupid to have these silly attachments she realised , but when you lived alone familiar voices on the radio orTV became part of your life .She felt Nellie`s wet nose pressing into her calf . This was the first signal that she wanted to go out . “ All right Nellie . We`ll go out soon .” Iris promised and appeased , the dog padded back to her bed .

Later in the garden centre , she wandered around happily trying to decide what to buy herself as a treat . She had promised herself one indulgence to go with all the workaday items sherequired . It would be wonderful if money were no object and you could just buy whatever you fancied she thought , looking covetously at some of the very expensive shrubs . Then , in a corner under a sign saying Reduced to Clear , she saw a pile of cracked and broken terracotta pots containing patio roses in several varieties

" Only need a bit of T L C . " said a voice at her side . "They`re a bargain .I`ve just bought three ." The speaker trundled his finds away in a trolley. He was right , thought Iris , taking a closer look . She chose three as well and felt very pleased with herself .

She drove back to the town centre where she was fortunate to find a parking space quite close to the bank . Her business there transacted , it occurred to her that she could save time by having a bite to eat now . Then she could forego lunch completely . There was a place only a few yards away she noticed .The coffee shop was self service but there was not too long a queue . Waiting in line Iris saw Thelma Honeyspan , deep in conversation with a middle aged man . Well , well , she thought.But then Thelma saw her and appeared to wave her over . Iris` heart sank . She had no wish to intrude on their tete a tete and was rather surprised that Thelma should want her to . In any event she would much have preferred to have her snack quickly and leave .Time was too precious today . Still , nothing else for it , she picked up her tray and walked across to their table .

"Oh hello Iris . This is Mr. Buttle but if you don`t mind I wont ask you to join us We are having a rather private conversation ." Thelma said smugly , seeming to be unaware how baldly rude her words were although her companion had the grace to look embarrassed .

" Do excuse me then ! " Iris moved away , her face pink with annoyance . Really ! that woman ! Did she have no idea how bad mannered she was ? Still she hadn`t wanted to join them anyway so there was no point in allowing this to upset her . All the same .....her danish pastry tasted like lead and she did not enjoy the coffee .

On the way home , as she drove through the lanes so pretty with spring blossom , Iris took a deep breath and determined to forget all about the incident . Poor Thelma should be pitied for her social ineptness she decided . She probably didn`t know any better . Why should such a stupid incident ruin such a lovely day ? She had her gardening to get on with and then a pleasant evening afterwards .

During the afternoon the weather became really summery . At about half past three Iris decided to finish work and go indoors . No point in exhausting herself . She had achieved all of her objectives in the garden and even completed some jobs she hadn`t thought of earlier . Now she felt pleasantly satisfied . She would run a hot bath and have a really good soak she decided .Sipping a cup of tea whilst the bath was running , she marvelled at the heat of the afternoon .It was more like midsummer than early April . She opened the french windows of her bedroom to let the sun in , then went to her wardrobe . The new suit she had planned to wear might be too warm after all . On the other hand the evening might turn chilly . She decided to stick to her original plan and went to fetch fresh underwear and a new pair of tights which she laid on the bed . Then , stripping of her gardening trousers and jersey , she undressed completely and climbed into the deliciously scented hot water .

After her parents` death , Iris used some of the money they`d left her in making improvements to the bungalow where they`d always lived . Not that it was in need of repairs but there were certain modern conveniences to which her parents had never aspired . Accordingly , she had treated herself to as new , streamlined kitchen and , something she had long coveted , a bathroom en suite. It had not been difficult for the builders to convert the small box room for this purpose and she had been delighted with the result . What she particularly liked was being able to lie in the bath and with the door open , listen to her bedside radio as she soaked .

Today`s Kaleidoscope was particularly interesting because the book of a local author was being reviewed , somebody she actually knew by sight . Strange to think that they were discussing somebody she had seen only yesterday buying cheese in Sainsbury`s . She lay back in the hot water with her eyes closed feeling the heat soaking into her aching legs and enjoying the pleasant scent of the bath oil . When the water began to cool she reluctantly climbed out and began to towel herself dry . Reaching for her towelling bathrobe she realised to her annoyance that she`d left it at the foot of the bed Naked , she walked into the bedroom.Something fluttered past her eyes – it was a butterfly . The first butterfly of the year. Smiling to herself she turned slightly and looked straight into the staring eyes of Cyril Gotes who stood in the open window .

For a split second she stood motionless , then terror , shock and horror sent her scurrying back to the bathroom where she grabbed the damp towel she`d discarded earlier and attempted to cover herself . She was aware of a hot trickle of urine down the inside of her thigh . At the same time she tried to shout " Get out of my house " but the sound that came out was a hoarse grunt unlike any sound she`d ever made before .

Cyril had walked into the bedroom now and it was this outrage which gave her back her voice .

" Go , get out of here before I call the police ." this time she screamed it and the sound terrified her .

" You don`t want to shout like that Iris " Cyril said " You`re frightening the dog . Look at her ."

It was true. Nellie was cowering in a corner trembling with fright . She hated loud noises .Iris became aware that she was shaking too and her heart was pounding as though she`d taken part in a race .

" For the last time , get out of my house " she shouted .

" You don`t mean that Iris " Cyril said advancing towards her . The use of her christian name was further outrage . How did he know it anyway ? He spoke in a strange , crooning voice .

" You don`t mean it because you want me . We both know what you want . You were lying there waiting for me weren`t you ? I knew you were when I came round the back and found the windows open . I thought first you were in the garden but you were here waiting for me."

The idea was so outrageous to her , made her feel so defiled that she almost lost her balance with shock .He gloated over her now . So close she could see white flaky patches of eczema or some other skin disorder round his receding hair line . His face was red and large pored and a strange but familiar , medicinal like odour emanated from him , a liniment type smell which Iris suddenly recognised . It was a brand of medicinal lozenges you used to get years ago . Bizarrely too , she realised that she recognised the motif on the tie he was wearing . It was a regimental tie -REME – her brother had once worn it Later she would marvel at how she had been able to notice these things .

Like a transfixed rabbit she stood frozen as he placed one hand on her breast whilst the other parted the towel and attempted to fondle her sex . He then muttered something so crudely obscene that she shuddered with shock and disgust . It was this that drove her to raise her knee and drive it savagely into his groin .

" Christ Almighty   ! " Cyril turned white and staggered backwards.

" Now will you go ? Because if you don`t…. I …I`ll kill you ." Iris screamed

" All right you frigid cow..I`m  going . Might as well shag a frozen carcase as you . You should be glad anyone even wanted to try it . Be like cracking open a safe I bet." Cyril`s mouth was set in a snarl . He turned towards the windows then turned back . "And what about my money ? You said you`d have it ready ."

Iris was too traumatised to be astounded at his audacity . She pointed to an envelope on the dressing table which he pocketed . Then he made his exit .

After a couple of minutes she went to the windows and locked them She then closed the curtains. Turning back she caught sight of herself in the mirror .Her face was mottled red and white. She looked old and shrivelled . Exactly as she felt inside she thought . Sick and profoundly depressed she went over the event again in her mind . Why had she opened the windows sheasked herself ? Was it a subconscious desire to invite what had happened? She could not believe it of herself , but how would it seem to others ? She felt defiled .

She sat on the bed partly crushing her new outfit but past caring about it . She would never wear it now anyway . Shivers ran through her body and seconds later she ran to the bathroom and retched . Everything was ruined she thought returning to her bed . The day which had begun withsuch promises of pleasure had turned into an evil charade . Crying hopelessly now she flung herself on the bed and sobbed out her despair . She knew then that she was not just weeping for today`s horrible event but for the futility of everything in her life . It was all a fraud .Even things that seemed good and pleasant were coated in an invisible cover of slime . What was the point of anything ? The dog , bewildered and upset by this strange behaviour tried to offer Iris the comfortof her body but Iris pushed her away .

In her misery she lost track of time but some while later became aware of the insistent ringing of the door bell . She knew she had to answer it . It was bound to be Rose come to collect her for their outing . She would assume something was wrong if there was no answer. She might even raise the alarm and have the door forced . She would have to tell her she was ill which was true enough anyway . Her appearance would confirm it . Iris dragged herself to the door .Two men stood there smiling benignly . Over their outdoor clothing they wore lurid yellow plastic waist coats emblazened "Christian Crusade " in large red letters . One of them carried a collecting tin . Iris recognised him as having been employed at the Mr. Minit shoe repairers in the High Street .The other man seemed familiar too although she could not place him . Then it came to her . It was the man she`d seen this morning having coffee with Thelma . He carried a pile of pamphlets .The younger man smiled broadly at her revealing badly decayed teeth . He had a pugilist`s face with a nose that had been badly broken at some time and a crew cut which gave him an even tougher image somehow . He looked a most unlikely person to be touting religion

.."Today is a happy day for you Sister " he said " We have good news about Jesus ."

"Alleluia ! " said the other " Our news can make this the happiest day of your life ." He handed Iris a leaflet . " What happens today is just a sample of the joy to come . Please give generously in the name of Christ ."

Unable to contain herself Iris burst into peal after peal of hysterical laughter but after only a few seconds this turned into uncontrollable weeping The two men hung back disconcerted, unsure of how to cope with the situation .The three stood there and seconds later it was this bizarre tableau that greeted Rose as she drew up outside the house .

Indoors at last , much time elapsed before Rose was able to discover what had taken place . She`d assumed initially that Iris had suffered some dreadful personal tragedy , the death of somebody close perhaps . After searching around she came across some brandy and persuaded Iris to drink a small measure . Even when the tears had stopped at last , Iris still remained mute until Rose became almost cross and insisted on knowing what was wrong . At first Iris said she was ill but this was so obviously not the cause of her distress Rose continued to question her . It was only when she attempted to telephone the doctor that , haltingly , Iris divulged what had taken place .

Rose was appalled . Her first reaction was that they should inform the police immediately but Iris absolutely vetoed this .

" Can you imagine what would happen then ? He`d only deny it . It would be my word against his and everybody would say I was a sex starved spinster . I`d have to go to court . It would be in the local paper . Can`t you just see the headlines in the "Echo " ? " Local man accused " or " Spinster claims sex assault by local plumber ."Can you imagine the gossip and sniggering ? I couldn`t bear it ." She began to cry again. Rose saw her point entirely . Even so she felt something should be done .

" But Iris, he can`t be allowed to get away with this " she insisted . " It`s made me feel .murderous !We `ve got to do something about it . You do realise he`s probably done this sort of thing before ?"

" I don`t care ." said Iris wearily  " I don`t care about anything any longer ." Again she began to cry . Rose was full of pity for her . She spoke gently

" Iris . I don`t think you should stay here alone tonight . Come home with me . We wont talk about this any more if you`d rather not but I know you wont sleep if you stay here I`m too worried to leave you ."

Iris objected feebly , mentioning the dog and trying to find other excuses not to go but Rose would hear none of it . Within minutes she`d helped Iris to dress and put together some overnight things as well as Nellie`s requirements and , after securing the house they all went on their way. Rose always kept her spare room ready for an occupant so it was the work of minutes to settle Iris in bed .

" I`m going to make you a milky drink and I think you should have a  sleeping pill " she told Iris . "And please don`t worry about Nellie . I`ll take her out in a minute and again in the morning ."

But although Iris swallowed the pill obediently and drank the hot , milky liquid she was unable to sleep . She kept on reliving the events of the afternoon and felt that the face of Cyril Gotes would be etched on her memory for ever . Rose had told her to think positively about what had happened . After all , she`d said ,  Iris had triumphed in the end .  She`d successfully defended herself and her attacker had not achieved his objective. She had done exactly the right thing in fighting back and should feel proud of her behaviour . But this gave Iris no satisfaction whatsoever . She knew she would never feel the same about her home again . She would never enjoy a bath again and how could she allow a man , any man , to set foot in her house ? It was not simply an attempted rape . Cyril Gotes had robbed her of her peace of mind , her trust in people and the security of her own home . She began to feel very angry and her anger was made worse by the knowledge that she could do absolutely nothing about it .

Chapter 28

Early next morning Rose telephoned Queenie and asked her to come to her house ."Iris is staying here for a few days . She's rather upset I'm afraid . The thing is I have to go out this morning and I don't think she should be left by herself" ."

" But what's happened ? " Queenie was agog .

" I can't tell you myself . Iris may tell you but I think she does not really want to talk about it yet so please don't press her ." Rose hated to be so mysterious but felt that she could not discuss the matter without Iris' permission . Queenie agreed to come immediately . Whatever could have happened she asked herself as she replaced the phone ? And why would Iris not want to talk about it ? Even more puzzling , why on earth was Iris staying with Rose ? The whole thing was most odd .

Queenie had planned to go to a jumble sale this morning , something she hated to miss in the normal course of events but this situation took precedence. Rose had offered to come and fetch her but Queenie told her she would much prefer to walk . It was such a pleasant morning and she could take the track that ran along the side of the golf course . It was only 10 minutes walk if you went that way . She went to change into her walking shoes and then the telephone rang . Again it was Rose .

" I'm so glad I caught you before you left the house . I'm coming over to you right away and bringing the dog .You can walk her back to my house if you don't mind . The poor creature is desperate to go out and I can't spare the time to take her ."

Queenie was delighted to do this .It was much more fun walking with a dog

" How is Iris?" she asked .

" Dead to the world I'm glad to say . I made her take a sleeping pill last night . The rest will do her good ." Rose replied .

Queenie was pleased about having the dog to walk . People looked at you so oddly when you went walking alone she had found . At least having a dog along provided some purpose and it made people want to talk to you especially with such an appealing dog as Nellie . But she must ensure the cats were out of the way before Rose arrived with the animal . Solly hated all dogs , even amiable old labradors like Nellie .

Rose meanwhile was looking at her street plan of the neighbourhood . She had decided to confront Cyril Gotes . She had made this decision last night in bed whilst listening to Iris` sobs from the next room . Cyril had chosen his victim well she thought . Iris was a particularly vulnerable target which made his actions all the more reprehensible . He would never have dared to try it on with someone like herself . First thing this morning she had looked up his address in the yellow pages but had been unsure of the exact location of Berringer Row . Now she saw that it was easy to find . Just north of the station , opposite the old brick works site .

Rose was thankful that Iris was still asleep otherwise she might have felt the need to tell her what she planned to do. She knew Iris would be against the idea .This way it would be a fait accompli . She coaxed the dog into the back of the car and set off . Queenie was waiting for her at her gate and after a few words with her it was simply a matter of setting down Nellie and then she was off again .

Within ten minutes she reached Berringer Row . Then she remembered that this must be the street where Hayley lived . Since she had had the termination Rose had seldom set eyes on the girl but as she now performed her duties in a satisfactorily manner , this was an agreeable arrangement to them both ..As she looked around her though she could well understand why Evied had felt doubtful about the relationship.This seemed to be the neighbourhood from hell.

She drove very slowly down the street as there were lots of small children about . Annoyingly , some of the houses had no visible numbers . But then she saw number fifteen and pulled up outside , noticing that the gate stood ajar . The net curtains in number 16 twitched and , in no 14 the other half of the semi detached house , a blonde woman came to her front door and made no attempt to conceal her interest . As Rose walked up the path the woman called to her .

" You`ll be from the social . Just go upstairs . Sandy`s in bed .
"

The house was joined to its neighbour at the first floor but separated from it at ground level by a tunnel which led to the respective back doors . It was obvious that these back entrances were seldom used because of the old bikes , motor cycle parts and what looked like part of an old fridge which blocked the entry . Rose stood at the front door for a few minutes after ringing the bell . In spite of the advice given by the neighbour she was reluctant to simply walk in without announcing herself . On the other hand , the business she had to conduct could not take place on the doorstep .

As she hesitated her dilemma was solved by a faint voice requesting her to come upstairs so she pushed open the door and went in .The smell hit her as soon as she was inside the house .It was the sweetish , nauseating odour of longterm filth , yet the hallway and stairs did not look obviously dirty . Nevertheless Rose was gaggingas she reached the top and the full force of the odour enveloped her . A small dog ran from the room at the top of the stairs and began to yap . There was a dim light burning in the room and the sound of a radio or television . Through the open door Rose could see a figure in bed . She moved nearer . At that moment the woman looked up and gazed imploringly at her .

" Thank God you`ve come " she said . " Oh  doctor . I feel so bad . I think I`m dying ."

" I`m not a doctor ." Rose answered entering the room and looking round her in wonderment . It was difficult to make things out in the gloom . The woman certainly did look ill she thought though it was not surprising given the foetid atmosphere and prevailing squalor . But she was certainly a frightening colour , almost bright yellow .

" Rita said she`d send for the social . " Sandy said " I`m glad you`ve come but it`s really a doctor I need . This just about finished me ." She picked up a piece of paper from the bed and offered it to Rose . " I don`t care what happens to me now ." She switched on a light over the bed and the full impact of the room hit Rose . She took a step back involuntarily and felt something squelch under her foot . She saw now the vastness of Sandy , the cats crouched around her and the piles of rotting food and assorted rubbish lying around the floor . The dog ran past Rose and leapt onto the bed next to his mistress . " Read This " demanded Sandy , thrusting the piece of paper at Rose . .She took it from her . It was a letter written in felt tip pen .

Dear Auntie Hilda ,

You say I should come home and look after my mum but I will never go there again . Mum knows what Dad did to me and did nothing about it . I have been having counselling for months . They say I should report him to the police but I could not put us all through it . I wont go home again so please don`t ask me to . Love Karen .

" I don`t understand ." Rose said at last . She was aware now that she was in the midst of something ugly and repellant , something entirely outside her experience " Are you Hilda ? "

The fat woman , crying quietly said ,

" I`m Sandy . That letter`s from my daughter Karen. Hilda`s my sister . Cyril`s my husband . Hilda brought this note round an hour ago . She said she wont come here no more . She said awful things to me ." She wailed pitifully " Oh I feel so bad .Help me please ."

" Has somebody sent for the doctor ? " Rose asked .

" He wouldn`t come . I`ve rung him over and over . Says I`ve got to come to the surgery . Says Cyril should bring me ."

" Let me try . Give me the phone ?" Rose could not conceal her disgust when Sandy handed her the sticky instrument but she had no choice but to use it . For the next ten minutes she was fully occupied . After speaking to the surgery and explaining to a sceptical receptionist that she believed Sandy to be seriously ill, a home visit was promised . Rose wandered whether she ought to do anything to prepare for the doctor`s visit . Perhaps help Sandy to wash ? Then , looking around decided against it . Where would she start ? It was simply beyond her .

She decided to consult the neighbour who would surely know what time Mr. Gotes was expected home . Try as she might , Rose could not fit the dapper little man who`d repaired her leaking plunbing into this squalid environment . She found Rita very forthcoming . In spite of being informed otherwise , she persisted in her idea that Rose was some kind of welfare official . Rita gave her a potted history of the Gotes family as she knew them describing Cyril as a " nutter ", and giving her own version of their peculiar menage . Rose listened incredulously . " Between you and me " she told Rose confidentially , " It`s him that`s made her like she is . "

" It was really Mr. Gotes I came here to see ." Rose said . " Where is he this morning ? "

"Out on a job I s`pose . He`ll be back soon though cos he goes down the football . He goes every week.."

At this point the doctor arrived . He was a brusque , world weary man in late middle age . He nodded curtly to Rita and said to Rose

" Was it you who sent for me ?". She concurred and he entered the house .

" My God ! " Rose heard as he got the first whiff of the odour there . She stood at the foot of the stairs and heard him questioning Sandy briskly and her piteous replies and then heard him calling for an ambulance . He came down then and seemed to assume that Rose was some figure of authority .

" You`ll be going with Mrs. Gotes to the hospital I imagine ? You were quite right to call me . She is seriously ill . The ambulance should be here before long ." He sat on the bottom stair writing a note which he placed in an envelope and handed to Rose .

" Take this with you . It might be an idea to have the council fumigation people round here don't you think ? Where is the bold Mr. Gotes by the way ? I've yet to meet him . I should have thought he'd have called me long before things reached this state."

" I don't know where he is ? " Rose answered "Actually it's him I came here to see . I ..." But the doctor was already on his way . Before he reached the gate Rita called to him ,

" Doctor , doctor what's wrong with Sandy ? Is she going to the clinic ?"

" No ." he answered brusquely not even bothering to look round .

" Where are you sending her then ? Is she going to Harley Hall ?"

This was the local psychiatric hospital . The doctor turned on his heel then and faced Rita squarely .

" If she were I wouldn't be discussing the matter with you Mrs. Beale . I think you should mind your own business . A little more neighbourliness on your part and a little less nosiness and perhaps Mrs Gotes would not be in this state . "

This was so unfair it brought tears to Rita's eyes .That doctor was a bastard she decided. .She would make sure she didn't get him next time she went down the health centre .

The ambulance arrived then . The two paramedics could not disguise their horror at the squalor they found in Sandy's bedroom but somehow managed to joke about it , even bringing a smile to Sandy's face . Problems were encountered in lifting the patient from her bed since her bulk defeated the combined strength of the crew who had not expected this problem . Eventually Sandy insisted that she could walk downstairs and did so carrying the dog . The cats remained where they lay . A dressing gown was not available which caused further delay but Rita kindly saved the day by providing a large , pink candlewick bedspread which was draped around Sandy like a shawl .

A small crowd of neighbours had gathered outside the house and were speculating about why an ambulance was required but seeing them caused Sandy to refuse to leave the premises until they were moved . Again Rose was assumed to be the authority figure who should deal with this .She was surprised how easily she fell into this role . She simply asked the people to move and they did . They knew they would get the whole story from Rita later anyway .

" What about this dog ? " the driver said to Sandy . " He can't come with you ." She began to wail piteously .

" Animals are not allpowed in ambulances love , it's against the rules ." He spoke kindly but firmly .

"Oh Rite ! What shall I do ? Can you take him ?" She appealed to her neighbour . " Cyril wont look after him ."

"Sorry Sandy . I can't . Rastus 'd kill him. I'll feed the cats for you but I can't take the dog . You need the RSPCA to take him ." Rita was firm too.

" I'll take him ." Rose heard herself say ." leave him here for now and I'll collect him when I get back from the hospital ." What have I let myself in for ? she asked herself .

Rita tethered the dog to a post near the broken down fence . Immediately he began to howl . Sandy began to cry again too . The ambulancemen , looking harrassed , ushered both she and Rose into the ambulance and they set off watched with great interest by most of the residents of Berringer Row . After Rita had given anyone who was interested the low down on the story , she returned indoors .

Hayley was just coming downstairs . She yawned widely

" Good afternoon " her mother said sarcastically . But she was joking . She didn't mind the girl having a lie in . It was Saturday morning after all , and it had only just gone eleven .

"You missed it all . " she told her daughter ." There was a woman from the social come to see Sandy . Next thing the doctor comes and an ambulance and now they've taken her off to hospital ." then changing her tack " There's bacon if you fancy a bit ." Hayley wasn't interested .

" Ooh no " she said in disgust . The thought of it made her almost heave . " I'm going round Darren's soon as I've had a cup of tea."

Chapter 29

Cyril had just opened up a can of beer and was about to sit down and drink it whilst perusing his newspaper when the door bell rang . The day had begun badly for him with a letter from the inland revenue . Since going into business on his own account Cyril had ignored all such communications He simply read the documents , placed them in a drawer in the kitchen and promptly forgot about them . This one though was threatening reprisals if he did not take action soon so he supposed something would now have to be done about it . Then he had had a frustrating morning when a supposedly simple , routine job had developed unforeseen snags which had caused hours of back breaking effort and still wasn`t completed. He`d have to go back there this afternoon . As he `d walked up the path a few minutes ago , Rita  Beale  had appeared and taken great delight in informing him that Sandy had been taken to hospital , she didn`t know where . Some busybody from the social had been to the house and sent for the doctor . Cyril had been aware that his wife was very unwell because he had heard her gasping and moaning for the last several days . He had hoped that the illness might prove fatal but obviously no such luck. This all added to his general ill humour . Therefore he decided to ignore the bell . Whoever it was could go to hell as far as he was concerned .

But the ringing continued . Whoever it was had no intention of going away it seemed . Then Cyril remembered that he`d left the van parked outside which was a dead giveaway that he was at home. He cursed to himself and put down the  "Sun ". If it was that Rita again he`d tell her to piss off !

Opening the door he saw a tall , well dressed woman . She was middle aged and looked rather official . He cursed inwardly again . Some nosey parker from the council no doubt . Then he realised that he recognised the woman . He`d done some work for her some months back . He assumed a pleasant expression and pulled the door behind him so that she couldn`t see inside .

"Excuse me Madam ." he said politely, " I don`t usually have customers to the door . They normally telephone . What can I do for you ? "

"There is a matter I need to discuss with you .I think it might be best if you asked me in." The woman spoke in the sort of plummy , cut glass voice that Cyril detested . The sort of voice that smacked of privilege and power . Then he remembered exactly who she was . His hackles rose immediately and he spoke now in his normal , truculent manner .

" I don`t invite customers into my house . What is it you want ? "

" I`m afraid my business can`t be discussed on the doorstep . It concerns your wife and some other matters . " Rose replied coolly . Cyril was cursing inside . He felt both intimidated and embarrassed to be cornered on his home ground like this..It put him at a complete disadvantage . It was partly this woman though who made him feel so at a loss . He detested the type – hoity toity , do gooding sort . Always poking into other people`s business . He supposed Sandy had somehow got in touch with her . The cheek of it ! His blood boiled .

" I never ask strangers into my house . It`s asking for trouble these days ." He blustered .

" I`m hardly a stranger Mr. Gotes , and don`t think for one minute that I want to enter your home, " She laid emphasis on the last word . "But I think in your own interests you should ask me in . Unless you want your neighbours to know all about your activities ?" Cyril reddened and looked about him . Sure enough , Rita stood on her front step taking in everything whilst on his other side Mrs Eccles and her two teenage children were also taking a keen interest and her husband stood in the hallway behind her .

"You`d better come in then ."Cyril said sullenly . Rose followed him into the kitchen  which , she  couldn`t help noticing , was clinically clean and bare . Cyril resumed his seat and stared at her aggressively " Well ?"

"I came here this morning to talk to you about what you did yesterday to my friend Miss Claye "Rose said , staring back at him equally fiercely .He did not intimidate her in the least. He seemed taken aback . Beneath his overall he wore an impeccably ironed shirt , Rose noticed and a smart tie . She saw that his shoes were immaculately polished too . Even in his working clothes he looks dapper , she thought .It seemed incredible that he shared a home with the woman whose odour was still clinging to her clothes .

" I did a job for her . That`s quite right ." Cyril said , taking a swig from his can . He did not look at Rose .

" You did rather more than that I think ." Rose said " You assaulted Miss Claye and terrified her .You would have raped her if she hadn`t defended herself ."

" It`s all lies . She`s making it up . I didn`t do nothing ."

Rose glared at him in contempt ." You attacked her . How dare you deny it ? You assumed that she was somebody who would not complain to the police . I wonder how many other women you`ve assaulted ?"

" You try and prove it . It`s her word against mine ." snarled Cyril slopping beer over the table in his anger ." Who`d want an old bag like that anyway ? "

" You`re totally contemptible . You might at least have the decency to show some remorse but I suppose that`s asking far too much from a degenerate like you ."

" Now look here . You`ve no call to come here insulting me ! Just because some sex starved spinster wanted her oats and I wouldn`t come   across."

"Mr . Gotes." Rose interrupted icily , wishing she had the nerve to throw the beer in his face ." I have spent the last three hours with your wife. We had a most enlightening conversation. I have also seen a letter from your daughter accusing you of incest . What do you think the police would make of that if I chose to tell them ? "

There was a long silence . Cyril`s face was ashen now . " What are you going to do ? " He asked .

" It`s not my business to report you to the police much as I should like to . I believe that is up to your own family. I think you should consider your position here . It would make my friend much happier to know that you no longer live in this area . If you promise me that you will move from here within the next four weeks I will do nothing . If you remain here I shall do everything in my power to persuade both Miss Claye and your daughter to press charges against you . And one other thing . I want you to return the money you took from Miss Claye yesterday . I think you owe her that at the very least .Why should she pay to be attacked ? "

" Why the fuck should I give her the money .I did the job didn`t I ?" But Cyril knew he was beaten . Close to tears he dug into his pocket and handed Rose the envelope .

" I might as well tell you that I have advised your wife to start divorce proceedings . As it happens , I work for the Citizen`s Advice Bureau and I can arrange for a solicitor to visit her in hospital ." Rose told him .

"Oh , fuck off to hell you interfering old bitch ! " Cyril turned his back on her . He seemed to be quite distraught now , Rose noticed with satisfaction . She was happy to oblige him .

On the way home , Skipper sat quietly on the front passenger seat on which Rose had placed a quantity of newspaper . He must be a Jack Russell cross she decided. She must stop at a pet shop on the way home and buy some products to clean him up . The first thing would be to bath him although he would probably be terrified. It might be best to do it outdoors .

She thought over the morning's events. She had never known anything quite like it . She had a wonderful feeling of power . It seemed she had only to say the word and people obeyed her . The most amazing thing was the way Gotes had caved in . She'd expected far more trouble from him – he could even have become violent . But he had cut a pathetic figure in the end . Not that she had the least sympathy for him . Possibly he had convinced himself that Iris might welcome his attentions ? But that did not explain his behaviour towards his own family . And what good would reporting him to the police do ? The man clearly had problems that would not be cured by custodial treatment . The best thing to hope was that he would move away soon. Sandy had told her that he came from the Yorkshire area originally . Perhaps he would go back there ? The most immediate problem was how to help Iris .

Chapter 30

Walking the dog along the track by the golf course Queenie noticed spring flowers in bloom.There were bluebells under the trees and here and there a primrose . It occurred to her then that it might have been a good idea to take Iris some flowers . Unfortunately there were no shops between here and where Rose lived and it was too far to do a detour to the florist.

She wondered again what could be wrong with Iris , but if she did not want to talk about it she would have no way of finding out .She wondered too , why Iris had chosen to go to Rose's house rather than hers . After all , Rose was rather a new friend whereas she had been close to Iris for years . I suppose Rose is more capable than me she eventually decided – more able to cope in an emergency . All the same she could not help feeling rather hurt .

As she turned the corner into the road where Rose lived Queenie was attracted by the lovely garden of a bungalow on the other side of the road . She crossed to have a closer look pulling Nellie unwillingly behind her   A clematis – Montana – in prolific bloom trailed all along one wall and right ascross the garden fence . A profusion of spring flowers bloomed in a wide border by the driveway and two flowering cherry trees added to the colour . A man emerged from a side door pushing a lawn mower . There was something familiar about him.

Queenie gasped as he came nearer . It was the man from the book shop . Even in his gardening clothes he looks special , she thought . She turned away quickly before he could see her . It looked so nosey gawping into somebody's garden. Then her heart sank . Nellie had chosen that precise moment to do her morning business . Right outside the gate . She had a choice , thought Queenie She could ignore the problem and walk on which would be very anti social , or she could tell the man what had happened and ask to borrow a trowel to remove the problem . She decided on the latter course of action .

Gerald , as he later introduced himself , was absolutely charming . He insisted on removing the mess himself and ended up having a long chat with Queenie whom , of course , he remembered from the other day . When she told him she was visiting a sick friend who was staying with Rose - she didn't know quite how else to put it – he was most interested and insisted that she should come to the green house and choose a plant for her . Queenie was totally charmed by him . After some minutes of dithering she chose a lovely Perlagonium . The white petals of the bloom were variegated with delicate shades of lilac deepening into mauve . She knew Iris would love it and later on she would ask her for a cutting .

What made things even better was discovering that Gerald was a cat person too. He made her laugh by telling her about his Persian Queen Purrfidia who had disgraced herself upon the pillow of a guest who was becoming de trop . Gerald had had to pretend to be angry whilst really he was delighted with the cat's behaviour , particularly since it seemed to persuade their guest that it was time to go .How they had chuckled . She went on her waylfeeling that she had made a new friend .

At Rose's gate Queenie caught a glimpse of Iris in the sitting room and was relieved to see her up and about . However when Iris opened the door and stood before Queenie she looked so drawn and unhappy that Queenie felt an immediate rush of sympathy and concern . Irislooked puzzled too

"What are you doing here Queenie and why have you got Nellie ?"

" Rose asked me to take her out . She had to go somewhere in a hurry . Iris , whatever has happened ? I can tell it's something awful because you look so dreadful ." Queenie thrust the plant at her friend whilst the dog went berserk upon seeing her mistress.

"I'm surprised Rose didn't tell you but I suppose she thought I should do it myself .You'll have to know . I was attacked yesterday at home . Sexually attacked ." Iris stated the facts baldly not looking at her companion

"Oh my god . How terrible !" Queenie was uncomfortably aware that her first thought was thank God it happened to her and not me . Immediately she felt guilty . "Do you know who...?"

Iris interrupted " Yes . It was the plumber . Mr. Gotes ." her voice was grim " He came round yesterday afternoon and ...." But it was all too much for her . Iris began to cry and remained unable to speak for several minutes . Queenie was full of concern . She didn't know quite what to do .

" I know " she said finally " I'll make some coffee shall I ? And you should have something to eat Iris . What about some toast ?"

" Oh I couldn't eat a thing " Iris said , moving restlessly around the room .She wished Queenie had not come . She simply could not put up with her fussing and her questions. Minutes later , Queenie came in with a tray

"What are you going to do Iris ? Have you told the police ? " she asked.

"I'm not telling the police " said Iris , sounding very defensive . "You may think that's very stupid but I can't bring myself to do it ." she was close to tears again . Then she said -

" Try to imagine how you would feel if this had happened to you . People sniggering about sex starved spinsters , whispering about you in the street . Headlines in the "Echo". Some people might even suggest that I encouraged him ! I've been able to think about nothing else all night ."

Queenie mentally kicked herself for being so tactless.She could imagine it all only too well. She left the room. In the kitchen she tried to banish the subject from her mind .Rose' kitchen really put hers to shame she thought . Everything that should gleam did so and the colour scheme was so attractive.Queenie particularly admired the Le Creuset saucepans which she had not noticed when she visited before . They were primrose yellow and the colour was echoed in the china displayed on the pine dresser . Rose had suggested that Queenie should prepare some lunch for the three of them , telling her to make free with anything she wanted from the freezer and now she was delighted with this prospect . Poor Iris ! she couldn't begin to imagine what she must have gone through . Such an occurrence was every maiden ladies' nightmare and once again Queenie thanked God that it had not happened to her

Yes , Roses' house was quite charming Queenie thought and , although like Queenie she had old furniture and traditional soft furnishings the overall effect was so much nicer . She could not put her finger on quite why this was and went to ask Iris about it .

"It's because she's got no clutter " Iris said immediately and right away Queenie realised that this was so . Perhaps the time had come for her to do something about her own clutter ? But even as she thought this she knew she never would .

"It's high time you did something about your clutter Queenie . You're going to leave a terrible job for some poor body when you've gone." Iris warned . She seemed to have a knack of reading her thoughts , thought Queenie in annoyance.

"Really Iris . I'm not quite in my dotage yet." She replied crossly " And I happen to like my clutter thank you very much ."

Chapter 31

After foraging in Rose's freezer Queenie rustled up a tasty lunch . The day had turned chilly again in spite of its promising start and something hot was in order she decided . There were a number of cartons of home made soup stacked neatly in the freezer . Queenie picked out one labelled Stilton and Broccoli . Further searching produced an apple tart . She marvelled again at how organised and efficient Rose was . All the containers in the freezer were neatly labelled with their contents and dates and stored neatly in their various categories so diffferent from her own chaotic freezer which was full of unlabelled contents stored wherever she could find space for them . It was not that she was too lazy to label things , rather than that it never seemed necessary at the time. She put things away thinking to herself oh I`ll remember that as it`s in the blue plastic box , only to have her memory fail her with predictable consequences .

Iris sat in the sitting room pretending to read . She probably wouldn`t want to eat much reasoned  Queenie so it wouldn`t do to prepare too much food . Anyway , soup was nourishing and there was a large granary loaf should anybody want some cheese .

" Shall we eat in the kitchen ?" She asked Iris . "It`s well gone one o clock . We could listen to "Any Questions " I missed it last night . I don`t think its worth waiting for Rose . She said she didn`t know how long she would be .

" Did she say where she was going ? " Iris asked . She had a sudden presentiment that Rose` urgent  business might concern herself . At that very moment she saw Rose` car turning into the drive and watched as she emerged from it carrying a small , dirty looking mongrel dog .Smelling the dog at once Nellie rushed forward only to be stopped in her tracks by the snarls of the smaller animal . There was much questioning and excitement . In spite of his appearance Iris was charmed by the little dog and attempted to stroke him .

"Don`t get too close Iris " Rose warned . "He`s very dirty and infested I`m afraid . His name is Skipper and the first thing I must do is shut him in the shed with some food . Then I shall need a bath . And before that dog is allowed back into the house he must be thoroughly bathed too. " Rose took the animal and disappeared to the shed .Over lunch , having first ascertained that Queenie was aware of what had taken place last night , Rose revealed her activities of the morning . Queenie was fascinated as the tale unfolded but Iris was simply furious . She put down her spoon and turned on Rose ferociously .

"How dare you interfere in my affairs Rose ? You had absolutely no right to go there without telling me first . It's none of your business ."

There was an uncomfortable silence . Then Rose said

" I'm sorry you feel like that Iris . I was trying to be helpful ." She continued with the story .Queenie was enthralled . At the end Rose turned to Iris and said

" I knew you would accuse me of interfering which is why I did not tell you what I planned to do ,but I know I did the right thing . Somebody had to face that man . If he had been allowed to get away with it who knows what he would have done next ? I know his type very well . He's a coward above all . If you could only have seen his poor wife or heard what she had to say about him you would realise..."

Iris was still angry but now it was because Rose had had the temerity to do what she never could have done . She realised how unreasonable this was however and tried to contain herself .

" What was actually wrong with that woman , apart from being so very fat ? " Queenie asked , deeply interested .

" Something called choleocystitis . It's a gall bladder infection apparently . And the rash had nothing to do with it . That turned out to be flea bites . She shared her bed with so many animals . If you had seen that bedroom ..." Rose shuddered at the memory . " That's why the dog has to be thoroughly cleaned up . Goodness knows what he's harbouring ."

" But what will happen to her now ?" Queenie persisted .

" I think she'll be in hospital for a while . She's agreed to be transferred to the psychiatric hospital after she has recovered from the gall bladder operation. She's been very depressed for ages apparently . Not surprising when you consider the circumstances . I've promised to keep in touch with her . In a strange way I feel I owe it to her to be of some help . She seems to have nobody else who cares about her . It's all quite tragic ."

"And what about Gotes ? " Iris enquired . She could not bring herself to utter his first name "Do you really believe he'll go away ?" It seemed far fetched to her .

"Iris I'm sure of it . I made him an offer he couldn't refuse . It was blackmail , I suppose , but who cares with a rat like that ?" Rose laughed . " And I almost forgot ...." She reached for her handbag and retrieved the envelope . " This is yours Iris . I made him return it . Why should you pay him for being attacked ?"

Iris dropped it on the table . " I don`t want it ! I couldn`t handle anything touched by that man .Give it to charity ."

" I`ve an idea Rose " Queenie butted in ." Why not put it towards cleaning up Sandy`s house? That means Iris will still have paid for her plumbing and at the same time she`d be helping Sandy . It`s a really good cause Iris , and at least one good thing will have come out of all the nastiness ."

" That`a a brilliant idea !." " Oh yes ." Both the others spoke at once Queenie felt pleased with her suggestion and Rose felt relieved that the situation with Iris seemed to have been relieved .

"Queenie , would you mind doing some shopping for me this afternoon Rose enquired . " I simply must get on with cleaning up that dog . And you`ll stay and have supper tonight wont you ." she didn`t really want to be left on her own with Iris . " I`ve got everything I need I think except eggs and bread for tomorrow ."

Queenie agreed happily . Then a thought struck her . "Do you think we could ask Thelma to come too ? She never gets out in the evening and you know how lonely she is "

" By all means . You don`t mind do you Iris ? It might even take your mind off things if we have a party ." Then seeing Iris` doubtful face she added " Now don`t worry . We wont say a word to her about what happened yesterday. Right Queenie  I`ll ring her now."

Queenie began to bustle about , searching for her bag and taking down her coat . " If I go right away I can catch the 2.15 bus .It goes straight to Sainsbury`s .What shall we eat tonight Rose ? "

" My freezer `s bursting with food . There`s a piece of beef or salmon if you`d rather . You should choose Iris . Get some cream Queenie and I`ll make a chocolate mousse . I`m still waiting to use up the chocolate Gerald brought back from France ."

" I`ll take Nellie for a walk . I need some air ." Iris said .

" Not before you`ve helped me to bath Skipper " Rose smiled . " I couldn`t tackle it alone ."

Chapter 32

Queenie pushed her trolley around the aisles in Sainsbury's . Saturday afternoon was not a good time to do your shopping she decided . There were too many family parties blocking the aisles and young children running about . People seemed to buy such vast quantities of food nowadays she observed .Some of the families even had two trolleys piled high with packets and boxes What on earth did they do with it all ?

She recalled her mother going out for a morning's food shopping armed with no more than a string bag . That easily carried the rations for a week . Of course in those days people shopped day by day in small quantities and shops were only too happy to deliver even the smallest orders . Imagine ringing Sainsbury's and asking them to deliver half a pound of sausage and a small brown loaf . Queenie giggled to herself at the thought of this and noticed a tall , athletic looking woman stare at her oddly .

She moved away quickly and bumped into a small child who fell to the ground bawling . Queenie wasn't sure whether to help her up or not .

" Roxanne " yelled a large woman who must have been the child's mother " Stay by me or I'll wallop you one ." Children had such peculiar names these days Queenie thought , selecting a melon . She was a fine one to pass comment though given her own name which invariably attracted comment .

Which Queen did your parents have in mind when they named you? people asked and Queenie then had to explain that she had been called after a music hall artiste whom her parents had admired during their courtship .

Italian cheese was on special offer today she noted , lingering by the cheese display . She herself was partial to gorgonzola but not everyone liked it. Better stick to something everyone would like she decided , lifting out a large piece of cambazola . She looked at the price £3.85 . Ridiculous to pay that for a piece of cheese . She held it in her hand thoughtfully for a moment then , rather like a conjurer , quickly inserted it into one of the large " poacher " pockets of her raincoat and carried on down the aisle .

The reality of what she had just done suddenly struck her like a gong . She would suffer all night from this action she knew . Was it worth it for £3. 85 ? No it definitely was not . She retraced her steps and waited until the coast was clear. Then , with rather more difficulty than it had gone in , she retrieved the cheese from her pocket and replaced it , rather crushed , back on the display .

Then she took another , unsullied , pack and placed it in her trolley. The relief she felt was immediate and almost tangible , like removing a pair of shoes that pinched . She moved towards the other dairy products and found the cream she required then wandered off towards wines and spirits . Rose had suggested a Chardonnay but would one bottle be enough ? Queenie browsed around the shelves for some time .There were huge queues at every checkout she now noticed and , stupidly , she had not kept her eye on the time . There was now less then twenty minutes before her bus was due . Still she should be out of here by then surely ?

She would definitely not come here on a Saturday again she decided . This checkout girl seemed particularly slow but at last it was Queenie's turn . She paid for her items and clutching two carriers she headed quickly for the exit . A woman approached her , the same woman in fact who had been staring at her earlier . .Perhaps she knew her from somewhere ? Queenie smiled at her inquiringly but the woman's face was expressionless .

" Excuse me Madam , but I'd like you to accompany me to the manager's office. I have reason to believe that you have not paid for all of your shopping "

The shock was like being doused by a freezing bucket of water . Then – seconds later – Queenie felt as if she'd been scalded . She stood stock still while these sensations washed over her . Strangely though , there was also a sense of inevitability . This was the moment she had been dreading but expecting for some time . But all she could think of was missing the bus .

" My bus is due in a minute . I can't miss it ." the words came out in a gasp .

" I can't help that Madam . Come with me now please ." She grasped Queenie firmly by the arm . She was a large, raw boned woman who made Queenie feel like a midget . Other shoppers gawped at the spectacle . Queenie heard someone say . " That's the store detective . She must have been shoplifting . " She felt her cheeks burning and did not dare to look about her as she was led towards a door marked " Manager ".

i n the small office a short , balding man sat behind a desk covered with papers . He looked at Queenie with dislike . " Another shoplifting ? " he enquired of the woman who nodded grimly .The woman released her grip on Queenie and began to recite a well used formula to him ending with the words "I then observed the lady taking a piece of cheese and concealing it in the pocket of her raincoat . I followed her through the store and observed no further thefts."

" Did you take the cheese ?" asked the man . He seemed thoroughly bored . Queenie was white with fear . " No . " She whispered .

" In that case I must ask you to remove your raincoat and allow us to search it ." He said . The humiliation was exquisite , but there was a part of Queenie that somehow welcomed it . She had been asking for this for a long time , it was only to be expected that it had finally happened . She thanked God that some thing had made her replace the cheese . This was the lesson she needed to bring her to her senses . She knew now that she would not steal again .

Trembling , she handed her raincoat to the store detective who received it confidently and started to go through the pockets . Her triumphant expression changed to one of chagrin when she did not find what she wanted. She scrabbled in all the pockets then , even the tiny one for bus tickets and then gave the raincoat a shake but she retrieved only some crumpled tissues and a few coins . She then seized Queenie`s bag and emptied it on the desk . All the usual items fell out including a card which said " I succeed at everything I attempt ."

The manager`s expression was not at all bored now , Queenie noticed . " She must have hidden it somewhere else " the woman said but looking at Queenie`s slight physique it was obvious that her navy jersey and slim fitting skirt concealed no incriminating bulges . Both people began to look decidedly uneasy and Queenie found her confidence returning .

"Please show me your receipt " the store detective said angrily . After this had been checked with every item in her basket an uneasy silence fell .

" It looks as though there has been a mistake " The manager said . He looked crossly at the store detective . " I must offer you my sincere apologies Madam . You must appreciate how difficult it is ..." His voice trailed away and he now looked embarrassed .

" I think you both must realise now that you have made a mistake " Queenie said in quite a different voice . " But you have made me miss my bus and now I have no way of getting home ."Amidst profuse apologies , a taxi was ordered for Queenie to be charged to the store she was told . Both the manager and the store detective were so abject in their apologies that Queenie began to feel sorry for the them . Of course they were probably terrified that she might sue. She decided that she could afford to be magmanimous . She told them them that she well understood their difficulties and would be making no complaint about the incident . The relief and gratitude of the manager was so hard to bear that she almost broke down and confessed what had happened .

Carrying her shopping himself Mr. Merriman , who had now introduced himself to her , escorted her to the exit and helped her into the taxi .As they pulled away from the store Queenie began to shake with shock and relief . Things could have been so different . She could have been on her way to the police station now where they would no doubt have placed her in a cell . Perhaps she would have had to ask Rose to bail her out ? It didn't bear thinking about . Thank God she had seen sense and replaced the cheese . It wasn't just luck she reasoned but divine intervention This must have been a lesson for her . Well she had learned it thoroughly . Never again would she take anything . Not so much as a toothpick !

" Oh thank you . thank you God for showing me the error of my ways before it was too late ." She realised she had said this prayer aloud . Then she almost laughed aloud thinking of her plans to find a manual to stop her stealing .It was never a book she'd required .This was what she'd needed all along . You could describe it as a short , sharp shock . In his mirror the taxi driver could see the lady in the back seat smiling to herself with her eyes closed and now and then muttering to herself aloud ." You get all kinds in this job ." he reminded himself .

Chapter 33

Preparing for bed much earlier than she had expected , Rose went over the evening in her mind .Somehow it had fallen decidedly flat . The food had been delicious yet nobody seemed to enjoy it much . At least nobody had wanted a second helping of anything and nobody except herself fhad even wanted a second glass of wine . Iris was quiet and withdrawn all night which was only to be expected given what she had been through , but Queenie was not herself either . She had eaten hardly anything and seemed to be deep in thought for most of the time .

Then there was the unfortunate argument between Iris and Thelma . Well , not so much an argument as a definite unpleasantness which seemed to upset Thelma so much that she had decided to go home without even having a cup of coffee .The plan had been that Thelma and Queenie should share a taxi home but she had left so abruptly the matter had not even be raised . It had ended up with Queenie sleeping unwillingly in the next room to Iris . She had only wanted to walk home, if you please , along that lonely track by the golf course ! It had taken the combined protests of Rose and Iris to deter her from this course of action and even then she had given in with very bad grace complaining that they were making her neglect her cats . Matters became so heated that neither Iris nor Queenie had bidden good night to each other and the atmosphere had been extremely uncomfortable .

All these difficult women , thought Rose How on earth had she got herself involved with them ? She felt as if she were the warden of some kind of female hostel and had just finished an evening shift with some particularly trying inmates .

" Don't bother to dress up , come just as you are " She had said to Thelma on the phone , " It's just the four of us ." and then she had turned up in taffeta and pearls . She had been clutching an enormous box of chocolates too , a quite uncalled for gesture . Trust her to do something completely over the top . It was unfair to criticise her for an act of kindness but , no matter what she did , Rose knew that there was something about the woman she could not take to and Iris obviously felt the same .

Accepting a small sherry ,Thelma had annoyed her by saying in a surprised sort of way "Your house is quite nice really ." Rose had been tempted to ask "Why shouldn't it be ? "

Thelma had continued " It`s almost as big as mine .Pity you haven`t got triple glazing though. It does make such a difference you know ."

" I don`t think I`d like it anyway ." Iris had said ." In the event of a fire you`d never get out ."

" Oh . I`d never have a fire " Thelma had said , as if such a contingency were a matter of choice . She had then proceeded to brag quite shamelessly about the various superior fittings of her bungalow to the boredom of everyone in the room . She then began to tell them about her villa in Florida saying at the end of her saga " We could all go there together if you wanted . It would only cost you the price of a flight ." There had been no positive response to this suggestion although Queenie had smiled encouragingly . Rose could imagine nothing she would rather do less .

During the meal , apropos of nothing , Thelma had begun again

" You know , we`re just like the  "Golden Girls " aren`t we ? It`s my favourite programme ."

"Golden girls ?" Iris asked , totally uncomprehending . " Who are they ? "

" You know Iris " Queenie said ." It`s that American TV programme about those women who all share a house in Florida .It`s quite funny sometimes ."

Iris had watched it once , at Queenie`s instigation she now remembered , and had found it puerile beyond belief . It was a combination of vulgarity and sentimentality which totally grated on her . She found it too American anyway . Typical of Thelma to enjoy it .

" What irritated me about that programme was that it insisted on peddling the belief that women are only interested in finding a man , no matter what their age . " Rose said " It was funny if you watched it once but then the joke wore thin ." At this Thelma had looked so deflated that Rose had felt forced to add " Of course , there are other American programmes I love . Sgt. Bilko always makes me laugh ."

The conversation then moved on to books . Thelma had not heard of any of the writers they talked about although previously she`d said she loved to read . Even names like Ruth Rendell and John Mortimer meant nothing to her it seemed .

" Who is your favourite author Thelma?" Queenie asked curiously . " I don`t think I`ve got one ." she answered . " I like those Readers Digest condensed books I suppose because . they`re not too long to get boring . But what I really enjoy are those little books of poetry by Patience Strong . I always keep one at the side of my bed ."

There was no answer to that . In fact the disclosure was followed by an embarrassed silence . Of course there was nothing wrong in Thelma's choice of reading matter , but condensed books ? thought Iris . If a book was worth reading what was the point in condensing it ?

Then , just as Rose had served the chocolate mousse , during a conversation about holidays ,Thelma had made the remark which had sparked off all the trouble .

" My late husband was planning to take me to Spain if he'd lived. He spoke of buying a place there to spend our retirement . He was very fond of Spain . Of course his death put paid to that ." She cast down her eyes to allow a respectful silence to elapse .

" I bet it was Benidorm he chose . " Iris said nastily and immediately regretted the remark . Both Rose and Queenie looked at her in surprise . It was so unlike Iris to be nasty .

" As a matter of fact it was . And why should you be so superior about that or anything else for that matter ? At least I had a husband which is more than you ever did ." There was a shocked silence . " Anyway , I've got to go now . " Thelma pushed away her dish and rose from the table

" Where did you put my coat Rose ? " She walked to the door and Rose hurriedly followed her . Iris looked at Queenie and sighed. Her eyes were full of tears .

" I don't know why I said that ." She muttered . " But it was completely out of order I know ." At the door Rose had put her hand on Thelma's arm .

" Please on't take offence Thelma . I shouldn't be telling you this but Iris has had a terribly upsetting experience and isn't herself at all . I'm sure she did'nt mean to offend you . And I'm sure she's taken no offence either .Can't we agree to forget all about it ? "

But Thelma was not at all interested in what had upset Iris . She refused to be mollified and had walked away in high dudgeon ..At the gate she had suddenly turned back

" They've always thought themselves better than me those two and no doubt you're just the same . But I could buy and sell you all . Just remember that ! "

Rose sighed , poor Thelma . One couldn't help feeling sorry for her but she was her own worse enemy . What a catastrophe of an evening ! She climbed into bed and was soon asleep .

....

Thelma meanwhile , had gone home and stayed up to the early hours nursing her anger . Even in bed she had hardly slept a wink such was her fury . Towards morning she fell into a doze but when she woke up she had such a bad headache she could hardly raise her head from the pillow .

Touching her throbbing head she thought she could feel a lumpy rash so she had to drag herself up to investigate it in the mirror . It turned out to be the impression of the broderie anglais trimming on her pillowslip which she must have been lying against whilst she was asleep . She should have recognised this pain she realised now . It was the same as the headaches she`d suffered from years before . She`d been told then that the pain was associated with grinding her teeth during her sleep , something she`d been prone to do as a young woman . She would simply have to have to lie here until the pain wore off . It sometimes took an hour or more .

She lay on her back and thought over the events of last night . She had been so pleased when Rose had telephoned to invite her for supper because she`d been feeling particularly down yesterday . It had been the anniversary of mother`s funeral . She`d gone straight out and bought the biggest box of chocolates she could find as a thank you gesture . She knew that it was only polite to offer one`s hostess a gift . Yet her gesture had not been met with the delight she had expected . If anything , Rose had seemed taken aback although she had said thank you .

Well , she`d burned her boats now and no mistake . She did not regret her angry outburst to Iris last night – it was no more than she`d deserved – but it meant of course that she had lost the only friends she had in the neighbourhood. Just when she was beginning to have some semblance of a social life . Well , she wasn`t sorry about Iris – stuck up bitch – but it was a shame to fall out with Queenie and Rose although she didn`t go a bundle on Rose anyway . She was a useful person to know though because she had so many contacts .

So what did she do now ? People spoke so glibly about how to make friends . Join an evening class , do some voluntary work , these were always the suggestions handed out by professional advice givers . Well she had tried all those things and they didn`t work . " What about your neighbours ? " Rose had asked her when they`d first met at the Citizen`s Advice Bureau . "Have you met them yet ? It might be a good idea to introduce yourself ." Thelma recalled one of her neighbours calling round the day after she`d moved in . She`d opened the front door and there was this attractive blond woman , expensively dressed , holding a potted plant . She had the sort of accent and confident manner which Thelma found intimidating so that her first instinct had been to make an excuse to get rid of her fast . Somehow though , the woman had managed to inveigle her way into the house where she had gazed about with great interest .

Margot Chasey – as she had introduced herself – told Thelma that her husband was involved with computers . She had then proceeded to cross examine Thelma about her background and interests , seeming to lose interest when Thelma admitted that she had never played bridge . " I would quite like to learn " Thelma had offered but Margot had not taken up this hint . Nor was she interested when Thelma began to show her some of her furnishings and tell her about what everything had cost . At the end of this conversation Thelma was left with the feeling that she'd been set some kind of test and failed badly .

One particularly lonely afternoon weeks later she had decided to call on Margot . After all , she had said "Do call round any time ." But she had received a very chilly reception . Margot had kept her on the doorstep and after saying " Settling in all right ? ", had explained that she was very busy and did not have time to talk . " So nice to see you ." She'd said insincerely . There were only seven houses in the close and so far Margot was the only neighbour to make herself known . Thelma had once plucked up the courage to knock at the doors at two other of her neighbours but nobody was at home . She sometimes caught glimpses of people driving in or out , other times had seen people gardening but they never acknowledged her and she felt too disheartened to introduce herself . After all , she was the newcomer . It was surely up to them to welcome her .

Some people were born unlucky , mother always said so and it seemed that it was true . But it was so unfair . It wasn't her fault .She tried to be nice to people but look where it got her ?Look how she had even offered them the use of her timeshare only to have it rejected . And then they'd had the nerve to criticise the television programmes she watched and the books she read .

Why was it that some people seemed to sail through life with no troubles of any kind while people like her had to endure poverty and bereavement ? None of them had ever had to worry about having enough money to pay their bills . Their parents had died when they no longer had need of them leaving them nice homes and money , whereas her own life , until recently , had been one long struggle . Nobody had ever given her anything . Poor mother had worked her fingers to the bone just to keep a roof over their heads and her reward was a harrowing death which she met screaming in pain . Yet both she and her mother had always led decent lives They were devout and lived by the Bible but where had it got them ? Thelma knew it was wicked to question her faith but sometimes things did not make sense .

Then a really scaring thought came into her head .Something which had never occurred to her before . What if it was just the same in heaven ? People like Rose Deacon lording it over people like her. Good looking and clever ones ruling the roost whilst people like herself slaved in the background . No , it was too awful to contemplate .

Now that she was better off financially all she wanted was a bit of friendship and respect but it seemed that this was to be denied her too . Was it some kind of test from God ? What had she done to make her former schoolmates be so horrible to her ? You'd think with everything they had they would be charitable .Instead they seemed to be deliberately unkind . And just what gave them the right to feel so superior ? Thelma tossed and turned , mulling over these questions .Then light dawned .Well of course it was obvious really . She should have realised it before . They were jealous that's all . It was as simple as that .
]

Chapter 34

The next morning had begun for Rose by Queenie bearing a cup of tea . It was only just after seven o clock she had noticed with irritation .

" I shan't stay for breakfast.I'm going to walk home now ", she had informed a sleepy Rose . " I feel bad about Thelma .Do you think I should ring her or perhaps call round ? She was so cross last night . I'd like her to know that I really didn't mean to upset her ."

" I should telephone ." Rose advised . Privately she was inclined to let Thelma stew in her own juice but she knew that she was not as soft hearted as Queenie . " The person I'm more worried about is Iris . Do you think I should get someone from Victim Support to visit her ? She wont go and see anybody off her own bat but if somebody actually called on her it might help her to talk about what happened ."

Queenie advised against this

" Iris is a very private person ." She said " She wont thank you for interfering I know . I should keep out of it"

Iris had stayed in bed late and when she came down complained that she had been awake for most of the night Rose sympathised because it had been exactly the same for her . Skipper , left in the kitchen at bedtime had howled mournfully until Rose had felt compelled to go down to comfort him . When she attempted to return to bed the howling had begun again . It was only to be expected , she reasoned . The poor creature had spent most of his life lying next to Sandy .It was too much to ask for him to be expected to sleep alone . So she had brought him upstairs and made a bed for him in the little Victorian arm chair close to her bed but he refused to remain there and , after several attempts to send him away , tiredness had forced her to give in and allow him to lie at her side. She consoled herself with the thought that at least he was clean now .

They had spent most of the day discussing Cyril Gotes .This had not been at Rose` instigation .Iris seemed to have a need to talk about it . In particular she needed reassurance that the man would really go away . During all their conversations Rose tried to reinforce the idea that Gotes was not the violent rapist Iris cast him as , but a pathetic inadequate who had acted in a purely opportunistic way and that by repulsing him she had emerged the victor.

" I think I might go home tomorrow " Iris informed Rose as they were out walking the dogs later that afternoon .

" Are you sure ? Why not wait until I can go with you ? I`m busy all day tomorrow  but we could go on Tuesday afternoon ? You can have a nice , lazy day tomorrow whilst I`m out ."

Iris agreed to this plan . One more day would not make much difference she thought . In one way she was dreading going back but , on the other hand , there were things to see to at home . Mail would start piling up . She had not cancelled her milk and the old ladies would think it most odd that she had disappeared without telling them where she was going . Also she did not want to impose on Rose any longer than was necessary . As somebody who also lived alone , she knew how difficult it was to adapt to having another person around .

The next day Rose left the house shortly before nine . It was her morning in the charity shop . She wondered whether Thelma would turn up and was just about to mention the matter to Iris but stopped herself in time . She rather doubted it but anyway her absence would be no loss . Iris had been quite happy to look after Skipper but as soon as Rose tried to leave the house the animal set up such a terrible racket that there was nothing for it but to take him with her .

After they`d gone , Iris took Nellie for a walk . She had slept badly again last night and felt particularly weary . She would spend the rest of the morning reading she decided or listening to the radio .Returning to the house she settled herself in an armchair and then predictably , fell asleep .

She was awakened by Nellie gently tugging at her sleeve . Heavens it was nearly two o clock .The dog wanted to go out again . Better take her now she decided . She ran a comb through her hair , fetched her coat , changed her shoes and off they went .They were out for almost an hour . It was another brilliantly sunny day although the wind was cold . Iris felt better for the fresh air . She decided she would prepare some supper . That would be a nice surprise for Rose .

She took Nellie in the back garden and left her there whilst she went indoors . The dog would need to be brushed and have her paws cleaned before she took her inside .Rose` very pale beige carpet was impractical when there were animals around .Putting her key in the front door Iris was aware of the noise of the radio , blaring out loud pop music . But I didn`t leave the radio on , I`m sure , she told herself as she walked inside . Then again , perhaps she had done . She was so tired she was doing stupid things .

She walked towards the noise which came from the sitting room and saw , first of all , a man`s shoe lying on the floor and then a collection of garments strewn all over the place . One step further and she took in the full , horrible scene . Darren Piper`s naked backside bobbing up and down obscenely as he and Hayley Beale engaged themselves in vigorous sexual activity on Rose` sofa . Neither of them were aware of her presence . Her heart thudding she quietly let herself out of the house .

She walked briskly , her mind in turmoil and her cheeks burning with embarrassment . Was the whole world obsessed with sex ? What would Rose say if she knew her house was being used for such purposes ? She had spoken so well of the young girl who cleaned for her. Then again , perhaps it was herself who was out of touch for finding this behaviour out of order ? She was an old maid after all . Iris was so obsessed by all these thoughts that before she realised it she was at her front door .

She let herself in and the dog bounded before her , wagging her tail furiously . At least she`s pleased to be back Iris thought . She went into the kitchen and filled the kettle . She hesitated outside her bedroom door . She would not go into her bedroom yet . But why not ? Why should she let that loathsome creature destroy her possession of her own home ? She went in . It looked and smelled just as it always did . There was no trace of Cyril Gotes there .

She remembered Rose` words . She had been the victor in their encounter . Keeping that thought in her mind she opened the curtains but kept the windows closed but she did not feel happy .

Later she telephoned Rose . She had decided to say nothing of what she had seen that afternoon .In the first place it embarrassed her to discuss it but she also felt that it was none of her business .If it came to Rose` attention she could sort it out herself . But she had to provide an explanation for her abrupt departure . As it turned out that was not too difficult Rose merely said " As long as you`re sure you are all right there . Feel free to come right back here if you don`t feel happy ."

Iris spent the evening writing letters and then tried to watch television but found she could not concentrate . She kept thinking about what she had witnessed this afternoon . It was completely....gross , she thought . She could not imagine herself ever taking part in such an activity , not even when she`d been younger . She imagined what might have happened if Cyril Gotes had achieved his objective and her face twisted in agony . She would rather die . Yet people made out it was one of life`s greatest pleasures . She supposed that proved she was " frigid " and "just an old maid " . But perhaps her attitude was nature`s way of making her happy with her lot ? It wouldn`t do if women like her without partners were forever craving male company . Yet to most people spinsters were seen as figures of fun and she knew that secretly she was ashamed of her status . Being a maiden lady was both a stigma and a disfigurement .

Rose meanwhile , was feeling cross . She had returned home to find the house empty but in spite of the fact that Hayley had been , the house did not have that freshly cleaned look that it had always had in Evie`s time . Rose assumed that Iris` presence had inhibited Hayley in some way , yet now she had learned that Iris had decided to return home before Hayley`s arrival . But why had she left all her things behind ? And why had Hayley not cleaned properly ?

Not that she was sorry Iris had gone home much as she sympathised with her . If anything , she was delighted . The last few days had been trying to say the least. She was already regretting her impulsive decision to care for Sandy`s dog . The animal was proving to be a liability . He had howled non stop in the back room of the shop this morning . Of course , it would be the one morning when May did not have her mother in tow . The very morning when she could have kept the animal company .

It seemed now that Hayley`s cleaning standarda were slipping again too . The house had obviously not  been cleaned properly this afternoon .In Evie`s day , Rose had paid her by the hour but had no objections to her finishing earlier so long as the cleaning was done .Hayley had adopted the same system of work , choosing her own hours and Rose had no objection to this . Now it seemed that she was simply taking advantage of her good nature . Rose determined that she would speak to her about it and if there was no improvement she would get rid of her , friend of Evie or not . She sighed . Now she supposed she would have to take Skipper out . She had never known such a totally dependant animal . The little dog required human company constantly showing total distress if he were left alone for a moment .At the sam e time he was a very appealing dog . He snuggled up to Rose at every opportunity so it was im possible not to like him .

Chapter 35

Tittivating at her dressing table , Thelma heard the chink of glasses and raised voices coming from the other side of the fence . Evidently her neighbours were entertaining again she noted enviously . She rose and closed the window with a contemptuous slam . It would not occur to them to invite her in of course ! Not that she would have accepted an invitation anyway since she was going out with Queenie tonight to see the clairvoyant . Still , it would have been nice to have been asked .

After nine months of living here she had not as much as crossed the threshold of any of her neighbours homes yet they all seemed to mingle socially amongst themselves . She could not help noticing the pre luncheon drinks parties on Sundays and the barbecues on nice evenings from all of which she was excluded . Why was she such an outcast to them ? She could only suppose it was because she was a single woman . On the other hand that didn't seem to make much difference to Rose Deacon who seemed to be out every night .How did she become so popular ? Oh well , life was unfair .There was no getting away from the fact. Anyway , here was the taxi to take her to Queenie . Thelma grabbed her bag , picked up her keys and hurriedly left the house .

Sitting in the back of the vehicle , Thelma felt both excited and scared about the visit to the clairvoyant . She had never done such a thing before . Mother would have been dead against it as would anybody associated with the mission . There had once been a sermon about it . Even though that was years ago Thelma still remembered it well . It had been the time when there had been a lot in the papers about people playing with ouija boards . An American preacher had come to the mission and given them a sermon called " Dabbling with the Devil" all about the frightening things that could happen to you when you meddled with the spirit world . Afterwards the congregation had been handed printed copies of the sermon just to make sure they didn't forget .

But Thelma did not go to the mission now and you could not be bound by your mother all your life . After all , she was leading a rather different existence Her life style , as they called it now , was vastly different from mother's . If she could only see what her daughter had spent on her appearance this last month she would have a fit . Times changed and people had to change with them . Anyway , fortune telling was just harmless fun – that's what Queenie had said and if it was all right for her it was all right by Thelma too . Why then was she feeling so guilty about the outing ?

Thelma had seen little of Queenie since the night of the supper at Rose` house . She'd been good enough to telephone her and apologise for what had happened , even though she wasn`t the one at fault , but when she had rung her back suggesting they go out for the day or meet somewhere for lunch Queenie always seemed to be busy . Something to do with some Indian friends apparently .Thelma thought it very odd but then Queenie had always been on the strange side .When she had telephoned and suggested the visit to the clairvoyant Thelma had agreed immediately , just for the sake of having somewhere to go , but really she would have preferred a visit to the theatre or the cinema .

Queenie was waiting at her gate as arranged wearing dark glasses of all things . She looked rather scruffy too , Thelma thought , dressed as she was in trousers and an anorak . She could have made more of an effort – whatever would the clairvoyant think ? Thelma touched the printed skirt of her Geiger suit . At least she was dressed appropriately for the outing .

" I seem to have a touch of conjunctivitis " Queenie had said , but when she removed the dark glasses in the taxi it looked more as if she had been crying . " Leah has just telephoned to alter the time of our appointment . Apparently she can see nobody before 8.30 tonight . " She told Thelma . " I think something urgent must have cropped up . I tried to let you know but you`d already left the house ."

" But it`s a quarter to eight now and we`ll be there in just a few minutes " Thelma objected . "We can`t just hang about the streets . People might get the wrong idea ."

Queenie stifled a giggle . Surely she and Thelma were rather old to be taken for streetwalkers?

"Don`t worry . She said we can wait in her house . It wont hurt us to wait . Obviously something important has delayed her ." Queenie was secretly quite pleased about the delay . She had made the mistake of discussing tonight`s venture with Violet next door and received a very dusty response .Vi reminded Queenie of her parent`s beliefs and made no secret of the fact that she found fortune telling evil . She had also made many uncalled for comments about visitor`s Queenie had received recently saying that she " didn`t hold with darkies leaving their own country " . She`d said that she `d felt it her duty to speak plainly since Queenie`s parents were no longer around to keep an eye on her . " What would your mum have said to you inviting darkies into the house eh ?" she`d asked . Queenie had told her to mind her own business whereupon Vi had become so upset she`d burst into tears .

This had made Queenie cry too . In the end they had both apologised to each other which had only occasioned more tears .

Leah's house turned out to be a very ordinary double fronted terraced property with a dark green front door and net curtains . Queenie felt disappointed and became even more so when the door was answered by a small boy who ushered them into one of the front rooms . It all seemed so ordinary . There was a strong smell of frying and the sound of a television coming from the back of the house . The room they were in had the anonymous air of a dentist's waiting room .There were chairs arranged around the walls and a coffee table with various well used magazines strewn on it . The room was badly in need of refurbishing too and smelt musty and unaired . There was a gas fire burning quite unnecessarily which added to the airlessness .

It was worse than waiting to see the dentist Queenie thought . Neither she or Thelma said a word for several minutes nor did either of them pick up a magazine to read .The small boy entered the room again ." Mum says the first one can come in at half eight – soon as "Eastenders" has finished ""he announced.

Queenie frowned . This wasn't at all what she had been expecting . Still , to be sensible , what should she have expected after all – a gypsy caravan ? Anyway , Jimmy Ng set great store by Leah so what did it matter if her surroundings were so mundane .

" I assume that was her urgent appointment " Thelma said "Eastenders! What a cheek ! " She glanced at Queenie nervously

"Which of us should go first? I think it should be you since it was your idea ."

"If you like ." Queenie replied . Her tummy was full of butterflies . At that moment the doorbell rang and there was the sound of several voices . The boy ushered four girls into the room . There was a smell of scent and cosmetics as they took seats around the room and much shrieking and giggling . Everyone began to talk at once ."You been here before ?"a pretty blonde girl asked Thelma . " No ." She answered nervously "Have you ?" It turned out that all the girls had been before . Leah had told them amazing things . She was uncanny they said .

This did not really make sense to Queenie . If they had been before why would they want to come again ?But suddenly the sound of music told her that " Eastenders " had come to an end . It was time to consult the oracle She rose to her feet and made her way to the opposite room .Leah turned out to be a jolly looking lady with curly yellow hair and very pink cheeks . She looked completely ungypsy like and put Queenie at her ease immediately .

" Sit down Duck .Sorry you had to wait for a bit but I can`t miss Eastenders and for some reason they changed the time tonight . Some people prefer "Coronation Street " I know , but I`ve always liked" Eastenders " . I can tell you prefer the street though ."

" Really ? How ? " asked Queenie , fascinated because what Leah said was perfectly true .

" There`s a lot of things I can tell about you . Give me your hand " Leah instructed . Queenie did so . There was a few seconds silence .

" I can see worry here . You` ve had a problem . Something that bothers you very much . It stops you sleeping at night and gives you a guilty conscience . Am I right ? " Leah looked serious . Bright red in the face , Queenie could do nothing but agree . This was astonishing .

" What can I do about it ? " She whispered .

" All I can tell you is that things will eventually get better with that particular problem . You must be careful to think before you act . You are inclined to be impulsive ." Leah paused . " You have many good friends who are concerned about you . Some kind of loss is indicated . There will be be tears but you will recover ."

"Oh no " gasped Queenie ." The loss will be a gain in the long term " Leah said enigmatically. She released Queenie`s hand and produced a crystal ball which she stared into intently .

" You have an interesting future ahead . I see travel – long journeys in aeroplanes . I see success in business but you must take care of your health Is there arthritis in the family?

Queenie nodded . Leah assumed a faraway expression . " There is an old lady here with a stick .She says her name is Doris – no Dorothy ." Queenie blanched . " That`s my mother ." she quavered . " She seems very agitated . I`m getting the message that she`s worried about you . She wants you to think before you act . She doesn`t like the company you`re keeping and she`s concerned about ..."Leah paused ". She`s gone now dear but I think she was bothered about your diet . Now there`s a man with a moustache , whistling . I get the name Fred ? Would it be yourfather? Queenie nodded . Her head was reeling . This was too much . It had to be true . Leah could not have known these things unless she had some supernatural power . Leah had much more to say which Queenie though she had taken in but later realised she had forgotten The consultation over , she stumbled out in a state of utter confusion.   Thelma pounced on her as soon as she entered the waiting room

161

" What did she say to you ?" she queried in a hissing whisper clearly audible to everyone in the room but already Leah was shouting " Next please " and she was forced to go . Queenie sat back in her chair and closed her eyes . The waiting girls forebore to question her as she looked so shaken .

Meanwhile , Thelma was surprised by Leah's appearance too . She hadn't expected someone quite so ordinary and friendly looking . She placed her lizard skin clutch bag on the table and it was immediately seized by Leah who stroked it several times before putting it down . She appraised Thelma silently whilst doing this .Her next words shocked her client .

" This bag is'nt yours is it dear ? " Thelma , embarrassed , had to agree . The bag had belonged to the late Mrs.Honeyspan .It had been far too good to throw away so Thelma had kept it although she disliked reptiles.

"It belonged to someone who has passed on I can tell ." Leah continued . " She suffered terribly but is at peace now . Now give me your hand dear.There's no need to be shy or frightened of me ." She held Thelma's hand for several seconds before looking at her palm .

"You've had a hard life . There's been lots of hardship and sorrow too but things are much better now , am I right dear ?" Thelma nodded

" Things haven' t been too bright lately but there's a lot of contentment in store , I can assure you of that. I'm getting the name"Kate" Would that be your mother?" Thelma gulped and finally managed to gasp out her agreement .She was terrified . This could not be right . Leah continued

" She says she's very peaceful now dear . She wants you not to worry about her . She keeps coming and going . Ah here she is again . She's trying to tell me something . She says she forgives you for keeping her illness a secret . You must not lose your faith she says ."

" Tell her I wont. " Thelma sobbed , but Leah was continuing "Somebody else is coming through . I'm getting the name Muriel . Does that mean anything to you dear ? "

"Yes. " sobbed Thelma . Muriel was the first Mrs .Honeyspan

.

" She's at peace too dear . She wants you to know she's grateful to you . She bears you no ill will whatsoever ." There was much more but Thelma was too upset to pay attention to it . She shouldnever have come here she told herself . It simply wasn't right .

On the way home in the taxi Thelma trembled uncontrollably . " We should never have gone there Queenie " she wailed ." I don`t know why I was tempted . The Bible warns against it . It can`t be right." Thelma tapped her fingers on her lap in an agitated manner . She had told Queenie what she could remember of Leah`s message but Queenie had been more selective in what she had revealed .

" Oh don`t be so silly Thelma " She replied irritably . " What have you got to worry about ? You only had good news ." Privately though , she agreed with Thelma . She was feeling very apprehensive about what Leah had told her . " It will be worse before it gets better" she had said What could that mean other than something very ominous ?

At home , Thelma tried to watch television but could not concentrate . Leah had brought it all back to her . All the worry and secrecy following the doctor`s announcement that Mother had inoperable lung cancer  Thelma knew that her mother would have been unable to cope with the truth so had allowed her to believe that she was suffering from TB ,an illness she`d had many years before. Three weeks before her death she had even colluded with her in the belief that she required a new winter coat to wear when she " was better ". She recalled clearly the visit to C&A in Portsmouth and mother so ravaged by illness they could find nothing to fit her properly . Still she had tried to joke " I always wanted to be slim and now I am . Shame I had to wait until I was 83 ."

They had bought a coat in the end – a heather coloured tweed with a velvet collar but Mother had never worn it . That had been her last shopping trip . In fact , less than two weeks later she had been taken to the hospice . Thelma had managed to convince her that it was a special kind of sanitorium . Several times she`d said to Thelma in a frightened sort of way

" You`d tell me if I had something awful wouldn`t you Thelma ? You wouldn`t keep it from me ? "

" You know I would mother ." Thelma had lied stoutly . Afterwards when she had discussed the deception with Pastor Mawson he had told her that she had done exactly the right thing and should not reproach herself Somehow , though she kept on feeling guilty about it .Now, from what Leah said Mother had forgiven her so she should be feeling better but she did`nt . And she could never tell anybody from the mission that she had visited a clairvoyant . That would really place her beyond the pale . It was true , she decided , fortune telling was the work of the devil . No good could come of it .

Chapter 36

Iris dragged herself up from the sofa where she had fallen asleep and looked at her watch . Good Heavens! It was after seven o clock . She must have dropped off just after 4 pm . What a waste of time ! She had planned to cut the grass , a job that was long overdue and then drop in on both of the old ladies since she had not seen either of them for weeks . She hadn`t walked Nellie yet either or made any preparations for her evening meal .Not that she felt at all like eating anything .Her appetite seemed to have disappeared . There was a sour taste in her mouth and she could feel the beginning of a headache behind her eyes It was so unlike her to fall asleep during the day though . She had brought her tea into the sitting room earlier on intending to have it and then take Nellie out , but the tea tray remained untouched . She must have fallen asleep soon after she`d sat down . This is what happens when you don`t sleep properly at night she told herself .

She had no fear of being alone in the house now . Cyril Gotes had definitely gone away . Rose had told her this two weeks ago . When she had first returned here after the attack she had contemplated selling the property and for a while could not bring herself to use the en suite bathroom . However she had forced herself to behave normally and this seemed to have paid off in that she no longer felt nervous in bed and was able to take a bath without thinking about what had happened .

Within herself though matters were far from resolved . She lay awake for hours in bed thinking about the futility of her life . About to go to the Ladies Floral Group social evening a few nights ago she had suffered what she could only describe as a panic attack and found herself unable to leave the house . She seemed unable to raise any interest or enthusiasm for any of her normal activities and even mundane chores like housework which one did almost without thinking required an effort she felt unable to make .

She went into the kitchen where Nellie bounded over to her with a reproachful look . For about twenty seconds Iris wondered irritably whether she wouldn`t be better off without a dog . Life would be so much easier . She would not have these demands made on her then . But Nellie sat down so obediently and waited for Iris to attach the lead to her collar , looking so expectantly at her the while , Iris` heart melted . She hugged the animal . How could she regard her as a nuisance ? The two left the house .

She noticed with surprise that it was a beautiful summer evening . Summer seemed to have happened without her realising it . With a slight shock she calculated that midsummer`s night had been and gone . What had happened to the time she asked herself , deciding to take the path leading to the common . As she crossed the road two boys came round the corner . They seemed to be arguing over a can of soft drink . One tried to drink from it whilst the other grappled with him trying to grab it . With a yell of triumph the first boy raised the can above his head and threw it into the air where it emptied some of its contents at Iris` feet and over her shoes . The can then bounced into the gutter . The other boy swore at his friend but neither of them apologised to Iris or attempted to retrieve the can . They simply walked on ignoring her complete .

Without thinking what she was doing she ran back and grabbed the perpetrator by the back of his tee shirt . " Scum " she yelled at him . " Go back and pick up that can . Go on . Pick it up and put it where it belongs !" Her voice was strident and sounded alien to her . The boy was clearly frightened . He couldn`t be more than twelve she realised . Suddenly she felt sick . What on earth was she doing ? This was not like her at all . Nevertheless the boy did not argue . He did as he was told while his companion looked on in silence . Then they both ran away . She continued on her way feeling sick and ashamed . She wasn`t in the wrong she knew that  But she should not have behaved like a harridan . Why couldn`t she control herself ?

On the way home Nellie disappeared into the undergrowth for several minutes . Iris called her irritably and she suddenly emerged carrying something in her mouth . " Drop it Nellie " she ordered and obediently the dog did so . It was a used condom . Iris shuddered in disgust . She kicked it away . It was all of a piece she thought . all part of the rottenness that was life today .Oh well ,she might as well go and see the old ladies and get that chore out of the way. Or at least ,one of the old ladies She could not face both of them this evening .

Ethel Jerram was cross . She made it plain that she thought Iris had been neglecting her and would not be mollified . She`s aged , Iris thought , even in the past month . The wrinkled face looked like a piece of dried fruit , especially now when her mouth was set in that disapproving downward scowl . Eventually Ethel invited her indoors . She limped slowly down the hallway ahead of Iris her dowager`s hump cruelly exposed by this back view . Once settled in her armchair she eyed Iris acidly . " If you hadn`t been so busy you might have known that I have been very unwell . The doctor almost gave me up . Still , I don`t expect you`re interested in my state of health . And of course you won`t know about Ada Simey . She`s gone now.“

“ Gone . Do you mean dead ? “ Iris was shocked .

“ No .Of course not . Gone into a home .” Ethel said querelously . “ Where I shall have to go before too long the way I feel .You`ll know all about it yourself one day . You`ll be old too .”

“ That was very sudden . “ Iris commented , doing her best to ignore Ethel`s umbrageous mood .She had learned from past experience that this was the best way to deal with it .

Pleased to have a visitor and eager to talk, Ethel soon overcame her hostility and proceeded to tell Iris all about Ada`s decision to move into the home . “ It`s not very far from here Iris . A lovely old house in beautiful gardens Ada says . They let her take several bits of her furniture to put in her room and she can have visitors whenever she wants . They have sherry parties and bridge evenings . Perhaps we could go and visit her one afternoon? I know she had her ways but now she`s not here I miss her, I must say .” She went on to tell Iris all about her own failing health , the various pills she had been given which did no good at all , and how she could not get off to sleep at night . Iris was her first visitor for some time and it was as if she had days of stored conversation waiting to be used up After a while Iris stopped listening .

How selfish the elderly were she thought . Ethel was only interested in herself . It would never occur to her to ask how I am . Is this what I shall be like in 25 years ? She looked at the old lady closely , seeing the wrinkled , prune like face , thin white hair and frail , humped body as if for the first time . Ethel`s nose jutted out of her sunken cheeks like a grotesque beak Iris saw , and in the sleeveless cotton dress she wore on this warm evening the flesh on her arms hung off the bones and jiggled as she spoke . Iris shuddered inwardly . This is what she had to look forward to she told herself grimly .

As soon as she could decently leave without antagonising Ethel , she did so promising her that , yes , they would visit Ada together soon and that she would call in again within the next few days . As Ethel let her out she reached for Iris` hand and pressed it saying “ You`re a good girl Iris .” This unexpected gesture brought tears to Iris`eyes so that she had to move away quickly ,fearful of breaking down . Nellie , waiting patiently in the front porch lumbered clumsily to her feet and they crossed the road to their home . It was still broad daylight Iris noticed

There was an untidy looking parcel lying on the front step . It was a brown paper carrier containing two pots of marmalade.There was no note but Iris knew that they had been brought by Queenie . Might as well put them straight into the dustbin now she thought . Queenie would insist on making the awful stuff which never turned out quite right and then palming it off on her friends . The last lot had not set properly but somehow she had not liked to throw it away so had taken it to the church Bring and Buy instead where it had probably been bought by some unsuspecting old lady . Then there was that awful chutney that was still lurking in her larder . Why on earth did Queenie bother she thought with irritation .

Indoors she could not face the thought of food . She made a pot of tea instead and took it into the sitting room . She would have to stay up as long as possible tonight to ensure she had a good night's sleep she decided . Perhaps there was something on television worth watching She switched on staring in puzzlement at the picture which appeared on the screen . It looked like two men or no , they were two dwarfs but one of them seemed to have only one leg , fighting in the nude . Odd . She raised the volume . It was a man's voice , concerned and thoughtful .

"Les and Danny are gay and disabled . All they ask is the right to a sex life like everyone else. Should we deny then this ?

" In the name of God ! " Iris shrieked as she turned off the set . Then the telephone rang . She was strongly tempted to ignore it . Bound to be somebody selling double glazing or even worse funeral savings plans . That was the latest thing on offer . Still , better see who it was . It was Queenie . Iris listened to her in exasperation . It became obvious that the gift of marmalade had been in the nature of a bribe . It seemed she wanted Iris to accompany her to a car boot sale of all things which was taking place the following Sunday . The thing was she had no way of getting to Plummet's fields without a car and she just wondered whether Iris would be interested in coming along

"Frankly, no" Iris answered her shortly ." Don't you think you've got enough junk Queenie ? I should have thought you'd be better employed getting rid of the stuff you've already got . I'm afraid I've got better things to do than hang around with all those peculiar people ."

Queenie chattered on but Iris was only half listening. Then her attention was caught,she could hardly believe her ears . Apparently that afternoon a strange man had called on Queenie with some trumped up story about being an antique collector . She had not only invited him in but given him tea and then shown him round the cottage

167

. " Are you out of your mind Queenie ? He was a complete stranger! He could have murdered you ! " Iris was outraged at her stupidity and even more so when Queenie chose to argue about it saying how nice the man was and obviously a gentleman .

" Listen to me Queenie . Didn`t you learn anything from what happenned to me ? And that was somebody I knew , not a complete stranger . I sometimes wonder where your brains are ! " Iris was so furious she put down the phone not caring whether she`d offended Queenie or not.

Chapter 37

After Iris 'rather churlish (Queenie thought) refusal to accompany her to the car boot sale she had regretfully given up her plans for the outing . Then luck intervened . Wandering around her front garden after breakfast that Sunday morning with no clear plans in mind for the day , Queenie had begun to deadhead a trough of pansies in a desultory sort of way . She noticed Bert Armstrong next door loading up his van with working materials and watched in some surprise knowing that Bert had been forced to retire from his work as a painter and decorator following a nasty fall from a ladder almost two years ago. Even then , he was well past normal retiring age .

Well into his seventies now , he occupied himself mainly with growing dahlias and was reputed to be something of an expert in this field Queenie could not help herself from walking over and enquiring about his activity .

" You're surely not going back to work Bert ? " She enquired , after bidding him good morning .

" In a manner of speaking , though I shan't get paid for it ." He replied ruefully . " Our Linda's eldest has moved into one of those places out Retford way and it needs doing up badly . One of those so called " starter homes " but so jerry built you wouldn't believe it . I said I'd give our Gordon a hand but none of these youngsters seem to have much idea when it comes to getting a job done ."

" Lucky for them that they've got such an obliging grandad." Queenie said . A thought struck her. " Don't you go past Plummets fields to get to Rettford ? " She asked and when he nodded she begged " Oh Bert , Please take me with you . There's a car boot fair there and I'm dying to go ."

" Of course I will midear , but how will you get home afterwards ? I shall be working until late ."

" Don't worry . I'll find a way somehow .Let me get my jacket" Queenie went back to the house breaking into a run when she reached the path . Bert couldn't help laughing to himself . Queenie was a rum one and no mistake . Fancy wanting to spend this lovely day looking at piles of second hand rubbish when she could be in the garden . There was nowt as queer as folk .

Nevertheless , he had a soft spot for Queenie . He remembered her as a golden haired little girl of about five , looking at h im through the garden fence and asking plaintively " Will you play with me Bert ?" Old Mrs. Mack had been a bit of a tartar and had not allowed her daughter to play with local children .

Three hours later , laden down with assorted bags and bundles , Queenie took stock of her situation .There was no way she could get this lot home without getting a taxi , but how on earth could she find one stuck out here in the middle of nowhere ? There wasn`t a phone box to be seen but perhaps if she started to walk there might be one further down the road ?   She tried to adjust her parcels to balance the weight and   realized that the last purchase she had made , a Chinese teapot in a wicker basket was about to burst out of the plastic bag into which it had been crammed .Why had she bought that stack of "Gourmet"magazines she asked herself . They were the heaviest things of all . All sense seemed to desert her when she was faced with a bargain she acknowledged . In fact she might have even have to ditch the magazines in a litter bin if a taxi was not available soon . Now it looked as if it might rain too She placed her bags on the ground to give haerself a rest and looked around her .A vehicle hove into view.Perhaps she could thumb a lift ? Even if they only took her to the nearest telephone box it would be something . She had never tried such a thing before but there had to be a first time for everything . Tentatively she raised her arm . The car slowed down as it neared her and she was aware of raucous , derisive laughter .Two tough looking young men were in the interior . " Wanna lift love ?" one of them sneered while the other laughed at her scornfully . Queenie looked away feeling scared and foolish and waited for them to drive off .

Another vehicle approached but this time she kept her head down . Thumbing lifts was not a good idea after all she decided . The car slowed down and then stopped . Then she heard somebody call her name and looking up recognised Jimmy Ng who was regarding her with concern .

" Queenie . What are you doing here ?"

Queenie was so relieved she could have hugged him . " Oh thank goodness you saw me , I don`t know what I should have done if you hadn`t appeared ." She repeated this remark at intervals all the way home . Jimmy was concerned that Queenie had put herself into such a vulnerable position and made her promise not to be so foolish again " If there is somewhere you would like to go I will take you . Promise me that you will ask me first. I , too , enjoy the car boot sales ." It was the strangest thing . Apparently Jimmy had been wandering around the car boot sale all morning yet neither of them had noticed the other .

Queenie was thrilled . " You`re the very first person I`ve met who likes to look at junk . Everybody else seems to turn their nose up .I thought there was something strange about me . Now Jimmy you must come home with me and have some tea . You can taste some of my cooking for a change. I made a cake earlier on And while you`re there I shall show you some of my things ." She was delighted with this knowledge she had gained about Jimmy Ng which seened to show him in an even better light than she had previously regarded him .

As they emerged from his car however , Queenie could not help noticing the net curtains twitching at the house opposite whilst Violet Armstrong her next door neighbour did not attempt to conceal her scandalised expression as she watched Jimmy Ng follow Queenie up the garden path .

Whilst they drank their tea , Queenie showed Jimmy her purchases . He admired the teapot and the Doulton figurine she had also bought which was only slightly chipped . Queenie showed him how she would repair it to make the damage unrecognisable .

"And then you will sell it again? " he enquired

" Well no . I hadn`t planned to .But perhaps you`re right .There is so much stuff here now . I suppose it would make sense to get rid of some . I`d love to do a car boot sale but then it would be impossible without a car ."

" I could help you . I`d like to ." Jimmy smiled at her " We could share a stall at an antiques fair first of all . You could sell some of your china and I would sell Asian artefacts .I have lots of things to dispose of . And what we don`t sell there we could take to a car boot sale ."

" Do you really mean it ? " Queenie`s eyes shone with delight . " I`d love to do that. You don`t know how often I `ve wished I had a friend who enjoyed the same things as me ."

Queenie was overwhelmed at her good fortune in meeting this remarkable little man .

" I`m really lucky to have met you ."

"On the contrary . I am the lucky one For me it is a pleasure to know you ." Jimmy said this completely without embarrassment as if it were a fact entirely beyond dispute and his attitude dispelled any self consciousness Queenie felt at the exchange . They smiled at each other in satisfaction .

Chapter 38

Iris settled Nellie in her basket and prepared to leave the house
. She was beginning to feel at ease there again . Now that Cyril Gotes
had definitely gone - news which Rose had passed on to her just a few
days ago - the worst feelings of disquiet about her home had
disappeared . She had tried to put the whole episode out of her mind
but once or twice she had had nightmares in which Cyril Gotes
featured and at one point she had moved to another bedroom and then
even contemplated moving house as a means of ridding herself of the
unpleasant associations . Then anger had forced her to rethink the
situation . Why should she allow the behaviour of one loathsome
individual to force her out of her home ?She returned to her old
bedroom and made a point of lingering in the bathroom and this
strategy seemed to have worked .

Within herself however , matters had not been resolved so
easily . She found difficulty in sleeping and was irritable and edgy as a
result . Sometimes when engaged in her usual activities she would feel
overcome with feelings of futility to the extent where her own
thoughts frightened her . Other times she felt unaccountably angry for
no reason that she could fathom. She also seemed to have developed
an unreasonable anxiety about meeting people to the point where even
normal , pleasant social occasions like her quilting group became an
ordeal to be avoided at all costs . She did not understand why she
should be feeling like this .

Last week at the dentist she had picked up a glossy magazine
and saw an article entitled " Are you a natural victim ? " Reading it to
the end she was forced to the horrifying conclusion that this was just
what she was . Since then she had been unable to identify the feelings
of what the article had described aptly as "unworthiness " which she
was unable to shake off . Was all this due to what had happenned to
her or was it the inevitable consequence of being a " natural victim "

And who could she talk to about it ? Agony aunts wrote
glibly about counsellors but the thought of obtaining professional help
made her feel worse . On the other hand , she could not carry on like
this . Perhaps she should visit her GP but he seemed to regard any
middleaged woman as sufferring from menopausal problems
regardless of what symptoms they presented to him . She did not feel
that HRT was the answer and she knew that this would be his
suggestion .

Now she was on her way to pick up Queenie , not that she felt
in the least like going out this evening but she knew that Queenie

would be disappointed to be let down at the last minute. Tonight was the club's annual "Bring and Taste " supper an event Iris usually enjoyed . This evening the speaker was to be Eamonn O'Riorden although what he could talk about to interest 80 or so ladies was a mystery , Iris thought .

At Queenie's suggestion , again stressing her loneliness , Iris had telephoned Thelma and invited her to come too . The invitation had been in the nature of an olive branch . Iris had not apologised to her as such but had made it plain that she was anxious to remain on friendly terms . Thelma however had been rather distant in manner and had turned down the invitation on the grounds that she was " far too busy thank you ." Iris felt snubbed . Even if she was busy which she doubted there were politer ways of declining an invitation . Never mind . She would certainly not ask her again . Lonely indeed ! She had never taken to Thelma during their schooldays and now felt just the same about her . People didn't change really .

In the car on her way to Queenie's Iris still felt cross thinking about Thelma . Then it struck her that the fact that people didn't change must apply to her too .What did that say about her ? She remembered that silly game they had played once when she'd been in the sixth form . At that age they were always analysing themselves and pointing out each others weak points , terribly hurtful sometimes like the time Beryl Savill had been told that she dressed like a tart . She'd been practically hysterical and stayed off school for over a week .

That particular day , Iris recalled clearly , they'd all been sitting on the grass after lunch and Caroline Beasley had said they should all write their names on a piece of paper and pass the paper amongst the group who would associate their name with a colour . She'd been reading about it in an American magazine she'd said . According to this American psychologist everyone's personality corresponded to a colour . So they'd played the game. When they'd finished Caroline collected the papers and distributed them to their named owners .

There was much shrieking and giggling as they were read . Iris looked at hers . There were five colours written on it . Somebody – it had to be Sylvia Crooke though because of the purple ink – had written eau de nil then crossed it out and put " classroom walls colour ." The classroom walls were a a dirty , wishy washy shade . Not exactly green or grey but an indeterminate colour . She had never liked Sylvia Crooke after that . Somebody else had written grey whilst another girl had written beige . Worst still , somebody had put " No colour " whilst the last one of all simply said   "Don't know ". That was CarolineBeasley because Iris recognised the backward sloping hand .

She felt crushed . Is that how she appeared to others ? Fortunately the bell for afternoon school had rung and prevented any discussion of the results because she knew she would have broken down in tears had they been discussed openly . Nobody seemed to notice her reaction . Iris felt again the smarting pain she had felt that day . She supposed though that it was all true . She wasn't a forceful person . She didn't stand out in a crowd . It must have been obvious even then .But was it so terrible to be colourless ?

Absorbed in these thoughts Iris almost missed the turning to Queenie's street and braked fiercely .There was an ominous rattling from the the basket containing her tuna surprise . The lid must have come off the casserole dish. She hoped it it wasn't slopping about in the basket. Queenie would have to carry it on her lap . She'd said she would be bringing some kind of dessert . Iris just hoped that the ingredients she'd used weren't past their sell by date . No matter how often she warned her about it she took absolutely no notice . It would be a fine thing if she poisoned half the local ladies but it would take something like that to make her learn her lesson Iris knew .

She pulled up at the kerb and there was Queenie waiting to close her front door . My God ! What was she wearing ? Iris stared . From this distance it looked like some kind of Hell's Angel outfit . As Queenie approached the car however Iris could see that it was a sort of all in one jump suit in a black , soft , leather type fabric . The things she'd thought were studs were in fact small silver buttons . How very unsuitable . Iris shook her head . Queenie really was over the top . Somebodywould have to tell her for her own good . Anyone would think she was a teenager and not a middle aged woman .

"What about my outfit ? Do you like it ?" Queenie asked delightedly , turning around to give her friend a really good look . Iris couldn't help noticing that her hair had reverted to its former piebald colour where it had grown out at the roots and was also badly in need of reshaping .

" It was on the "nearly new "rack at the Guides jumble last week and I just couldn't resist it . It was only five pounds . I bet it cost the earth new ."

" It's quite ridiculous on somebody of your age " Iris was about to say but something stopped her .Queenie seemed so pleased with herself why should she spoil it for her ?"

" It's grand. " she said instead . " Can you carry my basket on your lap Queenie ? I'm afraid it might spill otherwise . What have you brought ?"

" It's a prune and almond tart " Queenie answered " it sounds funny I know but it tastes really good . Especially if you serve it warm . Who is the speaker tonight by the way ? I 've lost the list you gave me ? "

" Oh ....nobody special " said Iris and they went on their way .

When they walked into the parish hall Selina Stanton was waiting in the lobby . She collected t heir 50 pence , took charge of their raffle donation and then comandeered their supper offerings which were placed on a side table . " I suppose she wants to inspect them before she lays them out " Queenie whispered to Iris . Selena turned and glared at her briefly . Iris forebore to remind Queenie of what had happenned at last year's supper when the lemon cream sponge she presented had shown the clear imprint of a cat's paw .

Queenie couldn't help but notice that the box of soap Iris had given for the raffle was one she'd given her for Christmas . Obviously she didn't like violets .Not that she could carp since she herself was disposing of an unwanted gift in her case some writing paper and envelopes edged with an ugly floral design .

" We have a very interesting talk for you tonight ladies " Selina said." Eamonn. O'Riorden has very kindly agreed to talk to us about his experiences over the years in the grocery trade . He's called his talk " 40 years in retailing ". Queenie blanched . She looked through the doorway into the main hall and sure enough there was Eamonn O'Riorden standing by the platform with his wife Margaret . She was dressed as if for a very grand occcasion in a satin dress and sparkling necklace and earrings . By contrast , Mr. O'Riorden himself was wearing a handknitted pullover under his tweed sports jacket .

" Come along Queenie " Iris said . "We should be able to get a seat at the front since we're so nice and early ."

"Er , I must go to the loo " Queenie said , panic stricken . "Don't wait for me Iris . I may be some time.And don't bother to save me a seat , I'm better at the back because of ... my eyes" She fled to the lavatory with both Iris and Selina exchanging puzzled glances after her. Queenie remained in the ladies room for a good ten minutes emerging only when she could hear Selina calling the room to order . She wished she could sneak off home but instead slunk into the back of the hall pretending not to see Iris or Rose who had saved her a seat and were gesturing wildly at her from the front row . Surely Mr. O`Riorden would not recognise her from this distance ?

Eamonn smiled warmly at the ladies and wished them a very good evening. Unaccustomed to public speaking ,he assumed an earnest , sonerous manner as he began his talk , almost as if he were reading the lesson in church but as he got into his stride his presentation improved . In spite of her discomfiture Queenie soon became interested in what he had to say . He described his early years as an order boy with Liptons just after the war when rationing was still in force . He spoke of the black market , weighing up pounds of tea and sugar by hand and carrying whole sides of bacon to be hung on hooks from the ceiling in the store . He described the introduction of frozen food in the ninteen fifties and the advent of self service stores . The talk was enlivened by many amusing anecdotes . In fact , Queenie had to admit that he was a really good speaker . How had he kept his Irish accent she wondered if he had lived here for all these years . She supposed it came from his parents .

Then came the surprise . Eamonn finished up by telling them that , due to his enforced retirement he had sold his shop to a Mr. Patel who would be taking over the business as from next Monday . There was a shocked intake of breath throughout the hall at this bombshell . Selina hurriedly rose to her feet .

" Now ladies , as we are running rather late I can allow just a few minutes for questions before we break for supper ."

A stout , elderly lady in the middle of the hall did not address the speaker but turned to her neighbour and said loudly " The only thing I want to know is why couldn`t he sell the business to somebody English ? " Selina rose to her feet again looking flustered .

" I should like to ask about shoplifting ." She said " Is that much of a problem in an area like this ? I`ve heard it`s on the increase ."

Queenie held her breath . She really could not bear this . It seemed to her then thar Mr. O`Riorden was staring straight at her as he gave his answer.

" I`m afraid I have to say yes to that question " He said ponderously , pulling down the welt of his fair isle jumper which had ridden up over his tummy . " Unfortunately , shop theft as I prefer to call it , is a very prevalent problem here and in my experience it isn`t the poor old age pensioners nor your widows or poor people who are responsible . You would all be amazed if I told you the people I`ve caught at it ." Eamonn had abandoned his public speaking voice now and asssumed his normal . chatty manner . Obviously this was a favourite topic of his and he wanted to tell all .

" Yes . " he continued " Some people round here are hardened shoplifters and it's always the last folk you'd expect......." Here he raised his finger and seemed to point it directly at her . Queenie stiffenned . She was going to faint unless she took control of herself . She'd simply have to look away and think of something else until he'd finished . Oh , why had she come here this evening ? Wasn't the experience in Sainsbury's enough ? she asked God . She had promised herself that never again would she take anything else without paying for it . Obviously her punishment was meant to continue . God meant to ram the lesson home . She forced herself to pay attention.

" And it's not the basics these people steal either , I can tell you . It's always cream and not milk . It's always your red salmon . not pink . It's always your four star brandy and fillet steak. I put it to one woman once . I said to her   " If you were that desperate , I said , that you had to steal a tin of fish why didn't you take mackerel eh ? That's only 35 pence a tin It's just as nutritious . Why did you have to take red salmon ? " It seemed that Eamonn was becoming carried away . Selina decided it was time to intervene . She got to her feet and waited foa pause in his monologue .

" Well I am sure that everyone joins me in thanking you for a most interesting and enjoyable talk Eamonn . And it goes without saying that both you and Margaret have our very best wishes for your retirement . Ladies please show your appreciation ."   There was prolonged applause and even more when Margaret was presented with a bouquet and Eamonn received a bottle of single malt . Then everyone was bidden to the buffet .

" You look terribly flushed Queenie are you feeling all right ?" Rose sounded concerned . " We saved you a seat .Why didn't you join us ?"

" Oh I'm fine now thanks . My tummy felt a bit funny before . I thought I'd better stay near the door . Just in case ."

" I know what's wrong with you . Youi've been eating that food from the market again ." Iris voice was accusing ." You'll never learn ."

" Now ladies , there's plenty of time to chat later . Please do come and help yourselves now"   Selina practically pushed them towards the supper table where , in spite of her haste , there was still quite a queue . Queenie saw that Eamonn and his wife had already got their supper and had seated themselves at a small table in a corner .

She relaxed slightly . Provided she gave them a wide berth everything might be all right .

"Shame about poor old Eamonn " She heard the woman in front of her say " His cataracts are so bad now he`s practically blind . He`s been waiting for so long for the operation he`s decided to go privately ." Her neighbour tutted .   "Such a nice man , too . That explains why he sold the business to the first person who offered ."

Suddenly Queenie felt positively light hearted . " Could we go and have a drink afterwards ?" she asked her friends . " My treat ."

Chapter 39

They didn't go for a drink after the meeting much to Queenie's disappointment . Iris said she didn't feel up to it and Rose did not try to dissuade her . Queenie was feeling so relieved and happy after the experience with Eamonn O'Riorden she would have liked to celebrate what she thought of as a reprieve , but she had no choice but to go along with what Iris wanted. After all she was the driver.

Queenie was worried about Iris . She seemed so strange these days. Sometimes so impatient she was positively rude , other times listless and apathetic . She seemed to have no interest in anything . Rose had noticed it too . Queenie had heard her ask Iris if everything was all right but she did not even get a response . Iris either did not hear her or simply chose to ignore the question . On the way home in the car Iris was silent . Normally she'd have been gossiping with Queenie about Margaret O'Riorden's over the top outfit or discussing the food they'd eaten.

Queenie made several attempts to start such a conversation but Iris did not take her up . After a while she , too , fell silent When they drew up outside Queenie's house Iris merely said "Good night Queenie " and started up the engine .

" Will you be going to the bring and buy at the parish hall on Saturday morning ? " Queenie asked , knowing full well that Iris would be doing the coffee as she alweays did . " No " Iris answered shortly , and with that she drove off . Queenie walked up the path feeling very perplexed and rather cross . Perhaps she had inadvertently offended her ? If so , she wished Iris would have it out with her instead of all this silence and sulks . Then she noticed something strange . Her garage door was ajar . But it hadn't been opened for months . She was suddenly aware of the beating of her heart and there was a horrid , sinking feeling in her tummy . There must have been a break in . There was no other explanation . Oh God what should she do now?

Better not go in . Whoever it was could still be there . Terrified now , Queenie took to her heels and raced next door where she hammered on the door .Bert Armstrong came to the door in his night clothes and was not best pleased .

" Bit late to come calling isn't it ? " he said shortly " We've been in bed for hours . Pensioners need their rest " he added , to make quite sure she got the message . He didn't have his dentures in she noticed .

Then Bert looked at Queenie and realised something was wrong. Immediately he was all concern , ushering her indoors and offering brandy Telephoning the police took longer than she expected . She`d never had cause to dial 999 before . In a quavering voice she explained her fears and was told to stay put and await the arrival of the police . Vi Armstrong came down then to see what was going on . " Oh hello Queenie " she said as if it was the most normal thing in the world to receive a visitor at 11 .10 pm . She wore a voluminous winceyette nightdress with a long gents cardigan over the top and her hair was done up in old fashioned metal curlers . Queenie couldn`t help staring because they were the same kind her mother had used years and years ago .Vi went pale when she heard Queenie`s news.

" My God , Bert . That van ! " Vi almost shrieked the words . Bert blanched too . " You don`t think ..." he began but Vi interrupted him .

" There was a van outside your house for a good half hour earlier tonight . I saw the men bringing things out . I said to Bert " Looks like Queenie`s getting rid of some stuff at last ." Those men walked in and out cool as you like. We didn`t think anything of it did we Bert ?"

" No , we didn`t " Bert said contritely . " I`m sorry midear . We should have been more alert but you don`t expect burglars round here ." He looked very upset and his sympathy seemed to make it all worse somehow . Queenie burst into tears . " You couldn`t possibly have known " she said through her tears .

Two policemen arrived and accompanied Queenie back to her house . At first nothing seemed obviously amiss and the house did not appear to have been ransacked as she had expected . But then she noticed gaps here and there . An old corner cupboard had gone together with its contents. Her television and video were missing and her collection of CDs . Two pictures had been taken from the sitting room walls and her silk rug had disppeared too. In the dining room her candlesticks had been taken and a number of small silver objects . Upstairs things seemed largely untouched apart from her jewellry box which lay upturned on the floor , empty of course .

The policemen told her she was fortunate the house had not been trashed but when they entered the kitchen they looked grave . There was a saucepan of water , almost boiled dry now , bubbling on the stove . She shrank back in horror when they explained that this was a common ploy used by burglars who were unarmed . If taken by surprise they could use the boiling water as a weapon .

The most upsetting thing of all came a few moments later when Queenie took the policemen into the store room leading to the garage . Apart from her bookshelves and a few odd items of bric a brac , the room was bare. Her precious collection of china had gone . All the tea chests had vanished as well as the boxes containing her prized collection of children`s books . It was all too much . Queenie began to sob brokenheartedly . She had an enormous collection of childrens books which she begun to collect when she was only a child herself   Quite apart from their value which was considerable now , they meant such a lot to her . And her lovely china which she had never enjoyed properly because there was nowhere to display it .

" These theives knew what they wanted." the older policeman remarked ." Any people round here know about your collection?"

" Only my friends ." answered Queenie . She was suddenly filled with a feeling of dread .No , it was impossible . She could never think badly of Jimmy Ng . But she had shown him everything she had and he had expressed particular admiration for her mother`s jewellry which was much too heavy and ornate for Queenies taste . No . It was out of the question . Then relief flooded through her

" I`ve just remembered " she told the policeman .  " A man called round here a few weeks ago . He was a really charming man  I thought , not a criminal type at all . He said he couldn`t help noticing a piece of china I had in the window and wondered whether I might consider selling it to him for his collection . I`m afraid I invited him in . It seems so stupid now but he seemed so genuine and nice . He admired all my things and I was stupid enough to show him everything . I must be a complete fool "

Queenie remembered Iris` warning now and felt even worse . The police would think she was absolutely batty and Iris would no doubt be delighted that her predictions had been correct . How could she have been so foolish ?

The policemen shook their heads . " It happens time after time " said one " No matter how many warnings we give about doorstep visiters , these people get away with it again and again. It`s usually the really old folk who are taken in ." Or the stupid ones like me Queenie thought feeling ashamed of herself .

After ensuring that Queenie was all right the police left saying that somebody would call in the morning to take a statement from both herself and her neighbours . They also promised to send a crime prevention officer around to advise her about future security . They were not at all optimistic about her prospects of retrieving her property however .Queenie could not wait for the men to leave her in peace . She felt drained of all feeling . She realised now that this burglary was no random misfortune . It obviously meant something . First there was the super market incident , then tonight's episode with Eamonn O'Riorden and now this .

It was God's way of balancing the scales she decided and all part of the price she had to pay for her past behaviour . Natural justice in a way . God was really working overtime to teach her a lesson . And how could she complain about being stolen from when she had been a thief herself , albeit an unconvicted one ? The kind policemen had been concerned about leaving her on her own . They asked if they could telephone someone to come and stay with her but Queenie assured them she would be quite all right . She did not feel at all nervous about being alone in the house. Why should she ? Nothing else would happen now she knew.   She did feel the urge to talk to somebody but it was far too late to ring Rose now . The cats lay cuddled up together on their cushion seemingly quite unperturbed about what had happenned . She supposed she should emulate their behaviour .

Chapter 40

Rose sat in her garden enjoying the sun . Skipper lay at her feet . He seemed to have become as attached to her as he had been to his previous owner and all her attempts to make him more independent had failed . Meanwhile she could go nowhere , not even to the loo without taking the animal with her . Failure to do so resulted in banshee like screams which could shred your nerves in seconds .

Then there were the cats , Furlong and Purrfidia . Rose had not bargained for boarding them but a frantic visit from Gerald on route to the airport had left her with no choice but to take them in. Shamefacedly , Gerald had confessed that the cattery had refused to accept them   because he had neglected to ensure they had been vaccinated . It had slipped his mind he'd said because he'd been so busy with all the other arrangements . Now with only hours to go before their flight to Athens he was desperate . " I know it's an absolute imposition " he'd said and Rose had rather taken him aback by saying " Yes , Gerald .It is .I'm beginning to feel put upon to say the least . "

And she meant it . But she'd felt bound to accept the cats . Fortunately Skipper was used to cats and the animals co habited peacefully . There had been a postcard from Gerald this morning . Apart from describing the weather and the view it said nothing . Rose was anxious about both the men . On their last day together in the bookshop before their holiday she'd felt she had to confront Gerald with her fears about Eric's health .

" It's AIDS isn't it that Eric has ? " Rose had just come out with it and was then amazed at her own temerity . Gerald was on his knees unpacking a box of books at the time . He didn't answer at once but simply looked at her in a strange , searching way . Looking for some indication of censure or distaste she supposed . At the same time his expression was one of
complete misery . Rose went straight to him and took him in her arms . For a moment he stood rigid then with a gasp he'd collapsed weeping into her embrace. Awkwardly , she did her best to comfort him . After a while she detached herself ,went to the shop door and put up the " Closed " sign .

" I'm going to make a pot of tea whilst we pull ourselves together." She'd said . Gerald had blown his nose and nodded .The tea making gave him the opportunity to compose himself so that when Rose carried in the tray he was almost himself again .

" I wish you`d felt able to tell me before about Eric . Gerald . " Rose said , handing him his cup and saucer . " Not that I could do anything to alter things . I`ve felt very left out though . Almost as if you didn`t trust me ."

Gerald shook his head . " Please don`t feel like that . First of all , it wasn`t my place to tell you .That was Eric`s responsibility . You`ve been such good pals I was sure he`d say something to you sooner or later . I`m afraid there`s something of the ostrich in both of us . But it isn`t just that. Until you asked me that question I couldn`t guarantee that you were even aware of our relationship . No Rose .." as she began to protest " I`m not suggesting that you are naïve in the extreme . Or like Helen . But we`ve never discussed it have we ? I would have been happy to but you never raised it . I assumed it was a matter you`d rather not know about . Most people seem prepared to tolerate people like us as long as we don`t thrust it down their throats as it were. There`s a tacit acceptance that we don`t discuss it . I`m glad it`s out in the open now ."

" What about you . Have you got AIDS too ?" Rose too felt relieved that she could talk openly at last . " I`m not even HIV positive . God knows why ." Gerald said heavily .

"And is Eric as ill as he looks ?"

" Yes . I`m afraid so .You always hope for a miracle of course but" Gerald became tearful again . " We`ve been together for over 30 years now . I just can`t contemplate life without him ."Gerald blew his nose loudly . Then he`d begun to talk of something else .

Rose` thoughts turned to Queenie . Poor thing . She`d telephoned this morning to tell about the burglary at her cottage . Strangely , Rose thought , although she`d been upset about losing her possessions , she`d seemed to adopt a very philosophical attitude to what had happened . Rose rather admired her for it . She would call on her later this afternoon she decided ..Meanwhile it was time she put in at least an hour on some weeding. She rose from her chair .

In the garden she saw a car pulling up outside the house . The driver , a stocky, redfaced man in his fifties , went to the passenger seat to help out the occupant , a heavily pregnant woman . With delight Rose saw that it was Evie, how nice of her to call with her husband . Rose had never met Stan Piper . She advanced towards them smiling broadly but stopped in her tracks whn she saw the look on his face . He was positively glowering at her . Evie too, looked equally grim .

" Is there something wrong ?" Rose feared she was going to be told about some terrible tragedy .

"Yes there is but it`s not something I want to talk about on the doorstep . We`d like to come in if you don`t mind ." Evie`s voice was menacing. Once inside the house though she immediately burst into tears .

"For God`s sake Evie ! I told you not to come here if it was going to upset you . I would have told her ." Stan advanced on his wife and clumsily tried to comfort her . Rose looked on in dismay .

" I don`t know how you could do it Rose knowing me like you do . I could hardly believe it when our Darren told me . He`s finished with Hayley for good now . My own grandchild ! "

Hayley had obviously spilt the beans about the abortion Rose realised . She had been advised to discuss it with no one .

" Evie , You know I would never do anything to hurt you . I know what you must think but it wasn`t that simple . The decision was Hayley`s . It was not for me to discuss it with you much as I wanted to."

"That`s not what Hayley said . According to her you were the one who told her to get rid of the baby . What do you know about babies anyway eh ? You`re a spinster and an interfering old biddy into the bargain . Why don`t you mind your own business ?" Stan said truculently . He was a man of few words usually and had surprised himself with his own eloquence .

" I understand how upset you must feel ...." Rose began but Evie interrupted her . She was redfaced and furiously angry now

"You don`'t understand at all . You`re nothing but an interfering busybody . You had no business getting involved in my family`s affairs . When I think of how much I respected you I could kick myself . We`ve lost a grandchild through you ! That child would have been a playmate for mine . I could have taken care of both of them. We`d have loved it wouldn`t we Stan" She began to sob again . The man looked on helplessly.

Rose felt the greatest sympathy for them both but knew she could say nothing to defend herself or make things better.

" Come on Evie . You`ve had your say .There`s no point staying here ." Stan took his wife`s arm and led her to the door .

" I`ll never forgive you for this . " were her words to Rose as she left the house .

Rose watched the car drive away. There was no question of her gardening now .She felt much too upset to stay in the house either . She decided to go and see Queenie . First of all she would call at the florist and get her some flowers she decided . She fetched her jacket and departed .

Queenie meanwhile , had just taken delivery of her new television set . She had decided to rent one for the time being and the shop was so obliging they had agreed to deliver it immediately . It was a particularly warm afternoon and she couldn't help feeling guilty about being indoors. There was something almost well …decadent about watching TV in the afternoon especially when the weather was so nice . Her mother would never have allowed it she knew . However it was tea time and it was just a happy co incidence that tea time and Oprah Winfrey seemed to happen together . She switched on and a picture appeared but the sun was so strong she was obliged to draw the curtains in order to obtain a clear view of the screen.

Queenie placed her tea tray on the coffee table trying to ignore the empty space her lovely rug used to occupy and the gap in the corner where her cupboard had been . She was determined not to dwell upon what had happened . It was useless to upset herself about it . She must only think positive thoughts – thst's what her booklet had recommended . This was something she'd picked up in the health centre last time she was there. It was entitled   " Coping with Loss and Bereavement - A Survivor's guide ." she knew her particular loss did not come into quite that category but the principle was the same .

After the police had been and gone this morning , Vi Armstrong had come round with a cake she'd baked especially . It was date and walnut she said , and the very least she could do in the circumstances . They both felt so guilty over what had taken place they would never forgive themselves Vi told her . Then she 'd sat herself down at the kitchen table and told Queenie that it was time for some plain speaking . What had happened last night was only to be expected bearing in mind the company Queenie had been keeping lately . Her poor mother would turn in the grave if she only knew the sort of people her daughter had been inviting into the house .

" I make no bones about it and I told the police the same , " Vi continued ." There's never been any break ins round here before and it stands to reason who's behind it . Whatever was she thinking about , inviting funny looking foreigners into her home ? All the neighbours were talking about it ." she'd said.

Queenie was upset but furious too .

" I've no wish to fall out with you Vi .Or Bert for that matter . You've always been very kind to me and you're very good neighbours .But what I do is none of your business . I shall invite who I like into my home and you can tell the neighbours that too ."

Vi had flounced out , very offended .The cake she'd left was excellent though, thought Queenie biting into a large slice . She'd

spent some time this morning ringing her friends to tell them of her misfortune . Iris had responded strangely , Queenie thought . She hadn`t said " I told you so " but had burst into tears and become quite distraught . In the end Queenie had felt so concerned about her it had quite taken her mind of her own problem.s .   Rose had been wonderful though , offering to lend her a TV and even
volunteering to do some shopping or any thing Queenie might want .

Thelma , though had taken quite a different approach when told of the burglary .

"That could n``t happen here ." She`d said . " If you lived in this sort of property you`d be properly protected from burglars . You need an alarm and security blinds like mine . Of course , its impossible to make old properties like yours really secure . If I were you I`d move house . I`d never feel safe in my bed again ."

Queenie began to tell her about the security precautions the police had advised her about but Thelma did not seem at all interested and began to talk about her own concerns . She didn`t even ask her what had been taken or express the slightest sympathy , Queenie thought afterwards . In the past she had always defended Thelma when Rose or Iris had criticised her but now she was beginning to understand their misgivings .

She settled down to her viewing . Oprah was interviewing two serial killers in prison . They looked so ordinary it made it all the more chilling somehow . She watched fascinated only to be disturbed by the doorbell . Damn ! thought Queenie . Now I`ll have to turn it off . Mustn`t be caught watching Oprah . But it might just be somebody collecting for something she decided , so left the set turned on . To her surprise and delight Rose stood on the doorstep clutching a huge bunch of cornflowers .

" I thought these would look nice in that old doulton jar you have " she said handing them to Queenie and seeing her face fall .

" How thoughtless of me . I suppose that was stolen too ?" Queenie nodded . Rose followed her indoors

" Oh but I`m interrupting your tea and your viewing . " She continued .

" I`m glad it was you who caught me and not Iris " Queenie said . "She`d be really shocked at catching me indoors on a day like this . She`d say I should be in the garden ."

" But it is so easy to watch too much TV Rose said , settling herself into a chair

" And you have to agree it is a terrible timewaster . I found myself wasting so much time on it I had to devise a plan to make myself stop ."

" What did you do ?" asked Queenie , thinking guiltily of many long winter afternoons spent watching old films .

" I moved my TV into the kitchen " Rose told her . " I know it sounds strange but it works very well . There are no comfortable chairs there you see so I`m not tempted to linger . It takes something really special to make me sit for more than half an hour on a hard chair .You should try it ."

" Oh I don`t know ." Queenie answered . " I`m not really a busy person you see so it doesn`t matter if I waste time ."

" Well , as a matter of fact , that`s partly why I`m here . I was on my way to place an ad in the "Echo" for somebody to help out in the shop when I suddenly thought of you . It`s only part time and not at all well paid but I know you love books and it would mean that I could have a bit of time to myself . What do you think ? " Queenie was blushing with delight .

" Oh Rose ! I`d love to . I can`t think of anything I`d like more . You are so kind and thoughtful to think of me . Now – let me offer you a cup of tea .Afterwards I`ll show you what the burglars did ."

The bell began to ring again at this point. Queenie went to answer it . Rose heard her talking and another familiar voice answering . She was surprised though when Queenie ushered May into the room . May was equally surprised to see her .

" This is a very kind lady from " Victim Support " come to offer me some help . " Queenie told Rose .

" Oh but May and I are old pals " Rose answered . "Aren`t we May ? " We work together every Monday in the charity shop . I never knew you did this though . How long have you been involved with " Victim support " ?

" Ever since I was mugged three years ago " May said , sitting heavily on the needlework stool .She was still wearing her winter woolly hat but had made some concession to the warm weather by exchanging her usual stout brogues for Scholl orthopaedic sandals which still constrained her bunions cruelly . Her use of this strange verb sounded almost as odd as if she had chosen to wear a baseball cap , Rose thought . Strange how people picked up these imported expressions . She remembered the " mugging ". May had been shoved to the ground by a teenage boy who ran off with her pension money outside the post office . She told the story frequently only now the boy had become a dangerous gangster whom May had gallantly fought off .

      " People do appreciate a visit when something nasty happens to them " May continued " of course I can`t do much to help but people seem to like to talk about their experience ."

      " I`m sure you`re right " Queenie joined in . " I`ll make some fresh tea if you`ll excuse me ." How fortuitous that Vi had brought that cake this morning she thought as she went into the kitchen .

Chapter 41

Queenie was puzzled and concerned . She could not get Iris to answer the door Having tried unsuccessfully to contact her by telephone for several days she had decided to walk round to Iris` house and see what was going on . The first thing she noticed was that the grass needed cutting but looking closer it was obvious that the whole garden required attention . There was a litter of dead twigs and flower heads caused by the high winds of the previous week still lying all over the path . A trellis nailed to the archway leading through into the back garden had partially blown down and several empty plant pots lay along the edge of the pathway . Queenie could see the weeds in great profusion all along the border and it was clear that no dead heading had been done for some time .

Iris must be ill thought Queenie . There could be no other explanation . She hated any kind of mess or disorder and would never leave her garden looking neglected like this .Unless something terrible had happened ? Alarmed now , Queenie walked round to the back door . If she couldn`t gain entry here she would have to call the police she decided . Before she reached the door however Nellie bounded out to greet her . Thoroughly relieved , Queenie walked into the kitchen.

Iris sat at the table in her dressing gown . She hardly raised her head as Queenie spoke ,

" Iris whatever is the matter ? Are you ill ? I`ve been ringing and ringing ."

" Oh hello Queenie " Iris` voice was dull  She looked tired and bleary eyed .    "Sorry I didn`t come to the door . I feel so tired . I`ve been sleeping so badly lately . "

" But it`s three o clock ." Queenie looked round the kitchen properly now . The bread bin was open and empty . Although the normally tidy room was cluttered and disordered there was no evidence of any food . However there was a pile of unopened mail on the table together with a stack of newspapers . " Have you had any breakfast ?" She enquired .

" I don`t feel like anything . Don`t fuss Queenie ." Her voice was irritable.

" I`m just going through to the loo "   Queenie made this remark to give herself opportunity of having a good look around . It was all as she feared . Iris normally the most particular of people had let her house get into complete dissaray . The bedroom was not too bad although dusty , but the sitting room was in a complete mess . It seemed that Iris had been sleeping on the sofa because the duvet and pillows were there and a litter of used crockery lay on the coffee table. The curtain were half closed and there was an umpleasant smell from some dead flowers . The plants on the window sill were shrivelled well past recovery and a layer of dust was on every surface .

Well she could sort out the worst of it quickly thought Queenie wishing she could sort out Iris` problems as easily . She busied herself with dusters and the vaccuum cleaner . Iris continued to sit at the kitchen table.She raised no objection to Queenie`s activities in fact she said nothing whilst this was going on . When she had finished the washing up Queenie turned to her friend .

" Iris why don`t I do some shopping for you ? Nellie can come along for the walk and when we come back we can have tea. I`ll just look in the fridge and see what you need ."

The fridge had not been disturbed for some time . Queenie could smell the milk as soon as she opened the door as well as a rank odour of stale bacon .

" I know , " she said brightly " I`ll run you a nice , hot bath . Then you can settle yourself down next door and perhaps have a little sleep until we have our tea ? "

Iris shrugged " If you like . " Queenie bustled about feeling uneasy . Iris was obviously not herself but what could she do about It ? Was it worth calling the doctor ? Iris might be cross and anyway it was hardly an urgent thing . What could she say to the doctor anyway ? But on the other hand the situation could not be ignored either . She puzzled over this dilemma whilst finishing off her work in the kitchen . She emptied the contents of the fridge into a carrier bag and carried it to the dustbin . That too , was malodorous and very full .

She tried to work out when she had last seen Iris . She`d thought first that it was two weeks but it  must be more than that . She remembered now . It was the night of the ladies supper . The night she`d been burgled . That was over three weeks ago . Iris had been strange that night too , she recalled . Of course she herself had been so preoccupied with her own concerns since then she`d hardly given Iris a thought until this week , she though guiltily .

In the Spar shop Queenie bought milk , eggs and some crisp apples She added cheese ,a packet of chocolate biscuits and some tomatoes . Then her eye was caught by a display of hair colours under a sign " reduced to clear ". There were only two shades to choose from though.In the past her attempts to colour her own hair had not been very successful probably , she decided , because she had been too conservative in her choice of shade . She would never have thought of giving herself the colour that expensive hairdresser had chosen yet that had looked wonderful . Everyone had said so.   It was worth taking a chance she decided . Raven black would not suit her at all but "Flaming Sunset the other option , was probably nearer her own natural colour . And for 99p you could hardly go wrong . She wouldn`t use it right away . It would give her a lift one day when she needed cheering up .

Walking back with Nellie a thought occurred to her . She had done all that shopping without once thinking of "taking" anything It simply had not entered her head . It was wonderful .Almost as if the awful things that had happened were worth it .

Whilst they sat having tea Queenie attempted to question Iris about what was wrong . At least she had managed to persuade her to eat something she thought later . She truly had not intended to quarrel with her , but somehow they had ended up arguing . Iris seemed to believe that she was getting at her , criticising her for not attending to her house and garden or not looking after herself properly . She claimed that she was not ill at all , merely tired and disillusioned . She said she`d been sleeping so badly that she didn`t feel like doing anything , that nothing was worth doing anyway .

" Oh Iris that simply isn`t true " Queenie had protested . " Just think of all the things you like doing . You`ve got more interests than anyone I know . Reading , dressmaking , the quilting group . And what about the chrch choir ? Then there`s the garden and all your voluntary work …and Nellie . You belong to the theatre club too . You have a very full life ". But even as she said all this she realised that she was not convincing herself . Then she `d tried to make various suggestions as to what they might do to cheer Iris up but they`d met with no response whatsoever .The last straw had been when she`d tried to persuade Iris to visit her brother in Australia . She had , after all made mention of doing this sometime this year . Perhaps she`d been too insistant though because Iris had suddenly lost her temper

" I`ll thank you not to interfere in my affairs " she`d said angrily . " Just go home Queenie and leave me in peace ." Much offended , Queenie went.

Chapter 42

Iris at at the kitchen table checking her bank statement . She`d been sitting here since before 9am and now it was after 10 she noticed . She forced herself to concentrate . She was better off than she`d thought . Earlier this year she`d toyed with the idea of taking a holiday in Australia . Her only brother had been living there for more than 25 years and she had never met his wife or seen the children who were now in their late teens.

Ronnie saw no point in returning to England now his parents were gone . He hadn`t even come back for their funeral although this Iris could not blame him fot this . He had been in hospital at the time . He had been generous too , in relinquishing his share of the family home to Iris . Not many brothers would have been as good she thought .

Although Ronnie did not write regularly he telephoned at Christmas and on her birthday and , give them their due , the children always wrote to thank her for presents she sent them . She supposed it was Roseanna , Ronnie`s wife , who made sure that contact was ensured . Men were oten thoughtless in these matters . It was Roseanna too , who invariably urged Iris to come and stay whenever they spoke on the phone . Last time , Iris had promised she would definitely make it this year but , feeling as she did now it was quite out of the question . She supposed she should write and make this plain before they began to make plans for her .

Nellie began to make impatient noises and Iris put her out in the back garden . The dog gazed back at her indignantly . Iris had not taken her for a proper walk for weeks now. She just didn`t feel up to it . But then her whole routine seemed to have gone to pot lately . She hadn`t been near old Ethel nor had she taken part in any of her usual activities . She seemed to have neither the energy nor the motivation . Iris had enough insight to know there was something wrong with her . She kept telling herself that she must pull herself together but whenever shebegan to feel slightly better something seemed to happen to drag her down again .

The latest thing was the burglary at Queenie`s which had really upset her although Queenie herself seemed just to have bounced back after the experience . Iris regretted her shortness of temper that day when Queenie had called on her and resolved to ring her her and apologise when she felt better . She heard the bell ring at this point so dragged herself up to answer it Glancing in the hall morror she saw her unkempt hair and pasty complexion but did n`r to remedy either . Whoever it was couldtake her as she was .

It was the vicar – Martin Croombeck . He was a nervous , diffident man who , although he`d been appointed to the parish three years ago , people still thought of as a newcomer . The Reverend Croombeck was a narrow shouldered , pear shapoed man who could never look tidy in spite of the constant efforts of his wife to keep him in that condition . He was not at all good looking and his appearance was undermined by its presentation . His hair now pepper and salt , was perpetually windswept and in need of cutting and his clothing in need of a brush . He drove a decrepit old volvo with two smelly old dogs in the back . The seats were covered in papers , parish magazines and bags of jumble . This morning though he simply looked concerned .

" Iris . We`ve been worried about you . May I come in ?" He walked in anyway without waiting for her permission .

In the kitchen he smiled at Iris . Although not in the least attractive to look at , he had a smile of great sweetness and sincerity . Somehow though Iris had never taken to him . His predecessor had been such a wonderful vicar whose untimely death had saddened the whole community . As far as Iris was concerned this man could never take his place .

She resumed her seat at the table and uninvited , Martin took the other chair . He could not help noticing the neglected state of the kitchen . The pedal bin was overflowing and the floor tiles were smeared . There was an untidy jumble of bottles and jars on the table whilst the sink was full of unwashed dishes which overflowed onto the draining board and surrounding surfaces . Although it was a warm morning the kitchen windows were tightly shut and there was a faintly unpleasant smell compounded of dog and , Martin realised human sweat which he knew was not emanating from him .

He spoke first . "You`ve been sorely missed Iris . We haven`t seen you for some time but I assumed you were busy with other matters . Several people have commented that you haven`t been involved in your normal activities and I did think of calling on you but , as I say I assumed you had other fish to fry . But last evening a friend of yours told me she was anxious about you and now I`ve just come from Ethel Gerram and she expressed such concern I felt I had to call . Now having seen you I wish I`d called much sooner . There is something wrong isn`t there ? "

" Who was this " Friend " ? I suppose it was Queenie Mack ?" Iris asked angrily . "People should mind their own business ." Her

194

eyes , as she looked looked back at him , had the look of his dogs when they had been scolded unjustly . A hurt , bewildered look .

"No . Actually it was your friend Rose Deacon ." Martin answered her gently . " And she mentioned you only because she was concerned I`m sure , not with any desire to be interfering .Your friends are worried about you ."

After a short pause Iris spoke .

"I dpn`t know what the matter is . " She shifted in her seat and continued

" At least in a way I do . Something very upsetting happened to me but I thought I was coping with it …and then….it was as if one day everything was normal and the next it was as if somebody had given me a pair of really strong glasses and I could see everything as it really was - rotten and nasty . It made me realise I`d been living in a fool`s paradise before . And every day that passes makes me realise just how terrible everything is .I can`t listen to the news anymore , it`s always some terrible disaster . The papers , even the local paper , are full of people being robbed or assaulted and other horrible crimes .People are so wicked now . Nothing seems worthwhile anymore . I wake up every morning and all I can think of is how futile everything is.

As for church , I don`t see the point of it anymore so don`t start quoting the bible or talking to me about Jesus . I can`t think why I`ve wasted so many years on it . I just don`t see the point in carrying on any more ." She began to cry , quietly at first but then abandoned herself to complete despair . The dog moved in then , trying to force her head into Iris` lap but received no encouragement from her .

There was a long silence . Martin sighed . He assumed that Iris` condition had been brought about by a failed romance . Nobody had told him this and , fortunately , he thought it better to make no mention of it .

"I have`nt come here to talk to you about God .I`m just here as a friend who is concerned about you . I think I understand something of what you`re going through . Something similar happened to me years ago . It`s something I never talk about but I shall tell you . This took place when I was quite young . Like you I was bowling along quite happily . I`d just taken my finals , had a job all set up and was about to get engaged . Life was wonderful but suddenly I was knocked for six . My father was involved in a dreadful scandal .Yes " noticing her surprise , " real "News of the World " stuff . I wont go into details but it was sordid and nasty . He went to prison . That was bad enough but it got worse . My mother seemed to be coping quite well I thought but then she suddenly committed suicide . To cap it all my fiance broke everything off . She said she could not cope with my grief ."

    Iris was looking at him in horror

    " Martin . I'm so sorry ."

    " Don't think I'm telling you all this to prove that my problems were worse than yours and I overcame them . There's a reason . For a while afterwards I carried on normally too , but then I started to feel exactly as you described . Life completely lost its savour . Sometimes I didn't see the point in getting out of bed . I felt a sense of absolute futility and didn't want to go on .As you feel now I think ."

    "What happened?" She whispered.

    " Some very good friend persuaded me to go to the doctor . He realised that I was ill . Yes " he continued " You may look as sceptical as you like but I assure you that your state of mind is an illness just as real as jaundice or appendicitis . And it can be treated . I am the living proof of that . It was the treatment I had and the self knowledge I gained because of it that led me into the church . I felt I'd been abandoned by God as you do now . But he was there all the time . He's here too Iris , working through me and all your friends who are so concerned about you . I know it's hard for you to believe that now ."

    She said nothing but continued to weep quietly . He took her hand .

    " Telephone the surgery now " Martin urged " and make an urgent appointment Tell the doctor everything you told me . There is medication available now which can make you feel better within a few days . All you friends will rally round I assure you . "

    That said , Martin certainly felt better whether Iris did or not . He rose from the table and went to the telephone where he dialled the surgary . Handing the instrument to Iris she had no choice but to make an appointment which was for that afternoon .

    " Iris . I will come and collect you this afternoon ." The vicar's voice was firm . He intended to make sure the appointment was kept . " I don't think you should drive at the moment " he added so that she would not feel unduly coerced . She protested weakly but eventually gave in .

    " Now . There's something else I want to say to you ." Martin sat down heavily and removed his glasses . His eyes were pink and sore looking and there were deep indents from his glasses on each side of his nose . He looked so vulnerable and unappealing that Iris felt a rush of warmth towards him . She noticed too that he was blushing with embarrassment .

        " I know I`m not a charismatic person . I`ve always felt that some members of the parish have found me wanting in some respects . It made me a bit defensive I think and not as open with people as I could have been . This is something I should have said to you long ago . I don`t think you realise Iris , just what a valuable member of the community you are . Women like you are the absolute backbone of the parsih . We couldn`t survive without you . Most of the married ladies don`t have the time or the commitment and I`m afraid we sometimes take you for granted . In fact I know we do . I just want you to be aware of how much we appreciate everything you do , not just for the church . Your neighbours value your help and concern just as much as I do . Please remember that when you feel depressed ….. There ! I`ve made my speech . Please believe that it came from the bottom of my heart" ." Martin replaced his glasses and got up to go Iris made no response but took him to the door and allowed him to leave .

Chapter 43

Queenie replaced the telephone feeling disappointed . Iris , having telephoned to apologise for quarreling with her last week , had suddenly turned nasty again simply because Queenie had raised the matter of the school reunion asking if she'd changed her mind about attending it . She'd said she found no enjoyment in such occasions , that they were just an opportunity for those girls who'd done well for themselves to show off and make people like her feel inadequate.

Queenie had never thought of it in that way . She was genuinely pleased to see those girls she had known so many years ago . It was interesting to hear their news and see the partners they had brought with them . Celia Hertridge had been married four times – once to an Italian Count – and at the last reunion five years ago , she'd brought along a much younger man who was said to have once been a famous pop star . Lucy Steiner was now an M P whilst Nymbia Drew was a well known scientist , occasionally to be seen on television .

Other old girls had interesting stories to tell about living overseas or fascinating careers . That's why the reunion was such fun . Still , thinking about it , she supposed that Iris was right really . Compared with some of the others , her life had been very unexciting really . They probably looked at the single women like them and thought poor old things , never been married or had children , never left home even . They were probably patronising them , secretly ridiculing them and finding them figures of fun . Queenie became quite cross at the thought of it . She would love to show them that she was just as interesting as they were . An idea formed in her mind . She would need to mull it over . Meanwhile she decided to ring Thelma . She felt sure that she would want to go , and so would Rose of course . But because Rose was a few years older than them Queenie had not really known any her contemporaries during their schooldays .

Anyway , the circular had requested any old girls living locally to offer accommodation to far flung people and today was the deadline for doing so . Queenie herself was prepared to do this and she knew that Thelma would be only too delighted to entertain guests . There was a list of people who required to be accommodated and several of the names were girls she remembered well . She dialled Thelma's number .

Thelma was excited about the reunion too . She had not been to one previously and relished the thought of showing herself off in her very smartest clothes to all those girls who had looked down on her years ago The thought of putting some of them up overnight was even more agreeable. That would open their eyes and no mistake . She had telephoned her offer of accommodation weeks ago she informed Queenie smugly and received letters of acceptance from all three of the ladies she had invited .

" I thought I would have a lunch party the next day so it would be nice if you could bring your guests along too " She continued . " I hope your're going to do something about your hair beforehand Queenie . It looked a rather odd colour when I saw you in town the other day . Almost two toned ....if you don't mind my saying so ."

There was a silence . In fact , Queenie did mind although she said nothing and the conversation was terminated coldly . Hurt , Queenie went to look at herself in the mirror . Could it be true ? Her hair was bound to have grown out at the roots she supposed and nobody could deny that it was in need of a cut . She had gone into the " Headmaster " shop last week only to be told that they no longer required models for their students but when she had asked the price of colouring and restyling , the quote had appalled her . She would colour it herself she decided and then have it cut at " Viola "s . It was a rather old fashioned salon but at least they charged more realistic prices and did not patronise you like those awful young men in the expensive shop . She ought to plan her outfit for the reunion too . It would be nice to have an opportunity to dress up for a change she thought .Shame Iris could not be persuaded to come though .

She reached for her jacket . She would have to hurry if she wanted to get to the wholefood shop before closing time . The whole point of the recipe she was attempting was cardamon pods and this had proved to be the very item she did not have in the cupboard . Queenie had been visiting Gishri for several weeks now to learn the basics of Indian cookery . She planned to hold a party soon when she would impress her guests with her new found skills and introduce Gishri and Jimmy to her friends . She could just picture Iris' face when she arrived and met them .

The shop was busy . Funny , Queenie remembered , because about ten years ago this shop had been on the verge of closing down because business had been so poor . There seemed to have been a sudden surge of interest in wholefoods and of course the shop specialised in organic vegetables too which had become increasingly popular lately . Although strictly speaking it was not a self service store , space was so limited that various large displays of items were open for customers to help themselves . Standing by just such a display whilst waiting to pay for her spices , Queenie helped herself to a large bulb of garlic and , quite without thinking , placed it in her pocket . It was not until she was back at home and removing her jacket that she came across the garlic .

Panic set in immediately . Please God , don`t tell me this is going to start all over again , she prayed . Just when she was beginning to feel that everything was all right . Matters had reached a pretty pass when " Taking " things had become such a habit that she did it without even thinking . Obviously her behaviour had become a habit .This would teach her to become complacent she thought . Next time she went to that shop she would make a point of paying for the item and explain that she had taken it by mistake .

She went into the back garden to cut herself a lettuce and saw that. Vi was in the garden too attending to her tomatoes . She turned away ostentatiously at Queenie`s approach . The two had not spoken since they had exchanged words after the burglary .I shall have to break the ice , Queenie thought , it`s quite ridiculous to be on bad terms after all the years we`ve been friends .

" Vi " she called " I wonder whether you`d like some raspberries ? I can`t possibly use all these and I know you like to make jam ."

Vi turned round immediately . She spoke as if nothing untoward had ever happened between them .

" Oh thanks Queenie " she answered . " I`ll come round after supper and pick them . I`ll bring you some of my tomatoes too. They`ve done really well this year .

Chapter 44

Iris was collecting her materials for the quilting group which met monthly in the homes of its members . There were fewer than 20 of them in all which meant that being the hostess was hardly a burdensome duty . In fact her turn was coming up within the next three months but all that was required of her was to prepare some light refreshmentt for the ladies and ensure there was enough seating .

The group had come about quite by chance about ten years ago . At that time Iris had been in the habit of spending an occasional evening with Ethel and Ada and taking her sewing with her . A former colleague of Ada's who'd taught needlework began to come along too and suggested that they should spend their time making kneelers for St. Stephen's . She had designed them herself to be completed in cross stitch . The vicar's wife had become involved then and several other ladies followed in her wake .

The group decided to make a huge hanging for the childrens' corner of the church and several other large scale projects had followed . Over the years various people had joined whilst others had dropped out . Both Ethel and Ada had left the group some years since and nowadays no large communal work was undertaken .Now everybody was involved in work of their choice which was sold twice a year at a special sale in aid of which ever charity was chosen by the group .About five years ago they had been joined by a younger woman , Ursula Ridditch , whose ideas had changed the group completely . Ursula , a personnel officer , was small , dark and dynamic .

The ladies had always enjoyed a pleasant evening attending to their needlework and chatting gently amongst themselves but , after about three sessions of this , Ursula had made the suggestion that they should choose a specific topic of conversation for the evening and talk only about that

." People who've never been here regard us as a lot of gossiping women . I am sure we will attract many more members if things are more structured ." she had stated .

There was a certain amount of truth in this Iris knew . Since the group had got bigger people did tend to discuss other people and gossip was almost inevitable . On the other hand , some people enjoyed the cosy , informal atmosphere and did not want to be organised by Ursula . The matter was put to a vote however and Ursula won .On the first occasion they had discussed Law and Order on which everybody had a point of view and this turned out to be an interesting evening .Other topics had been the Irish Troubles , the Welfare state and then the Menopause .It was at this point that several of the older ladies including Ada and Ethel began to drop out .They blamed Ursula for ruining their sewing club and even now , five years later , Ada could become quite vitriolic on the subject .

Iris continued to go however and the group continued to evolve . Ursula had been succeeded in the chair by Bridget Bryce , a teacher at the local comprehensive school and also the chair of the local Townswomens Guild . She had introduced speakers to the group and also been responsible for introducing their first male member , a middle aged batchelor called Robin Shea .Some of the ladies had been very much against this innovation but in the event it had caused hardly a ripple . Robin was something of an expert in gros point and his work commanded enormous prices at their sales . Apart from this he was a mine of useful information and had been the source of many of their most interesting speakers .

Although Iris had to admit that she was feeling much better lately , the medication she was taking made her feel drowsy . Tonight`s speaker was to be their local MP and she did not feel especially interested in listening to him . She decided to telephone Bridget to cancel but then remembered crossly that she had promised to introduce Rose to the group this evening . There was no way she could get out of it then . Oh well it might do her good to get out of the house for the evening , she thought resignedly .Rose called for her promptly at 7 pm . She was pleased to see the difference in Iris and , when asked , Iris agreed she was feeling much better . She put this down to the fact that she had now regained her normal sleeping pattern and no longer felt tired and irritable . She had obviously made an effort with her hair and dress which must mean she was on the mend Rose thought . She herself was dressed in trousers and a sweater . She still managed to look smart thought Iris enviously , whereas whenever she herself tried to dress casually she could not bring it off somehow . She got so bored with her safe old skirts and jerseys though .

Rose had laughed at her when she`d told her she couldn`t wear casual clothes . " That`s just a state of mind " she`d said ."Anybody can wear casual clothes these days . I`ve seen quite elderly ladies wearing jeans and looking perfectly all right ." Iris was not convinced though and continued to believe that trousers were only for gardening . Seeing Rose wearing hers so happily made her feel discontented .

They set off into the damp , muggy evening .Arriving at the home of Dorothy Hewitt , their hostess that night , the air in her hallway was that myriad compound of innumerable scents which is always found when women congregate together . Tall , plump and effusive , Dorothy greeted Iris with a warm hug . " So nice to see you Iris . I know you haven`t been well lately ." Iris shrank from her embrace . People had obviously been talking about her . She wondered just what they had been saying . Dorothy had overdone her perfume too . The scent of " Poison " was almost overpowering . Some time was spent introducing Rose which proved to be unnecessary when she and Dorothy realised that they had been schoolmates many years before .

Iris moved away and left them to their reminiscing .She was about to hang up her raincoat when somebody grabbed her arm .It was Ursula .

" Iris ! I was hoping you`d turn up tonight ." she was looking particularly animated . Why is she always so dressed up ? Iris thought irritably , looking at the violet dress and jacket in an expensive looking silky fabric which , she had to admit , flattered Ursula`s dark hair . There was something about her expression which alarmed Iris . Ursula`s eyes were gleaming and she was avid looking , as if she was about to impart some sensational gossip . She began

" What about out friend Queenie then ?Quite the dark horse isn`t she? I suppose you know all about it ?"

" What do you mean ?" Iris was puzzled.

" Her new boyfriend of course . They`ve been seen together several times now . They`re definitely an item I`m told ."

" What ?" Rose , about to discard her jacket , burst out laughing ." I don`t believe it Ursula. You`re just making it up to tease us ." But she then turned to Iris and said sotto voce

" Unless she`s been to that marriage bureau again ." She laughed once more . She seemed to find the whole thing very amusing whereas Iris just felt shocked and rather hurt too . She`d always thought that she was Queenie`s closest friend . Queenie might have said something she thought , although to be fair she had not seen that much of her lately . Then , too , she had hardly acted like a good friend of late – refusing to take her to the car boot sale as well as being rather short with her on the telephone more than once . Still , Queemie might have said something .

" I don't know anything about it " Iris admitted . " Who is this man ? Is he somebody local ?"

She hated that expression on Ursula's face . Her eyes were bright and nosrtils flared as she drew in her breath ready to speak . She was about to impart something staggering . Iris knew that look well .

" Well actually I'm told he's a foreigner . Rather a strange little man from all accounts .Asian I believe ." Watching their reaction to her news . Ursula's satisfaction was complete .

" Asian ? " Iris could hardly contain her surprise and incredulity .

" I'm sorry , but I simply don't believe it ." she said finally . Rose chuckled" I always knew Queenie had hidden depths but wherever did she find an Asian boyfriend in these parts ? there's hope for us all then , girls . However has she managed to keep it to herself though ? I saw her only yesterday and she seemed just like she always does . She's never said a word to me about a boyfriend . "

" Everybody's talking about it apparently ." Ursula continued . " My mother told me . They were talking about her in the OAP club . Violet , Queenie's neighbour is terribly upset . She said it would have broken her parents hearts if they'd known . He visits her regularly from all accounts but they've been seen driving in his car too and Vernon saw them together at an antiques fair last Sunday . He described him as a very strange little man - said he looked more Chinese than Indian .Of course , Queenie's always been rather" She searched for a word and came up with " Eccentric . Apparently he's years younger than her too . "

" An Asian toyboy ? Come off it Ursula" Rose was practically in hysterics now . Several other ladies were laughing too . Dorothy , being rather hard of hearing , did not know the cause of the amusement but was delighted that her turn as hostess was turning out to be such fun .

The evening was ruined for Iris then . She could not take her mind off Queenie . It was none of her business of course , but she was genuinely concerned about her and puzzled too . To the best of her knowledge Queenie had never had a boyfriend . That was why her revelation about the marriage bureau had been so startling . She remembered during their teenage years that Queenie had been unlike the other girls . Although she enjoyed a social life which involved the opposite sex , belonging to the tennis club and church fellowship group , she had never seemed interested in men romantically . That side of life had never seemed important to her . Nowadays of course people would simply assume she was a lesbian but Iris was convinced that this was not the case either . She supposed the word that described Queenie would be asexual .

So what did this relationship with an Asian mean ? It was all very well for Rose to laugh about it but it was not all funny . Queenie was so unworldly .This man could easily take advantage of her . He might already have done so . Queenie was quite capable of lending him money or getting involved in some stupid business deal . Were n't Asians supposed to be peculiarly business oriented ? Iris recognised the inherent racism of this opinion but the very fact that Queenie had never mentioned the friendship meant that something was not right .But what could she do about it ? She would have to discuss it with Rose on the way home .

Meanwhile all the others were having a good snigger at Queenie's expense which irritated Iris intensely . It was as if Queenie was letting the side down by giving them all cause to talk about her . It was all part of the stereotype of spinsters . They were supposed to act in a foolish way and to allow unscrupulous men to take advantage of them to provide titillating gossip for their superior married sisters ! Iris seethed as she worked on her quilted cushion cover . She realised that she was furious with Queenie . Trust her to make a fool of herself like this .

The guest speaker spoke at length about the proposed local by pass , a subject which had oncebeen of great interest to Iris because it could well affect her property but she hardly took in a word . Later , when Dorothy was serving coffee and an assortment of dainty savouries , Rose disturbed her thoughts . " Whatever is the matter Iris ?" she asked   " I thought you might have some questions for the speaker but you seemed hardly to be listening ."

Iris sighed , " I'm worried about Queenie and this boyfriend .She's so silly sometimes. This man could be taking advantage of her for all we know . I don't know what to do about it."

" But why should you do anything ?" Rose seemed genuinely puzzled . " It really doesn't concern us and anyway it's probably just gossip . Queenie's quite capable of managing her own affairs and she certainly won't thank you for interfering . If she'd wanted us to know about this man she would have told us . And if it is true – I say good for Queenie ! Now just try to forget about it and come and have some coffee ." Rose was becoming irritated Iris could tell . She left her seat and followed her to the sideboard where Dorothy was dispensing the refreshments .

" Just look at that " Rose gestured to Iris . Robin Shea was sitting at a small table with the guest speaker being waited on by various ladies whilst others hung around listening to their conversation admiringly .

" Bring a couple of men in and see how the women react ! They simply can`t stop doing things for them and deferring to them . Nobody else dares to have a conversation in case they interrupt the men because what they say is so much more important than our trivial chat ! " Rose sounded extremely scornful but Iris could not have cared less . Let them do what they want , she thought , she was still brooding about Queenie .

Chapter 45

Thelma sat at her dressing table . She had decided to turn out the drawers for want of something better to do but , on inspecting them , the job seemed to be unnecessary . She'd tweezed a hair from the mole on her chin , inspected the roots of her hair and now just sat there wondering what to do next . She really must do something about filling in her Saturdays she decided . In some ways they could seem more lonely than Sundays . Everyone else seemed to be so busy . She glanced at the clock radio . It was not quite noon . Too early still to think about lunch . Perhaps she should walk round the garden ?

She was groping for a pair of outdoor shoes when the bell rang . Delighted with this diversion she practically raced to the door but at the last moment remembered to tell herself not to seem to eager to open it . She allowed a few seconds to elapse and then the bell rang again .

It was Margot Chasey from next door . Evidently she had come straight from playing tennis judging by her clothing and the film of sweat on her upper lip . She smiled at Thelma in the most friendly way and began to chat about this and that as if they were the greatest friends . Thelma felt gratified . Margot declined to come in and got to the point of her visit . She and her husband were hosting a garden party in aid of a childrens charity next Sunday she explained and she wondered whether Thelma might like to come along ? As a matter of fact , Margot confided , she would be glad of Thelma's help as over 80 guests were expected. Thelma accepted with alacrity .

"I'd love to help Margot " she volunteered , visualising herself on the lawn handing round dainty canapes . Margot seemed delighted and made her farewell .As she closed the door , doubt overcame Thelma . Although she was delighted with the invitation which proved that she was being accepted by her neighbours at last , whatever should she wear ? She had never been to a garden party before . She must not make the mistake overdressing again . There had been too many instances of that already .Better review her wardrobe at once she decided . If there was nothing suitable there she could then spend this afternoon on a shopping expedition. .

It was on these sort of occasions that Thelma really missed her mother . It would have been so nice to share her pleasure in the invitation with her and have her advice about how she should dress for the occasion . If only she had somebody to confide in . Perhaps tonight she would telephone Queenie on some pretext or other and then casually refer to the garden party in passing ?

Now the day of the party was here , Thelma was still in turmoil about her outfit . She had decided that the only was to avoid a sartorial faux pas was to have several outfits ready and then to watch from her window the other guests arriving and see what they were wearing This had proved to be good idea . She observed now that a smart cotton dress seemed to be the appropriate attire for a lady of her maturity although some younger people wer dressed more casually.

A rnumber of cars were already parked outside her house . On previous occasions when the Chaseys had entertained Thelma had been furious about this but today she was delighted . However she was chargrinned to see Rose Deacon drive up and leave her car outside without so much as a glance . So they had invited her then ? Oh well She`d get her come uppance when she realised that Thelma was practically the hostess . Better get a move on she decided . There was already a pungent smell coming from the garden next door. It smelled as if they were barbecuing a pig You`d think that Rose might have telephoned to say that she was attending a party next door to her . Wasn`t that just typical of her sneaky behaviour ?

Minutes later Thelma stood eying herself in the hall mirror .The dress , though only cotton , had cost a fortune in the exclusive ladies dress shop in the village and it was certainly very stylish . All she needed to add were her pearls . She had already changed her court shoes for a pair of white strappy sandals and with her little white straw bag felt quite suitably attired .She had actually bought herself a very pretty hat but nobody else seemed to be wearing one . Never mind . It would always come in for a future occasion. Now feeling completely confident at last , she made her way to the party .

The property next door to Thelma was , she had to admit , far superior to hers . For one thing it was twice the size and stood in an acre plot. The Chaseys had had the garden landscaped in such a way as to give the illusion of even greater space she noticed enviously , wishing she had employed the same ideas in her smaller garden .

All the noise was coming from the back garden so she avoided the front door and made her way around the side of the house . She felt rather shy now she had to admit and perhaps these sandals were not the best choice of footwear after all . The narrow sling backs cut cruelly into her heel . She bent to adjust them just as a large red faced man emerged from a side door . He looked flustered but his face brightened when he caught sight of Thelma. Although they had never been introduced Thelma recognised him as Margot`s husband .

" Hallo .You must be Mrs Thingy from next door ? How nice to see you " he said insincerely.Thelma flushed with pleasure . What a nice man.

" Thank goodness you `ve turned up at last . I was just staring to panic. If you come this way I`ll show you the kitchen ." He ignored Thelma`s outstretched hand . Puzzled , she followed him indoors .They walked through a utility area into an enormous farmhouse style kitchen .

" There`s never enough space is there ? " he remarked " Even in a kitchen as large as this . If you let the glasses pile up though things get completely out of hand" He looked hard at Thelma then .

" You`re going to need a pinny I think and some rubber gloves . Dressed like that anyone might think you`d come to a party ." He laughed heartily , turned away and removed a large vynil apron from a hook on the door and handed it to her .There was a picture of a gollywog on it.

"There are some rubber gloves in that cupboard under the sink . Don`t bother to dry the glasses .Just leave them to drain " At the door he turned

" It `s really very good of you to help us out like this .Do help yourself to a drink or anything else you fancy ."

Chapter 46

Rose , leaving the CAB at noon , decided to call in to the bookshop to see how Queenie was getting on . She was inappropriately dressed for the weather she realised , stepping into the sunshine in her raincoat and sensible shoes . It was one of those September days that had begun cool and grey but had now turned out so warm it might have been midsummer . Other people had been similarly caught out she noticed , seeing two women in winter coats red faced and perspiring .

It was only a few minutes walk to the bookshop . Rose took the opportunity to call in to W.H.Smith to pick up a couple of magazines . She planned to visit the hospital later on and thought that they would make an ideal offering for Sandy .Whilst waiting to pay for her purchases somebody else joined the queue. It was Thelma , sporting a different hairstyle , or rather not a hairstyle as such since her hair was uncoiffed , merely hanging straight held back by a velvet band .

" I`m on my way to the hairdresser " Thelma announced as if reading Rose` mind . " But I`m glad I saw you Rose . I wanted to tell you that I shan`t be able to help you in the charity shop again . I`m far too busy these days ." She was clutching a newspaper in one hand and a large bunch of chrysanthemums in the other. " I`m involved in something rather special actually " she added enigmatically .

"That`s quite all right " Rose answered , determined not to give Thelma the satisfaction of being asked why she was so busy .

" There are always people willing to volunteer their help . I`m glad you`ve found something to occupy your time ".No matter how much she tried , she simply could not warm to the woman she thought . She had to admit though that Thelma looked much happier than before . That unpleasant sulky expression had gone from her face . Rose went on her way to the shop .

Queenie was delighted to see her and full of stories about happenings in the shop this morning .An elderly lady had taken a funny turn but had felt better after a short rest . A toddler had dropped his opened tube of Smarties in a box of books and screamed blue murder and then Queenie had accidentally short changed somebody and had not realised this until the customer had gone . Her hair style had changed too , Rose noticed . It was completely different , dragged back from her face now and secured at the back with a silk scarf . With the outfit she wore today , black leggings with a loose black and white striped tunic   Queenie looked totally   transformed . Younger and

somehow more " with it ". She saw Rose looking and explained "
All the young girls are wearing these leggings and they looked so
comfortable I had to try them . "

Rose chuckled ," I hope you're not going to try everything
these young people do .Where will it all end ? Drugs and sex orgies
?Or perhaps you'll turn your house into a squat ? " Privately she
thought that Queenie's boyfriend might have something to do with her
changed appearance . Perhaps she was trying to make herself look
younger for his benefit? Amazingly, Queenie had made no mention
of her new friend and Rose had been loath to raise the subject herself .
She knew , too , that the matter had not been broached by Iris either
although she continued to fret about it .They were both of the opinion
that Queenie would tell them when she felt ready to do so .

Rose began to tell Queenie about her plans for the afternoon.
Queenie took a keen interest in anything relating to Sandy Gotes and
was most interested in the ideas Rose had for refurbishing the house
before Sandy was discharged from hospital . To this end she had been
buying anything suitable that appeared in the charity shop and now
had a large collection of rugs, bedding and cushions . Other people had
donated items of furniture and kitchen equipment.

It had been Rose' plan to clean the house from top to bottom
before starting to redecorate and she had arranged for several
volunteers to help her tackle this job over a recent weekend but , at
the very last minute Sandy , greatly embarrassed , had begged her not
to go ahead with this work . She explained that her sister Hilda was
dead set against the idea and preferred to do the cleaning herself .
Something about not wanting strangers in in the house and "
Washing their own dirty linen ."

Rose realised then that she she might have been presuming .
In the past she had been accused of being a busy body after all and the
last thing she wanted to do was upset Sandy's sister . But surely she
could not object to the house being redecorated or to the new
furnishings ? It would be so marvellous for Sandy to reurn home and
find her house transformed . "Couldn't I persuade Hilda ?" she had
asked but Sandy did not answer.

" How is Sandy herself ? I know you'd said she 'd lost weight
but is she any happier ?" Queenie enquired .

" Much more cheerful and positive in outlook these days .
She's reconciled with her daughter now which has helped enormously
, and losing weight has made her much more mobile . They have her
exercising in the gym there every morning and now she actually
enjoys it . She loathed it at first . I think she expects to be discharged

before the end of the month . That`s why I was so keen to get on with the decorating . I`m, so looking forward to seeing her face when she walks back into that house . Of course I need to persuade her sister first ." Rose was full of enthusiam about the project .

"Talking of transformation " Queenie said , changing the subject " "Isn`t it amazing to see the change in Iris She`s almost back to her old self . I`m so glad she went to the doctor in the end "

"Oh yes ." Agreed Rose " I was so worried about her . It`s such a relief to see her responding to the medication . Now shall we have some coffee ? I bought some chelsea buns and if we have one now I shan`t need to bother about lunch . I mustn`t stay long though . I`ve got Skipper in the back of the car and you know how he hates being left alone."

Skipper was the problem later when Rose arrived at the hospital . It was much too hot to leave him in the car but she could not risk allowing him to see his mistress either fearing it would only upset them both . In the end she tethered him to a tree trunk thankful that the hospital buildings were far enough away to make his shrieks inaudible . The hospital had formerly been a stately home and still retained a large portion of the original parkland surrounding the house . Rose skirted her way through the beautiful garden . Although still imposing from the outside , the interior of the house had been disembowelled to create the specialised facilities required by the patients . Sad in a way , thought Rose looking at the partitions which disfigured the beautiful high ceilinged hall , but necessary no doubt .

The ward Sandy occupied was in a new outbuilding joined to the main house by a seemingly endless corridor . As Rose walked doiwn it she could observe various activities taking place in the rooms to the left . There were intriguing signs on the doors too whilst windows on the right of the corridor overlooked the well kept gardens . Apparently the patients themselves were responsible for maintaining the gardens which would be useful therapy Rose thought . As she approached the ward she could hear raucous laughter and soon she was able to see Sandy and some other young women enveloped in a cloud of cigarette smoke . The TV set was on , set to such a high volume it hurt the ears but nobody appeared to be watching it .

Rose had to approach the small room where Sandy sat through the main ward . Here several old ladies sat in chairs arranged around the walls . Some of them dozed but othere just gazed into space . No members of staff were visible An embarrassed silence fell as Rose entered the smoking room . Almost choking in the atmosphere , she asked if she could open the french windows but then unable to bear the stuffy room she suggested to Sandy that they should sit outside .

On a seat in the garden they chatted . Initially , Sandy had been shy of Rose but now she had lost all her former reserve . She told Rose proudly that she had now lost almost three stone in weight

" Well we must get you some new clothes then ." said Rose but Sandy said she would prefer to wait until she had reached her " target ". This meant , she said , that she would have to continue with her rigid diet for some time yet . Not that rigid , thought Rose who had been present last week when Rita had arrived with a large food parcel .

It amused Rose to hear Sandy using the jargon she had acquired during her treatment . She discussed her "addictive personality " and how for many years she had been " in denial " concerning her husband's behaviour . Today she was full of what she had learned about " Bio feedback" as a way of coping with cravings .

" Dr. Shah wants me to come back to the hospital as a day patient after I've been discharged " she told Rose ." I don't mind though .The girls are really friendly and I shall be able to use the gym free of charge . It's just for three days a week ."

Rose gave Sandy the home magazines she'd bought earlier and they discussed how the house could be re decorated and what colours and materials to use . Pink was her favourite colour , Sandy said , adding that she preferred a silk rather than a matt finish for the walls . A figure approached them across the grass . It was a woman and on seeing her Sandy coloured and became silent . The woman was tall and painfully thin with a pale complexion relieved by reddened , chapped cheeks and the sort of naturally curly hair that is so frizzy it looks like a bad perm .She had a thin , bitter mouth and a hard done by expression on her face . She did not smile when Sandy introduced her to Rose .

" This is my sister Hilda ."

" Pleased to meet you ." Hilda said , but she did not look it . Nor did she take the hand proffered by Rose or return her effusive smile . She did not join them on the bench either although there was plenty of room . Instead she stood awkwardly a yard or so away with a scornful expression on her face . It was hard to believe they were sisters Rose thought . They seemed completely different in every way . Rose attempted to continue the conversation about the house , trying to draw Hilda into the conversation by telling her about the plans they had already made but she made no positive response . Nor did she demur when Rose asked if it would be all right if they began their decorating at the weekend . Instead she just stood there . Sandy became tongue tied , obviouslyfinding her presence inhibiting and soon Rose began to feel uncomfortable too . Perhaps I`m in the way , she thought . Perhaps she wants to talk privately to Sandy ? Better make myself scarce .

Gathering her things she made her farewell promising to come again next week . She told Sandy she planned to make a start on the decorating this weekend .Coming to the end of the long corridor some minutes later , Rose was aware of footsteps running behind her . It was Hilda   redfaced and breathless from running . She gasped

" I wanted to catch you before you went but I didn`t want our Sandy to know I was going to talk to you ." She had a strange , hoarse voice and spoke the words awkwardly . She was wearing a washed out cotton frock Rose saw now , in a style that had been fashionable about 15 years ago , with a long white cardigan slung over one shoulder . She was obviously ill at ease , fiddling with the strap of her plastic shoulder bag and rubbing one foot behind the other The red leather sandals she wore were cracked and discoloured .

Whenever she saw badly dressed people Rose longed to introduce them to charity shops . In her experience it was the folk who needed them least who seemed to patronise such places . Yet people like Hilda seemed to think it was somehow demeaning to shop there . She wished there was some tactful way of telling her this . Then she pinched herself mentally . It was none of her business what clothes Hilda chose to wear . She smiled at her .

" Perhaps we could have a cup of tea . I`d love to have a chat . To be honest I think I owe you an  apology . I think I unintentionally offended you about my plans for cleaning the house . Sandy  said you were cross about it . I really didn`t mean to cause any ... " But Hilda interrupted her

" There`s a WRVS canteen near the entrance . We can go there if you like. There`s seats ."

Two elderly ladies , deep in conversation were in charge in the vast tea room .There were packets of biscuits to be had and small cakes wrapped in plastic but Hilda refused any of these . Nor would she allow Rose to pay for her tea although it cost only pennies . Not wishing to cause further offence , Rose did not argue the issue . The tea was unpleasantly strong and served in nasty little plastic beakers but at least there was nobody else in the room and they could hold their conversation privately .

Seated on bent wood chairs at a wobbly table , Rose waited for Hilda to speak . She took several gulps of tea before doing so . Eventually , not looking at Rose she said flatly

" You`re wasting your time helping our Sandy ."

" What do you mean ?" Rose looked at her in astonishment .

" No . Don`t say anything . I`ve got to say this . I know she`s my sister but she`s a dirty , lazy little bitch . Always has been ." Hilda spoke bitterly . This conversation shamed and embarrassed her but she had to see it through .

" Oh she`ll let you clean her placece for her , but I tell you straight , in a few weeks time it `ll be as bad as ever . And I wont be going round there any more to clean it up .I`ve had my fill of it ." She put the beaker down and folded her hands across her lap .

" But surely . Now that she`s had the treatment here and got rid of that dreadful man things will be different ...." Rose began .

"Don`t you believe it ." Hilda`s tone was vicious . " I`ve got no time for Cyril . Never had . He`s a nasty piece of work . She was warned not to marry him but she would have her own way . But at least he was clean . How he put up with that lazy , dirty bitch I`ll never know ."

" But ..She`s your sister " Rose said , immediately realising how stupid that remark was .

" It was our Mum`s fault , " Hilda continued ignoring Rose . " We were all grown up when Sandy was born . She spoiled her rotten . She gave her everything she could never afford to give  us , chocolate , toys , dancing lessons . Whatever she wanted she got . That`s why she was always so fat . Mum was forever stuffing her with crisps and sweets . Course we were all earning then and she could afford it . And she never asked her to lift a finger around the house .Treated her like Lady Muck , waited on her hand and foot .

Now me , I was scrubbing out the lavatory and peeling eight pounds of spuds before I went to school in the morning . And I wasn`t even 11 years old . But I was the eldest girl you see . It was expected of me . We all told Mum she was ruining Sandy but she wouldn`t have it " My little darling " she used to call her . Then her little darling got herself pregnant when she was only 16 ." Hilda was vituperative . " She wanted to marry Cyril . God knows why . Mum hated him . We all did , but Sandy had to have her own way . She got herself pregnant on purpose . I`ll always believe that . So they had a big white wedding . Mum cashed in her insurance and paid for the lot . Three tiered cake and everything . Me , I had to save up for three years for my wedding . And even then we couldn`t have a big do . I wasn`t dressed in a white dress . A suit from C&A had to be good enough for me . But that wouldn`t have been good enough for our Sandy . She had to have the full works ."

Again the bitterness was evident in Hilda's voice ." Her house was always a tip . If it hadn't been for Cyril those kids would have been taken off her ..I used to see them as babies lying there in filthy nappies crying their little hearts out while she sat in front of the fire reading magazines . She'd lie in bed on Sunday morning until midday while he got the dinner ready . If he hadn't done it there'd be no dinner . Mum used to go there when she could to clean the place up even when she was crippled with arthritis . Then when they went abroad she'd worry herself sick wondering how Sandy and the kids were getting on . It killed her in the end . The worry of it all . You don't know the half of it ." Hilda looked at her properly now for the first time , indignant , challenging .

Rose felt slightly sick . She said " Are you trying to tell me she can't have help because she doesn't deserve it ? If so I 'm afraid I can't agree with you ."

" You must please yourself . I can't stop you doing what you want . All I know is if she fell down a sewer she'd come up smelling of roses. Nobody ever helped me .I've always just had to get on with it."

" I can see you've had a very hard life . It's understandable you're bitter " Rose began but Hilda interrupted her again . She spoke fiercely , scornfully

"People like you don't understand anything . I know you mean well . You'll make the house look lovely . She'll be all smiles and gratitude . And you think you'll call round again in a few weeks and everything will still be nice .But I know our Sandy that's all .The place will be a filthy , stinking tip in no time and she'll be quite happy to sit back and let you clean it up all over again . You'll think to yourself " Why did I bother ? These people aren't worth it ." Hilda was crying now and wringing her hands in her frustrating attempt to make Rose understand .

" What I'm trying to say is that we're not all like our Sandy . I'd rather die than have someone clean up after me . But if somebody did that for me I'd ...keep my place like a palace .. Do you see what I mean ?"

" I do . I do . Please don't upset yourself like this ." Rose was almost in tears herself . She felt extremely foolish . How could she have been so .....lacking in perception ? What Hilda said had explained a lot . The half amused , half sympatheteic look of the medical social worker who 'd been there one day when she'd been visiting Sandy made sense now . She tried to give Hilda a reassuring touch but she snatched her hand away , then turned and faced Rose again . She looked really angry now . Her whole face was red .

" You say you understand but I don`t think you do. People like you get off on feeding on the problems of people like us . I can just see you telling all your friends " I  did everything for her but it was all complete waste of time . You  know what these people are like . They don`t know any better. " Hilda crudely parodied Rose` accent . " If our Sandy needs help she can get it from the social  Why don`t you just mind your own business ? "

There was a long silence . Eventually Rose , red in the face , spoke

" You`re right Hilda . I`ve made the most terible mistake . You must believe me when I say that I did not intend to offend anyone . I thought I was helping your sister . It made me feel pleased with myself to think that we were making things better for her . I did have expectations of visiting her and seeing her life transformed . I feel a fool now . Of course we`ll go ahead and get the house ready for her . I can`t go back on my promise . But whatever happens then is up to Sandy . How she chooses to live is her own affair of course ." Rose mopped her brow . She had seldom felt so ill at ease.

" You must do as you like . I`ve just told you the truth . And don`t you go telling her what I said . It`ll only cause trouble. I`m going now ." Hilda stood and put on her cardigan . She replaced the chair under the table and looked at Rose again

" I don`t hate her you know . She is my sister after all . It`s just I know her inside out. It`s not even her faultt. My mother made her like she is"

" I`m glad you felt able to talk to me Hilda ." Rose spoke sincerely . " It can`t have been easy for you . I know how hard you`ve worked to help Sandy . I only wish I had a sister like you ."

" Yes . Well I`ll be off then ." Rose heard her footsteps echoing down the corridor . She sat on until the noise faded away .On the way home she felt very angry with herself . She had done it again . It didn`t matter how good her motives had been . She had been a busybody . The worst kind of Lady Bountiful . And she had so little self perception it had to be pointed out to her ..... Well , she had to be grateful to Hilda for showing her what she couldn`t see herself . But would she ever learn her lesson ? Sunk in depression , Rose drove home .

Chapter 47

Iris was going to the reunion after all . It was Rose who had persuaded her . Apparently the numbers of people wishing to attend had been far in excess of any previous reunion .So many in fact that the small committee were quite unable to cope without calling on volunteers to help . Rose had volunteered to help with the catering and had then inveighled Iris to join her . " You `ll have to get involved Iris . We simply can`t manage without you " she`d coaxed , which was why Iris and several other middleaged ladies were now sitting in the draughty parish hall on a dull , autumnal afternoon making plans for the grand buffet .

At the start of the meeting Ruth Critch the chair person had read out a list of apologies from ladies who`d been unable to come today . Queenie`s name was among them.Iris had raised her eyebrows at this .

" Other fish to fry I suppose " she`d whispered to Rose who made no reply Ruth had continued

" And we have received a very generous cheque from Thelma Riley. She had hoped to be of help with this committee but has been prevented by another commitment . This cheque is in lieu of her help . A very nice gesture I thought ." There was some half hearted applause . Rose and Iris exchanged glances .

"We have two priorities ladies" said Ruth , getting on with the main business . Obviously there was no full length mirror in her bedroom . She was dressed in a handknitted suit which clung so tightly to her plump contours the ridges made by her underwear were clearly visible. Her large front teeth were slightly crossed and caught the light as she spoke . Iris remembered her arriving at the school from somewhere in the north of England when she was about 14 . Her parents had insisted that she outgrew her old school uniform before providing her with the bottle green outfit required by the girls grammar school which had led to her being given the nickname of " Bluebird " still used by her friends . She`d retained her Lancashire accent too and really didn`t look that much different than she had in 1954 apart from the fact that her hair was now snow white . She`d been the chair of the Old Girls Committee for many years now .

" The best possible buffet at the lowest possible cost ."

" But surely the money we are charging will be perfectly adequate for a splendid buffet ? We could buy everything in from Marks and Spencers Why should we be penny pinching ? " objected Penny Fleete . Some of the ladies sighed . Penny had always been awkward and argumentative even in the third form .

"The whole point of the reunion – or rather the reason behind it – is to raise money for the school fund ." reproved Ruth " The governors would not have given permission for us to use school facilites otherwise . Anyway we should regard it as a challenge . We have so many excellent cooks here tonight there should be no problem in providing an excellent buffet at a fraction of the cost quoted by outside caterers . Now – shall we discuss menus and give ourselves an idea of approximate costings ? " The meeting settled down to work.

An hour later Iris yawned and looked at her watch . The proceedings seemed interminable . Nobody seemed able to agree about anything and some people – Penny Fleete for instance –seemed to make objections just for the sake of it . It was always the same with these committees .You got the same old faithfuls ending up doing all the work and the same people wasting everyone's time . She wondered that Ruth Critch still had the energy after all these years . She herself certainly had n't . Why had she allowed Rose to rope her in for it ? Her mind wandered and afterwards she was surprised to discover from Rose that the two of them had been given the task of preparing two poached salmon and several pounds of sundry salads .

They were about to cross the main road on their way back to Rose` house for tea when a couple approached them pushing a pram . Rose spoke but the two walked briskly past without even acknowledging her . Iris looked at Rose in surprise and saw that her face was red and that she looked upset .

" Rose , wasn't that Evie Piper ? And that must have been their new baby in the pram ! How could she be so rude ? " She was astonished .

" It's my own fault , I'm afraid ." Rose said ruefully . " I upset them both very badly over that business with Hayley Beale . They `ll never forgive me for that . I seem to make a habit of offending people these days ." She sounded so fed up , so unlike her normal self that Iris felt alarmed .

" Nonsense Rose .You'd never deliberately set out to hurt anyone . I know you better than that .If the Pipers choose to take offence they can just get on with it . I've never heard such rubbish ."

" It's not just Evie I'm afraid . I've badly upset Sandy's sister too .I thought I was helping but it seems I was just interfering . I seem to have become rather an expert at it ." Rose realised she was upsetting Iris and strove to become more cheerful .

" Any new about Queenie ?" she continued . " I saw her yesterday but she still hasn't made any mention of her Asian friend ."

" I was going to ask you the same thing . I haven't see her for ages " admitted Iris " She didn't send me a birthday card either which is very unlike her . But I suppose she's busy with her new friend . That's if that story of Ursula's was true ."

" I think it must be . Several other people have mentioned it to me . In fact , Selena said she'd seen Queenie with a party of Indian people at that new restaurant in the High street . " Days of the Raj " it's called .You know what Selena's like . She was completely agog but I just pretended I didn't know anything about it. I've tried pumping Queenie once or twice but she just keeps mum ." Rose sounded amused

" I'm surprised she hasn't confided in you though . You are her closest friend after all ."

" I think it just proves she's ashamed of it ." Iris said triumphantly . " You know Quieenie . She's usually full of everything that's happenned to her . She's the last person to keep things to herself . She obviously knows we'd disapprove of this man ."

" But I don't disapprove of him and I don't know how you can . You don't even know him . It's thoroughly unfair to take a dislike to somebody you havent even met." Rose sounded exasperated

" Anyway , one lesson I've learned very thoroughly during the past few weeks is to mind my own business Now lets talk about something else . Where shall we prepare these salmon ? Your kitchen or mine ? I think I have a slightly larger oven than you." Diverted , Iris began to discuss salads .

Chapter 48

Thelma was preparing breakfast for her guests . It was such a pleasant , sunny morning that she`d decided to serve the meal in the conservatory . Given the choice . all three of her visitors had requested a continental breakfast which had necessitated her rising early to dash to the continental pastry shop for croissants . Of course she could have used frozen ones but they simply weren`t the same . She decanted orange juice into a large Waterford jug , so heavy she could hardly lift it and opened several varieties of jam which she placed in crystal bowls . There was cheese on offer too as well as yoghurt and a selection of cold meat . She sighed with satisfaction . There was just time to nip out and cut some flowers to place on the table to add the finishing touch .

Thelma felt very pleased with herself this morning . Her guests had been visibly impressed by her home and had all expressed their admiration to a gratifying degree . It had also been a delight to observe her neighbours taking note of the smart cars parked in her driveway . Let them wonder what I`m up to she thought . And then let them wonder why they haven`t been invited . She was still smarting from the shameful treatment meted out to her at Margot`s garden party. There had been no further invitations from next door and Thelma had made a point of being icily polite when Margot had telephoned to thank her for her services .

Perhaps the most gratifying moment had been when the ladies had arrived last evening . Thelma could hardly believe her eyes when she had seen the stout person emerging from her car. Deirdree was simply enormous. She must be a size 24 at least , Thelma had thought warming to her immediately . It made her feel positively sylph like in comparison . Maggie and Alice had arrived together a bit later and again Thelma was delighted to note that although they weren`t as large as Deirdree , they both looked older than she herself did . Nor was their clothing a patch on hers . In fact , Maggie looked as if she had come straight from walking her dog . None of them had bothered to colour their hair either she noticed in surprise though she herself had been for a root touch up yesterday morning as well as a manicure . Maggie was the only one to have married but since she was now divorced Thelma felt that she was one up on that score too . All in all she had been delighted .

The ladies had enjoyed a pleasant evening together . Thelma had prepared a sumptuous cold buffet and everyone had tucked in . She herself did not approve of strong drink but she had naturally provided it for her guests although it had surprised her to see Deirdree enjoying it in quite the quantities she had taken . It seemed to have little effect on her though But the most pleasant thing of all was just to lie in bed last night knowing that she had such a wonderful , full day to look forward to . And now the day was here .

The ladies enjoyed their breakfast and Thelma enjoyed bustling about , seeing that they had everything they wanted . Afterwards though , they began to chat amongst themselves and Thelma began to feel rather left out of things . She couldn`t join in their conversation of  university days and didn`t understand some of their jargon and allusions .

"And what do you do with yourself Thelma ?" Deirdree Dagdale asked eventually ."There can`t be too much work attached to running this bungalow."  The question was not meant at all in any disparaging sense but Thelma felt slighted . Although she had ben delighted to accept Thelma`s offer of hospitality , Deirdree was puzzled too . She could not make Thelma out .They had certainly not been friends all those years ago . As far as she remembered Thelma had left school early . She had not been the academic type whereas Deirdree and the other two guests had gone on to university and then into suitable careers .

" Actually , I`m very busy . I`m involved in religious work . Not everyone has the time to devote to helping other people you see . It wouldn`t do if we all had highpowered careers ." Thelma sounded self righteous . All her pleasure in the ladies visit had vanished now .To be honest she was suddenly wondering whether the plan of hosting these people was a good idea after all .

In her desire to show off her lovely home Thelma had quite forgotten that her guests had never been particular friends of hers . While she was fetching and carrying and being a good hostess she began to feel like a boarding house landlady . The guests chattered amongst themselves and did not include her in their conversation until Deirdree`s patronising question. The fact was that she had nothing in common with them then or now .

Deirdree , Alice and Maggie had all been clever and gone on to the sixth form whereas Thelma had missed out on her "O" levels as they were then called and had been forced to leave school . Mother had not thought it worthwhile for her to try again . Anyway , they needed her earnings . Even if she had been brilliantly clever her financial circumstances would have prevented her going further she remembered resentfully . Deirdree did some very important Civil Service job in the Cabinet Office whilst Maggie was a Vet on the Isle

222

of Wight . Alice`s job was apparently so very secret and important that she was not allowed to discuss it .   Something to do with atomic energy she had implied . Of course , she had always been scientifically oriented Thelma recalled . Her father had been a science teacher too . Anyway all three of them were in a different league to her . She hadn`t had their advantages of course .

It all came back to Thelma now . During their schooldays none of these girls had gone out of their way to make friends with her . She could well remember the day when Deirdree , then form captain , had berated her for not staying late for hockey practice . " Lack of school spirit " she`d called it . What she did not appreciate was that after 4.15 pm Thelma`s bus pass became invalid and she did not have sixpence to pay the fare . Staying late would have involved her in a four mile hike home . Nor could Deirdree know that Thelma`s school shoes already had a cardboard sole in them or that there was no way her mother could dry out her school clothes should she get home soaked to the skin . Of course *her* father would come and collect her in a motor car at whatever time she asked him to come . As would Maggie`s and Alice`s .

Forty years on   , Thelma could still feel the envy and resentment she`d felt then . They might have important jobs but none of them knew what a day`s work was compared to the way she`d slaved in the hospital for all those years . And now Deirdree had the nerve to patronise her by asking what she did with herself. It almost took her breath away . It was always the same she told herself She carried the tray of breakfast dishes through to the kitchen . The ladies were so involved with their conversation they did n`t even notice her leaving the room .

Thelma pondered on the unfairness of it all . Just because thery had got on in life they thought they could look down on her .Well she had got on in life too hadn`t she ? Her lovely home proved that . Never mind , she told herself she would see her day with them later. Wait until she got into her finery . The outfit she had chosen to wear for the reunion was particularly expensive. That would show them ! It didn`t matter how important their jobs were if they didn`t know how to dress .Her hair was better cut and styled than any of theirs. too and if the truth was known she could probably buy and sell all of them .

Loading the dish washer she began to feel more cheerful . Her moment of triumph was at hand . Later on at the reunion all those people who had known her in the past would get a surprise . There were a couple of people she remembered particularly whom she could

hardly wait to meet again . Let them see what she was like now !
From the conservatory somebody called
" Is there any more coffee Thelma ?"

Chapter 49

"Hello Queenie ." Iris` voice on the telephone was shy and tentative Queenie noted – quite right too considering the way she had virtually ignored her of late . She would give her no encouragement she decided .

" Yes Iris What can I do for you ? I`m rather busy at the moment so I can`t talk for long ." she replied coolly .

" I just wanted you to know that I am going to the reunion after all . Rose persuaded me . In fact I`m helping with the buffet . I just wanted to offer you a lift there . Only it will mean leaving a bit earlier than you might haver planned because ...."

"Oh thanks Iris but you needn`t bother " Queenie interrupted " I`ve already made arrangements . A friend is taking me . Now , if you`ll   excuse   me   .."

" Look Queenie .I hope I haven`t offended you in any way . I feel I owe you an apology anyhow.I know I was very offhand with you when you were only trying to help me , but I wasn`t myself then . I certainly didn`t mean to upset you and I do appreciate your kindness ." Iris sounded so upset Queenie melted immediately .

" Don`t be such a goose " She said " You know I don`t hold grudges. Lets forget all about it .I`m glad you`re better and I`m so pleased you`re coming to the reunion . I`ve got so much to tell you.Why don`t you come and have tea this afternoon and we can have a really good chat? By the way , what are you wearing to the reunion ? I`ve got the most amazing outfit and I`m treating myself to a really expensive hair cut . Oh dear , there`s my doorbell .I must go Iris but I`ll speak to you soon ." Queenie raced to the door . She was pleased that Iris had made contact at last .

Jimmy Ng stood there clutching a large parcel . His face was wreathed in smiles .Queenie smiled too with delight . She knew the parcel contained the sari which Gishri had ordered especially for her from a shop in the midlands which specialised in high quality Indian wear .

" I`m going to try it on right away Jimmy ." She said practically grabbing it from him ." You go and have a seat .I`ll be down in a few minutes ."

The guests Queenie was supposed to be hosting had cancelled at the last minute due to illness .She was disappointed . Sarah Dwyer or Shah as she was now known was married to an Indian doctor and Queenie had hoped to delight them with Indian cuisine as well as introduce them to Jimmy . She thought it would be easier for him at the reunion if there were other Indians there too . Not that he had any qualms about going . Queenie had never known anyone who had such self confidence as her friend . He was at ease in any company .

Jimmy picked up Queenie`s " Telegraph " and was just about to sit down with it when the bell rang . He hesitated , feeling it was not his place to answer the door of his friend but then Queenie shouted  " Will you see who`s there Jimmy ?" so he did as he was asked . He greeted the visitor with his usual beaming smile but Vi Armstrong did not return his greeting. In truth , she was too shocked . However she came inside anyway and walked a few steps into ther hallway only to be greeted by the sight of Queenie descending the stairs wearing a sari . It was a beautiful , pale blue garment in a light , diaphenous fabric . As Queenie reached the bottom she did a pirouette and was about to ask " How do I look ? when the expression on Vi`s face stopped her in her tracks .

Vi`s face was red and she looked as if she was about to burst into tears . Instead she turned on her heel and left the house , slamming the front door behind her .

" Oh dear . Now I`ve upset Vi again ." Queenie said resignedly . Jimmy looked upset too .

" I think she took exception to the sari ." He said ." Queenie , it is a beautiful sari but I think you should wear it only with your Indian friends . Your idea of wearing it to the reunion party is not a good one . It would be ....." he searched for words to use . " .. a kind of ostentation I think ."

" Yes . Perhaps you`re right ." But Queenie was disappointed . She had been looking forward to causing a sensation when she appeared in the beautiful garment . Still , if Vi`s reaction was anything to go by something less exotic was in order instead ." I`ll go and take it off . Put the kettle on Jimmy please and we`ll have tea when I come down . "

Next door, Vi Armstrong in tear, was telephoning her daughter   .

Chapter 50

Rose was putting the finishing touches to the buffet assisted by Ruth Critch . It all looked very impressive and smelled most appetising .Her eye was caught by a large platter of unusual looking items .

"Whatever are those things over there?They smell very exotic"

"I said exactly the same when Queenie delivered them . She said they're called samosas . She made them herself apparently . And those other things over there too . I never knew she was such a good cook or that she was married to an Indian . I suppose she learned to cook when she was in India ."
Rose was bemused

" No Ruth . As far as I know she's never been there . And she's not married ." Ruth always got things wrong she remembered . She'd been famous for it during her schooldays.

" I think you're wrong Rose . She was with her husband last night . They brought the food together and they were saying they'd both be here today . He was a very pleasant man . Do you know who he put me in mind of ? " Ruth didn't wait for an answer . " That American singer Sammy Davis junior ."

" But she's not married."

" Oh isn't she ? " Ruth replied with a complete lack of interest . Rose found her incuriosity infuriating . But then that was Ruth . She'd always been the same . One of those people who never questionned anything and with whom it was impossible to gossip .

" I think we've just about finished . People are starting to arrive . We'd better make ourselves scarce . By the way Rose do you think I look all right dressed like this ? I don't really want to change clothes again ." Ruth began to undo her apron revealing a faded floral skirt with a dipping hemline and a blouse that just about went with it . She had never been interested in clothes .

" Oh yes . Absolutely fine ." lied Rose . "Now I must hurry home to change into my finery ." She followed Ruth to the ladies cloakroom .

" I heard such sad news last night Rose . I simply can't stop thinking about it ." Ruth spoke in a low voice even though they were quite alone in the ladies room " Carol Cunningham – you must remember her Rose ? She was such a pretty girl . She married very young and had twins . She was due to come to the reunion you know but apparently she died last weekend. Breast cancer ". Ruth spoke the last two words in a whisper .

" Oh no ." Ruth shivered . This was the third such death amongst women known to her . And she remembered Carol well although it was years since she had seen her . There would be another reunion in five years time she told herself . How many of the present company would be around then . Perhaps she herself would be one of the departed ?She shivered again.

Returning to the hall some thirty minutes later , Rose was met with a cacophany of noise and throngs of people. Judging by the raised voices and laughter some people had been going overboard at the bar although it still was not quite noon . Or perhaps Janet and Les Hawkin were being over generous with the measures . They had volunteered to run the bar and were ideally suited to the job after their long years of of working in the hotel trade.

"Rose . I`m so glad you`re here . Maurice is dying to meet you again . " A large , grey haired woman with prominent teeth and a loud voice came upon Rose from behind . It was Marjorie Goulding dressed in a mustard coloured outfit which did nothing for her sallow complexion . Rose knew her immediately though she hadn`t seen her for forty years . Maurice Goulding had been her boyfriend originally and had taken up with Marjorie only after she had ended the relationship . She glimpsed Maurice a few yards away . Contrary to Marjorie`s insistance he appeared anything but eager to meet Rose again . He looked grey and was considerably overweight , a dispirited man with a peevish mouth wearing a badly fitting suit .He bore no resemblance whatsoever to the good looking , confident young man he`d been when Rose knew him .

Marjorie seemed as ebullient as ever though . She`d just retired from a teaching career she told Rose . Poor Maurice had been made redundant in 1990 and had not worked since . They chatted desultorily and Rose expressed her pleasure that Robert their son was doing so well in the Probation Service . She couldn`t help thinking that it might have been her in Marjorie`s shoes married to that bloated shell of a man . Then she laughed inwardly . Perhaps Maurice had looked at her and thought the same thing !

Deirdree Dagdayle joined them followed by her friend Maggie and the Gouldings drifted away .

" I saw that expression on your face Rose and knew exactly what you were thinking ." Deirdree remarked. "You were congratulating yourself on being single."

" How do you know that Deirdree ?"

" Because I've been doing exactly the same thing myself . When I see what some of the poor girls have ended up with I can hardly believe my good luck ." The three ladies laughed heartily. Iris appeared to be enjoying herself too , Rose noticed , eyeing her across the room where she was in animated conversation with a distinguished looking bearded man . She felt pleased that she had persuaded her to change her mind about coming . So that was all right . Rose relaxed and determined to enjoy herself too . About to join another group of people she caught sight of Thelma standing quite alone in a corner of the hall with that miserable , sulky expression on her face . Rose sighed . She supposed she'd better rescue her .

" My feet are killing me ." Thelma cpmplained as Rose approached her .

" I'm not surprised if you wear shoes like that ." Rose replied , looking at the five inch heels.

She saw that , as usual , Thelma's outfit was over the top . It was not that she dressed too smartly. Most of the ladies present were dressed well . It was Thelma's slavish adherence to the fashion plate look . Everything matched or toned even to the hanbag with silk scarf attached . There was something completely contrived about it . Expensive no doubt , but whoever had persuaded Thelma that she looked good in a short skirt should be called to account .That length just drew the eyes to those thick ankles and podgy calves which would have been better covered up.

Thelma had noticed Rose eyeing her outfit and had waited for some admiring comment . After all , when you thought what it had cost some remark was called for . She supposed Rose was jealous . Well she was bound to be . Her dress certainly wasn't new . That much was obvious .

"Doesn't the hall look wonderful ." Rose remarked . "Some of the committee were here until almost midnight last night making the finishing touches ."

"Really ?" Thelma looked about her without much interest . The hall certainly had been transformed though she had to agree . Of course , the colour scheme corresponded to the school colours she now realised . Everything was green and gold even the flower arrangements on the tables .

" We're donating the flowers to the old folks home later ." Rose said   looking around rather desperately for somebody for Thelma to talk with . Then she saw a likely candidate .

" Thelma , I've just spied Miss Carew . You must remember her ? Fancy her making the effort to come here today . She must be 90 at least . Let's go and talk to her shall we ?"

Thelma brightened . Miss Carew had been the needlework teacher , one of the few subjects at which Thelma had shone during her schooldays . On many occasions the class had been asked to admire and emulate Thelma's immaculate hem stitching and peerless embroidery .

In the ladies cloakroom Iris caught a glimpse of herself in the mirror and almost gasped in surprise at the happy face reflected there . She looked …. almost pretty she thought , feeling pleased now that she had worn her smartest dress , a floaty lilac and pale blue print . It occurred to her that she was enjoying herself for the first time for ages .

She had barely entered the building when a tall bearded man had accosted her .He had a lively , clever face and eyes of lightest blue .

" I knew you right away ." He'd said . "You're Ronnie Claye's sister Don't you remember me - Phillip Tewler ?" Of course she did although he looked very different from the young man who used to call at their house so many years ago . " You were a cricketer . " she recalled . " Ronnie was at your wedding I remember . Then didn't you go to Australia too ? I think it was you my mother blamed for giving Ronnie the idea ."

" I've only come back in the past few months . My wife died last year and now both the children are settled in England there was nothing to keep me there I'm living with Sarah my sister now. .She's been widowed too so it made sense to get together . But tell me all about you . Ronnie used to talk about you such a lot . He was very proud of his little sister ."

They talked for ages until they were interrupted by a fat , red faced man who told Iris he remembered her very well . " Jim Stanton " he introduced himself . " I believe you were my first love , Eunice . Don't you remember how I used to wait for you after school on Wednesday afternoons? You used to tell your mother you were staying late for hockey practice ."

Iris laughed . " I would never have been so bold ." She told him . "You're confusing me with Eunice Callaghan . She's here somewhere I think. I saw her earlier." Look - over there"

They all looked across to where a tall , bottle blonde was holding court amidst a circle of people. Eunice hadn't worn well . Years of chain smoking had played havoc with her skin and her eyes seemed almost to have disappeared into their sockets . Beneath her short skirt varicose veins disfigured her calves . Iris remembered her as a particularly attractive girl with the sort of physique which could have made her a model . She had married young however and gone on to have a very large family .

Jim Stanton seemed disappointed . He began to talk to Phillip about cricket and Iris excused herself . As she turned away Phillip said .

" Iris . you will join me for the meal later I hope ? We `ve got so much to talk about ." and smilingly she agreed .Thelma had enjoyed her chat to old Miss Carew but there were so many people waiting to chat to her too that , regretfully , she had to give way after only a few minutes . Rose was now amongst another group of people who were having a very good time judging by their gales of laughter . She approached them diffidently and the laughter died down as she insinuated herself into the group.

" I think they`re about to serve lunch Rose .Will you come with me to the buffet ? "

Rose sighed inwardly but agreed readily enough . It looked as though she would be dogged by Thelma for the day she thought ruefully .

"Rose Deacon ! You haven`t changed a bit ! " A tiny red haired woman clutched at Rose` arm .

" Nor have you Eileen . How nice to see you here . Have you travelled far ?

" From Ireland . Wicklow you know . But I didn`t come specially . I always visit my family at this time of year and I was just lucky that this reunion was taking place at the right time . I don`t recognise you though " Eileen said , staring hard at Thelma .

" I`m Thelma Honeyspan ." It still gave Thelma a thrill to mention her married name . " But I used to be Thelma Riley ."

"Riley , Riley . No .The only Riley I knew was that funny old dinner lady . You remember Rose ？ We used to call her Old Mother Riley . She was some sort of religious fanatic . Do you remember that day when she …...Rose interupted swiftly

" That was Thelma`s mother Eileen . " Thelma said nothing . She was too angry . Eileen was unfazed . She laughed loudly " Trust me to put my foot in it I always run true to form my husband always says . No offence intended Thelma ." But Thelma made no reply .

At that moment Rose caught sight of Queenie who had just entered the hall

" Look Thelma , there's Queenie . Perhaps she'd like to join our table for lunch ? Why don't you grab her ? "Then she noticed that Queenie was accompanied . Good heavens ! That strange little man must be her boyfriend . Rose stared incredulously .Queenie's arrival had created a minor sensation . Everyone was staring . Queenie seemed slightly ill at ease but her partner seemed quite oblivious to the stares . Everyone seemed to be giving them a wide berth however . Rose hurried over . Somebody needed to make them feel welcome .

At least Queenie wasn't dressed in any kind of ethnic garment she noticed with relief . In fact , she was looking rather conventionally smart in a well cut beige suit and her hair had been properly cut for a change although she had not had it re coloured .Rose was introduced to Jimmy Ng and invited the couple to come and join her table after they had been to the buffet At this point Iris crossed the room to join them . She was appalled at Queenie's nerve in actually bringing her " friend " to such a gathering . She must realise what interest it would invite . Why give people an opportunity to talk about her ? Sometimes Queenie seemed to lose all sense of propriety she thought .

"Rose " Thelma called "I've just met some old friends so I'm going to sit with them ." She proceeded to walk off with an elderly couple . Charming , thought Rose although she was delighted by this .

Despite Iris' misgivings Jimmie proceeded to charm the assembled company . Rose had been aprehensive that his presence would cause at atmosphere at the table because people would not know quite how to react towards him . In particular , she was worried by how both Thelma or Iris would respond . Her fears were unfounded . Jimmy began by completely altering the seating arrangements at the table suggesting that everybody should sit next to somebody they did not know . Much giggling ensued . Felicity Shariff together with her Iranian husband who was a cancer specialist decided to join them at this point , followed by Moira Renshaw who was a well known journalist and her partner Jack Hine , apparently a high powered financier in the city . This rasised the tone completely and made their group seem exotic and sophisticated . Having introduced himself Jack immediately ordered champagne for the whole table .

Whether it was the champagne or simply his personal charisma , Jimmy proceeded to charm the assembled company . He began by suggesting that they played a game which involved all the ladies having to guess the occupation of the man at their side . Much hilarity ensued particularly when Moira guessed that he was " something in show business ." Rose guessed that her partner Phillip

Tewler was a writer and Iris was amazed when he replied " You must have psychic powers ." When Queenie guessed that Jack Hine was a gangster the table was in uproar .

The party became even merrier after the wine was circulated and Rose noticed other people looking across at their table and envying their conviviality Towards the end of the lunch Jack Hine was accepting an invitation from Jimmie to visit his home for supper whilst Felicity Shariff was telling Queenie about the best bazaars to visit in Delhi where she had just been for a visit and offering her accommodation with her family should she ever come to Dubai .

On the way home afterwards Iris and Rose disected the events of the day .

" I was so relieved to see that Queenie was dressed normally ." Rose confided . " I was afraid she was going to wear one of her " Outfits " , but she looked really smart ."

" My heart sank when I saw her walk in with her friend ." Iris replied . But he went down rather well in the end ." Her tone was surprised .

"I thought he seemed a very nice person. Not in the least what I was expecting ".Rose agreed.

"I had a long talk with Queenie about him on Sunday ." Iris continued "You know Vi Armstrong rang me about it ? She was very upset . She`s terrified that Queenie is going to mary him and begged me to talk to her about it even though I told her it was none of my business . Fortunately Queenie didn`t take it the wrong way . She insists that they are simply friends and that the relationship is totally platonic , just based on shared interests . She says she`s become friends with the whole family . Vi was so relieved to hear that there was no romantic involvement . She said that Queenie`s mother would never have allowed it."

" I gather that they`re going to be involved in some joint business venture though ." Rose said ." I couldn`t help overhearing when Queenie was talking to Felicity . And Jimmy actually asked me if there was any chance that Eric might be selling the shop . He said the premises would be ideal for what they have in mind . I just hope Queenie knows what she`s doing . She is inclined to leap in to things ."

" Oh so do I ." Iris sounded anxious . " But when I tried to tell her to be careful she as good as told me to mind my own business . She was quite touchy about it . The last thing I want to do is fall out with her about it ."

"Oh well . She must make her own mistakes . At least Thelma seemed to be enjoying herself in the end . Did you see her talking to that elderly couple ? I think it's the first time I've ever seen her laugh . And when I asked if she wanted to walk home with us she said she was staying on . "

" Yes . I met them. Mr. Harker was the school caretaker wasn't he ? They are Jehovah's Witnesses they said. What about that girl from the Isle of Wight ? She was absolutely coated in dog hairs and she had the nerve to hand back her plate at the buffet because it had a hairline crack . She said it was unhygienic ."

Iris seemed so animated and talkative Rose could not help remarking " You seemed to be getting on rather well with Phillip Tewler. He looked to be one of the .few men who seems to have worn well . Some of them ..."

" Yes. I know what you mean . Did you see Marjorie Goulding ?

"I could hardly believe my eyes when I saw Maurice .He's aged so much . As for Deirdree Dagdayle , she looked as if she'd been inflated . Yet she was so skinny years ago ." They gossiped on and before they reached home Iris had admitted to Rose that she was glad she had been persuaded to attend the reunion .

Chapter 51

It was a Friday evening some weeks later . There was a performance of "West Side Story" taking place in the school hall and the ladies had arranged to go together . They had agreed to meet up outside the town hall to have an early supper beforehand . Rose was first to arrive and after only a few seconds saw Queenie alighting from a van at the other side ofthe street . She had said that Bert Armstrong would be giving her a lift on his way to the Knights.

Queenie was wearing her smart camel hair coat Rose noticed , but her head was wrapped up turban style in a brown paisley scarf . It looked rather odd . She greeted Rose in a subdued manner too , Rose thought , but after chatting for a while seemed to recover her normal good humour

"Did you hear "Desert Island Discs " this morning " she asked Rose. "Wasn`t Desmond Tutu wonderful" Rose agreed ."I felt just like hugging him at the end . Isn`t it strange how you feel you really know somebody just from listening to a radio programme ?" Queenie glanced at her watch . " It`s not like Iris to be late . She was the one who said 6.15 ."

" I know ." Rose said " The show starts at 7.30 and we need to allow an hour for our supper at least ." She looked at Queenie again . It was no good . She would have to ask her about that scarf . It looked most strange and it was not as if it was chilly or even wet .

"Here she is now ." said Queenie as Iris crossed the road to meet them . How smart she looks Rose thought , admiring the navy suit . Iris did look smart if a little thin and pale . She had had her hair cut in an attractive feathery style that was very becoming . Unlike Rose though , she had no qualms about questioning Queenie about her head wear .

" Why are you wearing that scarf Queenie ? " she asked immediately .

Queenie blushed and looked away . " Please don`t ask ." she said finally . Then "All right . I`ll show you if you promise not to say a word . " She pulled back the scarf slightly to reveal hair that was the strangest colour Rose had ever seen . It was bright red ! Not the carrotty colour or even the brassy shade sometimes produced by henna , but a bright poppy red like a carnival wig .

It looked dreadful , giving Queenie a rakish , grotesque vulgarity . Like an old whore , thought Rose . Poor Queenie . Iris was horrified , so much so that she could not say a word .Seeing their reaction made Queenie even more upset .

" I`ve spent the whole afternoon trying to wash it out ." she told them "It won`t budge . In the end it got too late to go to a hairdresser but I`m going first thing in the morning . I don`t care what it costs ." Queenie replaced the scarf looking very miserable . Iris pursed her lips whilst Rose tried hard not to laugh . She wouldn`t hurt Queenie` feelings for the world .

" Never mind Queenie . Don`t let it spoil our evening . I never thought anything of you wearing a scarf anyway ." she lied .

The three made their way to the Red Rose café , an establishment which specialised in high teas and early suppers . As a teenager Queenie had worked here on Saturdays . She`d done very well for tips she remembered although the job lasted for only a month . She`d been told she was too slow and had been hurt when Valerie Peathorn – whom she regarded as practically retarded - had been taken on in her place . Later on though Valerie had become a WREN so she couldn`t have been as stupid as she looked . She wondered what had become of Valerie and was about to enquire when Iris spoke .

"Our mothers used to come here regularly ." she said . " Do you remember Queenie ? Welsh rarebit and bakewell tart after shopping on a Saturday ? "

"Oh yes , " Queenie answered " I thought that`s what I would have tonight . With a poached egg on top ."

"Well don``t have that . I want you to have something really special . It`s my treat tonight . I`ve got something to celebrate ." Iris looked very pleased with herself .

"Really ? " "What is it ?" Both Rose and Queenie spoke at once .

" I booked my air ticket to Australia . And it cost almost £200 less than I `d expected .Something to do with staying for longer than six weeks . So I thought this evening would be my treat . I want to pay for our tickets later too ."

" Iris ! I`m so pleased for you . I hope you`ll let me have Nellie whilst your away ." Rose said .Having recently parted with Skipper she found she was missing having an animal around .

" Well actually …" Iris blushed prettily ,

" I`m afraid I`ve already promised Phillip . You know Phillip Tewler ? He`s been staying with his sister and I think its become a bit claustrophobic .Anyway , he very kindly offered to keep an eye on the place whilst I`m away and it made sense for him to stay there and look after Nellie . He`s so handy around the house too . He`s going to do some decorating for me and look after the garden as well . It`s all worked out perfectly ."

The others agreed that it had . Iris told them all about her plans . She was going to leave I;n mid November and return in March . " That way I shall be in time to see my bulbs come up ."

" I do envy you ." Rose said wistfully . "Perhaps I`ll do something similar next year ." At least by then Gerald should have made some definite plans , she thought . As things are it looks as though both Queenie and I will still be in the shop next spring . Although Rose had been pleased to learn that Eric was in a period of remission she was not totally happy about the way Gerald had assumed she would continue to mind the business whilst the two spent the winter in San Francisco . But according to Gerald Eric`s health demanded a mild climate . How could she refuse to help out ?

"Actually , I` m planning to go abroad too " said Queenie " But don`t look so alarmed Rose , it`s only for ten days . I`m going to Indonesia with Jimmy and his sister . We`re going to look at various products with a view to importing Batik and such like ."

"I suppose I shall need to look for another assistant in the shop then" Rose said "It looks as though you`re going to become a high powered business lady with no time for other concerns." She spoke jokily but to her surprise Queenie replied quite seriously ,

" Well actually we shall be looking for suitable premises shortly . Jimmy thinks we should be able to get the business started at the beginning of next year . But I wouldn`t let you down without notice Rose ."

"Oh Queenie . I do hope you know what you`re doing " Iris blurted it out at the same time becoming aware of  Rose`s warning nudge . Then she said

. " I beg your pardon Queenie . It`s your business entirely ."

" Yes - I know that ." Queenie replied calmly . They settled down to enjoy their supper . If it had been me , thought Iris looking at Queenie`s turbanned head , I should have been too embarrassed to come out this evening . I'd have strayed at home but in that case I'd have missed a nice evening out . On the other hand I wouldn't have been silly enough to mess about with my hair in the first place . But if I had I'd have been too embarrassed to tell anyone about it . I wouldn't want to look a fool . I suppose it all proves that Queenie's a nicer person than me . She's certainly more adventurous . She reached a decision .

" Queenie where will you go to have your hair seen to tomorrow ?" she asked .Queenie was finishing up her trifle

" The Headmaster " I suppose ..It's expensive but they do it so well . Why do you ask ?"

" Only because I want to come with you . I've decided I want to have my hair coloured too . I'm so bored with this pepper and salt . I thought I might try becoming ash blonde." Iris blushed but instead of the horrified reactions she expected from the others they expressed great enthusiam for the idea .

Leaving the café , it was obvious that something was about to take place in the street . Traffic cones had been placed in the road and people were standing about expectantly .

" What's going on? " enquired Rose of a spectator .

" It's the grand procession of that revivalist group , The Christian Crusade . They're marching from all over the county to a rally outside the tabernacle .There're hundreds of them marching it said in the paper."

Queenie remembered reading about it in the local paper . It said that up to 2000 people were expected at the rally . The parade should be quite a spectacle she thought . There was the sound of a brass band in the distance .

"Oh do let's stay and watch " She appealed . "We have plenty of time ." Strains of music reached them . " Hills of the North ." At the far end of the High Street the front of the procession began to approach . It was headed by a huge brass band all wearing blue and gold uniforms with huge sashes bearing the slogan "Christian Crusade ".

The band was followed by two men bearing a huge banner , simirlarly emblazoned . Iris recognised them as the men who had called on her once . Behind them was a choir , dozens of men and women all in the uniform singing lustily . They were followed by ranks of marchers kept in line by sidesmen who handed out leaflets to the people lining the street . Another band made up entirely of youngsters came into view followed by hordes of young people . A middleaged woman strode in front of them in her navy and gold uniform , her sash straining against her bosom .

Queenie stared . " Look girls " She cried " Look , it`s Thelma !"

Rose and Iris looked . Sure enough it was Thelma but not as they were used to seeing her .Resplendant in her gold sash and carrying some kind of wand , Thelma marched in front of a squad of young people . Obviously she occupied a position of some importance in the organisation . Drawing level , Thelma caught sight of them too and smiled broadly in recognition . She looked the picture of contentment . Glancing at Rose Queenie saw that she was watching Iris who , like Thelma , looked contentedly serene.